Mitch Engel

Deadly Virtues

iUniverse, Inc.
New York   Bloomington

iUniverse books may be ordered through booksellers or by contacting:

iUniverse
1663 Liberty Drive
Bloomington, IN 47403
www.iuniverse.com
1-800-Authors (1-800-288-4677)

Because of the dynamic nature of the Internet, any Web addresses or links contained in this book may have changed since publication and may no longer be valid. The views expressed in this work are solely those of the author and do not necessarily reflect the views of the publisher, and the publisher hereby disclaims any responsibility for them.

ISBN: 978-1-4502-3100-8 (sc)
ISBN: 978-1-4502-3101-5 (hc)
ISBN: 978-1-4502-3102-2 (ebook)

Library of Congress Control Number: 2010929443

Printed in the United States of America

iUniverse rev. date: 07/30/2010

To Kris, for the reason and rhyme she brings to my life.

Part I

*"Ah, but a man's reach should exceed his
grasp, or what's a heaven for?"*

Robert Browning, British Poet, 1812-1889

Chapter One:

Wednesday Afternoon; May 21, 2008

"… and isn't it true that every stressed-out soul in this crowded stadium could justify playing the victim from time to time? Twenty-four hour media machines inundate us with reasons to distrust the world around us … attacking anything, attacking everything so that we too easily dismiss the potential we have for making a difference in our own small parts of the world. Yet here's the sublime paradox. Refuse to succumb to those uncertainties … that mass-induced, mass-produced cynicism. Let yourself dare, no let yourself soar, to take chances … to think more noble thoughts, hope more noble hopes, achieve more noble achievements. No matter the outcome, the willingness to reach forward will prevent you from joining the ranks who keep score by missed opportunities … the ones who stand still and allow life to happen to them, victims of their own inertia.

"Our lives are a series of consequences. We alone own the consequences of our actions … or of taking no action at all. This afternoon you've heard a number of our country's most celebrated personalities intimately share their stories, their successes. You leave here with a choice. You can begrudge them, their fame, in some cases their fortunes. Or. Or, I urge you, follow their leads. Let their words and accomplishments stir something deeper within you.

"The social complexities of the next decade will generate more and more voices clamoring for entitlement … clamoring for what is rightfully theirs for no reason other than hapless views of their own potential. But the grandest rewards will continue to be reaped by regular citizens, plain folks possessing a conviction for personal empowerment … for controlling their own destinies. Starting today … right here, right now, let's grasp that control. Godspeed on our journey together."

The striking woman stepped back from the podium, paused for the slightest of moments, then tilted a humble bow to the audience. More than nineteen thousand arose in unison, an anthemesque Celine Dion song started pouring out of the fortress of speakers surrounding the stage. Under the glow of a solitary spotlight, her deep brown eyes, the flowing black hair, the perfect white teeth, the understated black Armani suit, they all seemed to glisten triumphantly. With images of Americana flashing across huge screens and colorful laser beams streaking through the rafters, she concluded a series of modest waves as she disappeared into the stage floor through the magic of hydraulics.

From a distant perch in the nosebleed section of Kemper Arena, Andrea Elizabeth Morrison never had been so thoroughly jealous of anyone. Riding a whim of sunrise determination, she'd squeezed another eighty-five dollars onto a MasterCard to bolster her undernourished self-esteem. However, at this very instant, Andie Morrison felt totally inconsequential. No one could be as damned together as that woman. My God, she'd been intellectually off-the-charts and the most captivating speaker Andie had ever heard. According to the program, this Stephanie Burton was dripping in pedigrees, both academic and professional. At a young age, she'd soared into the stratosphere of the ad industry because of her breakthrough ideas and a natural skill for motivating others. Then to top it off, she was drop-dead gorgeous. The woman's optimism and common sense messages had captivated everyone in attendance, including Andie herself. Any minute, legions of adoring fans might douse themselves in oil and light a sacrificial match at the mere suggestion. Andie Morrison was drowning in a pool of self-disgust and missed opportunities as this supernatural creature finally disappeared beneath the arena – Andie assumed to the subterranean laboratory from whence she'd been created.

Throughout a May afternoon, Andie's early morning optimism had been teetering under the weighty achievements of senators, generals, best-selling authors, Olympians, newscasters and CEO's. Then they wheel out some modern day Athena to deliver the kill shot. Maybe it hadn't been such a good idea to waste a day's vacation on the Personal Empowerment Tour's visit to Kansas City.

As she made her way to the dressing room, Stephanie Burton still was absorbing the crowd's fervent enthusiasm. She had meant every encouraging word she'd spoken to them. She always did. But the echoing dissonance was as strong as ever. *We alone own the consequences of our actions.*

Chapter Two:

Wednesday Evening; May 21, 2008

Andie Morrison was blessed with an enviable array of attributes, yet cursed with one monumental weakness. She lacked any ambition whatsoever. At least that's what family and friends had been telling her for as long as she could remember. She didn't know if she agreed, but Andie normally hadn't been inclined to dwell on it.

She possessed a highly analytic mind. With near-perfect college entrance exams, Andie had been accepted for admittance into Brown, Duke and a handful of other elite schools. Unfortunately, she never got around to applying for the financial scholarships that probably would have been granted. So as high school wound down, she withered under the monetary guilt evoked through the repeated conversations her mother initiated when her father wasn't within earshot. Not wanting to burden her parents with hiring a weekend hostess for their struggling roadhouse on the outskirts of Kansas City, she enrolled at the University of Missouri's nearby branch campus – no regrets, no looking back. She loved interacting with the dinner regulars and hometown life had remained pretty uncomplicated.

But as fate delights, before the end of Andie's freshman year a mall developer offered her parents a preposterous sum of money for the restaurant's property. Mother Morrison kicked into persuasive overdrive and convinced her husband it was time to retire to that A-frame in the Ozarks they'd always dreamed about. Of minor note, her dad couldn't recall a single prior discussion about an afterlife in the Ozarks.

With the roadhouse closed and weekends available, Andie had answered a campus job posting: "QUALIFIED COMPUTER SCIENCE MAJOR. DATA ARCHIVING, TWENTY HOURS A WEEK. CONTACT THE KANSAS CITY POLICE DEPARTMENT." Eight years later Andie was a full-time D.A. Not as in District Attorney, but as in Data Analyst, still working for KCPD. In the meantime, she'd finished college, earned a Masters after five years of night classes, and at present anticipated the completion of her PhD sometime prior to menopause.

Andrea Elizabeth Morrison epitomized unvarnished Midwestern wholesomeness … apple pie values with bread and butter looks. She made everyone around her feel so instantly comfortable that at first most people didn't notice how unusually pretty she was. Her large eyes were always happy, welcoming – sometimes shining green, sometimes blue, depending on the surroundings that they didn't merely reflect but seemed to absorb. The rest of her facial features were likewise easy to take, but too easily subsumed by those ever-friendly eyes. Her mid-length hair was a light streaky brown, which even after twenty-nine years leaned blond in the summertime.

Andie was no more committed to advancing her appearance than she was her career – but she really didn't need much help. The sun and wind provided enough year-round skin color to justify little to no make-up. Her morning mirror time consisted of running a brush down either side of her head followed by a couple swipes of eyeliner if she remembered.

She abhorred any form of regimented exercise, but in her free time Andie usually headed to some form of athletic facility. She loved games; she loved to play. Tennis, basketball, soccer … anything Pops had taught her. On nights she wasn't propping her head up in a post-graduate classroom, she tried to sub for KCPD on whatever softball, volleyball or bowling team that might need her – which was all of them. Anyone watching would have assumed she'd been a big-time college athlete. But Andie hadn't even bothered to participate on many of her high school teams. She couldn't stand all the politics and tension that went along with teammates and coaching staffs.

Her body's fitness wasn't something that Andie gave much consideration; it merely was the byproduct of all the physical activity. Under the loose sweats and jerseys she liked to wear was a foldout figure – long waist, toned limbs, slender hips and firm bust. Assets well hidden from others by the choices she made with wardrobe … hidden to Andie herself by a phobic self-denial of her sexiness. The limited number of times she'd allowed dating relationships to progress to the bedroom, Andie had been downright startled by male reactions to her body. She found it awkward when otherwise intelligent men would slip into a slobbering state of pubescent euphoria at their first sight of her without clothes on.

In fact, relationships with men in total were more awkward than Andie would have liked. She wondered why the whole cat-and-mouse game needed to be so difficult. Why couldn't everybody just be their true selves from the outset, rather than waste so much time keeping all those guards up? From her standpoint, all the good stuff was behind those facades anyway.

Mother (never Mom) couldn't fathom why her youngest daughter behaved so indifferently toward men and dating, not to mention marriage. She'd once worked up the nerve to probe. "Andrea, I'm sure your father and I would find it in our hearts to love you just the same, but by any chance are you a lesbian?"

To assure her mother that she was equipped with all the proper sexual urges, and perhaps to inflict a modicum of payback for her meddling, Andie revealed, "Don't worry about me, Ma, I periodically invite random male acquaintances under my hood for a tune-up." Mother Morrison never broached the subject again, which extended the lengthy list of topics that Andie and her mother took great pains to avoid.

Due to the long traffic lines exiting Kemper Arena, it was close to 8PM before Andie arrived home to her apartment. Originally she'd planned on meeting up with a few work friends at a bar to watch a ballgame, but she no longer was in the mood. Instead she plopped onto the corduroy sectional in front of her big-screen TV, but made no move for the remote control sitting on the coffee table. For once she wanted silence, some private time to think. She opened a spiral notebook and started skimming through her scribbled notes from the various speeches that afternoon. It was all pretty trite stuff and she wondered why she'd even bothered to put her pen to paper. But interestingly, she hadn't taken a single note while Stephanie Burton was speaking. She'd been too busy listening. Really listening. Hearing, absorbing.

As she thought about what the Burton woman had said, Andie reflected on the sedentary nature of her career, the superficial contentment she found so easily and so often. Her mind hop-scotched through other aspects of her life, which inevitably brought her to the awkward relationship with her mother. They hadn't bothered to wait until Andie's teen years for any of the classic mother-daughter frictions to develop; their dealings had been complicated for as long as she could remember. Sure, she loved her mother, but she'd never felt the closeness she did with her father, Pops. When it came to Mother, no matter how Andie acted or what choices she made, she somehow knew she was falling short of expectation. So much tip-toeing, so many withheld approvals. At first by her mother, but eventually by Andie in return. After so many years, the stalest of stalemates.

Everything came easier, more naturally with Pops. No matter what Andie did, her father found joy in it. As the youngest of three daughters, she'd been his little princess. As a tomboy, she also could be the sports and outdoor companion he might have wanted in a son. His affirmation was steadfast. Andie wondered what might have happened if Pops had pushed her a bit harder. Would she have developed that missing ambition everyone kept harping on? But she couldn't begrudge him; he remained such a positive force in her life. No, that Burton woman had been right. She alone must take ownership of her actions and their consequences.

Andie couldn't help but see the twisted humor in her situation. All and all, Andie Morrison managed to find a basic contentment in most everything around her. But such simple satisfaction only served to punctuate the severity of her problem. To truly be happy she apparently needed to stop being so darned content. Between her mother, her sisters and girlfriends, and even a guy pal or two, there'd been a steady stream of caring people in her life who insisted she was wasting her talents, selling herself short. That she too easily settled … was too much of a pleaser.

Andrea Elizabeth Morrison again resolved to become more ambitious, more assertive. This time, she'd finally stop accepting what was easiest or most convenient … stop camouflaging uncertainties with quick jokes and fast smiles. This time she would make a real attempt at that deeper sense of fulfillment everyone kept talking about. As Stephanie Burton's comments kept replaying in her head, she realized something different might actually be stirring inside her.

Chapter Three:

Wednesday Evening; May 21, 2008

At the ripe old age of thirty-four, Prize Calloway was already a timeless fixture at Uncle Charlie's Tavern. The other regulars could anticipate his every move ... for the most part, to avoid him. Prize had invested countless nights perfecting what he considered his personal trademarks, blissfully unaware of the rolling eyes and mutterings he left in his wake.

After guzzling cheap drafts and chatting up single women throughout a typical evening, Calloway triumphantly would call for his signature nightcap, a tequila shooter. A tradition he likened to the two-minute warning. Arrival of that final Cuervo Gold was timed to signal his imminent departure to any ladies who might be interested in accompanying him. Consensus of barstool opinion was that this signal hadn't piqued a feminine interest in more than four years.

Nonetheless, the locals conceded that Prize Calloway had provided some spectacular memories back in his days on the high school football field – which may have been why Prize himself never graduated emotionally from that precise point in time. Throughout the ensuing sixteen years, Prize had reenacted the same gridiron highlights many times at Uncle Charlie's, the crowning narrative being the county championship game in which he returned two interceptions for touchdowns and scored a third off a recovered fumble. In praising the team for its 35-to-nothing victory, Coach Hadley had uttered those fateful words in the locker room.

"This was a big win for the whole squad, but the real prize goes to Calloway over there."

The following week at practice, Ralph Calloway, Jr. decreed that his teammates should henceforth refer to him only as "Prize." None of them really had remembered the coach's exact remark or connected it to Calloway's pronouncement, but he was their star so they honored his request just the same. The name stuck.

Young "Prize" headed off to Kansas State on a football scholarship but blew out his knee in a freshman scrimmage, thus denying the Hall of Fame a future linebacker. With two D's, an F, and an Incomplete in his first semester, Calloway felt he'd accomplished enough in college and opted not to enroll for a second term. He returned to Grandview, Missouri, where his retired Truman High jersey hung prominently over the grandstands. After a dozen years as a personal trainer at Weight & See Fitness, Prize was promoted to assistant manager. But the gratification of his newfound title and salary were secondary to Prize. Foremost, he relished the working environment of a gym. A temple. A place where a sculpted, red-blooded hetero guy like himself could be properly appreciated, even admired, as he crunched and curled for hours on end. And with the preponderance of mirrors at Weight & See, the admiration for Prize's physique mostly was self-generated. He could catch glimpses of his tight abs or pecs whenever impulse struck, which was often. Before showering, body glistening with sweat, he might hold a naked pose or two, constantly amazed by his own magnificence. Height: almost six-feet. Weight: a constant 175 pounds. Wiry blond hair, short and cropped. Skin kept a deep bronze – year-round and all-over, courtesy of Weight & See tanning beds.

Before tossing down his tequila shooter on Wednesday night, Prize had held the pool table for five straight games. He was on a roll. Earlier in the week on *Laser Warrior Death Duels, Pinball from an Alien Galaxy,* he'd come within a few hundred gigazats of breaking the machine's record, already held by none other than "P. Calloway." Midway through this particular evening he had considered croaking out his inimitable rendition of *I'll Get By With A Little Help From My Friends,* accompanied by Joe Cocker on the jukebox. What made his version unique was how he exaggeratedly grabbed his crotch at each reprise to overtly stress which of "his friends" he was singing about. But tonight he ultimately opted to go with an Elvis number. Toward midnight, he cleared most the dance floor with *Jailhouse Rock,* remembering to surgically substitute his preferred lyric of "Jail Bait Rock" at every instance. He finished his Elvis tribute bare-chested, a discarded Hawaiian shirt circling above him on the ceiling fan. Just another routine night for Prize Calloway. Until he made his way to the parking lot.

Halfway to his car he was approached from behind, "Hey, Prize, why would a guy like you be leaving all by yourself?"

It was a woman's voice, but none he recognized. He turned to see a ball-capped silhouette approaching through the darkness. With each step she became more interesting. First, his eyes locked onto the narrow hips and *firm glutes* packed tightly inside black denim. Then, some *world-class cleavage* spilling out of the leather top that she suggestively unzipped another inch as she walked. She was tall, almost fashion-model tall, even without the high heels. He noticed hints of blond hair working loose under her cap. Finally, that incredible face. Hypnotic blue eyes … smooth white skin … and moist, full lips accentuated by dark red lipstick. Prize stood mesmerized.

"I repeat. Why are you in such a hurry to leave alone?"

"Uh, I decided I should grab a few extra hours' sleep tonight. I've been hitting the weight room pretty hard."

"It shows. I was impressed when you had your shirt off."

"Yeah, well, ya know, I think fitness is job one." Prize actually blushed a little before his reflex charm kicked in, "Hey, how come I didn't see you in there? I sure would have noticed a sweet gift like you wrapped in such a fine package."

"I was sitting back in the corner, taking it all in … especially you. My name's Stevie, by the way."

"So Stevie, do you live in the area?"

"No, just here for a few days of personal business. But my nights are wide open."

"Well then, maybe I can show you what Grandview has to offer."

"I'd rather spend that time showing someone like you what I have to offer."

Caught off guard by her forwardness, Prize's male arrogance suffered momentary uncertainty. "Hey listen, let's get one thing clear. Prize Calloway has never had to pay for it."

Smiling, she stepped close to him and lowered her voice to a near whisper, "And why would a guy like you ever have to pay?" She then reached out and slowly rubbed one of his biceps through his shirt. "Isn't there some place we can go?"

"Uh-h-h, sure. I know a place … an apartment. Uh, my apartment. Would you like to go to my apartment?"

"How wonderfully hospitable. I thought the gentleman might never ask. Why don't I follow you there?"

During the ten-minute drive to his apartment complex, few seconds passed without Prize checking the rearview mirror on his Blazer. Crossing each intersection he feared the trailing sedan might take an unexpected turn. *What if this babe-and-a-half changes her mind? What if she's just another head-case bitch who gets off on teasing guys?*

But no, this dream, this fantasy was coming true. She wrapped her arms around his waist as they climbed the exterior wooden stairway to his third-floor studio. Inside, the place looked like it belonged to a teenager, with nothing but high school press clippings and posters of body-builders pinned to the walls. The floor was littered with free weights, fitness magazines, empty energy drink bottles and an assortment of porn videos. Stevie didn't seem to notice. Before Prize could say anything, she turned to him and stretched her body upward to put those amazing lips next to his ear. "Go ahead, undress. I want to watch."

Calloway clumsily peeled off items of clothing until he was down to his lavender briefs. Unsure of himself, he looked boyishly at Stevie seeking final instructions, still in disbelief at what actually was happening.

"Please don't stop now. You have my undivided attention"

With the briefs removed, he stood dry-mouthed and naked before her, "I guess you can see that I don't need some little blue pill to show my appreciation to a woman."

She licked her upper lip. "My, what a Prize you are."

When she nodded him toward the bed, he hesitated. "Maybe I should grab some condoms."

"No, not yet, Prize. The first time, I'll use just my hands. That way you'll last longer for the second and third. I hope you won't mind."

Mind? He thought he must be dreaming. *Second and third time? I have this gorgeous sex-starved stranger so turned on that she wants to treat me to an orgasmic marathon. What could be more perfect?*

Then she spoke again, her eyes looking directly into his, "I think I should get more comfortable." At which point Stevie began to disrobe slowly, a playful smile teasing her prey.

As she revealed more and more of herself, Prize watched trance-like from the bed. He began to understand Stevie's natural attraction to him since it was obvious that she, too, was a fitness fanatic. Her abs, taut and smooth. The toned muscles in her thighs and calves, evident with each movement. Her firm breasts, perfectly formed. Naked except for the thin straps of a stark white thong that accentuated the narrowness of her hips, she allowed him to gaze at her for a few moments before sitting on the edge of the bed.

She reached into the purse she had dropped next to the bed and pulled out a bottle of scented lotion. After squeezing liberal amounts into her hands, she began to massage Prize's chest and torso. Then his thighs. She methodically maneuvered around his genitals until he was lifting himself off the mattress to draw attention to his manhood. She slowly worked her way there. As her hands caressed, her breasts swayed rhythmically. Her eyes, her mouth, her entire face glowed erotically. Closer and closer she worked him toward an unimaginable sexual height. With just her hands, this unknown Stevie was providing more pleasure than he'd ever experienced with any woman in any fashion. He was building to his first big moment, anticipating the lifetime of fantasies that would be fulfilled in a long night ahead. Feeling like he was practically levitating above the bed. So much wanting the moment, but not wanting it to pass quite yet. Trying to sustain as long as possible.

Then, release. Explosive release. Explosive satisfaction. Momentarily hovering between conscious reality and dream state. Panting. Heart racing. Bodily spent. Processing only fragments of thoughts. Those heaving, swaying breasts. That mouth, those hands. The reactions from the mopes at Uncle Charlie's when he described every glorious detail to them. Her incredible body. How good he must look to her, his muscles accentuated by perspiration. Masculinity on full display. How perfect they must look together.

As he writhed in pleasure, she reached again into her purse, thinking of the many disgusting men he represented. Their shameless arrogance as they succumbed to every guttural urge, unconcerned about whatever damage they might do. She smiled to herself. *So Prize Calloway has never had to pay for it. Maybe it's time …*

Chapter Four:

Thursday Afternoon: May 22, 2008

Andie Morrison's fingers started rocketing across her keyboard as soon as an all too familiar giggle slithered over the top of her cubicle. The cackle of B-Cup Benny's solitary laughter was a sure sign that he'd flung one of his unfunny jabs at some poor soul who failed to duck out of sight while he made his morning rounds through the Data Pit. The man's mastery of inappropriate humor was surpassed only by his perfect sense of bad timing. Though Benny was Andie's immediate supervisor, she wasn't worried about impressing him. She merely hoped that feigning preoccupation with some priority project might dissuade him from stopping at her workstation to *"spread honey with one of his dependable worker bees."*

Benjamin Atkins, Director of Database Research at KCPD headquarters, had been department head to nine senior analysts and more than thirty assistants, interns, part-timers and clericals for two-plus years. Previously a supervisor in Police Motor Vehicle Maintenance, he had moved into his current position knowing virtually nothing about police databases or the field of secondary criminal research. After twenty-eight months in charge, the same could be said and often was.

Like his father, Atkins was a lifer with KCPD. But in Benny's case, not out of any deep-rooted passion or proclivity for police work. His longevity with the department was due mostly to coincidence. In 1981, five marginal performance reviews since graduating from the Academy, he'd been assigned to Community Services on a probationary basis for what looked to be his last official chance. He was given six months to prove himself as Officer Safely, teaching Kansas City's elementary school kids about bicycle safety. In discharging this time-honored duty he miraculously had saved the lives of three first-graders. Or so it seemed.

On the historic afternoon, Officer Safely had just concluded his filmstrip presentation to ninety grade-schoolers gathered during their lunch period in the cafeteria. Teachers were organizing their respective classes into exit lines as tables were being cleared for the next wave of students. At this particular school the cafeteria staff used metal racks to transport trays of dirty dishes and flatware back to the sinks. The racks were about six-feet high and rolled on hard rubber casters. An elderly dishwasher had been trying to pull one of the racks up and over the film projector's extension cord. When the stubborn wheels stuck, the rack toppled toward a first grade class that happened to be marching single-file beside it. "Officer Benjamin Atkins heroically stepped in front of the massive descending tower before it tragically might have stolen three promising youths from our midst." At least that's how an incumbent mayor in a close re-election race recognized Benny's act of courage at a Civic Medal ceremony.

Neither the mayor nor the media people in attendance fully appreciated the unfettered honesty of Officer Benjamin Atkins's brief acceptance remarks.

"Thank you, I merely acted out of natural instinct."

Benny was a junk food junkie. In his public comments he chose not to reference how he'd spotted an unopened Twinkie left on a tray at a nearby table, or how he had been racing to intercept said Twinkie before the cafeteria staff cleared that table. In mid-dash, a big metal structure came falling toward him and he'd hurriedly shoved it off with his right arm so as not to block the shortest route to the uneaten snack treat. As milk cartons and Jell-O bowls pelted him, Atkins simultaneously swept aside three trembling seven-year-olds with his left arm. They, too, had stood between Benny and the Twinkie. Before he could even get his hand on the cream-filled treasure, the cafeteria had erupted into cheers and he stopped to see what all the noise was about. Next thing he knew, teachers were praising him for his courage and keen alertness in jumping between the kids and the falling rack. Then a flock of cheering kids began shouting their thanks to Officer Safely. Fortunately, Benny managed to suppress the primal urge to grab the unopened Twinkie that was still in his sights.

The mayor's promise forever was captured by news cameras from every local TV station. "The Kansas City Police Department will always find a place for selfless officers like Ben Atkins."

For twenty-seven years, KCPD had been trying to locate that place. With only a handful of years before Benny qualified for full retirement, it looked less and less likely that the Department would have time to uncover a single redeeming skill.

KCPD Human Resources Division had figured Database Research might provide a final safe haven for Benny to secure his pension. No weapons. No direct interface with criminals or the public. Minimal interaction with other police personnel. More importantly, the nine senior research analysts in the group didn't seem to need much direct supervision. They were proven professionals with one particular bright young star to whom the others looked for guidance. According to the evaluations in her file, this Andrea Morrison was highly skilled in data searches and seemed to get along well with everyone. Best of all, she'd never raised a single complaint about anything – unheard of in a police department. After checking with her previous bosses, HR was convinced Ms. Morrison was unlikely to make any noise about having a harmless amoeba like Atkins foisted over her for a few years. Thus far, they'd been correct.

During his decades of soft assignments, Benny found time to devour a lot more Twinkies, plus plenty of burritos, chilidogs and barbecued ribs. The first day Ben Atkins was introduced around the DRC (the Database Research Center, or more familiarly, the Data Pit), eyes were drawn instantly to the flabby rolls and man boobs that wobbled in competing directions under his sweat-stained shirt.

He lecherously had suggested to a cluster of young analysts, "You girls can call me King B."

But no sooner did he jiggle out of sight than they coined the real nickname by which he became known – "B-Cup Benny." Plain "Benny" to his face.

"Andie, you look far too busy for police work. You aren't logged onto one of those poker sites are you?" The hideous cackle followed.

Normally Andie ignored the inane wisecracks from her harmless joke of a boss, as he at least knew enough to stay out of her way on anything meaningful. But this morning she decided to road test her new assertiveness by toying with B-Cup. Pretending to take his question literally, Andie turned from her computer conveying a look of mock concern.

"Of course not, Benny, I hope by now you'd know that I wouldn't use department equipment for personal interests. But I'm glad you've raised this sensitive subject … there's something I'm afraid I must bring up with you."

Benny wasn't sure where she was going, but he already regretted that he'd tried to be funny.

Andie lowered her voice to confer utmost confidentiality, "On the monthly usage logs, I've noticed that one of our departmental PC's keeps finding its way to what would have to be described as … how can I say this?" She paused, watching him grow visibly uncomfortable. "Let's just say someone is logging onto destinations that certainly aren't work-related and are adult in nature. I've been meaning to verify whose computer it might be."

The whole time, she never broke eye contact. He finally did, pulling a handkerchief from a pants pocket and wiping it across the back of his neck.

"Now, dear Andrea, I simply was having some fun with you … I know you're too busy to play poker at work. In fact, you've got far more important things to worry about than what others are doing during their down time."

She stared at him for a few moments before offering a straight-faced reply, "You're probably right, Sergeant Atkins." Then Andie turned and started typing away on her keyboard again, leaving Benny hovering awkwardly.

"Uhh, Miss Morrison, I did have some official business to cover with you."

She swiveled back around, "I'm sorry, Benny. How can I help you?"

"We've got a homicide out in Grandview."

Andie dropped the games. "I really am sorry, what do we have?"

"Not a whole lot yet. They found a body this morning and Forensics is on their way to assist Grandview PD. But we can get started."

Andie pulled a pad from the drawer, feeling a queasiness she'd been unable to shake after eight years of homicides. It was strange to start jotting down the final details of a human life as routinely as a shopping list.

Benny pulled an index card from his shirt pocket and read the notes he'd taken from a phone call minutes earlier. "Male, Caucasian. Thirty-four years old. Single, lived alone. Royal Castle Apartments. 3576 Warwick Way, number 3D. Name, Ralph Calloway, Jr. Employed, Assistant Manager for Weight & See Fitness Club."

To keep personal emotions in check, Andie would as quickly as possible try to become a mere extension of her computer. She clicked into question mode, "Who found him and how?"

"Grandview Police. They were called when the victim didn't show up for work or answer his phone. And yes, he was at work yesterday. Locals are checking when and where he was last seen."

"Do we have anything on the body yet?"

"Not pretty. Found in his own blood, throat slashed ear to ear."

"Where?"

"In his bed. And apparently he died fast."

"Lucky for him."

"Luckier than you think."

"Meaning?"

"Meaning he was stark naked, dried semen all over his belly."

"Thank you for that, Benny. Anything else?"

"No, which makes this one pretty unusual. There was absolutely nothing else. No liquor, no drugs, no weapons at the scene. No signs of struggle. But the oddest part, no clothes."

"You already said he was naked."

"No, Andie, I mean there were no clothes on the floor, the furniture … anywhere. No sign of what he was wearing before he jumped in the sack. Kind of weird, don't you think? Maybe this Calloway was some sort of compulsive freak who needed everything hung up and put away before he could perform sexually."

"Or could be we simply have a perp who's careful."

Now what did that mean? B-Cup Benny admired, envied, but mostly resented how Andie Morrison immediately would start making those intuitive leaps of hers. "Andie, why don't you just start running your little matches and see what we come up with?"

"Police officials who need the public support of rank-and-file cops will never admit it, but the backbone of any police department today is its information systems."

She'd heard that from the keynote speaker at a professional conference a few years earlier. Andie may not have assigned that level of self-importance to what she and her cohorts did every day, but she was well aware that they shared the simple charge of keeping the entire criminal history of humankind within fingertip reach of the Kansas City Police Department.

It required extraordinary efforts to maintain and share information that encompassed the ever-increasing scope of modern civilization's criminals and criminal acts. From chronic speeders or scofflaws, to tax and alimony evaders. From parole violations and drug busts, to con men and molesters. From armed robberies or arsonists, to murders and murderers. From whatever the beat cop in a patrol car needed to know before making a routine traffic stop or domestic disturbance call, to what might help an undercover detective penetrate an international crime syndicate. The possibilities, the permutations were inexhaustible. Which was exactly why Andie loved her job.

She was hardly a techie. Andie had been drawn to computer systems because of her affinity for problem solving. From childhood puzzles to high school calculus, she'd viewed these mental exercises as mini-odysseys to finite closure. What other kids deemed as classroom drudgery, Andie had found exhilarating – finding the one irrefutable right answer. As far back as grade school, she'd recognized that computers afforded exponentially more opportunities to delve into complex problems and sort black from white.

Hence this analytical young woman, who so much loved to play, serendipitously had found the perfect career. The expanding labyrinth of police work databases offered up the consummate game board, each case a chance to navigate limitless possibilities in quest of a singular just solution. Andie attributed whatever job success she'd enjoyed to a relentless application of mathematical science, but others recognized something beyond. Her intuition. She had the uncanny ability to transform science into art.

Andie and her associates in the Data Pit routinely entered and screened tens of thousands of data points each day. KCPD, like all major police forces, was connected online to vast networks of databases from around the world, with the most critical being those licensed exclusively for police work. Round the clock, thousands of federal, state and local law enforcement professionals simultaneously submitted crime details or search requests tied to every known form of illegal activity. Petty misdemeanors to major felonies. The complexity of the databases fascinated Andie, as did the origins of each component part. She envied the FBI professionals who continuously launched and refined the sophisticated programs that were used across the country and much of the world.

If fingerprints were picked up at a crime scene, they'd be entered into AFIS, the Automated Fingerprint Identification System. If a crime lab picked up a DNA profile, it was entered into CODIS, the Combined DNA Index System. There were dozens of different systems being accessed and updated real-time with data gathered by police forces across all fifty states. Andie Morrison found it difficult to admit her highest aspirations even to herself. If she could just kick start that sleepy ambition of hers, maybe she could make a real difference in the world of database forensics.

⌒*∦*⌒

It had been close to 3:30 when Benny waddled away from her workstation and slipped out of the Data Pit, heading toward the vending machines. With a murder scenario as peculiar as the one in Grandview, Andie needed to prepare herself for countless data dives and the many blind alleys that she likely would travel. As much as the hard facts of a grisly murder were disturbing to her, the prospects of a new exploratory journey excited Andie. Her Thursday night doctoral class in forensic psychology didn't start until 7:00, so there was time to screen for some of the obvious possibilities. She might as well get a few out of the way.

She clicked open a new master file and typed in a name, GRANDVIEW MURDER: CALLOWAY. She then started keying a rapid series of questions into databases.

UNSOLVED VIOLENT CRIMES, MISSOURI OR KANSAS? Then the surrounding states. She scanned back over a two-year period, then five, then ten, methodically probing for matches that might offer a clue or establish a pattern.

MURDERS, THROAT SLASHED? She found [7].

Of those … HOW MANY REMAIN UNSOLVED? [0]

Next entry point, UNSOLVED MURDERS, NUDE CORPSES? [11]

Of corpses … MALES? [3]

Of males … TRACES OF SEMEN? [0]

Another subset. MALE CORPSES, IN OWN RESIDENCE? [5]

Of those … UNSOLVED? [0]

And so she queried for three more hours. The results were as expected. Violent homicides made for big headlines but their occurrence weren't all that frequent. This violent homicide appeared to be a sex crime and Andie recognized that the Calloway case already fell into an unusual category.

The victim was an adult male and historical data skewed dramatically otherwise. With sex crimes, the perpetrators were predominantly adult men, but the victims most often were adult females, adolescents or children – particularly when violent or fatal. When a sex crime victim was an adult male, likelihood was high that the victim, murderer or both would turn out to be homosexual or bisexual. She knew that detectives immediately would have started checking into Ralph Calloway's lifestyle preferences.

Andie scowled at the clock, dreading her professor's reaction to another late arrival. But by hanging in for a few more minutes, she could enter the Grandview homicide profile into the national screening services. Results of broader geographic searches would be awaiting her the next morning via classified e-mail. She assumed nothing would come back but she needed to cover off the basics as quickly as possible.

Chapter Five:

Friday Morning; May 23, 2008

As soon as Andie logged onto her computer, her eyes lost their welcoming sparkle. She stared at the messages flashing in her inbox. POSSIBLE AFFIRMATIVE MATCH – FILE ATTACHED. Not once, but twice. She took a deep breath and opened the first. SEATTLE: MARCH 27, 2007.

Surface facts seemed eerily similar. The body of a twenty-nine year old male Caucasian, Geoffrey Thomas Wegman, was found on a houseboat that belonged to his parents. They had allowed him to live there alone. His nude corpse was face-up on a blood-soaked double bed, throat slashed, dried semen on the chest and abdominal area.

Andie scrolled deeper into the file, feeling the adrenaline from chasing down a potentially significant break in the early stages of a case, but dreading the dire implications if the murders were connected. The forensics report indicated that the only readable fingerprints on the houseboat were traced to the victim or individuals eventually eliminated as suspects. A few natural hair specimens likewise traced to the victim, but a strand of synthetic blond hair had been collected from a bed sheet. Nothing meaningful from fabric or particle samples. No signs of drinking or drugs at the crime scene. The prevailing theory from investigators was that the victim and perpetrator had boarded the boat for the sole purpose of sexual interaction. Yet no samples of bodily fluids beyond his own were found on or around the victim, with no indication that the perpetrator had wiped away any such fluids.

However, two non-bodily fluids were noted in the report. Wegman's torso and genital area had been covered liberally with a massage oil, which Seattle Forensics sourced as Solace, readily available at most drug stores.

The second substance was a narcotic opioid, fentanyl, that had dried around his nose and mouth in a spray pattern. The autopsy report indicated fentanyl also had been absorbed into his central nervous system.

A link to a scientific write-up on fentanyl was included in the Seattle file, so Andie familiarized herself before moving on. She learned fentanyl first had been synthesized in the 1950's as a painkiller with up to eighty times the potency of morphine. It most commonly was found in pain medications for advanced cancer patients, but over the past twenty years also had grown in both popularity and availability for non-medicinal purposes. Laced into heroin or cocaine, fentanyl enhanced the desired highs. Hundreds, if not thousands, of scientifically trained entrepreneurs were operating clandestine laboratories that profited from an expanding market.

For medical treatment, fentanyl typically was applied in gel form via patches, with dose concentrations calibrated to a patient's pain level. If sprayed directly into a person's face in liquid form, unconsciousness could be expected within a matter of seconds. A final footnote described how the anesthetic properties had become more widely recognized after 2002, when the Russian Army utilized fentanyl in gaseous form to incapacitate terrorists holding 800 hostages inside a Moscow theater.

In the Wegman case, Seattle's medical experts concluded it highly improbable that a male could have been stimulated to ejaculation after being rendered unconscious by fentanyl. But medical and police investigators had concurred that the moments immediately following ejaculation would have been an especially opportune time to spray the liquid for maximum sedative impact. The drug's anesthetic potency was in great part due to rapid absorptive qualities. Through ingestion, inhalation or dermal contact, fentanyl quickly enters the nervous system to start shutting down impulses to the brain. The short panting breaths accompanying male ejaculation would have quickened the assimilation into Wegman's system through the mucous membranes lining his mouth.

The presence of fentanyl also contributed to Seattle PD's conclusion that the murder had been premeditated. The perp had possessed an illegal substance not readily accessible, then managed to manipulate the victim into a situation where it could be applied to maximum advantage. Hardly a spontaneous act.

The estimated time of death was between 2AM and 3AM on Tuesday, March 27. The body had been found Thursday morning after Wegman missed his Wednesday night poker game. The murder weapon was believed to have been a razor-like blade. A 19.15 centimeter incision had been inflicted rapidly from above or behind, left to right, without obstruction. Consistent with the presence of fentanyl, the victim appeared to have offered no resistance. Wegman's blood alcohol level was a manageable 0.0129, but according to the autopsy, even this amount in his system would have furthered the speed with which the fentanyl took effect. There were no traces of other narcotics in his system.

Whatever clothes the victim had worn that evening appeared to have been removed from the houseboat. Robbery was dismissed as a motive because jewelry and other valuable possessions were left undisturbed, openly visible in the boat's cabin. Wegman's wallet, cash and credit cards were found in the console of his car, parked on a concrete pad above the steps down to the boat's private pier. Investigators concluded another car had been parked on the pad, but found no evidence leading to make or model. Adjacent houseboats on the secluded waterway were usually unoccupied on weeknights, so there were no witnesses to any activity around the pier on the night of the murder.

Wegman last had been seen on Monday evening at a boaters' bar he frequented. According to the bartender and wait staff, Wegman had been drinking but not excessively. There had been no apparent confrontations. He'd engaged in conversations with five different women throughout the evening. All were prior acquaintances and each could establish where she spent the balance of the evening and subsequent early morning. According to regular patrons, Wegman liked telling off-color jokes and on the Monday evening preceding his death he shared several particularly raunchy ones with the bartender and fellow patrons. He also passed around pictures of a recent date he'd convinced to pose topless. He had exited to the parking lot with two male acquaintances at approximately 11:45PM, where they separated to their respective vehicles. Neither had observed anyone else in the parking lot.

The bartender and waitresses provided whatever details they could recall about unfamiliar customers during the evening, but none were seen interacting with Wegman. Andie glanced down the list. Two motorcycle couples that liked dancing. Three off-duty Navy officers, one female and two male. A middle-aged woman looking for her husband. A woman off to herself, preoccupied with a book. An out-of-state businessman seated at the bar watching a basketball game. And so forth. Nothing or no one stood out. Police had been able to identify the Navy officers through Northwest

Regional Headquarters in Silverdale. A few others who'd paid by credit card were contacted and interviewed. Nothing had gone anywhere.

Andie read through the summaries of interviews with the victim's acquaintances. Geoff Wegman had claimed to restore boats for a living, but his friends only knew of one finished project. He occasionally did other odd jobs around the waterways, but as a rule had relied on regular subsidies from his parents. He'd been cocky about his wealthy upbringing yet still reasonably likable to most. Three different times he was engaged to marry, and three different fiancés had broken it off. None of them had seen Wegman in several months and each found it difficult to criticize the deceased beyond a few "silver spoon" references.

Andie finished her initial read of the Wegman case. The murder investigation had gone dormant in the fourteen months since March of 2007, with no relevant leads. The similarities to the Calloway murder in Grandview were striking and Andie would notify KCPD detectives of potential ties to the Seattle crime. But first she wanted to take a quick look at the second e-mailed file – this one from Indianapolis and dated October 17, 2007, seven months after the houseboat murder in Seattle.

Robert Evan Huggins had been found in the backseat of his Explorer, parked in a vacant strip mall. His dead body was sitting up, leaned against the rear door on the driver's side, head back and pants down, an unused condom in his hand. No dried semen. No slashed throat. No fentanyl, or other form of sedative. Cause of death, a 38-caliber bullet through the forehead. The weapon, his own gun.

Huggins had been a thirty-eight year old Caucasian, married, with two children. He'd worked in a diesel engine assembly plant and was last seen alive by a group of co-workers. According to the police report, they'd played in a Tuesday evening fall softball league before heading to CoCo Lounge, an exotic dance club on the west side of Indianapolis. Huggins had left the gathering around midnight, presumed to be homebound. The vacant shopping center where his vehicle had been found was several blocks from CoCo's. His own home, a townhouse, was eighteen miles away in Avon.

In an interview with detectives, the victim's young widow indicated that she'd suspected her husband of being sexually active outside their marriage. She herself had taken up with Huggins during his first marriage. When she became pregnant, "he did me honorable by divorcing that first wife and moving in with me." Three years and two children later they'd been married.

Indianapolis PD had been unable to connect anyone from the victim's circle of acquaintances to the crime. Nor could investigators connect any of the prostitutes that worked the area around the nightclub, including a few who admitted prior business transactions with Bobby Huggins. Despite the fact the murder weapon was the victim's own gun, nothing else had suggested suicide. Nine months later, the investigation was still classified as "ongoing," but Andie saw nothing that indicated any recent activity.

The case had been flagged from a national database and e-mailed to Andie because it fit several criteria for which she'd screened – MALE MURDER VICTIM, PARTIALLY OR TOTALLY UNCLOTHED, SEX-RELATED. Andie noted that like Calloway and Wegman, the victim had last been seen exiting a drinking establishment. But otherwise, there were far more differences than similarities. At best, a maybe.

Chapter Six:

Patience

In 2006, when Stephanie Burton resigned as CEO of Gerber, Alton & Jennings at age thirty-five, her envious peers in the industry assumed she wanted to go out at the peak of an unprecedented four-year run. Thousands of company associates from around the world feared their charismatic leader might be facing some life-threatening disease or personal crisis. Stephanie had kept her real reasons to herself. Continuing to head of one of the world's largest ad agency networks would constrain her from the grander aspirations she at last felt prepared to pursue.

Little more than a decade earlier, GA&J had been a lumbering dinosaur, the final bastion of a flanneled gray gentry that ruled advertising from its 19th Century inception through the 1970's. By the early Eighties, enough baby-booming women and minorities had logged the requisite experience to start reshaping the industry's managerial ranks, a trend GA&J had chosen totally to ignore – which was exactly why Stephanie Burton applied for a job there while finishing up her MBA at Northwestern's Kellogg School. She was certain the gentlemen's club at GA&J would soon be forced to pull their heads out of the sand or risk losing high profile clients under increased pressure to hire agencies with appropriate diversity standards. Stephanie had been confident there would be leveragable advantages for a talented, ambitious woman already inside the organization once GA&J got its wake-up call.

Ten months prior to spring graduation in 1995, Stephanie had submitted her resume to the agency's Michigan Avenue headquarters in Chicago and persistently phoned the HR officer responsible for the management training program. Her inquiries were just as persistently deflected to a hiring coordinator whose sole function seemed to be telling applicants that GA&J wasn't currently hiring. But as Stephanie continued to overhear male classmates boast about how heavily they were being recruited by GA&J, her patience wore thin. The entrenched double standards were bound to crumble and she could help the agency make a more constructive transition – but in the meantime, the old rules remained in effect. Growing up, she'd witnessed enough of those and knew how to play by them.

She boarded a pre-dawn train from Evanston and parked herself in the lobby of the agency's executive floor. Finally at 9:25, she'd heard the receptionist's saccharin voice, "Good morning, Mr. Lumpkin." Stephanie jumped right up.

"Mr. Lumpkin, sir, my name is Stephanie Margaret Burton and I'm here to help you address your agency's looming problem on sex standards."

Jack Lumpkin's mind filled with a dozen questions at once. *What kind of bush league move was this? How'd this person get up here? Aren't six high-priced creative teams already waiting for me in a conference room? Where's my coffee? And … slow down … isn't this young lady about the most exquisite creature I've ever laid eyes upon? Wouldn't I just love to establish some new sex standards with that body of hers?"*

Two weeks later, upon accepting the offer to become an account executive, Stephanie fully recognized that the agency president had been far more impressed by her physical attributes than whatever professional capabilities she might happen to possess. After all, she'd carefully selected the slit skirt, high heels and tight blouse that made that crucial first impression. She was more than able to self-justify the cheesy ploy to contend with the likes of Jack Lumpkin and an outdated male guard. Constructive change would take time. Patience.

Besides, Stephanie Burton had no reason to doubt her legitimate talent and business abilities. She'd been pursued aggressively by many of the top marketing and consulting firms in the country. Her credentials made her one of the most sought-after students in the entire business school. Prior to Northwestern, she had graduated Phi Beta Kappa from Columbia University with degrees in Psychology and Economics. She'd earned both in just three years of heavy course loads. She then had worked for a year as an international intern with Nestle in Switzerland. Though top business schools preferred older applicants with a few more years of work experience, Northwestern had admitted her into its program at age twenty-two without hesitation. Due to her poise, maturity and intelligence, classmates and faculty members never picked up on her relative youth. As she neared completion of her MBA, Procter & Gamble, Pepsico and

Boston Consulting Group each offered her six-figure salaries plus hefty sign-ons to join their fast-track executive development programs. Stephanie instead stuck to the career path she'd researched and plotted for herself. She believed she could more rapidly build the foundaton of experience she wanted by joining sleepy Gerber, Alton & Jennings, starting at forty-three grand. The entire organization had been ripe for transformation, offering countless opportunities to ignite change and instill a more progressive culture.

Twelve months later, Stephanie's career was heading nowhere. Patience, she'd continued to remind herself. As a junior account executive she was buried several layers deep under male managers who refused to take any female seriously. Most of her project assignments entailed late night number crunching or writing backgrounders for faceless bosses several levels above. On occasion she'd been invited to attend client meetings, mostly as window dressing with explicit instructions not to answer or ask any substantive questions. Changing the culture of GA&J might prove harder than anticipated.

The day after her first anniversary with the firm, Stephanie donned another slit skirt ensemble and paid a visit to Jack Lumpkin. On her own time she had been analyzing how GA&J competed with other ad agencies in bringing strategic insights to its existing clients and gaining attention from prospective new clients. By detailing the breadth of fresh consumer-driven initiatives used by competitive agencies, she demonstrated to Lumpkin that GA&J was continuing to lose relevance in a dynamic industry. She proposed how the agency could leapfrog to the forefront by forming a small, dedicated group that identified salient market trends some 5 to 10 years out and then conducted themselves and their business as if those conditions existed today. Through this on-going simulation of the future marketplace, the unit could consult clients on how best to reshape current market activities to preempt the future. She presented Lumpkin a multi-year plan for building a practice called FutureScape.

Though he tried to project polite neutrality, every nuance of Lumpkin's body language had revealed his excitement for the concept. On Monday of the following week he phoned her back. "Stephanie, I want to commend you on your insights and inform you that Gerber, Alton & Jennings will announce the formation of FutureScape. We discussed it thoroughly at a management offsite over the weekend."

She figured that meant the agency's four top execs had played golf on Saturday and talked about her proposal over their single malts. "That's wonderful, Mr. Lumpkin. I look forward to making you all very proud of your decision."

"I'm counting on that and so is Kent Gillespie."

A few frozen moments passed before Stephanie responded, "Kent Gillespie? I'm not sure I understand."

"Well, you'll be happy to know that Kent has agreed to head up the unit."

"But I proposed that I run the group."

"Surely, Stephanie, you weren't serious. You're still barely out of grad school and, to be frank, you've hardly set the place on fire. But you should know that Kent is emphatic about wanting you as his number two."

As Stephanie reflected on the Gillespie choice, she recognized that she could have done a lot worse. Of course, Lumpkin and his cronies would never have bought into her as the senior point person. She'd known that. But her presumptuous proposal had generated two promising consequences. First, the number two position was hers, as she'd hoped. Second, but unexpected, was someone like Kent Gillespie. He was only five years out of B-School himself and not yet locked into the firm's closed fraternity ways. Her audacious proposition to senior management that Stephanie Burton, with only a year's experience, could manage the operation must have made Gillespie seem like a weathered warhorse by comparison. GA&J's inaugural youth movement was at last underway. With the younger Kent Gillespie in charge, Stephanie knew she'd have greater latitude to establish her own platform and profile. With the younger Gillespie in charge, she was optimistic about maneuvering past him and presiding over FutureScape much faster than planned.

Stephanie Burton had waited her turn. It seemed that for all of her twenty-five years she'd been biding her time, playing by other people's rules. Watching one person after another accede to what was easiest, to what was most instantly gratifying … so willing to abandon any loftier hopes. Indeed for her, patience had proven itself as a virtue. For Stephanie Burton, a real beginning, with so many other virtues still to be tested.

Chapter Seven:

Ambition

Three years after FutureScape was announced, the embryonic practice had mushroomed to nearly two hundred people and become the fastest growing operation within GA&J's global organization. Kent Gillespie remained its Managing Director, but Stephanie M. Burton had been appointed its first President. Winning over and moving past Gillespie was no particular challenge. Unforeseen was how much she'd end up liking the guy. In fact, more than liking, she ended up living with him.

It was as if Stephanie had been born to create FutureScape. She convinced Gillespie to let her assemble a team of young renegades who would rather live in the future than dally in the present. She pried them out of whatever modest contentment they found in doctoral programs, social work, seminaries and bartending … or lured them away from the claustrophobic rigors of white-collar tedium. The FutureScape staff became instantly hers, not Kent's and not GA&J's. Hers.

Burton was an impassioned mentor to her hand-chosen. Each was drawn to her intellect … her vision for FutureScape and an unyielding standard of excellence in everything they did. Each was drawn to her compassion towards their individual life journeys and goals. Drawn to her affirmative personality and calmness in any situation … the ease of daily interactions. How she collaboratively coached them. When necessary, how she went to bat for them. Her loyalty to them was unquestionable. Likewise, theirs in return. Late nights, weekends, holidays, the clock became incidental. Their family was each other, their home an old warehouse converted into a vast domed workroom with the firmament painted across its ceiling. None among them ever had experienced the exuberance of performing at such a high level, or would have thought it possible. Previously, none among them would have believed such respect and dignity was attainable in a workplace.

Beyond what they could accomplish together, Stephanie Burton was uplifted by the FutureScape team on a whole different dimension. She connected to them with an intimacy and genuineness that she hadn't been able to experience with other personal relationships. These feelings had provided new hope that dark inner voids might someday disappear … that nobler ideals could prevail.

Initially the ad agency's traditional account managers were reluctant to introduce this merry band of oddballs to important corporate clients who were more conservative by nature. But soon their impact was undeniable. Clients were enthralled by Burton and ecstatic with how FutureScape forced them to rethink their business fundamentals. They couldn't get enough of Stephanie Burton, her insights, the charisma. Clients wanted her to participate in management conferences, to motivate sales forces, to speak at shareholder meetings. Buzz on the street prompted clients of other agencies to call GA&J and request introductory meetings just so they could see the remarkable Burton woman in action.

By 1999, GA&J became the hottest agency in the industry and twenty-eight year old Stephanie Burton was named to the agency's board of directors, taking home three quarters of a million a year. Jack Lumpkin was arguably the most propitious beneficiary of Stephanie's vision. When Clifford Gerber, grandson to the agency's founder, retired as CEO in early 1999, Lumpkin was named successor. Jack had been an average executive at best, but he'd hired Stephanie and subsequently advocated FutureScape. With a nest egg more obscenely immense than he ever could have fantasized, Lumpkin announced his own retirement three years later. One final glass ceiling remained and the board was left no choice. Just seven years after flashing her charms at Jack Lumpkin in the 18th floor lobby, Stephanie Margaret Burton was named CEO of what once had been the impenitent archetype of trousered chauvinism. To say the least, her career strategy had worked.

With Stephanie at the top, the ensuing four years for GA&J were even more phenomenal. The agency intensified its creative and media resources in every corner of the world to attract more and more global clients. GA&J demonstrated a superior readiness for the Internet explosion that forced other agencies to play catch-up. GA&J and Stephanie Burton repeatedly were recognized within the ad industry as the best in the business. The agency's network of 132 offices jumped from ninth in the world to third in overall media billings and was unquestionably the most profitable.

Paralleling the impressive business growth, Gerber, Alton & Jennings also set new standards for diversity – upholding ethnic, gender and cultural standards that were as progressive as any company's anywhere. Throughout its explosive global expansion, young talent flocked to the agency under Stephanie Burton's leadership. She tirelessly inspired and applauded as waves of promising new stars grew in confidence, experience and specialized strengths. Likewise, veteran professionals rediscovered lost passions or stretched their once rigid envelopes of curiosity and ambition.

But regardless of how historic and lucrative these four years as CEO might have been for Stephanie, they weren't nearly as stimulating or emotionally rewarding as the seven that preceded – those years when she'd formed FutureScape and for the first time in her life bonded so trustingly with a semblance of family. As with many accomplished executives, life at the top was less fulfilling than her climb to get there. But for Stephanie, a secret part of that fulfillment had been derived from beating men at their own game.

Without exception, Stephanie downplayed the countless industry recognitions and client tributes that came her way. When awards were presented to the agency, she found convenient reasons to have other executives accept them. It wasn't out of modesty, either real or false. It was her inner feelings of unworthiness. She constantly was tormented by the hypocrisy of her outward behavior as she struggled to contain the malicious thoughts that roiled within. Yet whatever her private demons, Stephanie Burton had established GA&J as a paradigm of loftier principles. She had proven to herself that ordinary people were indeed eager to reach higher … and that she possessed a natural ability to connect with these latent desires and help inspire them. Now, by leaving the ad industry, she intended to do it all again, but on a much grander scale.

Chapter Eight:

December, 2006

A week before Christmas in 2006, business cards and stationery were delivered to her LaSalle Street address. "The Stephanie M. Burton Consultancy" consisted of Stephanie, an administrative assistant and twelve hundred square feet of office space. She purposely had sought an office in the Loop, the heart of Chicago's financial district. Real power invariably was found near the money source, and as long as she stayed in Chicago that's what she wanted her address to convey.

Stephanie could distill her short-term business plan down to a simple statement, at least to herself. *Exploit every opportunity to gain exposure.* Because of her natural disdain for blatant opportunism, she was conflicted with this approach. But she knew there had been other occasions when she'd felt compelled to make distasteful choices in anticipation of the longer term good she hoped to accomplish.

Burton believed she now possessed the appropriate credentials to climb into the ring with the big boys. As a noted ad exec, she'd rubbed elbows with the country's corporate elite – but always as a service provider rather than a true equal. She was ready to establish a broader reputation that transcended her specific industry background, as well as her gender. With a broader platform she might inspire others to pursue their highest potential, to not succumb to destructive urges or influences, to soar toward glorious realms that poets and philosophers envisioned. This was the type of self-actualization that too few people were even willing to ponder. These were the noble principles to which she'd clung since youth, despite the many destructive behaviors that had surrounded her. Despite her own destructive tendencies.

Following her telephonic farewell address to GA&J's worldwide staff in September, Stephanie had escaped to a Mediterranean Island with Kent Gillespie for a month. They read, ran, swam, played, ate and slept like teenagers. By 2006, they'd lived together for nine years and she was looking for commitment. Not from him, but within herself. Stephanie long had wondered whether she could commit to the kind of loving relationship that two people deserve from one another. She'd wondered if she loved Kent Gillespie or was even capable of true romance with someone at all.

Kent was a decent, caring, talented man. After nearly a decade, she still enjoyed being with him. He was the first man who had kindled any kind of positive feeling inside her. But was that love, or simply deep respect and comfort? Amidst the intensity of busy careers, their relationship had been built upon available time fragments. It had been too easy to dismiss or defer the nagging questions she carried. Before jumping into a whole new chapter of her life and pulling Kent along, he deserved to know. For the inner peace she desperately sought for her own journey, she needed to know. Thus, the first priority upon wrapping up her ad career was spending an uninterrupted month alone with Kent.

Then Stephanie had taken off for a second month by herself, to tend to other questions she'd kept shelved over the years of laser focus on her career. By December of 2006, she had answers. Though many of those were not to her liking, she at least had answers. She was prepared to launch into the next phase of her life, hoping to help others in search of their own answers, in search of more meaningful purpose.

Stephanie hadn't bothered to line up consulting assignments in advance of opening her practice. She suspected that business would find her once she was duly prepared to accept it. She placed calls to business columnists at the *Wall Street Journal, New York Times,* and *Chicago Tribune.* Each owed her more than a few favors and the following day all three made reference to Stephanie Burton's new consulting practice in their columns. None of them bothered to report much detail about the type of consulting services she intended to provide. It was enough to know that a talent of this magnitude was available. The phone immediately began to ring, practically non-stop.

Chapter Nine:

January, 2007

Stephanie never had heard of P.E.T. when her assistant slipped a note across the desk that a Mr. Cummings, its executive director, was on the other line. Four weeks into her new enterprise, Stephanie Burton had been presented more opportunities than she could tackle in several years – board positions with public corporations, guest columns for national business magazines, retainers to serve as a confidential advisor to several *Fortune 100* CEO's, and countless strategic assignments from respected companies and institutions throughout the world. Stephanie cherry-picked the offers that would help her gain exposure and most rapidly build the broader platform she sought.

She churned through her memory trying to recollect anything resembling P.E.T., but nothing registered. *Some start-up company? Some animal rights group?* She punched Line 2, expecting a quick conversation and a polite decline to whatever offer Mr. Cummings wanted to extend.

An hour later, after further background explorations on the Internet, Stephanie was trying to temper her fervency. P.E.T. stood for Personal Empowerment Tour. In recent years she'd noticed the growing number of advertisements for daylong mega-conferences featuring big-name presenters. Everyday folks were paying outlandish sums to sit in a sports arena and be emboldened by recognized achievers. But she hadn't given a thought to how the mechanics of these forums worked, or what kind of people were behind all this perceived goodwill. Until now. P.E.T., Inc. was a private corporation headquartered in Philadelphia that appeared to be making tons of cash inspiring the masses. Since its inception, P.E.T. had been holding one event per month, each in different cities across the country.

Following her phone conversation with Mr. Cummings, Stephanie pulled up P.E.T.com, where she checked out ticket prices and attendance figures. P.E.T.'s organization and staff also were profiled at the website. Elsewhere, she found its S-Corp filing, which detailed the ownership structure. She searched through articles to get an idea of how much speakers might be paid for each engagement. She applied some rough numbers and the arithmetic was incredible.

Put fifteen to twenty thousand folks into a stadium at somewhere between $75 and $150 apiece. Pay six or seven living legends fifty-thousand each to make a speech. Budget a few hundred grand for renting the venue, security, equipment, etc. … a similar amount for advertising to fill the seats. Pay standard commissions to a few ticket brokers. Allocate a twelfth of the annual overhead to each monthly event for administrative staff, road crews, and so forth. Allow for a little slippage here and there … you still net more than a million bucks per city for a handful of partners.

It hadn't taken Stephanie long to understand why those partners might have heard a higher calling to inspire America's masses.

Sam Cummings had invited Stephanie to become one of the featured speakers at the next monthly event, in early February of 2007. It had been revealed that a former U.S. Attorney General, who was slated to appear, was under investigation for not disclosing her Cayman bank accounts. If Stephanie did well in her debut, P.E.T. might want to include her as a regular in future events.

The fifty thousand dollars per engagement wasn't what attracted her.

In part, it was the exposure she could gain through being affiliated with such a company of speakers – a retired Chairman of the Joint Chiefs, a former New Jersey Senator who once had run as the Republican Party's vice presidential candidate, a gold medal winner in the Olympic decathlon, a semi-retired network news anchor, the author of a string of best-selling books, and a former Detroit CEO who was credited with reshaping domestic car design.

In part, she was intrigued by the opportunity to learn more about what was behind P.E.T. and how its impressive list of partners had been brought together in such a venture.

But mostly, Stephanie Burton was eager to stand before large live audiences and speak to them not about advertising and marketing plans. No, at last speak directly and unashamedly to people about pursuing their own potentials … about experiencing greater fulfillment from searching inside themselves for their own positive energies and aspirations. She was eager to discover if she really could connect with them, if she could touch them as meaningfully as she'd always hoped.

⸜𝓂⸝

Stephanie Burton may not have had the name recognition of P.E.T.'s established roster of personalities, but the Memphis audience inside FedEx Forum took very special notice of her the first time she stepped up to the podium. She was younger than the others by at least twenty-five years. She definitely was more attractive. And she spoke from the heart, not some script that might have been used hundreds of times before. While the others recounted their pasts, she looked to the future, as she'd done so many times with FutureScape. Her passion, her flair, her pulse beat with the audience was evident in every phrase and gesture … the impact obvious from the audience's overwhelming reaction.

Sam Cummings immediately recognized that P.E.T. had found its missing piece for the new age revival meetings. The marquee value of celebrities and retired dignitaries would continue to sell plenty of high-priced tickets, but this woman finally could assure that everyone left an arena feeling that they got their money's worth. P.E.T. occasionally had freshened its cycle of politicians, actors, athletes and academicians, but no one ever had captivated a crowd like Stephanie Burton. Starting the next month, Cummings would make her the last speaker before the prepackaged finale. P.E.T. traditionally had needed its slick, high-tech multi-media module to rally worn-down audiences into a perfunctory standing ovation … but this Burton gal had people practically leaping out of their seats before she'd even completed her remarks.

After Stephanie signed a contract for the balance of the 2007 tour, she hardly could wait for the next opportunity to stand before a massive assembly and feel the electric connection again. Having watched how her fellow speakers behaved in Memphis, she'd felt other anticipations building as well. These men, these living legends had flaunted their clubby ways … they'd been completely dismissive of her, of the audience … so blusterous in the mutual stoking of their manly egos. Yet she knew she had outperformed them where it counted, on the stage, with the audience. She looked forward to the next monthly showdown. And privately, another impulse stirred.

Chapter Ten:

Saturday; May 24, 2008

The body of Prize Calloway was found on Thursday. By Saturday afternoon, KCPD concluded the murder was linked to the Wegman case in Seattle – most probably committed by the same person. The likelihood of a copycat was small since the Seattle homicide had received little media coverage outside Washington State, plus a number of undisclosed crime specifics were identical. Either way, the possibilities now crossed state lines and the FBI had been notified.

Andie Morrison sacrificed a weekend in the Ozarks to prepare a report comparing and contrasting the early findings from the Calloway investigation in Grandview with the fourteen-month-old Wegman case in Seattle. An FBI expert in serial homicides, en route from Denver, would be taking charge. He likely expected a detailed briefing upon his arrival and Andie wanted to make certain that KCPD came across as buttoned up. Golfing with Pops and galling Mother could hold for another weekend.

The unfolding facts from Grandview revealed that Calloway had been murdered with a razor or razor-like instrument from above or behind – just like Wegman in Seattle. The left-to-right incision was made cleanly and measured 20.62 centimeters. Forensics concluded Calloway was in a vulnerable supine position, face up on the bed, when his exposed throat had been cut. There were no signs that he'd offered resistance. As with Wegman, fentanyl had been absorbed into Calloway's central nervous system and exterior amounts were found around the nose and mouth. No trace of other narcotics. His blood alcohol level was a moderately high 0.0213.

The amount of semen on and around Calloway's body suggested that the preceding sex acts were likely to have been prolonged. It appeared sexual activity consisted solely of manual stimulation of the victim. Neither saliva, vaginal fluids nor residues from a condom were present on the victim – but liberal amounts of the massage oil, Solace, were.

The only identifiable fingerprints belonged to the victim. The doorknob and deadbolt at the entry to the apartment had been wiped clean on both sides of the door. The only human hairs from the crime scene were likewise the victim's. However, two fragments of synthetic hair, blond in color, had been found amidst the bed linens and would be turned over to the FBI for analytical comparison to the single strand from Seattle. There was nothing else present from which a DNA sample might be taken.

Calloway's wallet had not been located. A Seiko outdoorsman watch valued at several hundred dollars, and also wiped clean, was still on his wrist when the body had been discovered. There was no evidence to suggest that any possessions in his apartment were touched or that anyone besides Calloway had been inside his Chevy Blazer in recent days. A co-worker indicated Calloway rarely had carried more than thirty dollars in his wallet, so robbery appeared an unlikely motive.

Questioning by Grandview police revealed Calloway last had been seen exiting a local nightspot, Uncle Charlie's Tavern, at close to midnight on Wednesday. The report established Ralph "Prize" Calloway as a regular patron of the bar. Interviews conducted thus far with Uncle Charlie's staff and clientele revealed that though his showy behavior during his final evening might have been considered unusual by most standards, it was viewed as customary for him. As yet, interviews had produced no material leads. Over the course of approximately four-and-a-half hours, Calloway had interacted with most persons in the bar, whether he knew them or not. But no incidents of note. No arguments or confrontations, no intimate conversations or outward advances with females. He had departed Uncle Charlie's alone, with no perceptible urgency or agitation. In fact, he'd indicated to the bartender and a number of regular acquaintances that he planned to join them at the tavern the following night.

Thus far, these preliminary soft interrogations conducted by Grandview Police had uncovered nothing to suggest any suspects. KCPD or the FBI, perhaps both, would follow-up more thoroughly with many of those who'd been at Uncle Charlie's on Wednesday.

Early interviews with employees and known patrons had generated descriptions for a variety of unfamiliar customers in the bar that night. Four UCLA grad students on a heartland road trip who stayed until 2AM closing. Three Grandview gals celebrating a 21st birthday by hitting every bar in town, who ordered a quick round of fuzzy navels before moving on. A middle-aged married couple with an hour to burn before a late movie at the nearby Cineplex. Two salesman types seated at the bar, making dinner out of popcorn, chicken wings and vodka. A middle-aged businesswoman doing paperwork in a booth away from the noise. Two couples in their thirties or forties, who stopped in after a late movie at the Cineplex. Efforts were underway to identify and locate as many of these people as possible.

No residents at the Royal Castle Apartments recalled having seen Calloway or possible companions arrive or depart in the time frame of the murder. A second floor neighbor thought she remembered being awakened momentarily by footsteps on the exterior staircase and the sound of a woman's voice. She was unable to specify a time.

Interviewed family members and close acquaintances had scoffed at the questions about Calloway's interest or tendencies toward homosexuality.

⌒⁄⌒

Andie Morrison always had been thorough in her work, but this time she was bordering on obsession. No less than a dozen times had she reread and re-edited the report detailing the parallels between the Calloway and Wegman homicides. Some FBI know-it-all wasn't going to swoop in and conclude that her team was a bunch of Midwest bumpkins.

Standing at the Xerox, dutifully printing multiple copies of her final document, she felt her energy dropping. She realized that once she transferred the annotated bundle over to the FBI, her work on the case file would be suspended. The FBI's Data Section, the largest and most sophisticated criminal research network in the world, would pick it up from there. She then could look forward to the clueless one, B-Cup Benny, instructing her to refocus her energies on the kind of rote cases for which KCPD had jurisdiction. Back to car thieves and shoplifters.

For Andie, the two bizarre and mysterious murders represented a highly perplexing minefield of stops and starts. These were the kinds of cases she was cut out for. She'd felt the adrenaline rushing through her as she worked on them. Her confidence, her ambitions were actually kicking in. Now, the prospect of not tackling these murders seemed incomprehensible.

Chapter Eleven:

Saturday Evening; May 24, 2008

The last time Zachary Peterson had been stuck in Kansas City was the Buckman Imports investigation, more than ten years ago. Looking out the window of his cab from the airport, he wasn't sure whether he really disliked the city or not, but he carried no positive recollections from his three weeks in a Holiday Inn plodding through crates of overseas invoices. He hated white-collar cases and the relentless tedium required to identify the exact points at which too much opportunity had intersected with too little character.

Strange that within the Bureau renowned for its "Ten Most Wanted" heroics, an agent working up today's chain of command was better off carrying a calculator than a sidearm. The combination of his law and finance degrees had made Zachary Peterson a sure bet for a rocket ascent. But who could have foreseen an irrepressible attraction to good old-fashioned street crimes? Zach certainly hadn't when he joined the FBI, but a dozen workaholic years later, he'd become a willing slave to this special calling in law enforcement. Since leaving a safety net of sisters who had rallied to raise him, he'd been looking for something substantive to which he could anchor himself. Until that something revealed itself, his recognized niche within the FBI would have to suffice.

✑

At 10:30 on Saturday night, when Agent Peterson entered the briefing room, Andie Morrison barely managed to suppress an urge to verbalize her first impression. *At least he doesn't have a crew cut.* Otherwise, Zachary Peterson could have been sent from central casting. A standard issue

G-Man. Clean shaven, square features. Dark suit, white shirt, dull tie. Tall, but not too. Fit, but not muscle-bound. Carefully trained to blend in, to appear average. But probably more apt to stand out because no one looked that kind of average anymore.

"Gentlemen and Ma'am, I am Agent Zachary Peterson of the Federal Bureau of Investigations, and as of this moment I assume full authority over all investigations into your Calloway murder of May 21."

Oh brother, this clown was cloned from of an old movie.

Glancing around the table, Andie could see mutual resentment in the faces of the assembled KCPD detectives and forensic specialists. Even the Grandview Police Chief was rolling his eyes.

"Okay, that takes care of the official department crud. Way to go on making the connection to Seattle so quickly. That's terrific police work ... really terrific. Let's get into what else you guys have so far."

A hint of human life after all? And were those dimples when he flashed that grin?

Agent Peterson removed his suit coat and tossed it across an empty chair. Rolling up his sleeves, he turned to close the door behind him. As he did, Andie's attention was drawn to the splotch of color visible through the white oxford cloth of his dress shirt. She made out the words on the back of his T-shirt, "The Dave Matthews Band."

She couldn't help but smile. *Who knows? Maybe even a superior life form!* She'd driven as far as three hundred miles to see Dave Matthews concerts.

As Zach Peterson turned to face the table, he was caught totally off guard by how a simple smile had just lit up the lone female face amidst the sea of unfriendly male faces glaring at him. In fact, that face now lit up the entire room, at least for him. Her riveting blue eyes made it impossible to look elsewhere. They danced with a sparkle like none he'd ever seen.

After a few moments his unflinching gaze grew awkward, so Andie diverted her eyes back-and-forth to the men on her right and left, hoping to prod Agent Peterson back to the business at hand. It worked, and he regrouped to address the room at large. Nonetheless, while tossing questions at the assembled group for more than an hour, he monitored any and all vibes from this fascinating young woman. There was something so natural and instantly likeable about her, an attraction bolstered by the way those welcoming eyes retained their warmth throughout the briefing.

Upon reflection, Zach Peterson realized that he felt rather positive about Kansas City after all.

Chapter Twelve:

Sunday; May 25, 2008

Working Sundays never seemed right to Andie, even when she'd pulled weekend rotations back in her earliest days in the Data Pit. Today was different because nobody had remembered to remove her officially from the Grandview case. That most certainly would happen on Monday morning, so she was eager to have one last shot at digging among the possibilities hidden between two murders. One more chance to leave her mark on the investigation.

Besides, anything Andie uncovered might require additional discussions with the rather interesting Agent Peterson. *Zachary Peterson.* She saw something there. All the ingredients someone needed to be successful, with just enough rough edges left intentionally rough. He seemed to be his own person. No doubt, he loved his work; it showed, and she admired that. Still, it was obvious he did the job his way, not necessarily the prescribed way. She liked that, too. He definitely was the kind of guy Andie Morrison wanted to know better.

Following Saturday evening's briefing, Andie and Agent Peterson had exchanged a few pleasantries when she'd handed him the copies of her report. He seemed to want to stay and talk with her, before being whisked off to Grandview and the crime scene at close to midnight. A missed opportunity. *What was it that Stephanie Burton had said about hapless souls who kept score by missed opportunities? Or having the courage to take chances?* She saw no downside in playing this one out further.

Andie pored over the files from the two homicides, hoping to find any obscure, incidental fact that might prove to be the bridge in explaining how Calloway and Wegman had wound up identically dead some fifteen hundred miles and fourteen months apart. Their backgrounds appeared similar but not connected. Both lived alone and neither had married. Calloway had spent his entire thirty-four years in Grandview … and Wegman, his twenty-nine in Seattle. Neither finished college. Calloway, a single semester at Kansas State; Wegman, three years at three separate private schools in the Pacific Northwest. Both Caucasian. Both regulars on the bar scene right up until the times they died, whether by chance or not. Neither with a known history of homosexuality, leaving strong likelihood the murderer was female. A particularly unique aspect for two such cold-hearted sex killings. *Perhaps a woman drawn to their similarities … a woman diligent enough to uncover them.*

Uncle Charlie's Tavern in Grandview and Pier Pressure in Seattle were in no way connected, yet they also were similar. Local hangouts. Somewhat off the beaten path. Both dependent on a long-standing clientele of locals; not flashy singles joints. Neither a typical choice. Someone hoping to go unnoticed while seeking out sex partners, and ultimately murder victims, was more likely to choose someplace larger, more crowded … more anonymous. *She would have planned carefully … would have been highly cautious in carrying those plans out.*

After rereading the various police reports, Andie logged onto the *Seattle Times* website to read how the local newspaper had handled the Wegman murder and investigation as the story broke. The body had been discovered on Thursday, March 29, so she started with the Friday morning edition and it didn't take long to spot the headline on page one. "Houseboat Homicide." She was several paragraphs into it when a picture from an adjacent column caught her attention. It was a photograph of Retired General William A. Clements saluting a group of local veterans in wheelchairs. Andie had heard the celebrated general speak just a few days earlier at Kemper Arena, which prompted her to skim the accompanying story about his busy visit to Seattle. During his four days there, he had met with more than a dozen organizations and spoken to tens of thousands of citizens … "including a large crowd that paid to hear him on Monday at Key Arena, as a featured speaker with the Personal Empowerment Tour."

At first Andie was amused by the sheer coincidence, but soon her mind began processing. Wegman's murder had occurred in the early morning hours on Tuesday … the Personal Empowerment Tour event in Seattle had been Monday afternoon. In Kansas City, she'd attended the tour event on Wednesday … Calloway had been killed during the early morning hours of Thursday. Had to be random coincidence. How could a couple of bizarre and bloody murders correlate with a bunch of famous talking heads being in town? Yet, how could she simply ignore the pattern? In Andie's data world, she couldn't. Little was random. She searched for an Empowerment Tour website, not sure what she'd find but hoping for something that might lead somewhere.

The website provided background on the Personal Empowerment Tour, details on upcoming tour dates, biographies of featured speakers, and lots of ways to order tickets and tour merchandise. Andie was reading through general information when she came to the multi-year calendar of past and future tour dates. She pulled up 2007 to confirm the Seattle date – MARCH 26 (MONDAY): SEATTLE (KEY ARENA).

She scanned the rest of the 2007 schedule. One event per month. SAN ANTONIO and MEMPHIS before SEATTLE. Then, PHOENIX, HARTFORD, CLEVELAND, MILWAUKEE, BALTIMORE, SALT LAKE CITY, INDIANAPOLIS, ATLANTA and LOUISVILLE. She scrolled through it again, her inner sense clawing. Something else was there.

Once more from the top. JANUARY … SAN ANTONIO? FEBRUARY … MEMPHIS? She worked her way down. SEPTEMBER … SALT LAKE? OCTOBER … INDIANAPOLIS? Wait. OCTOBER … INDIANAPOLIS. That was it. OCTOBER 16 (TUESDAY) … INDIANAPOLIS (CONSECO FIELDHOUSE).

Andie pulled up the file she'd been e-mailed a few days earlier, hurriedly seeking a date that would have held little significance when she first read it. Her fear was realized … October 17, the day Robert Evan Huggins had been found dead inside his SUV in an Indianapolis parking lot.

Fourteen months … three murders in three different cities … maybe more. An apparent female serial killer … apparently sex driven. But somehow tied to a tour of motivational speaking events. *What kind of woman could pull this off … more importantly, would need to?* Andie Morrison couldn't possibly dislodge herself from this case. She picked up the phone.

Chapter Thirteen:

Monday; May 26, 2008

Zach Peterson returned to his hotel after midnight, receiving the message that a Miss Morrison had phoned late Sunday afternoon. She'd left her home number with explicit instructions to call at any hour, no matter what. He reflected on what a magnificent proposition that might represent under different circumstances, but figured she needed to discuss something about the case file. Either way, it wouldn't hurt to hear her voice. He'd spent a long day and evening in unproductive conversations with the regulars at Uncle Charlie's and wondered if he'd ever be able to look at another bowl of popcorn.

Before he even had a chance to say something charming or witty, she hijacked the phone call. She immediately launched into a litany of details of what now sounded like three murders in three cities and their coincidental timing with some Personal Empowerment Tour. After a few minutes he interrupted more abruptly than he meant to.

"Miss Morrison, there is the possibility that you've made a critical connection, but let's be careful not to get ahead of ourselves. Please meet me at your office at 7AM. Thank you and good night."

Then he actually closed his cell phone like some FBI hard-ass ... hanging up on a woman he'd thought about numerous times over the last twenty-four hours. He wanted to kick himself. *Smooth, Zach, really smooth.*

~

The next morning Zach Peterson arrived promptly, carrying two tall cups of convenience store coffee and a bag of doughnuts.

"I brought breakfast to apologize for my poor manners on the phone last night, Miss Morrison."

"Why Agent Peterson, you certainly are a charmer. I fear I don't have the proper china for such an elegant meal."

He looked down at the meager offering he held and suddenly felt awkward, "Oh … I guess this isn't really helping my situation, is it? I'm not very good at the flavored latte and croissant thing."

"No, Mr. Peterson, you're not making the right impression at all … at least as a top-notch investigator. If you'd bothered to interrogate even one person at your hotel's front desk, they could have told you to go just a half-block further east … to Dagwood's, which is only the best doughnut place in North America. Let's hope you at least have something in that bag with chocolate frosting. And, please, call me Andie."

There it was, that smile. He relaxed, again feeling instantly at ease in her presence. Something about those eyes.

"Andie, I didn't mean to be so abrupt last night, but I guess my FBI pride got the best of me. At times I tend to obsess over our performance. You found something we missed, something potentially enormous. I apologize. Anyway, I barely slept, eager to see what you've got on that computer of yours. And, by the way, I hope you'll call me Zach."

It was as if they'd worked together for years. Andie brought Zach up to speed on the Huggins murder, its parallels and contrasts to the other two, and how the timing for all three corresponded to the Personal Empowerment Tour's schedule. She then took him through the detailed brief she'd begun compiling on the tour itself.

Duly impressed, Zach interrupted her with a question that caught her off-guard. "Andie, if you were to continue on this case, what would you do next?"

He couldn't have sensed how much she'd anguished over the fact that this case was swinging over to the FBI, or he wouldn't be toying with her. "I'm sure your Data Section will want to explore other unsolved murders surrounding the dates and locations of every Personal Empowerment Tour event, starting with the most recent and working back."

"How would you feel if I requested that KCPD headquarters assign you to this case under my direction?"

She tried at first to maintain a modicum of professional composure, "Agent Pearson … Zach, I certainly would remain open to the possibility." Then she let her real feelings show, "In fact, I have to admit that I'd be thrilled if you made such a request."

He flashed a playful grin, "Andie, I received approval on my way over."

"I guess I should thank you for showing such confidence in someone you've barely met."

"Andie, that someone has already made several monumental breakthroughs on what looks to be a highly complicated and unusual case. We'll need all the top talent we can put against it. So please, as of now, I officially request that you start searching for those coincidental homicides in the other tour cities."

Andie displayed a playful grin of her own, "I already sent queries to the data centers in those cities earlier this morning."

She didn't bother telling him that she'd grabbed her customary cup of coffee and doughnut at Dagwood's before the sun had come up.

Chapter Fourteen:

February, 2007

The first time Stephanie Burton stepped up to the Personal Empowerment Tour's podium she'd been overwhelmed by the connection she felt with the Memphis crowd. The instant electricity. As a successful ad executive she'd spoken to many sizable business gatherings. This was different. These people weren't attending as part of their jobs. These twenty-two thousand were in those seats on their own accord, at their own expense, because they were looking for stronger direction in their lives. They filled a sports arena not to drink beer and cheer a home team, but to find greater personal meaning. Stephanie knew this in advance, but the full impact hadn't registered until she stood before them … until she looked out into near darkness and saw masses of people on the floor below her, in the tiers of seats around and above her. In every direction, thousands of motionless heads, silent in their anticipation of whatever insight she might be able to share – the intensity of those needy stares making her not the least bit nervous, instead elevating her sense of confidence and purpose.

On the surface, to the audience, she was calm and soft-spoken when she needed to be, yet forceful and passionate when it served her message. She could elicit spontaneous shouts of affirmation for the path to self-improvement, or just as easily engender compassionate laughs with a self-deprecating sidebar. She intuitively gauged the pulse of her audience, knowing precisely when to seize an emotional need, tease it, then satisfy it completely.

But inside, Stephanie Burton had battled her own emotions. She battled to suppress and channel the disgust she was feeling toward the men who preceded her to the podium and those still to follow. Men who dared to exploit the thousands looking on. *Oh, how they love to strut into the spotlight when their names are announced. Turning on their disingenuous smiles. Spewing their disingenuous words. Self-righteous with their pontificating ... then ridiculing this crowd and every crowd like it when they're back behind closed doors. Taking their hard-earned money ... stealing their dignity without them even knowing it.*

She battled a disturbing inner force that had been reawakened the previous day – a prep day spent with her fellow speakers. Watching them, absorbing every offensive nuance of their familiar behavior. *Oh, how they basked together in the testosterone of their smug little brotherhood ... flaunting the indecencies of their private codes of conduct. Behind their fame and accomplishments, no different than all the others.*

The dark rumblings probably had started several weeks earlier as she'd dug into the background of P.E.T., its partners and their connections to one another. She had recognized the signs of another old boys' club ... just as she'd understood the unspoken implications of that first phone call with Sam Cummings. P.E.T.'s executive director had been in desperate need of a token female to replace the tour's other token female, the one stupid enough to get caught in the time-honored practice of secret offshore bank accounts. Stephanie had ignored Cummings' patronizing manner. The ends didn't necessarily justify the means, but at times they did require a controlled tolerance. To become part of a tour where she might help thousands pursue their higher potential, she easily could suffer the transparent fawning of a Sam Cummings. But she hadn't been prepared for the appalling behavior she encountered when she'd arrived in Memphis.

She'd expected better from a former senator, a popular author, a revered news anchor, an Olympic decathlete, a Detroit CEO and a retired general. A most esteemed group ... at least on paper. She had joined them in a private dining room at the Madison Hotel, near the FedEx Forum. Following lunch, they were to be shuttled to the arena for their customary walk-thru on the day before a tour event. They'd risen in unison as she approached the table, but eye contact was delayed as they formulated their first impressions of her from the neck down. She wasn't sure if General William Clements had meant for her to hear his aside to Cummings or not. "You were dead on, Sam. The men in the audience are going to love what we've just done for them."

During lunch, she'd listened politely as first they regaled her with personal histories of their individual accomplishments. Then came the stories – meant to be amusing, at least to them. With each glass of expensive wine, accounts of their past travels together contained more and more innuendo. A few turned completely off-color. Intermingled were their personal commentaries on the tour's original purpose.

"Easiest money you'll ever make." That came from the newscaster.

"It's amazing how you can satisfy so many underachievers with a few simple anecdotes and a word or two of encouragement." That from the CEO.

Nods and laughs around the table.

The Olympian chimed in, "Heartfelt encouragement, of course."

Another round of nods and laughter.

They viewed the tour as a monthly trip to the pay window. Plus, it became obvious that the regular gatherings provided extracurricular opportunities for these celebrated men to act like frat boys again. By the end of the meal, the presence of a female hadn't seemed to impose any boundaries on the conversation whatsoever. Between the lines, with clumsy attempts at subtlety, they even bragged about sexual conquests, both past and recent. By dropping their guard, perhaps they thought they were accepting Stephanie into their midst, but she certainly saw it otherwise. They arrogantly were trivializing and dismissing her ... as men like them would have done with women throughout their privileged lives.

When she'd accepted the invitation to speak, when she had traveled to Memphis, Stephanie wasn't looking for another reason to be agitated by men who never understood or cared about the damage they inflicted. Anything but. She'd been eager to reach out and try to help thousands of people, not be drawn back to the memories and pains that forever roiled beneath her polished exterior. Those certainly weren't the thoughts she wanted to have as she took her place behind the podium and looked out over the crowd.

But, oh, how they love playing to one another ... accepting, affirming their denigration of women. Cock-wielding creatures who care only about themselves, just like the others. So smug with their glances and comments when they're together. All that clever banter at breakfast ... taunting one another about last night's escapades. Parading around like respected family men ... daring to hold themselves up to these people ... people they're already ridiculing in the privacy of their dressing room.

But dare they be so dismissive at the conclusion of that afternoon's speeches. Or so inflated by ego as to ignore how she'd spotted them each a few decades of fame and still won the audience hands down. She had anticipated that joining the P.E.T. roster would place her into a more powerful circle, but not the conflicting emotions that these men had triggered.

It would have been impossible for her not to be overwhelmed by the adulation of the crowd and the command she held over it. She had stirred the audience to levels not approached by the assorted living legends before and after her. The difference in audience receptivity would have been obvious to anyone. She was practically climbing out of her skin with an insatiable desire for more. Another opportunity to genuinely touch lives. Another opportunity to separate herself from the self-absorbed frauds who dared to belittle the real-life needs of others. Men who dared to ogle and objectify her, even while they were dismissing her as their equal.

After she exited the FedEx Forum stage, only Sam Cummings and a few of his minions managed to stop by the women's dressing room – where she, of course, was the sole occupant. Those P.E.T. staff members were tripping all over themselves with heavy praises, yet none of the tour's veteran speakers had bothered to travel the short corridor from the other dressing room and its closed-door camaraderie.

She'd known too many men like them. *Concerned only about what serves their egos and makes their pricks hard. Oblivious to the pain and damage they cause. Recklessly destroying what could be … what should be.*

Stephanie Burton departed Memphis with an undeniable determination. Notions that flowed in and out of her mind while she was at the podium had clarified. Solidified. Yes, she would win future showdowns with these disgusting men … but not merely on the stage, where everyone could watch.

Men like them needed to be made examples in other ways. Men like them needed to pay. For the harm they do, yet so conveniently ignore … for what they steal from the world around them. For what they'd stolen from her.

Stephanie returned to Chicago much different than she'd departed. The change was apparent to Kent Gillespie as soon as she entered their lakefront condo. He met her in the foyer, inquiring about how things had gone. Uncharacteristically, she didn't want to talk about her day, her presentation, or anything having to do with her trip. She threw her arms around him, said she had other ideas in mind and pulled him into a long breathless kiss. Kent wasn't sure how to react. In their decade together, she'd never been the sexual aggressor. Their love life had been tame, more friendly affection than erotic passion. Even when they'd been alone for a month on a Greek island, the occasional lovemaking she initiated had seemed mostly for his benefit. Now she was exhibiting actual lust, an emotion for which Stephanie hadn't previously demonstrated a noticeable capacity.

For the next few hours Stephanie performed and reinitiated sex in ways Kent wouldn't have imagined possible from this woman whom he thought he'd known so well. Even as he fell asleep, satisfied and exhausted, she continued to caress and explore his body with curious fascination.

Kent awakened the following morning to sounds from the kitchen. He arose and hurried toward them, jubilant that their mutually comfortable relationship had taken a promising turn toward genuine passion after all these years. Stephanie, already dressed for work, was at the center island filling her travel mug with coffee when he slipped behind her and kissed the back of her neck.

"I don't know what flows through the water pipes in Memphis, but I'm going to write and thank the mayor. You were remarkable last night. What do you say we both try to get home early tonight for the second verse?"

Stephanie's body tensed while she fumbled with the mug's lid, "Can we not talk about last night?"

Kent pulled away to allow Stephanie adequate space to overcome the obvious embarrassment she was feeling about her raw behavior. "Sure, Steph, I understand."

But he didn't.

When Kent eagerly arrived home that evening, all that met him was a sealed note. In it, Stephanie requested that he relocate himself and his possessions as soon as possible. She would stay at an undisclosed hotel in the meantime and he could expect a check that would more than cover his portion of the condo's value.

Kent Gillespie was more baffled than forlorn. The woman he admired for poise and stability in any circumstance had turned certifiably erratic. From model of decorum, to sex starved, to downright cold-hearted in a matter of forty-eight hours. Efforts to contact her were futile, thus he ultimately had no choice but to accept her decision. He knew their relationship wasn't rooted in an all-consuming love, but there always had been respectful harmony. Only rare evidences of friction. They'd shared endless conversations and so many common interests ... in fact, cultivated a great number of those interests together. For nearly ten years they had been seemingly comfortable and open with each other, yet now Stephanie makes the abrupt and unilateral decision to end everything.

Kent only could conclude that Stephanie Burton had met another man – presumably someone connected with the Personal Empowerment Tour. She'd become preoccupied with this tour in the weeks since she first was invited to speak. A new lover was the only logical explanation for her sudden appetite and mastery for bedroom gymnastics ... for why she couldn't face him after the most intimate night they'd ever shared.

Chapter Fifteen:

Temperance

Her second appearance with the Personal Empowerment Tour was scheduled for March, in Seattle. She would need the full month between events for her preparations … both practical and emotional.

When Stephanie Burton left Gerber, Alton & Jennings a few months earlier, she'd been intent on pursuing what seemed to be a singular, clear direction in her life. With the rush of feelings that had hit her in Memphis, she unexpectedly found herself contending with two very real but conflicting directions. Two deeply rooted yearnings that had driven conflicted actions in her past. She now recognized, and on some level relished, that these two yearnings would continue to drive disparate actions in her future.

Following their trip to the Greek Islands, she'd already made the rational decision to end her relationship with Kent … the events of Memphis merely prompted her to do so more abruptly than anticipated. She liked and respected Kent Gillespie more than any man she'd ever dated. More importantly, she trusted him. During their years together, the fact that she could trust a man with whom she was intimate had given her hope that someday she could love him … that she someday could love at all. But she'd been unable to cross that threshold, to open the emotional curtains that darkened her innermost thoughts. Their month away together had left her feeling empty about romantic dreams and the hopes she'd carried since childhood.

With what had been reawakened in Memphis, she needed to end the relationship immediately. Having Kent around would complicate her plans and preparations. As importantly, he deserved better than what she would be able to offer him going forward.

Years earlier, Kent had been a most worthy professional colleague. As their personal relationship had continued to intensify, they determined it wasn't appropriate for both to continue working at GA&J. Stephanie was able to make a few calls and help line him up with a senior position at a major public relations firm in Chicago. Now she wished she could do the same for his next romantic interest … but Kent would do just fine, and some very lucky woman would be the beneficiary.

Returning home from Memphis, she selfishly had spent one last night with Kent. Ultimately, he might remember those hours of uninhibited sex as suitable punctuation for all their years together. She hoped so. But in truth, she purposely had used him to attend to her own needs. Not physical needs, but practical ones. She had needed to reacquaint herself with an assortment of sexual techniques. During a past episode in her life, she'd been able to improvise and tend to a man's bodily impulses. But that had been years ago.

Indeed, Stephanie recognized that controlling men through sex was easy; she'd learned that basic truth in high school. More satisfying conquests were better achieved through other means, so those were the ones she'd been developing ever since.

Stephanie Burton barely recognized her father when he died of pancreatic cancer a few weeks after her ninth birthday in 1980, but she carried memories of how he looked prior to his illness. In the twenty-seven years since, she'd managed to piece together a reasonable mosaic of Kyle Burton's life – even though her mother, Leslie, had avoided most discussions about her husband and their marriage.

The last year of Kyle Burton's life was spent fighting and succumbing to disease, while Leslie Burton struggled to find her first outside job and manage the household. He had earned a decent living as a political science professor at Ohio University, in the small town of Athens. His doctoral thesis had built a case for nationalized life insurance, whereby the government would use the same actuarial tables as private insurance companies to offer citizens voluntary term-life coverage at reduced rates. A staunch liberal, he'd opined on how earnings from the government's investment of revenues could fund needed welfare programs, while the private sector would be cleansed of at least one parasitic faction. Brandishing a new PhD, Professor Kyle Burton had proceeded to drop his own life insurance policy out of a sense of intellectual integrity. Unfortunately, five months later he was diagnosed as terminal.

Stephanie's free-spirited mom previously hadn't bothered to pursue a serious avocation, let alone anything resembling a practical vocation. As a faculty wife, she'd been content to enjoy the carefree life of a college campus.

From those months when her father slowly died and she was shuffled from babysitter to babysitter, Stephanie still remembered how her mother progressed from carefree to melancholy … ultimately to cynical and apathetic. A personality transformation so obvious that a child could notice and remember the phases. Many years later, Stephanie remained convinced that it was during this maudlin year that her mother committed herself to a permanent quest for finding the meaninglessness in life. But Stephanie couldn't discern whether that spirit of hopelessness was borne from the loss of a spouse to the randomness of cancer, the awkwardness of reaching the age of thirty-two without a marketable skill, or the stupidity of a husband's academic principles that had left her practically penniless.

Stephanie carried another vivid memory of her mother from that tragic year. After the school bus had dropped her off at the street corner one afternoon, she immediately recognized Uncle Paulie's car in the driveway. Her dad was getting much worse, the mood in the house more sullen. Uncle Paulie at least brightened things up with his visits. Paul Scanlon was an associate professor who worked with her father and was younger, funnier and more interesting than all the other visitors who streamed through their home. As a close family friend, he'd been "Uncle Paulie" to Stephanie for as long as she could remember.

For some reason Uncle Paulie looked to be sleeping in the backseat of his car, his body wedged against the door, his head stretched back against the window, his eyes closed. Stephanie decided to sneak up and scare him under the cover of early dusk. When she approached the car she heard him moaning and feared something might be wrong, so she hurried to peer in the rear window. As a little girl, she was unprepared for what she observed … her mother's head in Uncle Paulie's naked lap, kissing his most private parts. Stephanie froze for several minutes, absolutely fascinated that a woman could make a man so strangely happy in such a ridiculous way. As a youngster she didn't even consider the rightness or wrongness of what the two were doing. Only several years later did it register that while her father lay dying inside their home, her mother was having sex in the driveway with his best friend. But at the time Stephanie simply had been intrigued by the act itself, the odd influence men and women could have over one another by touching body parts.

In the years that followed, her mother's lifestyle exposed Stephanie to numerous other influences a woman could exert over men. Countless men.

Puberty and its attendant body changes arrived late for Stephanie, but she'd been patient ... confident her time would come. In her early teens she conducted her own experimentation, allowing a few guys to paw her undeveloped chest, occasionally meting out a gratuitous rub to a boyish bulge. Such promiscuity was no reflection of any youthful desires, but merely a methodical exploration of various primal urges that seemed to cross genders – a fascination that stemmed from having watched her mother in the backseat of a car.

By high school, Stephanie's body was catching up to her mind. She noticed how girls who once joked about her plain looks and ironing board figure had begun to eye her somewhat enviously. She noticed how guys would gawk at her from a distance. And Stephanie had liked having that distance between she, classmates and high school life in general. It was safer, less painful. She preferred journeying into a more idealistic existence that could be found in books. She viewed her high school years as temporary inconvenience on the path to independence, to permanent escape from a home life where daily occurrences tarnished every virtuous notion she might ponder from her tucked-away corner of the local library. She lived those formative years in a state of continual conflict. With how glorious the human potential ... yet how vulgar and pervasive the reality.

Recognizing the lowest common denominators that abounded, during her junior year Stephanie had decided to hone certain skills she might need for more important years ahead. Ripe for target practice was the town's prototypical high school hero.

He went by Gunner, a name earned on the basketball court because he took most of his team's shots. He was a senior, a year ahead of Stephanie. He had transferred into Athens High School a year earlier, when his father was hired as an assistant basketball coach at the University. The addition of Gunner that first year had catapulted a mediocre basketball squad into the semi-finals of Ohio's state tournament. Entering his final year, he'd been expected to take them to the championship – a preseason favorite for Mr. Basketball of 1988. By flaunting every ounce of abrasive cockiness that his athletic limelight afforded, he became the target of Stephanie Burton's attention. She harbored no interest in associating with someone as insufferable as Gunner, nor any desire to venture into the school's popular crowd that she abhorred for its pointlessness. But manipulating this clueless oaf and knocking his ego down a few pegs had seemed a worthy extra-curricular exercise for a semester or two. She knew that connecting with this boorish jock on an emotional or intellectual level would be impossible, which is exactly why she chose him. She'd wanted to lure then control young Gunner purely through sex.

He'd never seen it coming. Three weeks after first approaching Gunner, Stephanie had him by the zipper. She enjoyed publicly demonstrating the hold she had on this high school hero. It was easy and she went out of her way to make it look that way to ogling schoolmates. He was completely mesmerized by the magic of her body and her willingness to push new boundaries of sexual expression. All the while, she concealed her disgust for his inept attempts to satisfy anyone but himself. He possessed the equipment but none of the technique. At times he'd even become physically forceful with Stephanie, but she channeled her contempt and strung the relationship out until the end of the basketball season was near. A few days before the state tourney, Stephanie notified Gunner that the game clock with her had run out; she was done with him. He was a wreck, the team lost in the opening round due to his abysmal play. An entire student body had watched its falling star be shot down by this enigma of a girl who also happened to be the school's best student, and who otherwise wasn't known or understood by anyone.

In retaliation, Gunner dedicated his energies to destroying Stephanie's image and reputation, broadcasting to the few who cared that she was a closet nymphomaniac, an apple off her mother's tree. The slurs were inconsequential to Stephanie. For the balance of her high school years, she remained an ardent loner, usually buried behind a book of some sort. At the time, she was content that this fun little diversion had advanced her high school education as intended. Looking back as an adult, she knew there were other lasting consequences.

Chapter Sixteen:

Thursday; May 29, 2008

Fellow agents relentlessly ragged him about his perpetual tunnel vision. He refused to allow anything personal to interfere with a near-compulsive focus when he was on a case, which was almost always. Yet all day he had looked forward to the call, waiting until evening when they both might have time for a longer conversation … anticipating, hoping it might drift personal. Like some nervous teenager, he finally punched the numbers on his cell phone and was treated to a very sleepy-sounding "Hello" on the other end.

"Hey, Andie. I just wrapped up an evening with a couple Seattle detectives and I'm headed for Indianapolis first thing in the morning. I thought we ought to compare notes."

Suddenly she was more alert, "Zach, it's after midnight. Do you ever call at a normal hour?"

"Oh, I'm sorry … you know, the time difference. I didn't interrupt anything did I?"

"As a matter of fact, I'm in bed. Give me a second … I'm not alone."

Zach's mood plummeted from the convergence of embarrassment and jealousy. *What an idiot!* Why hadn't it dawned on him that a woman as appealing as Andie Morrison might actually have a special man in her life? He closed his eyes and cringed while he listened to her talking to that intimate someone in a muffled voice, her hand covering the mouthpiece.

"Okay, Zach, I'm back."

"Andie, I'm terribly sorry. I don't need to bother you now, please let me call you in your office tomorrow."

"I'm sorry, Zach, I didn't hear you. Just a minute." Then with the phone pulled away from her mouth, she was talking to the other person again. "Please, could you just go wait for me in the living room? This is official police business and I'll need a few minutes."

There was momentary silence and Zach grew even more uncomfortable.

"Okay, Zach, the guys are gone. What did you want to talk about?"

"The guys? Andie, I thought you said you were in bed."

"I was … we were. I am."

Another awkward pause for Zach as his mind tried to process. "Uhh, it's none of my business, but are you having some sort of strange party?"

"No, not really. Just my normal Thursday night thing … entertaining a few of the fellas from the Kansas City Chiefs in their off-season. During the winter, it's the Royals." More silence. She wanted to let it sink in longer, but with the deadness on the other end of the phone she couldn't contain her laughter more than a few seconds.

Zach realized he was being had.

"I guess I forgot how friendly you Midwestern girls are. But point made, I'm sorry about the late call."

"Zach, I couldn't resist. And I'll take a call from a good-looking federal agent any time, day or night."

Zach's spirits instantly were restored by her sense of humor, the receptivity in her voice, and especially that last comment suggesting her interest might extend beyond professional. Maybe there was no significant other in her life after all.

His emotions had done a full three-sixty in a matter of minutes. Zach Peterson wasn't used to those kinds of gyrations. Measured. Controlled. Those were the traits he could count on to confront the absurdities and atrocities of his job. Traits he had counted on to guide him through everyday interactions since life had been turned upside down by the tragic death of his parents at a young age. But he hadn't been prepared to meet someone who could totally disarm his most trusted weaponry. Let alone that it actually felt good to let down his guard.

Their phone conversation stretched well over an hour, with neither Andie nor Zach the least concerned about the lateness. Each content to keep listening to the other's voice, like two teenagers in a budding romance. Ignoring, of course, the fact that they were exchanging details about a series of brutal murders.

Andie now was working out of the FBI's office in Kansas City, where Zach had set her up with a workstation that provided authorized access to the Bureau's extensive data files. She already was in daily contact with

Washington DC, receiving long-distant supervision and assistance from Dr. Justine Abernathy, head of one of the FBI's largest Data Section teams.

Zach had spent two days in Seattle familiarizing himself with details of the houseboat murder. Prior to arriving in Kansas City five days earlier, there would have been no reason for him to open the file on what had been classified as a local homicide. Now he was busy assimilating every detail of this first of three apparent serial killings. Not yet knowing if there were others, or if Wegman even had been the first.

Chapter Seventeen:

March, 2007

To say the 2007 killing of Geoff Wegman had been premeditated would be misleading on one key dimension. Indeed, Stephanie Burton had arrived in Seattle with her murderous actions planned to the smallest of details. She had known exactly the profile she sought. She just had no idea whom the victim would be and Wegman suffered the fatal misfortune of being in the wrong place at that wrong time.

After disentangling her relationship with Kent Gillespie in February, Stephanie had been able to focus her attention on Seattle, where a P.E.T. event was scheduled for March 26. She spent little time preparing the content of her actual speech, knowing she would work from sparse notes and shape her comments according to the reactions of another eager crowd. She instead devoted the month tending to details required for a separate, more private performance.

Stephanie Burton long had benefited from innate self-awareness, able to measure her steps and channel her ample talents accordingly. What had been reawakened in Memphis both frightened and excited her, revealing inner needs and passions far deeper, far darker than previously imagined. Once in her past, she'd allowed, perhaps willed them to surface – having convinced herself the catharsis of that experience was necessary and total. She'd wanted to believe her tormenting, malevolent urges finally had been extinguished by that one act. Instead, they merely had been suppressed.

In the span of a day-and-a-half in Memphis, she had experienced feelings beyond any from her past. Extreme empathy. Profound compassion for those thousands in the arena, collectively searching for more out of their lives. The deep fulfillment of connecting with them, of possibly helping them. Of wanting, needing to help so many more like them. But also, there had been the provocation, the rage toward a coterie of hollow men who could trivialize those people and their hopes. Men who had trivialized her so cavalierly ... as they did any woman. Like the many other men she had watched ... whom she'd known ... by whom she'd been disappointed, hurt. Memphis had triggered an explosion of emotions. Conflicting, simultaneous extremes ... disparate memories. She'd been unprepared for that explosion and her reaction to it ... the awakened need. A hunger to once again experience the liberating catharsis.

A downside to being the singular female on the Personal Empowerment Tour's roster was that upon leaving the podium, Stephanie returned to an empty women's dressing room for a second time. She was left wondering if her male counterparts could acknowledge, even amongst themselves, how the Seattle crowd had responded to her. She gathered her belongings to head for the airport. She had outperformed and outclassed every one of them in front of seventeen thousand approving witnesses. Her head pulsated, holding on to the echoes of the crowd ... further fueling the anticipation of the night ahead.

Outwardly relaxed during the late afternoon ride to Seattle-Tacoma International, Stephanie skimmed through a stack of newspapers on the backseat of the limo. For tour events, P.E.T. arranged private ground transportation and hotel suites for its speakers, as well as first class seats on all their flights. She thanked the driver and proceeded with her carry-on luggage to the gate for her scheduled flight to San Francisco. She canvassed the gate area. First to assure there was no one on the flight who might know her, then looking for female passengers traveling alone. Spotting an isolated woman scrunched over on a corner bench doing paperwork, Stephanie approached her.

"Excuse me, I was wondering if you might do me a tremendous favor?"

The woman looked up, at first a little perturbed, but much more receptive once she saw Stephanie and the professional aura she exuded. "I'm not sure. What do you need?"

"Are you flying coach?"

The woman nodded her head tentatively, "Yes."

Stephanie flashed a sheepish smile, "I know this may sound like an odd request, but could I trade you my first class seat?"

More tentative, "I don't think I understand."

"I'm a consultant up here on business and the client covers all of my travel expenses. Well, I just saw that their CFO is on our flight and he's a stickler about flying Coach. I really can't risk having him see me in First, so I was hoping to trade seats with someone."

The now accommodating stranger pulled a boarding pass from the side pocket of her briefcase. "You're an easy person to do favors for. Glad to help."

After she'd watched the woman join the other first class passengers for early boarding, Stephanie slipped in amongst the crowd at an adjacent gate area and waited there to make sure the plane took off without complications. She then made her way to a restroom back toward the main terminal. Inside a stall, she rubbed off her makeup with towelettes from her purse and changed out of a designer suit into casual clothes from her suitcase. With disposable contacts, her dark brown eyes became blue and she exchanged the wallet in her purse for another from the suitcase, then headed to the rental car counters.

Twenty minutes later a counter attendant handed her a set of keys. "Yours is the Toyota Camry in space C-26, Miss Vincent."

A week before, Stephanie had issued a personal credit card to her administrative assistant so that Joyce Vincent could use it for office supplies and meeting expenses. When ordering the card, Stephanie had requested a duplicate which she'd kept for herself.

To secure fake ID's, she'd driven three hours from Chicago to Madison on a wintry Saturday. There she checked out the bars surrounding University of Wisconsin, her face obscured by a stocking cap and hooded sweatshirt. A friendly bartender connected her to a source that produced fake ID's for college students at $20 a pop. Stephanie had given the guy an extra fifty along with an unflattering photo of herself. A couple hours later she was handed five Wisconsin driver's licenses with five different names – one being Meredith Joyce Vincent. Stephanie had taken the ID photo a few days earlier – make-up removed, color contacts in place, and a blank stare for the camera.

Using the assumed license and credit card, a plained-down Stephanie would leave no trail in accessing the rental car she needed. Upon returning the car she simply would elect to pay in cash, at which point the charge card imprint would be torn up and no transaction would hit the monthly statement sent to the real Joyce Vincent.

Scoring the fentanyl had been easier than anticipated. For a female wanting to maintain anonymity, a trendy nightclub like Chicago's *Tinsel* offered the safest, most natural access to the illicit drug scene. Stephanie had blended right into the younger crowd with a revealing micro-dress and lots of glittery face make-up – along with a blond wig and color contacts. She worked her way through a handful of guys on the prowl before finding the source she needed, a twenty-something grad student buried under student loans. He couldn't imagine and didn't inquire as to why anyone would be willing to pay two-hundred-and-fifty an ounce for fentanyl, but a quick call to one of his buddies had confirmed the price would net him a tidy sum for simply becoming a middleman. An hour later, he was back with a ten-ounce supply.

Leaving nothing to chance, she purchased a pair of guinea pigs and sprayed proportionately diluted amounts to assure the desired effect. She'd chosen fentanyl the old-fashioned way … an evening with reference books and periodicals in a public library. No check-outs, no log-ons, no way for anyone to trace the research she had done.

In addition to having rapid sedative qualities, she learned that fentanyl transported well. It needed to be stored in dark glass bottles over long periods, but could be kept in a regular plastic one for several days without any loss in potency. A three-ounce plastic bottle would clear airport security and carry more than enough for her purposes.

Stephanie's first stop after leaving the Seattle airport was a shopping mall for clothes and make-up. Next, a grocery store for trash bags and a paperback. After a few quick stops for the remaining items on her memorized shopping list, she headed toward the outskirts of the city, in search of just the right bar for finding just the right man. At every step, her excitement mounting.

She cruised by a variety of nightspots before settling on Pier Pressure, a boaters' hangout a quarter-mile inland from Puget Sound. The rustic building sat on isolated property with a parking lot that was minimally lit. It was large and crowded enough so that she could sit off by herself without drawing attention, but not hot and trendy by any definition. The kind of place that was likely to appeal to a requisite assortment of *"guys'*

guys" – links in an age-old chain of morons who feel the need to bathe publicly in their own testosterone.

Upon entering, a ball-capped Stephanie slid inconspicuously into a small corner booth where she ordered a sandwich and buried her face into the paperback she'd purchased. For close to two hours she pretended to nurse a couple of drafts, discretely emptying them into a plastic jug inside her purse so as not to dull her senses. She listened intently to the insufferable banter of a self-lubricating group of guys clustered around the main bar – thinking that she could have handed scripts to the macho half-wits and their discussions would have been no less predictable. The male rituals of top-this braggadocio and machine gun sexual innuendo had been repugnant to Stephanie ever since her mom began inviting so many men back to the house. More offensive to her was how women like her mother could pander to this behavior in order to make themselves more desirable to pathetic creatures whose singular value system hung shamelessly between their legs. How often she had watched her mother laugh at their boyish humor in order to stoke their man-sized egos.

From fragments of conversation and occasional glances up from her book, Stephanie gleaned enough details to identify her sacrificial prey. Amidst the peacocks, one stood out. She observed the way Geoff Wegman treated women with his eyes. How he looked right through their essence, looking instead for the slightest signal of invitation. Then the contempt when none was there. She listened to his lame jokes about fornication, flatulence and femininity. She watched as he passed around his digital camera so cronies could see his latest conquest bare-chested.

He looked as though he'd just stepped off the pages of a J. Crew catalogue and it was obvious that he worked hard to give that appearance. He was on the short side of average, maybe five-nine. Not a single dark hair was out of place, a filmy mist of hairspray still evident. Despite having arrived well after sundown, the latest top-of-the-line Oakleys rested neatly atop the perfect hair. He was dressed in his sailor uniform. Not the kind the Navy issues, but the one seemingly required for entry into friendly neighborhood yacht clubs. Docksiders, no socks. Khaki shorts, freshly pressed, heavily starched. Lime green polo shirt with anchor emblem, also freshly pressed, lighter on the starch. Superficiality incarnate.

Stephanie had a unique appreciation for the sophomoric proclivity that guys have for teasing one another, because she recognized that the flurry of barbs inevitably would pinpoint real truths about character. Wegman was the target of a disproportionate share. Living off wealthy parents.

Still floating alone through life on their houseboat. Perpetually chasing after attractive women greedy enough to balance his mood swings and perversions with his daddy's checkbook. He was physically handsome enough, but few women probably cared due to the reeking smugness. With all his faults, he was perfect.

Shortly after 11:00, Stephanie left a twenty on the table, quietly exited the bar and returned to her rental car. During the preceding week she'd spent hours practicing each step in near darkness. She removed the black-rimmed eyeglasses purchased at a local discount store and pulled off the oversized sweatshirt that had extended over the hips of her skintight blue jeans. She unbuttoned her silky blouse halfway down the front. From her suitcase she pulled a blond wig brought from Chicago, then adjusted it into place over the long dark hair that had been pinned under her ball cap. After slipping a different ball cap over the wig, she applied the make-up – heavy mascara and dark red lipstick. Within a matter of minutes she had transformed from intentionally bland into someone more youthful and much more noticeable. Finally, she prepared and organized a variety of items in a newly acquired shoulder bag.

She sat waiting and watching until Wegman came out the door with two of his drinking buddies. She feared they might be heading somewhere together, but sighed a silent relief when they separated toward their respective cars. The others already were pulling out as Wegman still walked toward a Porsche parked in the furthermost perimeter space. The irony was not lost. If this clown hadn't been so concerned about protecting his precious boy toy from the dings of car doors, he might have driven off before they were alone in the parking lot. She glanced back at the bar to make sure no one else was leaving, then started her car.

Wegman was turning the ignition key when she angled and stopped her car behind the Porsche, blocking his path. She calmly got out and walked over to his window. As he lowered it, she bent well forward to allow a full view of pushed up cleavage.

"Sorry to cut you off this way, but I was just leaving myself when I saw you over here. I wanted you to know how funny I thought you were tonight. Most guys really can't tell jokes, but you have the gift."

It didn't take much longer to maneuver Geoffrey Thomas Wegman into inviting her back to his place. Before pulling onto the street, Stephanie took one last look around. If anyone had seen them, she would have turned the other way and Wegman would have headed home alone, confused and frustrated by the whole teasing exchange. But as luck would have it, he was followed all the way to his houseboat by the fun-loving Stevie he'd just met.

For a month, Stephanie mentally had simulated her erotic, murderous actions to the point of obsession. A few hours earlier she had captivated thousands at Key Arena. Now she was entering a completely private stage for a much more highly charged performance.

At age thirty-six, Stephanie's morning regimen still included thirty minutes each on the Nautilus and treadmill, maintaining the firmness and conditioning she'd had since college. In other ways, without anyone suspecting, she had prepared herself to know exactly when and how to exploit her body, beauty and sexuality. Since high school, Stephanie had conditioned herself to the sexual urges of men. She could call upon an assortment of mindless techniques that had been explored and honed with the pathetic Gunner … and others on occasion. So simple. She was confident that her toned body and carnal proficiencies could arouse and sustain any man's interest long enough for the intended purpose.

The sight of Geoff Wegman's hardened phallus had provided Stephanie Burton an immediate erotic rush, but much different than he would've understood. The acts she proceeded to perform on it were purely mechanical to her. She derived a deeper stimulation from having lured a man to his ultimate demise through the very organ that always would betray him. So easily, so predictably. She knew men like Wegman inevitably would allow their judgment to be clouded and compromised by the goatish impulses of a penis. The root of pride, the downfall of ego. Freud understood. Wegman was but another prototypical specimen.

With his eyes closed, he didn't see the smile take shape. She couldn't help herself. *A strange woman simultaneously flashes some breasts and your groin takes over. If men like you were offered last blowjobs on death row instead of meals, you all just might kill one another to get there.*

Stephanie teasingly worked him toward completion, her method perfect. She brought him near, then eased off. Then again. Once more. Assuring his ultimate climax would be explosive, exhausting. All the while, she built toward a different release for herself – in total control of the situation, the victim, and finally the precise moment of his ejaculation. Sending his mind adrift in a helpless state of euphoria. His eyes clinched shut, his pulse racing, his breath panting, she reached into the purse at her side and wrapped her free hand around the plastic spray bottle. A final enticing whisper into his ear.

"Trust me, lover, you won't believe what's coming next."

In those few moments before fentanyl produced its sedating effect, she watched Wegman contemplating the erotic possibilities she'd just suggested. If doubts or fears ever crept into his mind, it would have been too late.

Once he was unconscious, Stephanie again reached into her purse, this time for the carpet knife she'd purchased at a local hardware store. His exposed throat stretched in sacrifice. As she pulled the blade across, her gaze fixed on his spent manhood. So often in her life she had found occasion to ponder how men could be predicted, placated or destroyed because of this pitiful lump of flesh. How many men had met their downfall because they couldn't gain control over a singular bodily organ? From great men, to common men, to common criminals. From frat houses and whorehouses, to houses of God and the White House. Reputation, livelihood, even life itself sacrificed to a hard-on.

She sat motionless, experiencing the inner calmness she had remembered from years earlier. The conflicted torment she'd lived with for so long, now quieted completely as time stood still. The scars healed, the damages undone, the disgust erased, if only for these precious minutes.

She'd been careful not to touch anything on the houseboat. She used Wegman's shirt to wipe the blood from her hands and the splattered drops on her body, then gathered the rest of his clothes and placed them into a garbage bag from her purse, taking no chance of leaving a partial fingerprint that might have grazed a button or belt buckle. She used towelettes from her purse to more thoroughly clean any traces of blood off herself. She wrapped the towelettes around the carpet knife and dropped it and the wig into the garbage bag. When disrobing, she purposely had tossed her clothes well away from the bed and the eventual blood that would flow from it. She collected them and dressed. Avoiding the streaks and spots near the bed, she made her way to the door. She pulled a cotton cloth from her purse to cover the doorknob as she turned it to exit the houseboat, then dropped that into the garbage bag. No more than twenty minutes after Wegman's final breath, Stephanie was on the highway. No remorse. Reveling in the total satisfaction she'd been granted, thinking ahead to the next time.

An hour later she stopped at the side of the road and changed into a second outfit purchased from a Seattle mall. She pulled another trash bag from her purse and threw in the clothes she'd just removed, plus the sweatshirt, ball cap, make-up, book and eyeglasses used earlier at Pier Pressure. Then the contact lenses, and finally the roomy purse she'd used to carry her criminal necessities. Before daybreak she stopped for coffee at a 24-hour drive-thru south of Kelso. In the rear, with no one watching, she dropped two sealed garbage bags into a dumpster where they would be joined by dozens more within hours – and within a day or two, dropped into a landfill some hundred and fifty miles away from Seattle.

She had planned and prepared meticulously. If any particles from her clothes or shoes were picked up at the crime scene, they only could be traced back to off-the-rack items broadly available. That morning she carefully had shaved off all body hair. The hair on her head had remained tightly bound beneath the wig. No physical evidence would be traced to Stephanie Burton back in Chicago – the same Stephanie Burton, who according to flight manifests, had flown first class from Seattle to San Francisco some seven hours prior to the murder.

She returned the rental car in Portland and caught the morning Amtrak to San Francisco. She traveled as Eileen Mecklin, needing only cash and a driver's license to purchase the train ticket. Adrenaline made sleep impossible. She departed the train in San Francisco with plenty of time to make her scheduled meeting with a potential consulting client. Following a dinner with two former associates, Stephanie Burton caught the red-eye and slept during most of the flight back to Chicago.

Chapter Eighteen:

Saturday; May 31, 2008

"Why Agent Peterson, is your watch broken? It's only eight o'clock at night … you surely must have thought it was later."

"No, the Bureau changed its phone packages and these just became the cheapest minutes."

Though they'd known each other for exactly one week, comfortable routines had formed between Andie Morrison and Zach Peterson. In fact, they already seemed to have agreed to one unspoken rule. Nightly phone calls couldn't possibly start with something as simple as "Hello" or "How was your day?" They evoked and enjoyed each other's quick wit. Following their opening banters, the free flowing conversations would integrate updates of what Zach was finding from his field visits and Andie was finding from her computer searches.

In Indianapolis, Zach had familiarized himself with the life and death of Robert Evan Huggins. After two days of reactivating what had become a stagnant case file, he was convinced of one thing. There probably weren't a lot of people who'd mourned the passing of Bobby Huggins.

Huggins had been charged twice for domestic abuse, once by each of his two wives – with both eventually dropping their charges. In his early twenties, he'd gotten off with probation for a drunk-and-disorderly. But a few years later, he did serve three-months for kicking an undercover policewoman during a prostitution sting.

On the night of the murder, Huggins had been verbally abusive to one of the exotic dancers at Coco's before one of the club's bouncers settled him down. According to some of his friends, it wasn't unusual for Huggins to harass and try to intimidate women. One remembered him as, "a hot head with serious aggression issues toward the opposite sex." His first wife simply attributed his bad behavior to "not getting over the fact that God gave him a little wiener ... and by the way, it served him right."

His drinking pals affirmed that Huggins kept a .38 handgun in his car, which they thought was a pretty good idea based on the number of people who might have wanted to take a first shot at him. Apparently that same gun had provided a convenient weapon for someone to follow through. Though there were plenty of folks who didn't like Bobby Huggins, no legitimate suspects had been identified. The case file had gone as cold as the act that killed him.

Chapter Nineteen:

Wednesday; October, 17, 2007

Indianapolis was Stephanie Burton's ninth speaking engagement, her seventh since the Wegman murder in Seattle. She'd been biding her time. Anticipating. Preparing. Once an identical murder was committed, she figured it wouldn't take long before the link was made between Wegman and whomever she might select in Indianapolis. But she assumed it would be quite some time and several more victims before anyone tied the killings to the Personal Empowerment Tour. Eventually some FBI computer jockey would make the connection and at that point she'd stop. Until then, she would have to squelch the inner conflicts caused by her immoral actions – those moments of supreme satisfaction were too sublime to be denied.

She'd contemplated the possibilities around the prior month's tour event in Salt Lake City, but a tight appointment calendar made the timing too risky. Her anticipation continued to build. Logistics for Indianapolis offered less of a challenge. She again would trade out her first class seat to a woman in the gate area, then rent a car. There would be ample time to tend to her private needs and drive the three-and-a-half-hours to Chicago … easily arriving in advance of a mayoral task force breakfast that would confirm she'd returned home the evening before. Later in the day she could return her rental car and settle in cash – this time, as Cheryl Lanville from Hyde Park. The real Cheryl Lanville was her interior decorator. Months earlier, she'd handed Lanville a company credit card so that any furnishings ordered for Burton's office could be billed directly. Again she'd retained a duplicate card.

After experiencing the electricity with the crowd inside Conseco Field House, Stephanie had made her various stops and scouted a number of nightspots before selecting Coco's. She was dressed in men's clothes with several layers underneath to bulk up her appearance. Wearing work gloves and a Colts cap pulled low, no one inside the strip club recognized that a woman had taken one of the back tables – well behind an all-male crowd clustered around the dancers' runway in the center of the room. Several other men sat alone toward the rear, away from the lights – their body language obvious to Stephanie … none of them wanting to be noticed, yet clearly needing to be there. Blending in was easy. Just another lone soul hunched over a beer, leering at the faux eroticism from a shadowed recess.

Bobby Huggins and his softball cronies weren't the least bit concerned about being noticed. They were right next to the stage occupying several tables crammed with shot glasses and beer pitchers. They had been there awhile.

When Bobby got into a heated verbal shouting match with one of the performers, Stephanie knew she'd found her man. He was viciously taunting a pole dancer about being a sleazy lesbian because she wouldn't go out with him again. The teary-eyed stripper, Amber, finally had spat back that she didn't date guys who hit women. Huggins rose in anger but quickly was quieted by the doorman who moved in like a walking sequoia. A few minutes later Stephanie settled the tab and headed to her car to fix herself up for this new Mr. Wonderful.

By the time Huggins staggered out to the parking lot forty minutes later, Stephanie Burton had completed the transition into her Stevie persona. When he exited alone, her emotions piqued, knowing what was imminent. If he hadn't been alone, she simply would have allowed him to drive off and continue tormenting women for years to come. She would have changed back to nondescript and made one more attempt at a different Indianapolis nightspot. If unsuccessful there, she would have pointed her car toward Chicago and begun making plans for the Empowerment Tour's next stop in Atlanta. But he had been alone. Gloriously alone.

Huggins was fumbling around in his pockets looking for his car keys when she approached him.

"Hey, Bobby, need a little help?"

"Do I know you? How do you know my name?"

"I heard your little conversation in there with Amber."

"Oh, her." He shook his head in disgust.

"Yeah, I've been hoping to work with her."

"So you strip?"

"From time to time, I'll undress for the right audience."

"Do you also turn tricks on the side like that lesbo dyke?"

"Again, let's just say I might tend to the special needs of the right audience."

His interest was mounting rapidly. "You don't buy that crap she was throwing out about me, do ya?"

"Amber and I have different views on men. Different needs. My name is Stevie, by the way."

During the exchange Huggins had been taking in her body, her outfit, the exposed skin, the sexy look on her face. He very much liked what he saw. "How much is this going to cost me?"

"Why don't we see how things develop? Maybe no money at all."

With the visual impression he made, it wasn't surprising to Stephanie that he sometimes needed to pay for companionship. Dark brown hair with gray on the edges. Around six-foot and well over two hundred and thirty pounds, probably two-forty. The pockmarks on his face mostly obscured by several days' growth. While the rest of his teammates had kept their softball caps on, he'd felt a need to switch to his cowboy hat. The top three buttons of his jersey were undone – placing abundant chest hair and multiple gold chains on full display. Also exposed was the top of a protruding stomach that swelled beneath the remaining buttons. Instead of the uniform's canvas belt worn by the rest of the team, he sported a wide leather one with an oversized buckle. Engraved on the front, a logo – "2005 National Drags." Everything about his appearance screamed that Bobby Huggins needed to be certain that his manliness was never in question. She was intent on providing him a final affirmation.

She asked if she could follow him home, but he responded that his wife might not take too well to the idea. He suggested they get a cheap motel room. Not wanting to be seen someplace so public, Stephanie offered a better idea.

"Why not the backseat of your Explorer … like a couple of high school kids? Think you might be up for a little nostalgia, Bobby?"

There was a deserted strip mall a few blocks away that he'd used "with other women in the business." But when he told her to hop into his car she hesitated, not wanting to tip the balance of control for the period of time he would be driving. Staying in control remained crucial to all of her plans.

As she stood there thinking, he scoffed, "Come on Hooker Babe, I thought time was money in your line of work. Don't worry … I'll drive you back to your car if you're as good as you look."

His crudeness was enough to convince her to take the risk. The prospect of bringing this guy to his ultimate climax heightened. She got in. The inside reeked of stale cigarette smoke; a pile of butts spilled over the edges of the ashtray.

Behind the wheel, he barked an order her way. "Why don't you grab us a couple rubbers out of the glove compartment?"

When she opened it, she saw a holstered handgun hooked to the side. She removed a few condoms and placed them in his extended hand, casually leaving the compartment open as she continued to throw flirtatious comments his way. She eyed the chamber of the revolver to make sure it was loaded. A few minutes later they were at the abandoned shopping center where one end of the parking lot was filled with brand new Hondas, space that an adjacent car dealer rented for overflow inventory. She suggested that he pull in among the new cars so any patrolling security guards wouldn't notice them. Once parked, he wasted no time in telling her to join him in the backseat. As he unhooked his seatbelt and moved out the driver's door, she discretely removed the handgun from its holster and dropped it into the oversized purse she'd opened next to her feet. Now armed with a gun, a utility knife bought earlier in the evening and a spray bottle of fentanyl, she felt entirely back in control. She had options not even anticipated.

In addition to the low cut leather vest, jeans and heels purchased at a nearby mall, she had rounded out her seductive ensemble with fake snakeskin gloves to assure she left no fingerprints. During the drive, she had contemplated how best to manipulate the situation to reach the desired outcome within the confines of a car. She simply could open the vest and reveal her breasts to help arouse him while she worked him towards a manual climax. She needed to avoid the possibility of her skin making contact with vinyl or plastic surfaces inside the car.

By the time she slid into the backseat he already had his treasured belt down around his ankles and was waving his manhood at her. He roughly grabbed her arm and started to yank her toward him, "Why don't you get started on this?"

His abrupt physical act prompted her instinctive reaction. There would be no more fun and games for Bobby Huggins … she carried too many horrible recollections and associations. She smiled and asked him to let her loose so she could get some oils that she liked to use. When he released her arm, she reached into the purse, pulled out his gun and unflinchingly shot him through the forehead. She had forgone the teasing, the build-up, the exquisite act of bringing down a man at his vainest masculine moment. Everything she'd been savoring from Seattle for the intervening months. But this cretin wouldn't have the chance to lay another hand on her, or anyone else. The satisfaction of that knowledge would suffice on this particular night.

On impulse, she propped his fallen head back against the corner of the opposite rear door, exactly the position she remembered from that car in her family's driveway so many years before. She calmly walked back to her rental car parked at Coco's, reflecting on Uncle Paulie and the other men who had polluted her memories for so long.

Chapter Twenty:

November, 1990

She was three months into her second year at Columbia, living in a studio apartment off Washington Square. As soon as she heard the first few words on the other end of the phone, she'd recognized Gunner's voice. His drawl, his unfamiliarity with proper grammar.

Despite his poor performance in the state tournament during senior year, Gunner's previous high school accomplishments combined with his dad's coaching credentials had been enough to earn him a basketball scholarship to Bowling Green State University. Now in his junior year, Bowling Green had advanced to the semi-finals of a pre-season tournament in Madison Square Garden.

Stephanie was surprised he'd bothered to learn she was studying in New York City, let alone that he'd managed to track down her phone number. He wanted to come and see her. He explained that in the years since she'd dumped him, he had done a lot of thinking about the kind of guy he was in high school. Being in college, traveling the country playing basketball had caused him to grow up. He'd gained new respect for the right way to treat women and wanted to see her while he was in town to make amends for any mistakes of the past. She had no desire whatsoever to see him again but figured if this intellectual dwarf was attempting to evolve from his sexist cave, the least she could do was acknowledge the effort.

Looking back many times during the years that followed, she realized she should have suspected something. He'd handed her a glass of cheap champagne that he brought, but poured himself ginger ale – apologetically explaining that alcohol for any reason was strictly off-limits during basketball season. She never had occasion to find out what drug he used.

How he must have relished the ambiguity of his toast, "Here's to putting past mistakes behind us, Stephanie."

After a few minutes she barely could keep her eyes open. But she remained conscious enough to remember every detail of him slapping her around ... laughing as he congratulated her for all the laughs she must have had while embarrassing him in front of the whole school ... in fact, "the whole shitty state."

She heard the sinister pleasure in his voice. "Oh, how you musta loved teasing me with all your sex tricks. Well, now we're gonna try a different kinda sex ... this time, with me in control."

It actually was more domination than control. "You're gonna love this new technique I been usin' lately."

After a few preliminary coital thrusts, he flipped her over and anally raped her. She'd been helpless. Once finished, he put his mouth to her ear.

"Now, you bitch, I hope you'll always remember me the way I been rememberin' you."

On final impulse, he'd kicked her in the ribs, emptied the rest of the champagne bottle onto her exposed and violated body, then left the apartment merrily whistling to himself.

In the aftermath, Stephanie hadn't allowed herself to drift asleep. She stayed on the floor for several hours as the effects of the drug wore off, collecting her thoughts. Reflecting not on what had happened in the preceding hours, but on the totality. All the way back to high school. Contemplating her actions and their consequences. She silently chided herself for the way she so blatantly had toyed with Gunner's pride and masculinity in high school. Yes, it had been youthful prankishness, but also utter arrogance on her part. Those past mistakes were compounded by her naiveté when he'd called earlier that day ... by thinking men like Gunner ever could change ... by agreeing to see him again. She committed to learn from the attack. Inure from it. From this point forward, never deny her natural instincts for the Gunners of the world ... the others she'd known. As men like them might need to be dealt with in the future, she must remember the repercussions of too easily flaunting an upper hand. No matter the circumstances, she must contain her ego ... prevail through patience, discretion, humility. Nothing overt. No lingering trail, physical or emotional, with any such man.

After considering the possible retaliatory actions for Gunner, she elected not to notify the police or pursue legal recourse. That would cause others to see and treat her as a victim. Worse yet, she'd have to acknowledge the incident to her pathetic mother who'd been making herself a susceptible victim to men her entire life. In order to bring Gunner to justice through the court system, too many others would gain the satisfaction of seeing another woman's vulnerability put on public display.

Prone on the floor, body aching, chilled and damp, but with eyes dry, her mind continued to clear from the effects of the drug. Her mind cleared about a lot of things. Men like Gunner and the others could not dissuade her of the virtuous ideals that had taken shape during childhood. Those noble thoughts were in no way shaped by the reality of her youth, but instead were a means of escaping it. She was determined to experience life's poetry. With enough encouragement, maybe just maybe, more people could rise to where the poets soar.

The scholarship to Columbia had enabled her to flee the cesspool of her home life, so she'd enrolled with expectations of starting fresh and never again yielding to baser mindsets ... every intention of seeking the loftier humanities embraced by her cherished poets and philosophers. Not the seamy realities to which her parents had devolved ... to which misguided masses of people succumbed every day.

Here, too, she'd been naïve. She was naïve to think she could scurry out of Athens on a yellow brick path and never look back. Naïve to think she simply would leave the hurts and anguish behind. Burying one's past required more than clicking the heels of esoteric hopes. Just like Gunner, other dark memories would continue to worm their way back into her life and she must find the means to cope with them. To prevail over them.

In the aftermath of Gunner's sexual assault there was a clear recognition for the first time. A reality she would accept. She was driven by two separate sets of emotions and ambitions ... compelled by coexistent, conflicting forces. To achieve her highest aspirations, she must at some point contend with her most guttural memories. The premeditated rape by a trivial lowlife had caused her to become even more resolute about her high-bound aspirations, the constructive differences she could make. But for that to happen ... in fact, for sheer sanity, she also had recognized that a haunting internal force would need to be expunged. On this day, Stephanie Burton had vowed a private justice for Gunner ... a private justice through Gunner. A justice in her own way, at her own time.

Part II

"Hope is the thing with feathers that perches in the soul -- and sings the tunes without the words -- and never stops at all."

Emily Dickinson, American Poet, 1830-1886

Chapter Twenty-One:

Friday; June 6, 2008

"Canceling the remainder of this year's Personal Empowerment Tour because of some sociopath is tantamount to succumbing to terrorism. Any time our nation or its institutions start yielding to the deviant behaviors of a few, we threaten the security of our communities by encouraging more lunatics to surface. That's the philosophy with which I commanded this nation's military forces and the one General William A. Clements will carry to Arlington Cemetery."

The camera pulled back from a close-up of William Addison Clements, retired Chairman of America's Joint Chiefs. Sitting next to him was Sam Cummings, P.E.T.'s executive director, who was trying his best to appear indifferent. On the adjacent split screen was a close-up of Stephanie Burton, calmly awaiting her turn to speak.

Almost instantly after the FBI announcement two days earlier, the cable news networks had shifted lockstep into their in-depth coverage of what loomed as a story of intense national interest. The videotape of a Bureau spokeswoman reading an official statement was re-aired repeatedly in those first few hours. Serial murders spanning the continent … sexually rooted … mysteriously attached to a tour of celebrity icons. Stephanie Burton had recognized this was the kind of story that cable news executives prayed for when they went to bed each night. During her ad years, she'd seen first-hand how networks hungrily chased even the smallest fraction of an audience rating point so they could justify higher rates to advertisers. As this story developed, viewership was destined to swing each time one of the networks unveiled some new fact or simply invented a fresh twist for recycling a familiar one.

⌒𝓂⌒

Two days earlier, on Wednesday morning, Stephanie had been running on her treadmill with the TV on in the background when CNN went live to a FBI press conference. The Bureau's spokesperson was identifying three known victims of an apparent serial killer whose actions corresponded with the exact dates and cities of a popular motivational speaking tour. Burton was caught off guard. After successfully replicating the Seattle killing in Kansas City a few days before, she'd anticipated that those two homicides would be quickly linked. Indianapolis hadn't gone as planned and she'd adjusted accordingly. She was somewhat surprised that the shooting of Huggins in a parked SUV had also been tied in, but what Burton hadn't expected at all was the practically instant connection to the Personal Empowerment Tour. That should have taken months or years, not days. She recognized that someone had done some pretty impressive police work. Her plans to rid the world of a few more Neanderthals would have to be scrapped. Whatever dark, private urges she might feel in the future, she had no choice but to live with them. So in many ways the FBI's public announcement would make her life simpler. Now she could focus her full attention in one constructive direction.

Stephanie Burton was well aware of how the news media worked. She anticipated that her affiliation with the tour would likely present her opportunities she hadn't been counting on, and thus began to mull over the ways she might optimize them. How could she best expose P.E.T.'s group of overblown has-beens as nothing more than the chauvinistic, hypocritical greed merchants she'd discovered them to be? More importantly, how might she best establish the higher profile she sought for her loftier ambitions?

As the morning story continued to break, Stephanie decided to work from home for the balance of the day so that she could watch the networks' assorted talking heads report unfolding details in the sensationalized fashion she'd come to expect and deplore. Pompous psychologists waxed ignorantly on the deviant motivations of the perpetrator, though they'd had virtually no time and the sketchiest of details to form their opinions. A hotshot district attorney ranted cartoonishly about how careless mistakes inevitably would expose the psychotic killer. A criminal historian was practically salivating with his observations on the unprecedented nature of such violent sex murders being committed by what appeared to be a female. Amidst the escalating media carnival, the three victims were briefly profiled and their immediate family members were introduced through teary sound bites.

With each of the three killings, Stephanie had followed local newspaper coverage through the Internet. In reading those accounts, Stephanie hadn't paid much attention to the victims, because to her they'd been nothing more than symbolic womanizers … metaphors for the reprehensible double standards and attitudes that had plagued too many lives for too long. Now seeing actual living relatives, she was forced to consider their individual humanity; but any momentary remorse soon waned as she remembered the degrading behaviors she'd observed at each of those bars. How quickly, how carelessly men like them revealed their true selves when an unknown woman exposed some skin and offered a few come-ons. How easily their primal urges had betrayed them … rendered them vulnerable. Part of her would miss that.

The day before the news release, P.E.T. headquarters was paid a surprise visit by the FBI. Sam Cummings immediately placed emergency calls to the tour's principal partners. They'd recognized that the foreseeable future of their highly lucrative enterprise would be called into question. P.E.T. couldn't remain silent, as silence might suggest that tour officials were unsure about the appropriate actions to take. Instead, their mutual interest needed to somehow be adopted as the public's.

World News Live, WNL, was first to raise the question of whether the Personal Empowerment Tour should be suspended because a serial criminal was still loose to commit murders corresponding with future speaking engagements. WNL execs anticipated how this could become a deliciously divisive issue and were hell-bent to drive that angle. If developed correctly, the viewing audience would split on their opinions and divergent views always made for stronger programming. The other cable networks quickly would follow suit, but the ratings advantage usually stayed with the one that fanned the earliest flames.

Meanwhile, P.E.T. had prepared its own game plan. Counseled by a celebrated crisis expert, the principal partners grew increasingly confident that their gravy train could stay on track. Sam Cummings was to become the visible, responsible face of P.E.T., projecting a thoughtful neutrality on the tour's immediate plans. He would reflect a genuine desire by tour management to act according to whatever was determined to be in the public's best interest.

To advocate their actual and more self-interested point-of-view, P.E.T. would call upon its proven big guns, the arsenal of retired legends that filled stadiums every month. Each would respectfully offer different reasons why the tour should continue uninterrupted. America revered these time-tested personalities, their proven accomplishments, their integrity. Their collective voices would carry great impact as public opinion took shape.

Though Cummings and his cohorts valued what Stephanie Burton had meant to tour audiences, they viewed her as an outsider. With each stop on the tour, she'd displayed more and more indifference towards the other speakers; they had no way of knowing whether she would adhere to any central communication strategy. Though she'd received substantial speaking fees, Burton didn't share in P.E.T. profits and would be less financially motivated to maintain a company line. So as the P.E.T. brain trust hurried to provide television networks easy access to its various speakers, they chose not to include Stephanie Burton on that list.

Nonetheless, a production staffer for WNL's nightly panel forum, *Beneath The Surface,* had reviewed recent tour literature and noticed that the lone female wasn't offered up. On a hunch, she contacted Burton directly.

When Stephanie picked up the voice mail that a Ms. Kelly Amaker, from *Beneath The Surface,* would like her to return the call, she knew exactly why. In flipping from network to network, it had been evident that WNL was fueling an ignitable controversy on whether the Personal Empowerment Tour should be suspended over concerns for public safety. It also had become obvious how P.E.T. was prepared to play their side of the developing debate. In an early interview on WNL, Nelson Hefferton, the former New Jersey senator and one-time vice-presidential candidate, expressed his "utmost confidence" that law officers and private citizens now would remain properly alert to suspicious behaviors when the tour visited their cities. As a tour speaker and longtime public servant, he went on to applaud the media for being thorough and responsible in bringing the unfortunate crimes to the public's attention.

Stephanie had little regard for Nelson Hefferton, having heard his real opinions about the gullible public when the microphones were off. But on camera, the polished and prepped Hefferton had been a great deal more credible than the guest WNL hurriedly scheduled to present opposing views. She was head of a citizen's watch group who became carried away with her assertions that the FBI probably wasn't disclosing numerous other murders in order to protect right wing propaganda machines like the Personal Empowerment Tour.

Stephanie figured P.E.T. would keep rolling out its living legends to woo public support for the tour's continuance. Thus, the cable networks would be scrambling for other relevant guests and some staff person was likely to happen across her association with the tour. The call from Kelly Amaker had been eagerly anticipated.

c√c

"Miss Burton, do you agree with the general's concern that canceling the Personal Empowerment Tour plays directly into the hands of terrorists and the lunatic fringe?" This wasn't a question being asked. It was a fireball hurled in the unmistakable style of Gordie Jacklin, the popular host of *Beneath The Surface*.

In preparation, Stephanie had studied up on Jacklin and watched a sampling of past telecasts. With his large shaved head sitting atop thick rounded shoulders and barely a trace of neck between, Jacklin took on both the appearance and personality of a bulldog when he was animated. She'd decided the only element out of character was his ever-present bowtie, an odd wardrobe preference from early in his career that he'd superstitiously held onto. Bowties were approachable, bowties were happy. Ice cream men; Maytag repairmen; Mickey Mouse; they all wore bowties. Not hardcore investigative journalists. To make matters worse, she'd noticed that when Jacklin stepped from behind his broadcast desk with his bowtie, bald pate and rounded shoulders, he visually transformed from bulldog to bowling pin. At this moment, however, it was the bulldog incarnation that glared menacingly at Stephanie Burton.

"First off, we all can appreciate what the retired general has meant to this country. For over a year, it has been my privilege to hear General Clements recount his many accomplishments in city after city as part of the highly successful tour founded by him and the very impressive group of silent business partners that he personally assembled." Stephanie Burton's polish and poise were on full display; her calmness conveyed an unbiased genuineness to the viewing audience. On the opposite split-screen, Clements and Cummings leaned their heads in whispered conversation, bracing for whatever she might say next.

"I certainly will miss being with the other speakers ... they all have accomplished a great deal throughout their remarkable careers ... each no doubt worthy of the lucrative fees they earn by traveling the country as part of such a tour. However, I no longer can continue. With all due respect, General, we're not dealing with either a terrorist or national security. We're dealing with heinous, inexplicable murders. For sure, the Personal Empowerment Tour provides inspiration to tens of thousands of people who are willing to purchase those expensive tickets. But until these crimes are solved, I can't imagine that any arena audience would feel too inspired, knowing that the very presence of the tour in their city could cost a fellow citizen his life. No business venture is worth such a price."

William Clements tried to redirect the dialogue. "Gordie, Miss Burton seems to have little confidence in our law enforcement agencies. We have to assume ... "

Jacklin cut him off. "General, we all hope the killer is apprehended in short order, but we know an apparent murderess has traveled the country at large for at least fourteen months. We shouldn't assume anything. Let's get back to something Miss Burton mentioned. How much of a second career does the Personal Empowerment Tour represent for you and the other notable personalities that have been making the rounds doing these media interviews in recent days? How much money do you receive each time you speak?"

Cummings jumped in. "I'm sorry, Mr. Jacklin, we're obligated to keep that confidential."

"Miss Burton, then? Can you tell us?"

"The terms of my agreement with Mr. Cummings specify that if I reveal my compensation, I will be dropped from the tour. But since I no longer wish to be a part, I have no qualms. I don't know what General Clements receives and presume it's more than me. I was a more recent addition, plus let's face it, I don't pretend to have the kind of reputation that he and the others do. Nonetheless, my fees still were considerable at $50,000 per engagement."

The pit bull lit up, raw meat in his grasp. "We're talking staggering amounts here. If General Clements speaks every month, he's pulling in at least six-hundred grand for twelve 30-minute speeches! And what you make as one of its principal partners is on top of that. General, no wonder you and the others want this tour to continue."

The program's director cut to a quick shot of Clements and Cummings seated side-by-side, trying to contain their uneasiness. The camera then mercifully cut back to a full close-up of a serene Stephanie Burton.

From off-camera, Gordie Jacklin softened his tone, "Miss Burton, do I understand that this morning you donated last year's speaking fee from Indianapolis to a trust fund set up for the children of Robert Evan Huggins, the victim there?"

She gently shook her head and gazed down from her eye contact with the camera, "I prefer not to go into that on the air, but I felt it was the right thing to do."

The WNL call-in poll during *Beneath The Surface* revealed that 93% of the viewers favored suspension of the Personal Empowerment Tour. A strong start. Stephanie Burton was feeling the familiar rush of obliterating another old boys' network.

Chapter Twenty-Two:

Tuesday; June 3, 2008

In the twelve days since Prize Calloway was found dead in Grandview, Andie Morrison had connected his murder to the two other homicides and then the tour. Zach Peterson had spent several days in Seattle and Indianapolis interviewing relevant parties and visiting the bars and crime scenes. He also had requested more teams in all three cities to expand the investigation, but there was no reason to believe the unusual case would be solved any time soon. The next tour date, scheduled for June 19 in San Diego, was fast approaching. The FBI had been obliged to go public, but first Zach needed to make a trip to Philadelphia.

⁂

"Agent Peterson, I guarantee you will have our full cooperation in your investigation." Sam Cummings had meant that. They always did.

Zach Peterson knew Cummings was completely sincere during this first conversation, but also knew that practical realities soon would prevail. They always did.

Zach had arrived unannounced at P.E.T. headquarters, located in one of Philadelphia's newer commercial high rises. He entered alone, six of his agents waiting downstairs. By notifying P.E.T. officials in person of an apparent connection between three unsolved homicides and the dates of their tour, he was following FBI protocol. With a serial murder case in its infancy, any individual was a potential suspect, any fact a potential lead. When people know in advance that the FBI is planning to rummage through their work space, they tend to discretely eliminate things that might prove awkward – their computer file of ethnic jokes, the bottle of

Jack in the bottom drawer, even that suggestive picture from a company Christmas party thumb-tacked to their cubicle. And when the FBI is short on clues, it's important to eliminate any possibility that some pivotal loose end might be flushed down a toilet, carried home in a briefcase or deleted from a computer.

The FBI had no legal grounds by which to subpoena P.E.T.'s staff, files or office contents. There was no probable cause for taking legal action against the company or any of its employees just because the three murders coincided with its tour. The FBI's ability to gain full investigative access would rest on P.E.T.'s willingness to cooperate. Zach had known the odds were good.

In every such instance in the past, Zach Peterson had watched executives essentially hand over the keys to their corporate kingdoms. When companies have nothing to hide, they feel a moral and civic duty to cooperate with the FBI. Or if companies truly might have a few skeletons stashed inside their corporate closets, executives still don't want to draw suspicion by showing anything less than full cooperation.

Sam Cummings certainly didn't disappoint. He'd been as surprised as anyone would be if a government agent were to pop into his or her office on a routine Tuesday to discuss serial murders. After Zach detailed the three homicides, their similarities and the parallel timing with tour events, Cummings was at a loss as to how to react. So it was at this precise and opportune moment that Zach had moved in.

"Mr. Cummings, the assistance of the Personal Empowerment Tour, Incorporated could prove vital to solving and stopping these horrific crimes. The Federal Bureau of Investigations respectfully seeks your permission to review all relevant records and to speak with your staff. Can the government count on your full cooperation, sir?"

Bingo. Cummings had been right on cue. "Agent Peterson, I guarantee you will have our full cooperation in your investigation."

After expressing the government's heartfelt appreciation, Zach then disclosed an important next step he had neglected to mention.

"Tomorrow morning, the FBI will make a public announcement about the serial murders and their apparent ties to the timing of Personal Empowerment Tour events."

Cummings had paled a few shades, contemplating the negative impact. "I need to notify our partners as quickly as possible."

Zach had felt sorry for the guy. From a dossier that one of his agents prepared, he knew Cummings was merely a puppet for General

William Clements and the lifelong friends he'd invited to become P.E.T. partners. Through marriage, Sam Cummings had catapulted up several socioeconomic stations and ever since, made a career out of being the extremely loyal son-in-law to a prominent Philadelphian, who was another close friend of the general.

Sam Cummings was in his mid-forties, but country club living had helped him preserve the boyish look of someone much younger. His outer self must have grown taller and lankier than his inner self ever anticipated, because Zach noticed that the genteel Mr. Cummings was in a perpetual state of uncertainty about what to do with his lengthy limbs when he walked, sat or simply attempted to stand still.

After extracting Cummings' cooperation, Zach pulled P.E.T.'s eleven staff members into a conference room and introduced them to the six agents who'd been waiting in the building's main lobby. The severity of the crimes and the startling manner in which they were revealed caused all the employees to fall quickly in line with whatever requests were made. It was important to take advantage of this cooperation while it lasted.

Zach and his team knew the pattern. Most citizens naturally started with a high level of respect, a borderline reverence for what FBI agents represent. Perhaps it was national pride ... perhaps perceptions built because of the ways in which Hollywood glorified G-Men. Regardless, that hallowed admiration was destined to fade during the coming investigation.

After a few days of pestering the P.E.T. staff with relentless, redundant questions about every mundane detail surrounding customer lists, payroll records and travel schedules, the agents somehow wouldn't seem so formidable. No longer would they be seen as heroic protectors of the public's security. Instead, they'll come to be viewed as pests ... a nuisance ... a bunch of anal-retentive clerks crawling all over everyone's personal space. The agents could count on the eventual strained moods, terse responses and visible exasperation. But Zach also could count on his unfazed agents to plod onward.

Chapter Twenty-Three:

Humility

On April 1, 2005, the offices of Personal Empowerment Tour, Incorporated had opened. The first tour stop was scheduled for six months later at the nearby Philadelphia Spectrum, so newly assembled staff members could closely manage and observe the multitude of logistics required to put on such an event. Those same details were to be replicated many times in many cities in the years ahead. The proximity also had allowed General William A. Clements and his silent partners to monitor their investment in what looked to be a windfall opportunity. The tour was the brainchild of Clements, whose roots were deep in the City of Brotherly Love.

Throughout his life, people naturally had assumed William Addison Clements was the product of a wealthy upbringing – mostly because he'd done everything possible to leave that impression. Even his name carried that loftiness. Point of fact, his father worked in the boiler room of a hospital and his mother was the manicurist in a hotel barbershop. That is, when one or the other wasn't serving time for another drunk-and-disorderly. When Clements was growing up, the most frequent visitors to his family's small apartment had been police officers responding to domestic calls from neighbors.

Clements had attended school halfway across town and taken extraordinary precautions to assure that classmates never saw the rundown building where his dysfunctional family resided. He walked an extra fifteen minutes each morning and afternoon to ride a city bus that routed through more upscale neighborhoods – areas to which he felt much better suited. Hard work and exceptional grades had earned him his scholarship to a prestigious Catholic high school. Though the student body included teenage boys from every rung of the economic ladder, Clements was most visible and comfortable with those on the higher end. Since he never referenced his own family, yet projected such an air of self-confidence, no one suspected he deliberately was compensating for a deep-rooted embarrassment about being poor. Except Harry Yates. But then, that was exactly what Yates had been looking for.

~*~

In 1961, at age thirty-seven, Harold Yates was being groomed to run Yates Brothers Steel in Allentown, Pennsylvania. His birthright. The 120-year-old company was founded by brothers Stanley and Thomas Yates, two blacksmiths who became proficient at rigging covered wagons during the nation's western expansion. By the mid-1840s, the brothers recognized there was more money to be made by simply manufacturing wagon parts for the burgeoning number of middlemen who organized and equipped the westward caravans. The subsequent Yates generations successfully built on this foundation by manufacturing quality steel parts that paralleled America's changing lifestyles – from plowshares and bicycle frames, to automobile drive shafts. But no amount of marketplace ingenuity could have fueled the phenomenal growth that fell on the factory's doorsteps during the Second World War.

To support the war effort in 1942, the family's fourth-generation president, Timothy Yates, agreed to re-engineer his largest production lines for the manufacturing of light artillery gun barrels. By 1945, Yates Steel had earned a broadened reputation for quality barrels used with heavy cannons, armored tanks, anti-aircraft guns and assorted other weaponry. Production capacity increased tenfold as the government paid breakeven prices for everything the company could manufacture. Once peacetime arrived, appropriate profit margins were added to the healthy volume of military orders that continued flowing to Yates Brothers, which by then was a well-entrenched provider to the U.S. Army.

A few years into the postwar boon, the family's fortune had multiplied many times and Timothy Yates wanted to express their patriotic gratitude. To that end, he pledged that the family annually would underwrite five full ROTC scholarships for Pennsylvania high school seniors. The only stipulation was that Yates Scholars must attend one of the twelve in-state colleges or universities that comprised the "Steel Battalion" of the Reserve Officer Training Corps.

Once a year, ten Scholar finalists were brought to the Yates boardroom in Allentown for formal interviews with a panel of Army officials. The family was granted one seat on the panel, and with that seat, the privilege of independently designating one of the five scholars. Timothy Yates relished this participation each March, but after a decade felt obliged to pass the honor on to Harry, the only one of his three children who'd taken an interest in the family business. The de facto heir to the corner office.

Though Harry possessed the Yates penchant for identifying lucrative new sources of growth, he'd felt less constrained by the family's strong ethical fabric. Harry thought his father's nationalism sappy, but viewed the Yates Scholar program as a highly worthwhile investment that could be better optimized. So in 1957, he gratefully picked up the mantle of screening elite high school prospects, but with an intensified focus on each candidate's level of character. The less the better.

Harry recognized that a Yates Scholar would graduate from college as a commissioned second lieutenant in the U.S. Army, and from there, any number of them might wind up in positions that directly or indirectly impacted military procurement. Thus, he sought a more tangible understanding with each Yates Scholars he selected personally. In a world on edge with Cold War, real wars loomed on the horizon. Hot and cold running wars were likely to be good for business.

The walnut, leather and marble on ample display in the Yates Brothers lobby had made a forceful impression on Will Clements. He wanted to fully absorb every sight, sound and aroma of the money and power emanating from every direction. As Harry Yates welcomed the scholarship candidates for 1961, he couldn't help but notice how this one kept separating from the rest. The young man's neck craning, mouth agape, eyes wide, as he checked out the paintings, sculptures and tapestries. This was precisely the sort of behavior for which Harry screened when he met potential Yates Scholars, but he couldn't remember another having been so wantonly conspicuous. Before the daylong selection process had even officially begun, Harry Yates had chosen his next scholar.

Chapter Twenty-Four:

Gratitude

Will Clements entered the ROTC program at Lehigh University in the autumn of 1961, his far-reaching ambitions bolstered by personal convictions that were unusually clear for an eighteen-year-old. Strong nations must be founded on a unified military industrial complex. Such unity required visionary officers who understood mutual interests – the concerns of an army that needed to be properly equipped, balanced with the concerns of corporations needing to remain strong in order to serve the national interest. This convergence was the highest form of capitalism and the very backbone of a global supremacy that the United States had enjoyed since its declared independence. Young Clements was sure he'd been formulating these beliefs while studying history in high school … the conversations with Harry Yates merely had helped him crystallize his points of view. After all, Harry Yates was a well-educated, influential man who understood how things really worked in Washington.

By the time Clements graduated from Lehigh in 1965, well-connected private citizens already had made certain his pending active duty would keep him outside of harm's way. Too many of America's brightest were being sacrificed in Southeast Asia, which had erupted into open warfare the prior year. With a few political strings appropriately tugged, there were guardian angels in place to assure that Clements would stay near important military action, but not too.

Though public opinion may have waffled and waned during America's involvement in Vietnam, there still was no opportunity like wartime for ambitious soldiers who looked to work their way up the chain of command. In November, 1965, Second Lieutenant W. A. Clements was assigned to United States Military Assistance Council, Vietnam (USMACV) – the sanitized name for the Army's command center in Saigon. He rotated out to Xuan Loc in 1966, then Bien Hoa in 1967, but after only a few months at each regional base was transferred back to central command where he remained until Saigon fell.

The young officer performed ably in one senior staff position after another. Importantly, W. A. Clements also was routinely assigned as an attaché to private sector representatives on their visits to Vietnam. For military suppliers to secure the really large government contracts, it was crucial for Capitol Hill to hear compelling expressions of field level needs from officers who'd been in the line of fire. Clements demonstrated an uncanny knack for uniting the right corporate and legislative delegations with the right commanders to make that happen. As he ascended up the ranks in Vietnam, his numbered bank accounts, set up by Yates and others, ascended in other parts of the globe.

Clements landed stateside in 1975, a heralded and decorated lieutenant colonel. Though citizens at large may have ignored or impugned the soldiers who returned home from this senseless debacle of a war, the Pentagon wholeheartedly affirmed its elite senior officers for having fought the good fight – or at least having muddled the good muddle. Upon returning home and for years to come, the name of Will Clements appeared near the top of whatever candidate lists were compiled for the most coveted commands and assignments.

Clements effectively parlayed a network of political connections and the cache of ten years in Nam to become one of the youngest officers since the Civil War to achieve the rank of Brigadier General. In relative short order he earned his second and third stars. A fourth was added midway through his three years as Chairman of the Joint Chiefs of Staff for America's Armed Services – thereby the top military advisor to the President and Secretary of Defense. Like most of the generals or admirals who had presided over the Joint Chiefs since the office's inception in 1949, W. A. Clements periodically was approached about running for political office. But each time he declined, proclaiming his steadfast desire to be remembered only as a soldier. Of course, Clements had recognized that the required disclosures for political candidacy would generate unwanted scrutiny of his very significant assets. This man, who as a young lad had worked so hard to mask his poverty, now had needed to obscure his wealth.

He retired from the U.S. Army in 2002, to begin enjoying the fruits of his patriotic servitude. In excellent physical condition at age sixty, he anticipated good health and a quality lifestyle for many years to come. Since his bug-eyed introduction to the privileged world of Harry Yates as a high school senior, Clements had gone on to acquire many high-end tastes of his own. Many he chose to share with his wife, children and grandchildren. Some of his higher-end habits were enjoyed more appropriately when he was away from them.

He took particular pride in his appearance. His thick white hair was neatly razor-cut at all times – to the tune of seventy-five dollars every Monday, plus another twenty-five to the manicurist. His dress shirts were custom-made with button-down collars and epaulets to perpetuate his military image. Under expensive suits and sports coats, he wore suspenders, or braces as he preferred to call them. Over the years, he'd received dozens of sets as gifts – almost all featuring eagles, stars, stripes or some such military insignia.

Clements walked away from his distinguished career with a sizable lifetime pension, plus a well-concealed nest egg that could fund quite a few lifetimes. But too much still hadn't been enough. As a new private citizen, the combination of greed and ego caused Clements to accept virtually every paid public appearance that came his way. It seemed all he had to do was answer his phone and someone was on the other end offering him five thousand to help open a shopping mall or ten thousand to deliver a college commencement address. Easy money, and all legitimate.

Popping up throughout the country were various business groups and associations that put on special motivational days or weekends for the general public's consumption. They recruited big name speakers to lure big crowds and big ticket prices. The sponsoring interests tended to organize around one or two dates a year, but none of them had attempted anything resembling a regular national tour. Clements had been enlisted for two such separate forums – once for thirty-five thousand dollars, once for fifty. After the second engagement, Clements was convinced there was room in the marketplace for a sustained tour and that he needed to be part of it. He easily could assemble other notables to join him as featured speakers, plus recruit a few old friends to front the money required to hire a staff and book some venues. Then he could ride the gravy train to fifty grand a month in appearance fees and, if his math was right, a lot more as a principal partner. The enterprise also could allow him to repay in kind, three venerable gentlemen who'd consistently looked out for him over the years – Lawrence Mendel of Brighton Chemicals, Carl Henderson of Henderson Industries, and the fatherly Harry Yates.

Chapter Twenty-Five:

Early June, 2008

P.E.T. maintained an active database that contained the names, addresses and phone numbers of every person issued tickets to any tour event. Most tickets were ordered in advance on credit cards, meaning the FBI could use cardholder records to verify identities and addresses. The few individuals who paid at the door with cash or checks still were asked to register, so that they could receive *Empower Yourself,* a commemorative magazine included in the admission price. P.E.T.'s ulterior purpose had been to collect as many addresses as possible because those ticket purchasers proved to be a highly profitable target for mailings that featured Personal Empowerment Tour books, tapes, calendars, coffee mugs and assorted other merchandise.

Approximately 53,000 names had been captured from the tour stops in Seattle, Indianapolis and Kansas City. Disks containing the profile data on these individuals were downloaded then entered into the FBI's data system for analysis in every way imaginable. Separately, the employee lists of outside vendors that helped promote and produce each P.E.T. event were screened, as well as the road crews who assembled, dismantled and transported the staging and special effects.

Itineraries on file with P.E.T.'s travel agency reflected that only Sam Cummings, three staff members and six P.E.T. speakers had traveled to all three cities. In most every case, each had departed within hours of the events. Travel records were being verified through flight manifests from the airlines, along with appointment calendars for the dates surrounding each murder.

Zach Peterson checked in with his Philadelphia teams several times a day. It would have been fortuitous if a significant lead had emerged from these obvious starting points, but none had. Anticipating a lengthy investigation, he received approval to beef up his teams in Seattle, Indianapolis and Kansas City. Three different haystacks. Hopefully, the murderer had slipped and left a needle somewhere amongst them.

Back in Kansas City, with unrestricted access to FBI data files, Andie Morrison systematically worked her way down various data paths identified by agents in the field. Lots of data, every possibility needing to be checked out. Standard motions that had to be gone through … routine wheels that had to be spun.

If the road ahead was to be long, neither Zach nor Andie appeared to mind the notion of traveling it together. Nightly phone conversations drifted into more personal territory, at times bordering on intimacy – something both had tended to avoid in prior personal relationships. As each had grown closer to past someones in their lives, those someones had wanted to start changing aspects of their personalities. Whatever might have created the initial attraction, those qualities no longer seemed good enough for some reason. But these latest conversations were different. There wasn't any need to put up guardrails … each was experiencing a natural comfort with the increased familiarity.

Chapter Twenty-Six:

Tuesday; June 3, 2008

Fran Rothenbach was one of only a handful of public relations veterans who at different times could represent both political parties and their various sub-factions inside the Beltway. The power figures rooted to the nation's capitol mostly referred to her as Frothy, a clever compression of her first and last names, but also an apt description of how she stirred things once she rolled up her sleeves on behalf of a client confronting potential image problems. She was the crisis queen. Behind the closed doors of a controversy, she was known to take total control of all the pointing fingers and squirming torsos. Frothy's sixth sense for public opinion, combined with a battle-tested capacity for developing messages to reshape it, had helped salvage the reputations of too many politicians, corporations and causes to remember.

She operated with the energy and career passion of someone much younger than her sixty-six years. Gravity may have won a few battles with Frothy, but it still was apparent that in addition to being mega-talented, she once had been a looker. She'd never been receptive to a trip down the aisle, but she did wear a platinum band with forty-two diamonds on her left hand – adding a new diamond each December to celebrate the years of blissful marriage to her career.

Within hours of the FBI's first visit to P.E.T. headquarters, Sam Cummings had phoned her. Later that day, Frothy was cabbing her way to Reagan National for the next flight to Philly. Just like other clients in need, the P.E.T. partners hadn't bristled at her fee of $40,000 per week and the minimum commitment of six weeks. Her terms were non-negotiable.

For their initial afternoon work session, Frothy and Cummings were joined in person by General Clements and his three silent partners, plus five of the tour's regular speakers via phone. After Cummings recounted the details revealed to him by the FBI, Frothy began an all-out interrogation into how the Personal Empowerment Tour had come into being, how it operated, how much revenue it generated, and who benefited from the lucrative profits. Once she understood the lay of the land, she slowly began to establish the foundation of an eventual game plan.

She'd been certain the question would be raised about suspending the tour in the interest of public safety. She also warned that the media soon would start chipping away at the tour as a business proposition, and in particular, the incredulously high returns on investment for its founding partners.

"Not that anything about your enterprise is illegal or unethical … it's simply a popular parade route for the mainstream media. Average Joes might hail all those gutsy entrepreneurs who pull themselves up by their bootstraps to make a first million or two. But you gentlemen and your mega-millions can be certain that the populist deck will be stacked against you. You silent partners will need to stay silently in the background.

"Oh, and gentlemen, I don't know what other business dealings some of you may have had in the past, but I encourage you to be certain your respective pantries are in order. As this serial murder story gathers steam, there's no telling where the media's appetite might lead them."

By the time the prep session adjourned at close to midnight, Frothy Rothenbach had outlined the tenets of P.E.T.'s media strategy – the various positions from which P.E.T. could attack or defend in the days ahead, depending on the swinging pendulum of public opinion. She convinced them of the importance of maneuverability when a company is about to be thrown under a vigilant media microscope that ignores blacks and whites en route to dissecting the delectable gray areas between. Against a backdrop of fears, she'd had this group of proud and powerful men bobbing their heads like dashboard dogs.

P.E.T.'s recognizable personalities would advocate a variety of reasons the tour should continue uninterrupted, while Sam Cummings would project consistent neutrality on behalf of a management team concerned only with the public's interest and safety. "If we want folks to believe the Personal Empowerment Tour was conceived for the purpose of bettering people's lives, it must outwardly appear that management is determined to assess the will of the people and act accordingly."

She determined that the esteemed William Addison Clements was the ideal person to argue that the tour should continue based on principles of strength. "Pull out the stops, General. Altering our activities ... constricting any form of personal freedom in response to some lunatic will show weakness to our enemies. Remind Americans that we shouldn't cower into even the vaguest form of self-imposed police state."

As a five-term New Jersey senator, Nelson Hefferton had attracted many voters by being a staunch proponent of greater funding for police forces, fire departments and public safety in his highly urban state. With his statesmanlike demeanor, Frothy had deemed him the perfect person to bear a message of confidence. "Reinforce the public's confidence in our cities ... in our law enforcement agencies ... in ourselves. Senator, with the serial crimes now exposed, citizens will be properly alert and prepared. Praise the media, praise the FBI ... praise the Lord if you need to ... for continuing to lift the public consciousness."

Similarly, Frothy Rothenbach crafted relevant messages for a corporate CEO, an Olympic gold medalist, a popular author and a retired newscaster. Like a well-crafted play, each had been cast into appropriate roles for the media stage.

During the course of the meeting, she was told the various reasons that Cummings and Clements had chosen to exclude Stephanie Burton from any plans; but Frothy identified what she believed to be a much more cogent one. "Though this Miss Burton may have enjoyed quite a career in advertising, her name is unknown to the general public and therefore of no value to our overall game plan."

Fran Rothenbach hadn't given another thought to Stephanie Burton.

Chapter Twenty-Seven:

Monday; June 9, 2008

Five days after the FBI's public announcement, the cable news networks had dialed their rheostats to full feeding frenzy over the P.E.T. serial murders. They reserved five or ten minute segments at the top of each hour to run a few video clips of conflicts, natural disasters or political events constituting the rest of the news that might happen to occur across a globe of 6.5 billion people and 200 nations. Allowing for twenty minutes of ad time to ring the network cash registers, the networks' programming staffs were left with more than thirty minutes out of a viewing hour to milk every conceivable angle of America's latest infatuation.

P.E.T. had wheeled out its full artillery of notables. Their rented limos were rolling round-the-clock as they made the media circuits in New York City, being interviewed, debated, paneled and polled during any available time segment – in some cases, sixty-minute circus acts that masqueraded as legitimate news programs. A few interviews with newspaper journalists were thrown in for good measure. From a Midtown hotel suite, Sam Cummings and Frothy Rothenbach operated a central command post, handling the non-stop media requests for P.E.T.'s spokes-legends.

～✎～

On WNL's *Issues Of The Day,* Cameron Fowler, a P.E.T. fixture speaker who cranked out best-selling expose´ books, was doing his level best to come across as a scholarly author.

"Let me summarize, Gwenn. The FBI has no hard evidence that a single one of these three murders relates in any manner to the tour's presence in their respective cities. It could be sheer coincidence. For all we know, the

FBI may not have uncovered or disclosed additional victims from other cities … victims with no ties whatsoever to our tour dates. Amidst the thousands of unsolved murders in this country, the FBI wires together a few facts around these three and announces a crime spree. I submit that the FBI has been utterly irresponsible in foisting this whole tour connection onto the public without reasonable proof. I would hazard to guess that if the FBI were inclined, it could select another three cities from the tour and find any number of like crimes for the same dates … from wife beating to child molestation. Should we blame the tour for those, too?"

Gwenn Townsend, the red-haired and fiery host of WNL's nightly debate on topical issues, swiveled around on her stool in customary emphatic fashion, "Miss Burton?" Townsend possessed an innate ability to go minutes without blinking, while at the same time flaring her nostrils as though a bad odor had infiltrated her studio.

Stephanie Burton calmly smiled at Townsend, then at Fowler. "Cameron, with regard to wife beatings and child molestation, I must defer to your experience."

She momentarily paused, leaving host and audience uncertain as to whether some shocking revelation was being insinuated about Cameron Fowler. But then Stephanie continued, "With the infamous personalities you've chosen to profile in your colorful paperbacks, you've obviously invested a great deal of time researching those and many other sordid acts. I don't take them lightly and assume you don't mean to either. However, if I heard correctly, it isn't really the nature of the crimes that concerns you but the motivation for the FBI's announcement … which you categorize as irresponsible. Cameron, I only hope you haven't spent so much time digging into scandals and questionable individuals that you now automatically assume the worst in everyone."

She redirected her eye contact from Fowler to Gwenn Townsend, as though she'd finished dealing with some mischievous child and now was ready to address the adults in the room.

"Miss Townsend, I genuinely respect what the FBI is charged to do for this country, and in this situation the difficulty of weighing the upside versus the downside of disclosing the details that surround a potential serial killer. No doubt, its own investigation is now complicated by an onslaught of inquiries and irrelevant leads. The immediate public awareness also must intensify the pressure it is under to solve these homicides. Yet the FBI determined that the public's interest and safety would be better served by releasing the facts as currently understood."

Momentarily looking over to Fowler, "We can't have it both ways in this country. We want our officials, our institutions to be accountable, to be transparent, to be forthcoming with information. Yet when we don't like what they have to reveal, we condemn them for recklessness."

Once more looking calmly toward Gwenn Townsend, "There is something so misguided in our nation today. With a population predominantly comprised of hard-working, well-intentioned individuals, there still is a growing tendency to distrust our institutions. Not just the ones where wrongdoing has occurred … but all of them … to immediately undercut and thus undermine the duties we expect them to execute properly on our behalf. We do so without a moment's hesitation. I hope we can be better than that … that maybe we each can hesitate at least long enough to think for ourselves before reaching for those hatchets. I'm no criminologist, yet I certainly can understand why the FBI has linked the facts around three such bizarre killings. I think the FBI is to be commended for its full disclosure."

Inside P.E.T.'s makeshift war room, Frothy Rothenbach flipped off the television and shook her head, "Cummings, that token broad of yours is killing us."

When the studio lights dimmed, Stephanie could feel the contempt emanating from Cameron Fowler. She would have loved to ask him to pass along her best to the general and his clannish pals, but she refused to play that way. She knew she'd landed a few more punches to the face of P.E.T., but what had excited her most was having the platform to express heartfelt views about the need for people to exhibit higher levels of trust and respect. She'd meant every word. Her hopes were building that she might be able to make a difference.

"Have you been following the media's coverage since you guys released the details on our murders?"

Only after posing her question to Zach over the phone, did Andie Morrison give any thought to the fact that most people weren't inclined to share something like murders in the course of a normal conversation. *Maybe our schedules … our hobbies … even our hopes or ambitions … but OUR MURDERS?* Yet somehow it felt okay to her.

Zach must have felt the same way, because he didn't hesitate to respond, "I hear the cable guys have been crawling all over the case, but I've only been able to pick up a few bits and pieces. It's hard when you're bouncing from city to city."

"Did you catch Stephanie Burton on WNL last night? She's the tour speaker who defended how the FBI has been handling things."

"I downloaded the clip a few minutes ago. I received no less than a hundred e-mails that had it attached. There may be a hint of bias, but I think our field agents like what she's been saying."

"Zach, all the points she makes in her interviews seem to be hitting home. And I have to admit, that's exactly how I felt when I heard her in person. I can't remember ever seeing anyone with the aura she has. There's this calmness about her that makes you believe she's got answers to questions the rest of us haven't gotten around to asking yet. I think we'll be seeing more of her."

"Then I guess we should be glad she's on our side."

Stephanie Burton was pacing herself carefully, applying a disciplined patience that would be vital to her ultimate effectiveness. As an ad executive, but also as a member of the media-consuming audience, she closely had followed the misguided trends in broadcast journalism. It wasn't enough that commercial decisions had long been based on underlying assumptions about the types of sinister stories that drew big audiences. But no longer was it just the sensationalized stories, it also was the people who reported them. On-camera personalities were doing more than simply skewing the stories, they in many ways were making themselves parts of them. Normal, objective demeanors weren't adequate to satisfy the stirred-up expectations of viewers and sponsors. She'd watched disappointedly as one after another, respectable journalists sacrificed their dignity by stretching to become more unusual, more celebrated than the stories they reported – or in many cases, as old-line newscasters had been displaced by exaggerated characters who possessed only an inkling of journalistic talent to begin with. She'd watched disappointedly as more and more newsmakers and media guests had succumbed to the same media currents. Lured by the swelling attraction of grander spotlights that required more colorful antics, accomplished individuals were throwing themselves into a voracious gristmill that chewed up their creditability. She knew how the game was played, which made her all the more determined to establish her own set of rules.

After her first impressive appearance on WNL's *Beneath the Surface*, the phone kept ringing and Stephanie Burton decided to make herself more available by handling her regular consulting projects from New York City while the news story played out. Amidst the heat of the public debate over the fate of the tour, she easily was receiving ten or twelve television invitations a day. From those, she cherry-picked the best ones, her criteria being twofold. First, she preferred programs, hosts or time slots that reached the largest audiences. Second and whenever possible, she wanted there to be a P.E.T. representative appearing alongside her. Not only did she relish face-to-face confrontations that might create opportune moments to expose their hypocrisies and chauvinisms, but she also could count on their predictable behaviors to provide perfect foils for counterpointing with important messages she sought to impart.

Regardless of the program format, no matter how exaggerated the antics of hosts, moderators or other guests, Stephanie Burton kept herself above the fray of sensationalism and argument. Everything about her on-camera demeanor conveyed calmness, common sense and respectful compassion. Amidst the frenetic efforts of the camera-hungry trying to force their points and clamoring for the last word, she exuded an understated grace and humility. With her careful soft-spoken delivery, it seemed as though she would prefer to be anywhere besides the middle of a brewing national controversy. But she left an impression that she was willing to sacrifice her own privacy due to some deeper sense of responsibility because of her past affiliation with the tour. Her concern for seeing the public's best interest served was apparently so genuine, that she would tolerate the media carnival around her.

In every television appearance she found a natural, appropriate way to inject a solemn reminder – a reminder to others on the program, to those in the viewing audience, that any debate over whether a speaking tour continued or not was only of minor significance. Foremost was the fact that three innocent people had been brutally killed. Three families had lost loved ones. A cold-hearted, perhaps demented murderer was still on the loose. Yet she did this with no air of self-righteousness, pointing fingers at no one –reflecting only a heartfelt respect for human life, for human dignity.

Beauty, poise and messages centered in common decency. The camera loved Stephanie Burton. Calls and e-mails to the networks showed that growing segments of the American public were taking notice, wanting to know more about this inspiring woman. Stephanie Burton not only was winning the head-to-head media battles, she single-handedly was winning a public opinion war. She'd become a one-woman wrecking ball to P.E.T.'s future.

When the murders first were disclosed, ticket sales spiked noticeably for upcoming tour stops in San Diego, Tampa, and Buffalo, because of novelty seekers who wanted to attend events that were sure to be the focus of national media coverage. Several days later, after these new ticket orders slowed, the refund requests from pre-existing ticket holders began flooding into P.E.T. headquarters. For Sam Cummings and the tour's partners, the economics of continuing the tour were making any further philosophical debates unnecessary.

Because of a few well-timed comments from Stephanie Burton, the media was boring into the exorbitant ticket prices that P.E.T. charged average people searching for self-improvement, as well as the exorbitant speaking fees that those prices funded, and the even more exorbitant profits that still remained for the tour's silent partners. And when it came to those partners, Burton paid special attention to planting a few innocent landmines.

Over the course of her fourteen months with the tour, Stephanie had watched the pompous, hedonistic General Clements strut and brag about his lifelong bonds to his tight, little power circle. She also had done her homework on Harry Yates, Carl Henderson and Lawrence Mendel, their respective companies and business dealings. She had no outright evidence of improprieties from their decades of military contracts, but she knew men like them and the corruption they bred. She was confident that packs of hungry investigative journalists pointed in their direction were likely to come up with something. Already, the P.E.T. partners and their immense wealth were being profiled by the media. Questions were surfacing about the levels of profit they had earned by supplying the military.

The decision made by the partners was not simply to suspend the Personal Empowerment Tour until the capture of the murderer, it was to disband the S-Corp entirely … to get out of the spotlight as soon as possible and stay out of it for good.

After less than two weeks, Frothy Rothenbach went scurrying back to Washington – for the first time in an illustrious career, choosing to refund the unused portion of her retainer. She knew she'd been whipped soundly. She also had been categorically wrong about the influence this unknown Stephanie Burton could wield.

Somewhat perversely, while the tour was being dismantled by a media storm, orders for tour merchandise were jamming P.E.T.'s phone lines and website. Suppliers in Shanghai and Singapore expanded their production lines to crank out enough Personal Empowerment Tour coffee mugs, paperweights and ballpoint pens. At online auction sites, collectors were shelling out double the original price for logo T-shirts and hats from previous tour events – triple or more when the items were from Seattle, Indianapolis or Kansas City.

Chapter Twenty-Eight:

Tenacity

Devoid of significant leads, no one involved in the P.E.T. murders investigation was making plans for any summer vacations. In addition to his nightly calls, Zach increasingly found reason to check in with Andie during the workday. He wanted updates from her computer searches. He wanted to brainstorm random details that his field teams were turning up, in case they prompted any substantive directions to pursue. He wanted the benefit of her uniquely keen instincts on every aspect of this perplexing case. But mostly, he just wanted to hear her voice, her laugh, and the uncomplicated comfort of their conversations.

Deep down, Zach couldn't help wondering if his request for Andie's temporary assignment to the FBI had pushed the limits on appropriate protocol. Rationally, he could convince himself that any senior agent in his position might have done the same thing. With unsolved serial homicides and the potential for more if the perpetrator wasn't captured, the FBI was empowered to seize reasonable control over whatever resources necessary to serve the public's safety most expeditiously. No one could argue that Andie hadn't advanced the investigation well ahead of where it otherwise would have been by first connecting the crimes and then tying them to the P.E.T. events. The data gurus at FBI headquarters were extremely impressed with Andie's skills and how well she integrated her efforts with others on the team. On a professional level, Zach could justify his precipitous action to himself or anyone else.

But the emotional benefits of a growing personal relationship were too spectacular for him not to question the objectivity of his original requisition. He remembered the feelings when he first saw her ... those eyes, the warmth they emitted. The promising gleam of something special.

And now that something special was developing … a something special like he'd never felt before. Zach willingly was opening up in ways he hadn't known he could … ways he'd always guarded against. He was smitten and he knew it. For that very reason alone, Zach Peterson could justify his precipitous action on any level –a justification reinforced by how fantastic he felt every time they spoke. In his years with the Bureau, he rarely had asserted his hard-earned seniority. For once, he had allowed that rank to produce one of those storied privileges, with no regrets whatsoever.

⌒⁊⁄⌒

Zach Peterson traveled like every other modern-day government agent –with a laptop, PDA, two cell phones, a pager, plus assorted adapters and spare battery packs wedged into every available pocket in his arsenal of carrying cases. His electronic survival kit kept him in constant contact with the masses of information and people involved in a serial murder investigation. But at heart, Zach was a dinosaur. At night, working alone in a hotel room, he'd pull out his trusty spiral notebook – the lines and margins typically darkened by handwritten notations. Unfortunately with this investigation, what he mostly saw was white space. In the back of the notebook were two extended timelines that he neatly folded accordion style. When he spread them side-by-side, the elongated sheets provided Zach a panoramic view of the sequence of events. The center point was the Calloway murder in Kansas City, the incident that triggered the FBI's involvement. The first timeline worked backwards to the inception of the Personal Empowerment Tour, with the locations and dates of every tour event noted. Indianapolis and Seattle were highlighted, with key facts about the murders hand-printed neatly below. The second timeline started from the Calloway murder and moved forward, with more than ample space remaining for critical information yet to be uncovered.

As Zach scanned the sparse content of his notebook and timelines, he felt the heavy burden of responsibility. It was up to him to call upon whatever resources necessary to identify and capture a serial killer before another life might be sacrificed to her twisted mind. Just because the speaking tour had stopped, there was no reason to think the killer would.

Zach was back with the field teams in Seattle, revisiting Geoffrey Wegman's houseboat and the Pier Pressure bar. By persistently replaying possible ways that events might have unfolded at each location in each city, he tried to gain a feel for how this murderer acted, how she thought

… hoping his latent sixth sense would kick in. It had been part of what originally drew him to solving street crimes and serial killings – an almost mystical instinct for certain crimes that he investigated. It didn't always happen, but without any overt acknowledgment, he would do everything possible to awaken the mojo, to prod it into action. Zach desperately wanted to get inside the head of the woman who had enticed three men into lurid compromised positions, then maliciously and intentionally compromised them for good.

He'd instructed the FBI forensic labs in Quantico, Virginia to retrace the limited evidentiary material collected by the police departments in Seattle and Indianapolis, along with what the FBI's Kansas City field teams were continuing to collect in Grandview. The strands of artificial blond hair, the massage lotion, the ammunition from Huggins' gun, other isolated random fibers, all were being run through databases to source where those materials might have been manufactured or sold. They likewise had been entered into the Evidence Control System, seeking potential matches with materials collected from other recorded criminal investigations.

Zach had met with FBI psychological profilers, who were compiling theories on the type of person most likely to have committed the three murders.

Meanwhile, the teams in Philadelphia continued to chase down every possible loose end related to the tour. Airline manifests had been checked and rechecked to verify that the P.E.T. staff members attending tour events had departed the three murder cities on the flights listed on their itineraries. Likewise for the six notables who spoke at each event. Their travel arrangements, along with their schedules and whereabouts for the hours and days surrounding each murder had been confirmed.

Though circumstances suggested otherwise, there was still a possibility that the murders had been committed by more than one person … some sadistic cult, some confederation of extremists, whatever. To that end, Zach had dialed in the Cybercrime Division, which was the FBI's most rapidly expanding operation. Teams were searching the cyber-world for websites, secured blogs and e-mail chains that might connect the murders or murderers. As these specialists had become accustomed, their investigative efforts were complicated by a flurry of new blogs and chat rooms, in this case dedicated to a country's fascination with the P.E.T. serial killings. On numerous websites, on-liners were exercising their freedom of expression to attack the FBI and police authorities, in some cases even glorifying the murders and their gory details.

From Kansas City, Andie Morrison continued partnering closely with Washington teams to systematically explore whatever investigative paths could be identified. Going back more than a decade, related crimes and criminals in the vicinities of Seattle, Indianapolis and Kansas City had been studied and restudied – likewise, criminal activity or anything unusual in the weeks surrounding P.E.T. events in the other twenty-eight cities that had been visited since the tour's inception. Also, murders and sex crimes that correlated with cities and dates for other motivational speaking events, not part of the Personal Empowerment Tour. Known enemies of P.E.T.'s partners and speakers. Related crimes involving fentanyl … related crimes somehow tied to bars or strip clubs. Andie was putting in fourteen-hour days as they chased down any and all related details.

During her limited waking hours away from the computer, her thoughts rarely strayed from the case or Zach – the two so bizarrely interwoven. These serial murders not only represented the highest profile investigation with which she'd ever been associated, but also the most stimulating challenge to her analytic skills. Her competitive instincts were fully alive; she was experiencing legitimate feelings of ambition. Maybe it was the acclaim of being credited with the biggest breakthroughs in the case thus far. Maybe it was working closely with Zach … benefitting from his encouragement … wanting to both help and impress him. Maybe it had been the way Stephanie Burton's messages had stayed with her. Maybe and probably it was all of these things, but amidst the grizzly murders and ridiculously long hours, Andie Morrison never had felt so exhilarated.

In conversations with Zach, she regularly was sharing things she wouldn't have acknowledged to anyone in the past – even herself. In their most recent call she'd felt the sudden urge to confess her penchant for settling, for avoiding confrontation. She previously couldn't have imagined actually wanting to divulge those weaknesses to another soul, let alone feeling good that she'd done so.

Chapter Twenty-Nine:

Mid-June, 2008

With the debate over the future of the Personal Empowerment Tour out of the way, Stephanie Burton closely monitored the media's shift of focus to other aspects of the murders and the investigation. Slightly bemused.

A few years before, as the country was being whiplashed through another series of celebrity misconducts, Kent Gillespie had offered up one of his disarmingly insightful observations. "If I remember my high school text book correctly, it sure seems like the news media's energy operates according to the same laws of physics as other forms of energy. It cannot be destroyed or dissipated … it only can be converted and redirected."

Since the inception of cable news networks, Stephanie had studied their evolution with profound professional interest. The first Bush-commanded Iraqi conflict was the event that passed a torch and legitimized cable news. It was then she'd started to become fascinated with the future prospects on a more personal level. With Desert Storm, Americans found they could come home from work, park their tray tables in the den and watch a war 'live' in prime time. Desert Storm – even the name had sounded more like a television mini-series than a war to which actual men and women were sent to kill and be killed. Convinced that cable news could become a more substantive part of the broadcast fabric, she convinced some of GA&J's major clients to start moving portions of their ad dollars to those networks.

A few years later, she only could observe with disappointment as coverage of the O.J. Simpson trial materially transformed how cable networks might serve up the news. Day after day, she, along with growing millions, watched the potential for a superior purveyance of real-time information being surrendered to lower common denominators. Over that prolonged trial of thirty-seven weeks, the cable networks proved there was no tidbit too small to help slake the public's unquenchable thirst for juicy, often horrid details. The networks went into creative overdrive to conjure up new program formats so that viewers wouldn't tire of simply hearing the same facts in the same ways. The networks even invented their own instant celebrity experts – formerly obscure ex-prosecutors, psychologists or DNA scientists, who were invited to help fill airtime. One interview had led to another and eventually annuities for many of these niche specialists.

Stephanie's interest in the cable networks' current energy went well beyond that of objective observer – watching as they resorted to their familiar trick bags. Fox News dusted off one of its celebrity experts. He was a retired big city detective who often struggled to align his subjects and verbs within the same sentence, but his real-life anecdotes and colorful flair for imparting gruesome details had made him a fixture in that network's coverage of crimes. Amidst a panel of other celebrity experts who were conjecturing about how three different victims might have fallen prey in such similar and vulnerable situations, Detective Vincent Gykos tossed in his two cents.

"You can take it to da sperm bank, ladies and gents. Da woman slicin' deez poor mopes is a looker. Dis touring temptress may be usin' some kinda blade to seal a deal, but her most powerful weapon has gotta be what she's totin' to turn em on."

The words barely had passed through Gykos's lips before a control room director was instructing someone to superimpose them across the bottom of the screen, "P.E.T. serial killer … a Touring Temptress." Just like that, the killer had a label. Fox News locked onto "Touring Temptress" in the hours that followed. Within a day or two, the titillating moniker was picked up by the other networks and the rest of the media world.

As coverage drilled deeper, more and more media correspondents were sent to the three murder cities. Among those soon interviewed were the divorced first-wife and widowed second-wife of Bobby Huggins, in Indianapolis. They were invited to appear together on CNN, an opportunity for Springer-like sparks to fly. But instead of sniping at each other, both spouses broke bad on the dearly departed. Their responses to initial questions had reflected measured remorse and respect – until the first-wife finally acknowledged that Huggins was prone to check out other women. From there the commentary on his character spiraled, with both wives ardently agreeing that Huggins had been an outright cheat and abusive womanizer.

Over the course of the next few days, other networks lined up their interviews with the same two wives. The duo's comfort with railing on Huggins escalated and their on-camera chemistry made it obvious that the two had become fast friends, feeding off each other and enjoying newfound co-celebrity.

Soon Huggins' workmates and drinking buddies were agreeing to be interviewed – one by one hurling another stone or two at the memory of their murdered colleague. A few told stories of his extra-marital dalliances. Amber, the stripper from Coco's, had provided the coup de grace. Tears in her eyes, she described Huggins's proclivity for pounding down rum and Cokes before punching out women.

News correspondents traveling to Seattle and Kansas City pursued similar trails, keenly aware that dirt on the victims was further stirring the public's fascination with the Touring Temptress. Basking in their fifteen minutes, two of Geoffrey Wegman's three ex-fiancés revealed that he had expected them to engage in unusual sex acts as fair exchange for the money he lavished on them. One even chose to sell the racy pictures Wegman had taken of her to a subscription website. One-time drinking pals from Pier Pressure now seemed to rejoice in relating how Wegman sponged off his parents … or how he probably possessed but one notable talent. He could tell more utterly raunchy jokes than anyone they'd ever known.

In exchange for their fifteen, the close acquaintances of Ralph Calloway, Jr. in Grandview, regaled in the memory of their one-time "Prize." How he routinely accosted women night after night. How he loved to brag about past conquests. How he wantonly shared intimate details of the experiences he'd once had with various local girls, exhibiting no regard for their reputations.

As more and more was reported about the crude, chauvinistic behaviors of the serial victims, a few feminist cable personalities began to portray the Touring Temptress as some sort of Robin Hood for unsuspecting women. In stark and purposeful contrast, the one consistent and effective voice in separating the victims from the criminal was Stephanie Burton. She was intent upon traveling a different route across the landscape of mainstream media. Every day or two she'd make a television appearance, calmly and compassionately attempting to center the conversation back to the need of finding the violent killer, of finding justice. Never exploiting or sensationalizing the media exposure, cautious to protect the dignity of three unfortunate victims. Through understated genuineness, she tried to re-instill the dignity of a public that displayed its collective fangs by devouring whatever dirt the latest media storm could kick up.

Stephanie remained inwardly mindful of grander, nobler hopes. She envisioned a platform from which she could encourage others to unashamedly pursue more constructive passions in their lives ... to not be constrained by the prevalent cynicism. To not be afraid of building upwards, when surrounded by so many who were eager to tear down. Poets and philosophers had forever painted such a bright canvas with their lofty, flowery language. But why couldn't others ... why couldn't she, in plain and simple terms?

⌒⑀⌒

During a month of coverage of the P.E.T. Murders, Stephanie Burton unquestionably had become the hottest media property. As she continued to choose appearances carefully, she felt a certain loyalty to WNL due to the original call from *Beneath the Surface*. She also had formed an instant bond with Kelly Amaker, the assistant producer who'd contacted her. With the same affirming style she had developed during her ad career, Stephanie was mentoring another young talent.

Burton insisted that Kelly be involved in all of her WNL appearances, not just the ones on *Beneath the Surface*. Of course, this collaboration was good for the young woman's standing at the network, and together they were helping WNL win a hard-fought ratings competition with the other cable networks.

To hype its on-going coverage of what was a sizzling hot story, WNL began using a montage of memorable clips to lead in and out of commercial breaks. It started with a segment from the FBI's original press conference, which was followed by a series of black-trimmed photos of the victims and a close-up of a Personal Empowerment Tour program, and then various sound bites from related WNL interviews. The final sound bite was Stephanie Burton making one of her earliest comments on *Issues of the Day*. "I hope we're better than this." As a close-up of Stephanie's attractive and now familiar face remained on the screen, the bold letters of a stylized graphic faded up beneath it – THE TOURING TEMPTRESS MURDERS.

One person alone could grasp the inconceivable irony.

Chapter Thirty:

Devotion

Years before any thoughts of full professorships, before even the slightest thought of marriage or children, Kyle Burton and Leslie Sutherland thought they had fallen in love. What they really had done was become mutually addicted. Addicted to the sexual explorations that were so much a part of the cultural revolution being fueled by a flower-powered generation. Addicted to a live-for-today attitude, a lack of boundaries. To smoking marijuana, on occasion dropping acid. Addicted more to pushing new envelopes than the narcotics themselves ... the liberation, the intimacy of illicit experimentation. Of thumbing their noses at whichever social convention that got in the way. Amidst the seemingly endless good times, with minds and bodies intertwined, repeatedly stimulated to new heights, it was easy to become convinced their two karmas had crossed and locked forever. Kismet. A pair of like souls destined to journey through earthly life in blissful union.

As things turned out, Stephanie Burton had been anything but destiny's child. The much anticipated Age of Aquarius never quite dawned for the Burton household and Stephanie's childhood was lived amidst the gaping voids that resulted ... trying to make sense out of a relationship between two parents that could never make sense ... eagerly, sometimes desperately, searching for comfort and security where no blanket of family had existed.

Kyle and Leslie had met during college at a peace rally, a sit-in on the lawn of the Administration Building at Ohio University in 1968. After sharing a blanket and conversation for the duration of a cloudless spring afternoon, they did what many earnest protestors of the Vietnam War were prone to do. They went back to an off-campus apartment, smoked pot and banged their brains out. There were definite advantages to being part of this generation intent on changing the world.

Stephanie Burton had seen old pictures of her mother. Leslie Sutherland looked like the quintessential flower child – her long, straight hair draped down her back to below the waist, usually a single braided strand on one side or the other. Her hair was black, not the color black, but darker – like the end of the universe where there's no color at all. Her eyes, the same deep darkness. She was tall with a long, lithe figure. Her breasts were unusually large but she refused to sheathe them in anything resembling a bra. One or both often escaped the halter-tops she preferred, but no matter to her if anyone saw … she was proud of their size, their shape, the way they bounced when they moved. She wore no make-up, and didn't need to. In fact, Leslie wore as little as possible as often as possible, preferring to display the natural gifts bestowed upon her.

Kyle Burton was decent enough looking to have dated other attractive girls, but Leslie Sutherland had established a much higher personal standard. In fact, she helped him set many new standards. For the rest of that first spring together, college became a living experiment for Leslie and Kyle, with neither enrolled in a single science class.

By the next school year they'd decided to join seven other like-minded souls in renting an off-campus house. Five young men and four young co-eds jumped bellbottoms first into communal living. Symbolic of their kindred spirit and repugnance toward social barriers, they removed all doors between the rooms of a rundown Victorian. Whether one was sleeping, shaving, screwing or on rare occasion studying, housemates were free to amble in, out and through each other's space. *What's mine is yours, what's yours is ours. What is ours … well, that doesn't matter because existentially speaking, we're all just passing through nothingness anyway.*

For two more years the enlightened young couple had let freedom ring. Housemates came and went. The number living harmoniously in the Victorian could vary for days, weeks or a semester, but Kyle and Leslie remained a steady and contented presence. He, the political science major, drawn to the free form conversations. She, of the strict Catholic upbringing, drawn to the free forum love and attendant lovemaking. In pairs, groups or whatever the circumstances, *if it felt good, why not?* For Leslie, it had felt good a lot.

No doubt, those living in the house had ascribed great importance to what they were doing together, the statement they'd been making. They had become a unified part of a movement that would right the world of wars, social injustice and the nethermost affliction of humankind, materialism. Only the unenlightened might have confused these virtues of a liberal humanitarianism with capricious indulgence.

Neither Kyle nor Leslie had felt any particular urgency about graduation and the looming real world. Their respective relationships with two sets of traditional Midwestern parents had been strained. Kyle needed to work various jobs to cover his costs of school, but Leslie inexplicably kept receiving her checks from home. Some terms they'd take full course loads, others not. Along the way, Kyle managed to earn his undergraduate degree and seamlessly slip into graduate work. Leslie changed majors repeatedly but never managed to accumulate enough of the right credits to merit a diploma of any kind.

Similarly, Leslie cycled through more than her fair share of life-changing philosophies and theologies. If one of the Beatles or numerous other in-tune personalities became devotees of some new guru or maharishi, she'd been apt to swiftly follow their leads. Most of these lifelong answers would last a few weeks, some even extended to months. On one such road to self-actualization, the one on which her body had become her temple, she'd needed to cleanse herself of smoking, drinking and pills. Her commitment total, she flushed every such substance in sight, which happened to include her birth control pills. Unaware, Kyle took no alternative precautions and soon Leslie's bodily temple was housing an expanded congregation. Fortunately her temporary adherence to healthier living also had included sexual monogamy, so paternity wasn't the issue it often might have been.

Kyle deemed himself ready for the pending obligations of parenthood, which was really the first semblance of responsibility either had accepted since their first fateful afternoon together. He now was prepared to start stepping through the looking glass into more serious adult life. Leslie also recognized that pregnancy and motherhood would require changes to their free-spirited lifestyle, and so began her fervent but fruitless attempts to make time stand still. She couldn't willingly surrender her piece of the Baby Boom birthright. For Leslie Sutherland, the high-bound tenets of social revolution had afforded her everything she sought from life – hedonistic gratification.

The first-time Leslie acquiesced to Kyle was on the institution of marriage. Leslie had proposed there be no superfluous legal union. Girl or boy, they simply could name the child 'Starlight' with no last name, then continue their communal existence in the Victorian. Kyle was having difficulty wrapping his mind around the concept, but a sudden disinterest among the other housemates protected him from becoming the lone killjoy. Since they needed to rent an apartment and succumb to dirty diapers and early morning feedings anyway, he counter-proposed marriage. By the time delivery rolled around in early 1971, Leslie's resolve had eroded further. Finding it harder to relate to her feel-good past while waddling around with swollen joints in late stage pregnancy, she caved once more by acceding to Kyle's schmaltzy urge to name the baby after an aging grandmother. So into this world was born Stephanie Margaret Burton.

Overcome by a feeling of postpartum oppression, Leslie became steadfast in her determination never to acquiesce to her husband again. During the ensuing years of marriage, they seldom were together, leaving Stephanie to be raised in rotating shifts.

Kyle surprised himself by getting turned on to graduate work, even accepting a teaching assistantship in the political science department. His enthusiasm eventually grew to the point that Paul Scanlon, his closest friend from the Victorian, enrolled in the same graduate program.

Leslie also continued to spend time with their friends from the Victorian, getting turned on in her old familiar ways. She chose not to alter the special bonds she, too, enjoyed with Paulie and the others. It would have been hypocritical for Kyle now to attempt to establish behavioral boundaries because of some arcane legal ceremony. Nonetheless, deep down he'd been ready, in fact desirous that their relationship might evolve to a more traditional level of shared commitment, as husband, wife and daughter. Though disappointed and hurt by Leslie's rejection of normal matrimonial attachments, he remained hopeful she might view things differently as Stephanie grew up. Instead, the ex-hippies settled into an even more plutonic relationship, content to share accommodations, occasional meals, pleasant-enough conversations, and lest they forget, a daughter. Otherwise, there were no questions asked.

A few years later, Kyle found himself yielding selectively to the once dreaded ways of the real world, while still trying to hold onto whatever ideals he could from the Sixties youth movement. Teaching at a large university offered the perfect setting for straddling one's values. The faculty in the Department of Political Science was large enough to provide upward mobility, material gain and intellectual status – while at the same time, an academic platform from which to trumpet cynicism and anti-establishment sentiments to eager young faces. Kyle found his element. He loved what he was doing, he mesmerized students, he rapidly accumulated an impressive portfolio of published articles, and he steadily climbed from teaching assistant to instructor and associate professor. Finally, a full professorship. To students, he looked like a campus figure plucked from some contemporary novel, uniformed in his blue jeans and tweed jackets, sporting a beard and moustache, oozing with liberalism and fair-mindedness. Away from campus, the upward climb had brought with it a cozy two-bedroom Cape Cod, a well-maintained used Volvo, and a growing appreciation for life's amenities … amenities he would have preferred to share with his wife, better still with his wife and daughter as a family. But with each passing year, the once college soul mates continued to drift farther apart. The satisfaction of his professional success was more than offset by a constant feeling of inadequacy from not understanding the emotional needs of the woman he still adored.

In the meantime, Leslie remained tethered to what was most comfortable to her – pot, alcohol and partying. After a few years, the old gang from the Victorian mostly had moved on, so she tapped into other fledgling groups and hangouts that perpetually took shape on the fringes of a large university. When at home, Leslie tried her best to give Stephanie undivided motherly love and attention. But as Kyle became more successful, his schedule demands increasingly encroached upon her time for less motherly pursuits. A trapped-at-home mom, her resentment built. Toward Kyle, toward his intensifying ambition. Often spilling over toward Stephanie, whose very existence had altered and complicated the pleasures she really sought.

It had become evident to the Burtons and their acquaintances that Stephanie was an unusually bright and inquisitive child, able to fully engage with any roomful of adults. Her innate intelligence was stimulated by constant time alone with one parent or the other. Doing word puzzles, learning history, studying maps with her dad. Singing, making rhymes, doing crafts with her mom. During the periods that neither parent could devote their full attention to Stephanie, she most often occupied herself with books she found around the house. Not just children's books, but grown-up books on history, philosophy, poetry. Savoring the words, wondering about what the writers were feeling when they wrote them.

As a young child, Stephanie was unable to recognize the dysfunctional nature of her parents' marriage or the absence of a close nuclear family. At the time, she had nothing with which to compare. Still, she'd been hoping and looking for something more sustaining with her parents. She became adept at melding her personality around her mom's changing moods – mood swings that became more frequent and noticeable over time. She could sense when her mother was turning melancholy or distant, and tried to find unobtrusive ways of comforting her. "Mommy, can I rub your forehead?" "Can I read you rhymes?"

She looked for more and more ways to help around the house with cleaning, the laundry and any of the other chores her mother mostly ignored. But Stephanie usually was left wondering why her mother didn't notice or appreciate her attempts ... why she couldn't feel close to her mother. Wondering what she herself was doing wrong with one parent over the other.

Her relationship with her father was, if nothing else, predictable. Stephanie absolutely idolized her dad, craving any minute he could be at home with her. She would sit by his side or on his lap and hang on every word as he explained how presidents were elected, how one war after another had been caused by religious differences, or how an airplane flew. But with him, too, she'd sensed an emptiness. She did everything possible to please him, to keep his spirits up, to make him feel loved, to make him feel important. Stephanie practically glued herself to his side after dinner and until bedtime. She cherished the moments when she could bring a sparkle to his saddened eyes. Arriving home with his leather satchel on his shoulder, her mother literally passing him in the doorway as she grabbed the car keys from his hand and headed out for her evening's activities. So many times, Stephanie would watch him shake his head with the most forlorn expression as he listened for the sound of the car driving off.

Stephanie learned not to question one parent about the interests, whereabouts or motivations of the other. Similarly, neither would ask Stephanie how she spent her private time with the opposite parent. Unwritten rules had been established, unmarked but clear borders. A shared roof that housed completely separate relationships.

One such private interaction was bath time. Most nights, Kyle Burton would put Stephanie to bed while Leslie was out doing her own thing. For him, it seemed like a particularly special time to be alone with his daughter. As far back as Stephanie could remember her father would join her in the bathtub. Since they'd always bathed together, even as she got older it didn't seem unusual when he would drop the robe from his unclothed body. Or when he would slide into the bathtub facing her. He would take his time soaping and rinsing every part of her body, first with a washcloth, then with his hands. Once she was thoroughly clean, he would hand her the soap and lay back so that she could take her time doing the same for him. As with so much they shared, he frequently reminded Stephanie that she needn't talk to her mother about their nightly baths. She was more than willing to comply because of how especially happy this time together would make him and she didn't want her mother to somehow spoil that pleasure.

Not until several years later, after Kyle Burton was dead, did Stephanie fully comprehend that the man she most revered had been habitually molesting her.

Chapter Thirty-One:

Hope

Kyle and Leslie Burton chose to wait several months before explaining to eight-year-old Stephanie that her father was dying of cancer. The news hit her exceedingly hard because the months preceding were amongst the happiest of her childhood. Her father had been spending much more time around the house and her mother was usually there with him. It actually had felt like they wanted to be together. Talking, caring about each other. A family of three taking walks, reading stories and poems, cooking dinner and cleaning up the kitchen afterward. On clear nights, naming the constellations from a blanket in the backyard. Having assumed that her family had ascended to some higher form of relationship, Stephanie experienced not just grief when they told her about the terminal illness but also betrayal. The newfound devotion had been due only to the fact her father was dying; it was predestined to last no longer than a few months.

Kyle and Leslie Burton had hoped to share those months with their daughter under seemingly normal circumstances ... to provide her lasting, positive memories of her father ... of her father and mother together. Like so often in their misdirected lives, Stephanie's parents had chosen what felt good only to them ... what out of momentary guilt had allowed them to feel better about a failed family. As a result, Stephanie carried even more hurtful artificial memories – reminders of the kind of childhood she'd coveted but been denied. The missed opportunities, the lost joys. A childhood she never could have experienced with her destructive parents.

Soon after Stephanie had been told the truth, her father slipped into his final surrender to cancer. Within weeks he never left the house. Within a few more, he rarely left his bedroom.

At the same time, she watched her mother visibly wear down – feeding her husband, giving him his medications, assisting him to the bathroom, tending to whatever needs she could. One afternoon when Leslie was especially exhausted, Stephanie had offered to help.

"Let me give Daddy his bath … I've done it lots of times."

Her mother casually dismissed the offer with a chuckle. But Stephanie never would forget her father's reaction – at first a smile of awkward discomfort, then the look of pained sorrow that quickly replaced it. In that moment, Stephanie recognized that their special baths had somehow been wrong. His expression left no doubt. What they'd been doing together must have been very, very wrong.

As her father lay dying, visitors poured through the house. Stephanie took it all in, fascinated by the parade of human behavior. She saw grandparents and relatives she barely knew, some she would never see again. She met lots of important people from the university, as well as her father's students. Most evenings there was a regular group that hung around, including Uncle Paulie. They would sit with her mother in the living room, drinking and reminiscing well past the time Stephanie went to bed.

After she'd seen her mother in the driveway with Uncle Paulie, Stephanie started noticing that this group seemed to touch each other a lot. Then she started noticing the noises late into the night. It became obvious that her mommy liked touching the private parts of more people than Uncle Paulie. *Was this something Daddy knew? Was this something Daddy liked, too?* What kind of life did her parents live?

The day after Kyle Burton's funeral, most the visitors stopped coming – all except the ones from the late night group. With her father gone, her mother at first made new commitments. "Stephie, I promise I'm going to be there for you in whole new ways. You'll see … we'll be closer than ever."

Unfortunately, old habits die hard and this phase proved to be another passing fancy in Leslie Burton's life. However, she did manage to complete a bookkeeping class in order to secure a job in the university bursar's office. Though widely known that Professor Kyle Burton's wife was a non-stop party girl, the department dean felt obliged to take care of one of their own and had lined up the position for Leslie. She soon demonstrated that she could handle the bookkeeping part, just not the part about starting at 8AM. Empathizing with the complications of being a single parent, the bursar tried 8:30, then 9:00. But as Leslie's arrivals kept pushing well beyond 10:00, it became apparent that her lateness had more to do with nightlife than motherhood. As a last attempt, the bursar suggested Leslie might better serve the university on a part-time basis – afternoons only. Miraculously, it worked.

But raising a daughter and maintaining a house on the salary of a part-time bookkeeper was impractical, especially since Kyle's modest savings hadn't been supplemented by any form of life insurance. Initially it was out of friendship and gratitude that Leslie's regular male friends started showing up with food and gifts. Throughout any given week, Stephanie could look forward to a variety of dinners brought in by interesting gentlemen who then would take her mother out for the evening. Night after night, Stephanie was left alone to do the dishes and pick up the house. Once she finished her homework, Stephanie would escape into books from the public library until bedtime. Books in which she would find encouragement to keep trying with her mother. Books that would offer her hope for what life could be someday.

She often was awakened when her mother and the male friends arrived home, late into the night. Laughing and talking loudly, after hours of drinking. But even when they tried to be quiet, the Cape Cod had been too small to insulate Stephanie from hearing. Sometimes they continued drinking a little longer in the living room, sometimes they moved straight to her mother's bedroom – so noisy that Stephanie had no choice but to accept the oft-heard rumors. Fighting back tears and nausea, she would try thinking of faraway places, hoping she might regain the sanctity of youthful sleep. But regardless of what might have gone on in the house during the night, the different men always had left by the next morning. Stephanie would get herself out of bed, make her own breakfast, then quietly slip into the bedroom to kiss her sleeping mother goodbye.

By the time she entered high school, Stephanie was savvy enough to have seen through her mother's arrangement with an endless string of male visitors. As best she could tell, her mother never accepted actual money from any of them. But it seemed to be understood that they were expected to help somehow. Not just meals or token gifts. Clothing, pieces of furniture, car repairs, a lawn mower.

Night after night, Leslie would click into party mode, turning on the good times to turn on her companions. Year after formative year, Stephanie had observed in both wonder and disgust. Wondering why … wondering what pleasures, what release her mother might be seeking, and whether she ever might find it. Disgusted by seeing her mother dressing and behaving like someone much younger, making a spectacle of herself. Year after formative year, watching her mother succumb to a cancer that was every bit as destructive as the others that had invaded their home. Watching her mother get used by men, using them in return. Year after formative year, unable to dislodge the thoughts of how her own father had used her. Remembering the deep adoration she'd once felt for him, knowing it had been completely displaced by anger and repulsion for the putrid thoughts he must have carried.

An intelligent, sensitive teenager with her whole life ahead, Stephanie had witnessed enough sordid behaviors and experienced their destructiveness to question the romanticism of the books and ideals she treasured. Based on her real-life experiences thus far, classic fiction books had been just that … classic fiction. The rutting behaviors of her mother and her various visitors were better explained in zoology books. Their sexual urges no more amorous or controllable than those of farm animals … more curse than blessing, more whimsy than fulfillment. She even had allowed herself to slide into the sewage through her own games with Gunner. Yet despite these many torn thoughts, Stephanie Burton had remained convinced that she could rise above the hurts, the negative influences and the vulnerabilities.

Chapter Thirty-Two:

Resolve

Each day the public's infatuation with The Touring Temptress seemed to grow as the media kept boring deeper into the backgrounds of Geoffrey Wegman, Bobby Huggins and "Prize" Calloway. Some reporters found it convenient to categorize them as a threesome of underachieving narcissists. The disregard, at times disdain, for the victims became evident in the media's coverage. On-camera experts spent more and more time speculating on the sequence of events that had led up to the crimes, hypothetically recreating how the victims might have been chosen, lured and debilitated.

From her hotel room, Stephanie followed the various media theories being advanced, knowing some were substantially close to how the three murders had occurred. The more that various theories became accepted, the more it seemed that certain broadcasters and their audiences wanted to paint the P.E.T. murderess as an artful, mysterious siren. Larger than life. But Stephanie knew better. The three victims had behaved predictably. It was she who had answered a siren's call ... a dark inner voice she had been suppressing since the first time she'd killed a man.

꙳

In the autumn of 2001, she'd presented a futuristic view on the green movement to the board of directors of GA&J's largest automotive client. Several months earlier Stephanie Burton had been invited to that meeting, and it was then she decided the time had arrived. The November meeting date would be almost eleven years from the exact day he visited her in New York City. Stephanie had kept close tabs on Gunner, who was working just outside Toledo, less than sixty miles from downtown Detroit.

He'd played out his four scholarship years, helped Bowling Green to four winning seasons, and climbed to fifth on the school's all-time scoring list. The coaching staff had pulled rabbits from one hat after another to preserve Gunner Parravano's academic eligibility, but there was never any thought of him earning an actual degree. His last day of college basketball had been his last day of college classes. He dropped out to marry his pregnant girlfriend and take a shot at pro ball in South America. But before he even secured his passport, he was arrested for taking a different type of shot at his bursting bride and nearly causing her to miscarry. This was hardly Gunner's first time in front of an Ohio judge for his various misdeeds. Once again, local alumni pulled strings and he got off with a year's probation – the terms of which forbade him from leaving the country, or even the state. The judge also issued a marriage annulment and stipulations for future child support, which Gunner proceeded to ignore.

Gunner had no choice but to stick around northwestern Ohio, play basketball in a few industrial leagues and try his hand at coaching the girl's team at a local high school. Unfortunately, he couldn't keep that hand off the girls and in his second year of coaching found himself before a familiar judge, this time for multiple charges of statutory rape. No alumni wanted to go near this one and no strings had been pulled. His sentence was forty-eight months, with no time off for good behavior due to repeated incidents during his stay at the Ohio State Penitentiary in Youngstown.

Once Gunner Parravano had made full restitution to the sovereign state of Ohio, a Bowling Green alum and sports fanatic from Toledo magnanimously stepped forward with a convenient fresh start. Gunner could help operate one of the driving ranges he owned out in the sticks. The alum had a hunch that the guys who hung out there might spend more money with a recognizable ex-jock working behind the counter. Gunner was given the early shift, pre-dawn to three in the afternoon – running the sprinklers, driving an old tractor to pick up range balls, and manning a combined sales counter and short-order grill. The jump in sales had been immediate. For the nominal price of a fried egg sandwich, customers could be treated to the inside skinny on either college hoops or life in prison. Their choice.

Gunner's off-hours were spent searching for female companionship. According to those who knew him, he had an insatiable libido and preferred the certainty of a steady bedmate every night. Nonetheless, his reputation for punching out the ones he loved and groping the ones he legally shouldn't, made it more and more difficult to meet women interested in dating. So he mostly relied on prostitutes to gratify his needs, or periodic one-nighters with gay men. Prior to prison, Gunner Parravano would have decked a suspected homosexual for simply smiling at him, but the prospect of years in a cell with nothing more than self-stimulation had changed his outlook. For sanity's sake, he had elected to temporarily compromise his standards on gender. Back in circulation, he still craved the rawness of another male now and then.

For two years he'd paid paltry rent to live in a rundown motel out near some fishing lakes. It consisted of fifteen one-room cabins that in the busiest of seasons might have seen six occupied. Though no reduction in rent went with it, he had selected the most dilapidated unit, set off by itself, behind a maintenance shed and some overgrown shrubs. Whatever few folks might be around the motel, he didn't want them observing the various guests he invited into the privacy of his cabin. It was there that Stephanie Burton had chosen to pick up on where they'd left off.

Through public records it was relatively easy to ascertain where a recently released convict had established employment and residence. She'd done that in 1999, and each month since made calls from pay phones in the various cities to which she traveled on business. By memory she would punch the number to the driving range, always early in the morning. As soon as her calls were answered, she quickly would hang up. She simply needed to hear the voice she remembered so clearly – the unmistakable voice that confirmed where he could be found whenever she was ready.

Following her morning presentation in Detroit, Stephanie headed to Toledo in the nondescript rental car she'd driven from Chicago. An hour later she spotted him through the front window, working the counter with a couple of customers. She pulled into the parking lot of a nearby grocery store and waited, never questioning the rightness of her intended actions or her ability to go through with them. It was something that had to be done. When he left work in a beat-up Firebird, she stayed behind him at safe distance. Once she watched him park and enter the isolated motel cabin, the decision on where to approach him had been easy. She drove several hundred yards before finding a dirt trail off the main road, then followed it back and parked in a secluded spot. She grabbed her purse and set out on a calm, leisurely walk toward a much anticipated reunion with Gunner.

He was just out of the shower and pouring his second shot of Wild Turkey when he heard the knock. He hadn't arranged for any professional companionship so he figured it was one of the *faggots* he called on occasion. Wouldn't they ever learn that their little get-togethers needed to be on his terms? He needed to be in the right mood, and if he wasn't, the last thing he wanted was a pansy on his doorstep. *Time to slap some sense into another flaming dirt bag.* He barely had gotten the towel around him as he opened the door.

He was thirty-one years old but the years hadn't been kind, or more accurately he hadn't kind to those years. As he stood in the doorframe, it was like she was seeing him through a faded yellow filter. A once tall muscular body had turned gaunt. His once thick brown hair had gone thin, discolored by years of peroxide that for whatever reason he'd used to become blond. Only the dark bushy sideburns belied him. His teeth were yellowed, as were several fingers on each hand – clearly stained from cigarettes, a habit probably picked up in prison. Across the back of his right hand, a faded tattoo of the name Gunner. *How many women had felt the back of that hand?* Even his skin had an unhealthy yellow pallor, most likely from drinking – his person, the room itself, reeking of alcohol. *How fitting that this disgusting coward of a man would now appear so yellowed by his past.* She'd smiled as she took it all in.

"Hello, Gunner."

Seeing her after ten years, in this hellhole, was so out of context that it had taken several moments to register. But it was her all right. Nobody else had a face like that. Or even here in the middle of nowhere, that I'm-so-damned-special way about her.

"Can I come in?"

"Why the hell would you want to?"

"Because I think we have some things to talk about."

He started to shut the door, but paused. "That was a long time ago. You'd never be able to prove anything now. And besides, I still think you deserved it for the head job you did on me in high school." Then he continued shutting the door.

"I couldn't agree more."

The door stopped slightly ajar, froze there, then slowly opened again. "You mean that, or are you just here to play with my head some more?"

"You gave me a lot to think about. What I did to you in high school was inexcusably mean and self-centered."

Gunner hesitated because he wasn't sure it was a good idea to raise the subject again, but ultimately couldn't resist asking, "What about what I did to you in New York?"

"Like you said, that was a long time ago. And who knows, maybe if you'd been more open-minded toward me at the time, I might have made a more willing partner?"

She'd seen the look and known she had him. That gleam. His male ego stoked. He was thinking with his prick. Here was a woman who had emasculated him in high school, whom he'd maliciously raped and beaten a few years later. He hasn't seen or heard from her in a decade, during which time he has taken up permanent residence at the bottom of the barrel. But based on the simple exchange of a few suggestive pleasantries, he was ready to believe all that history no longer mattered. Flesh conquers all. Stephanie Burton had stepped inside.

"I heard you'd become some hotshot ad exec or something … "

Because the murder occurred in an unincorporated area, jurisdiction belonged to the Lucas County Sheriff. The office already was stretched beyond its limited manpower trying to keep up with intensified security procedures resulting from the 9-11 attacks, two months earlier. Conclusions on the murder had been drawn quickly, and due to the nature of those conclusions there'd been virtually no public pressure to find the killer. News stories dealing with anything other than fighting terrorism and national security had received little coverage by the media, even the Toledo papers.

The motel's owner had been called by one of the regulars at the driving range when Gunner didn't show up for work. His naked body was found face down, spread-eagled on his bed – his head caved in by what was believed to have been a small sledgehammer, which never was located.

Parravano's reputation for switch-hitting was hardly a secret. Official records revealed that several male intimates had filed previous reports of physical attacks before withdrawing their formal charges. The crime scene practically screamed that Gunner had been repaid in full for whatever abuses he might have inflicted on one of his gay hook-ups. There'd apparently been some heavy partying. His blood alcohol level was .35, enough to cause severe impairment or unconsciousness with most any man. One empty and one partially empty bottle of Wild Turkey were found on the kitchen table. At some point the partying had turned ugly. Extremely ugly. And extremely bloody. After having his skull battered, Gunner Parravano's genitals had been severed and jammed deep into his

rectum. One more sign that he'd probably pushed the limit with one of his homosexual companions.

In a matter of days, the sheriff's office had completed the investigation into Gunner's acquaintances, as well as known vice peddlers in the area. They had turned up no leads or physical evidence from the killer. The locals didn't care all that much about who killed a has-been jock that had blown all his chances and finally turned pervert. It had been easy to allow this case to slide quickly over to open but inactive status. With Lake Erie as its northern border, a nuclear power plant in the adjacent county, and the industrial interests of Toledo, the citizens of Lucas County were much more concerned about the ominous issues of homeland security.

Nearly three hours after knocking on the cabin door, Stephanie Burton had made her way back to the hidden rental car. Dealing with Gunner required more time than anticipated … a full two hours of drinking and pandering, even some rudimentary physical contact before he finally passed out. Afterwards, almost an hour to clean up, change clothes and assure nothing in the rundown cabin could ever trace its way back to her.

She made several stops along the two hundred mile drive home to Chicago. The bag with her bloody clothes and the various cleaning supplies she'd purchased were tossed into a restaurant's dumpster near Goshen, Indiana. The sledgehammer was bleached clean and thrown over a junkyard fence near Gary. The bleached knife went down a storm sewer inside Chicago's city limits.

Throughout the drive, throughout the days that followed, Stephanie had savored every moment. Every step from the car to the cabin. Every word he'd uttered, every sound he'd made. Every reaction to how she'd played him. Every ticking second that he'd laid there naked before her, splayed over his bed in appropriate submission. Every drop of blood that had poured from open wounds, where the hammer struck his head. Every glorious quiver of her body as she'd watched him die. Every rush of adrenaline when she still needed more and had grabbed the kitchen knife out of the sink.

The wait, the anticipation had been worth it. Lying on that apartment floor eleven years ago, feeling the mixture of blood, cheap champagne and Gunner's semen drying on her thighs, she had vowed this single act. For eleven years she had known she must take his life. Never a second thought.

And she had been right. She was overwhelmed by the ebullient satisfaction. The cathartic release. The separation immediate from the pains inflicted by so many poisonous men that had trampled through her life. In those moments she had felt the palpable demise of every demon residing within her. This singular act had given her the most wondrous, ecstatic sensations of her life. But she was resolute … just this once. Now she had jettisoned the scarred memories; she could cleanly move forward with everything she hoped to accomplish.

She'd allowed the thoughts and feelings to linger in those immediate weeks. Then she forced herself to bury the whole experience along with much else from her past, sealing off mental passageways she was determined never to travel again. She had feared the attraction, the addictiveness. She couldn't permit herself to relive the awakening she'd felt with Gunner's death. For more than five years, her conscious discipline prevailed. Those innermost doors had remained locked. Until she'd stepped onto a Memphis stage and been overwhelmed by a tidal wave of past and present.

Chapter Thirty-Three:

Late Summer, 2008

Twelve weeks after Prize Calloway was murdered, the media engines finally started running out of steam. The tour organizers had pulled their plug in the early innings. The victims and their various foibles had been dissected from every conceivable angle. As much public pressure as could be mustered had been heaped upon the FBI. There were no new revelations to keep the bonfire blazing.

As television coverage of the serial killings had worn on, Stephanie Burton frequently found herself part of panels that segued into discussions about other news items. She was careful not to step overtly outside her bounds … at least on her own accord. But moderators couldn't resist asking such a popular new voice to weigh in on a corporate scandal or some celebrity's latest fall from favor. Exactly as she'd hoped; she kept to her game plan. The calming, compassionate and dignified perspectives that had counterbalanced the fire drill frenzy surrounding three murders were just as evident. No matter the topic, her common sense decency was welcomed by the audience. Her impact on ratings welcomed by the networks.

꿈

For the FBI, the dialed down media intensity allowed them to go more routinely about their business. No longer did they have to answer daily, even hourly questions about what they were turning up. Good thing, because they weren't turning up much.

The Bureu's forensic psychologists concurred; in all likelihood the murderess had acted alone. Three male preys, one huntress. She was profiled as a highly resourceful, detail-oriented woman who harbored virulent attitudes towards certain types of men. Pieces continued to fall in place as to those certain types of targeted men, but little more to go on regarding the woman herself.

For the time being, Zach's investigative teams would operate under the assumption the killer had been inside each of the bars while the victims were present during the evenings that preceded their murders. Each victim had gone to moderately crowded bars and departed alone. The lay-outs and activity levels within the establishments had offered ideal settings for the killer to enter and leave without drawing attention – and while there, spend as much time as necessary selecting her victim.

In two of the bars, the staff had referenced lone females among the unfamiliar patrons described to police officers. At Pier Pressure in Seattle, "a woman off to herself, preoccupied with a book." At Uncle Charlie's in Grandview, "a middle-aged businesswoman doing paperwork in a booth away from the noise."

Unless someone was rowdy or an especially generous tipper, the dancers and staff at Coco's in Indianapolis rarely bothered to notice specific individuals among the transient crowd inside a strip joint. On the night preceding the Huggins murder, they'd remembered numerous single patrons moving in and out of the club's dark recesses. "Just like every other night."

Seattle and Kansas City field teams had run into repeated dead ends trying to source where an unknown female might have purchased the limited amounts of fentanyl needed to sedate Wegman and Calloway. Even as they dug, they'd recognized the perp more likely would have transported her own supply – meaning it could have been purchased anywhere in the world, over any period of years.

Other agents across the country inquired their way to countless underground labs and middlemen, but the quantity simply had been too small to be singled out. With the same lack of results, Cybercrimes had exhausted their known Internet sources.

cyc

"I think your parents would be pretty darned proud of the man you've become."

"The family jury's still out as to whether I've made it all the way to adulthood. I'm guessing that a couple of my sisters would vote that I've still got some growing up to do. And, for sure, they all think I need to open up more."

The burgers and beers must have contained some sort of truth serum. It couldn't be the alcohol; he hadn't even finished his second beer. Zach surprised himself with how much he was willing to confide to someone he was dating ... or to anyone at all. He wasn't sure if Andie would categorize their recent times together as dating, but he hoped she would. Over the three months of the investigation, he'd been back to meet with his field teams in Kansas City seven times, more than double the trips he'd seen fit to make to Seattle or Indianapolis. The Beck Street Grill had become their regular spot.

"It would be fascinating to meet your sisters sometime, but probably not all six at once."

"Sorry, it's an all or nothing proposition. Whenever I get back to Wilmington, for some reason they feel compelled to put on a full-court love fest for baby brother."

"It could be because they adore you."

"I've considered that, but concluded it's much more likely they just want to remain in good favor with the FBI. We're talking about some pretty shady characters down there. One lets her kids have pet ferrets. They didn't even ask for dogs or cats ... only ferrets. Then there's my oldest sister ... she plays the oboe in the Wilmington Symphony Orchestra. Did you ever think anyone really played the oboe? Odd behaviors if you ask me."

During Zach's fly-by the week before, they'd spent the evening mostly talking about the investigation – clanking their last Harps in mock toast to the growing number of dry wells. Then Zach had walked Andie back to her car at the Bureau office, where they'd shared a first short kiss. Followed immediately by a first long one.

Tonight it had been obvious that both wanted to major in off-duty conversations, so they cautiously had journeyed into each others' pasts. Neither had been married, or seriously close ... apparently good news to both, since they couldn't conceal their smiles.

Andie had been the first to open up about family, predominantly her parents. In the case of Mother, she and Andie as yet hadn't worked through the typical mother-daughter thing from her teens. "Given another twenty or thirty years, I'm sure we can learn to let our defenses down. In the meantime, we usually can manage around enough of the issues to feel reasonably close. Heck, she doesn't make me go through a metal detector at the front door anymore."

With Pops, it was easy. "We've always had so much we could share. The outdoors, ethnic food, Springsteen, The Three Stooges ... having to manage around our respective issues with Mother."

Pops was the one person she always could count on to affirm her potential, rather than constantly critique her for falling short of it. "But, hey, I was his tomboy daughter. He's always had an enormous blind spot when he looks my way. And now that I'm trying to be more honest with myself, I wish I hadn't been so quick to shrug off what other people who really cared were trying to tell me."

After they'd laughed through some of her favorite family stories, Andie had let loose with a string of words that would make many a man cringe. "I just know you'll like my dad." But Zach wasn't the least put off. Pops sounded like the kind of guy he would like.

At first, Zach was reluctant to reciprocate when Andie demanded equal time about his family. Not that he wanted to be evasive. He merely was trying to postpone the inevitable downer when they were in the midst of such an enjoyable evening. His parents had died when he was eleven. Tragically. Though he'd certainly been able to move forward in the twenty-five years since, anyone new in his life still had to process the harshness.

He was the youngest of seven siblings and his six sisters ranged from seven to twenty-two years older than him. His parents had wanted to keep trying for that elusive son – so much so that they were in their mid-forties when Zach was born.

"I wasn't even out of elementary school when my dad decided to sell his dental practice at age fifty-seven. My mom was his hygienist, so she called it quits, too. They were pretty devout Methodists and had always dreamed of doing more serious missionary work than the volunteer stuff they could do on weekends. One of the reasons they'd retired so early was to give them the time.

"They got connected to a Christian group that was helping rebuild the Church of Uganda. This group had gone in there in 1979, when Idi Amin was overthrown and the new president, Milton Obote, welcomed back outside missionaries. Then Obote's government was tossed out in 1985, a few weeks after my parents arrived for what was supposed to be a four-month stay. Unfortunately, as Obote and his supporters were fleeing the country, a group of zealots mistook a civilian flatbed truck for a military transport. When the grenade hit their truck, my parents and three others were killed instantly."

Andie realized that in the many years since, Zach would have related this story hundreds of times, but the moisture in his eyes showed he still missed his mom and dad. She resisted any instinct to reach across the table for his hand, not wanting to make the situation too awkward or trite. But seeing her watery eyes looking back into his had spoken volumes to him – those expressive eyes that had been the gateway to their relationship.

"Originally the plan was that I would stay with my oldest sister and her family while my parents were in Uganda. Well, as it turned out, she and her husband became my surrogate parents. Plus, my other five sisters and their families got plenty of chances to help raise little brother, Zach, because they all live within short drives of Wilmington.

"Andie, I can't tell you how much everyone down there means to me. And unfortunately, I don't do a very good job of telling them either. But I'm going to do better, I promise. I just hope the FBI is ready for agents that are properly in touch with their inner emotions."

Andie's eyes were watery again. She had no doubts that Zach and Pops were going to get along fine.

Chapter Thirty-Four:

Autumn, 2008

"Who were the powerful men behind the curtain of the Personal Empowerment Tour? We'll profile them and their unusually strong allegiance to one another, tonight on *Beneath The Surface.*"

Retired General William Addison Clements and his cronies may have washed their hands of the Personal Empowerment Tour and the media attention it had drawn. But that didn't mean the media was done with them. Any number of hungry journalists were turning up the volume on the tour's silent partnership. Harry Yates, Lawrence Mendel and Carl Henderson had made untold fortunes in the private sector, mostly from contracts with America's military. Their close friend, General Clements, conveniently had been a lifetime military officer. Even for a former Joint Chiefs Chair, he seemed too comfortably ensconced within this circle of mega-ton checkbooks. Microscopes were out and the retired general found himself in the center of most of their lenses.

For forty years, William Clements had avoided any intensive scrutiny of his personal assets. He carefully had followed the advice of close confidants that he trusted to have his best interests in mind – because his interests were also theirs. His hidden wealth had been sheltered in all the right accounts, in all the right countries. With the rest of his visible assets and income, he'd paid every applicable tax in full and on time.

Back when he became Chairman of the Joint Chiefs, the appointment process had been less rigorous than it would have been now. The Secretary of Defense had recommended him to the President, who then announced his appointment pending a perfunctory approval by the Senate Armed Forces Committee. At the time, a rubber stamp because the sole focus was one's military record and his had been exemplary. Since senators felt no compulsion to have their staffs dig into Clements' personal life or finances, the President's advisors hadn't bothered with anything more than a cursory review. The various financial facades in place for the general had been more than adequate. But if the *media termites* kept at it, William Clements knew the government's forensic accountants would eventually be set loose. A very agitated public servant braced himself for the next media storm moving in his direction, this time with consequences much more dire than seeing his brainchild tour shut down.

⁓

Within days of the murder back in May, Forensics had identified the lotion present on Prize Calloway's body as Solace – the same one found on Wegman in Seattle. Zach had instructed one of his rookies to do some homework on Solace.

Thompson & Dowell (T&D) had been selling their popular brand in the United States for more than twenty years and the company estimated the product was present in over thirty-two million homes. More than sixty-one million bottles of Solace were sold each year. Daunting numbers, but T&D reported that neither Seattle nor Kansas City represented more than 450,000 annual units – around eleven hundred bottles a day. Still outrageously long odds, but the kind the FBI was used to tackling.

After Zach had mentioned these facts to Andie during a late night call, she threw one more long shot into the mix. "Just because Solace wasn't found at the crime scene in Indianapolis, it doesn't mean the killer hadn't come prepared to use it." Meaning another twelve hundred bottles a day to consider.

The only legitimate chance this particular lead might go anywhere would be if the perp had bought the Solace shortly before the murders, so Zach instructed field agents in the three cities to initiate a tedious process of checking local purchases during the weeks preceding each homicide. They were to start by gathering sales records from retail establishments located within five miles of Pier Pressure, Coco's Lounge or Uncle Charlie's Tavern. Plus any additional stores along the main arteries that represented direct routes from Key Arena, Conseco Fieldhouse or Kemper Arena to those bars. "Maybe we'll get lucky and something will turn up so we won't have to expand our radius."

They got lucky. Very lucky … or at least it had seemed. After five months of exhaustive efforts, checking out hundreds of stores and reviewing tens of thousands of receipts, they held three similar receipts from three local drug stores, each time-stamped during the early evening hours that preceded the three murders. Each respective drug store was within a few miles of each respective bar. Each receipt reflected purchases of the same items, and only those items – a tube of Maybellene Dark Secrets Washable Mascara, a Revlon Crimson Fantasy Lip Gloss stick and an 8-ounce bottle of Solace.

After the amount of time that had passed, the various sales clerks on duty had been unable to remember anything about the specific nights in question, let alone one particular customer. None of the small, independent drug stores had installed security cameras, so there were no videotapes of the transactions. Zach recognized such coincidence hadn't been lucky happenstance for a meticulous murderess.

Dark Secrets. Crimson Fantasy. Solace. At times Zach Peterson had to wonder if his perp was taunting them.

When Kelly Amaker proposed the idea during a late October production meeting, everyone on the *Beneath the Surface* staff had started nodding their heads like they'd just taken lessons in synchronized body language – including Gordie Jacklin. That was particularly encouraging since Jacklin rarely affirmed anyone's ideas but his own, especially one that took him out of center spotlight for precious minutes. But because Stephanie Burton had made her very first television appearance on his show back in June, any credit for launching this popular new personality should rightfully come his way. Besides, he really did like the woman and what she had to say.

The segment was to be called "From America's Heart" and they'd run it only two or three times a week instead of daily, to help preserve its authenticity. Each would be a three-minute piece featuring unsung acts of decency that occurred in the same locations or organizations that were dominating that day's headlines because of controversy or scandal. Regular counterpoints, reminders that there still was a strong fabric of morality amidst any negative situation. The staff would have little problem generating the required content or uncovering the human interests. Kelly Amaker was almost certain she could deliver Stephanie Burton to provide the commentary that would allow these stories to hold their own, even stand above the rest of the bilge. It was obvious that the idea, the opportunity to work the positive side of the street, had struck a chord with everyone in attendance.

Two weeks later, the calls, e-mails and letters, even the newspaper editorials, came pouring in. Stephanie Burton and "From America's Heart" had struck a chord with the public at large. A sound, a voice, a message that had needed to be heard.

Several weeks later, when Gordie Jacklin was scheduled for vacation, it had become obvious that Stephanie Burton was the right person to fill-in. The previously announced substitute was sent on "other assignment." Burton's popularity and this unexpected shift in plans was hitting Jacklin a little closer to home, but he'd been playing the role of career benefactor so nobly that it was too late to start backpedaling.

In front of a camera, Stephanie Burton was totally comfortable in each and every situation she encountered. She missed the electricity, the cues she picked up from having an audience live in front of her, but she still spoke to them through that lens as individuals rather than some faceless mass. She displayed the same natural instinct for what people were feeling and how to connect with them as she had in those crowded arenas.

She and Kelly Amaker had grown close. Though the young assistant producer was conspicuously ambitious, there was a genuine goodness about her. Stephanie admired that, wanted to help nurture it. Be surrounded by it.

As 2008 drew to a close, Stephanie Burton looked excitedly toward the New Year. With audience ratings and enthusiasm climbing, she was on the threshold of incredible opportunities, which also caused her to reflect on her journey. It had been two years since she'd left the ad world that had provided her a needed foundation. Seventeen since a soul-searching elucidation on the bare wooden floor of a New York apartment. Seventeen years since private vows had been made and bold aspirations took shape.

She had carried scars, everyone did. Hers from losing a father so young, then recognizing the abuse of his molestations. From a mother whose reputation followed her to school day after day … whose weakness of character saturated their home life and followed her still. From the many men who had been eager to exploit her mother's weakness. From knowing and watching countless men who always were eager to exploit, to leverage an upper hand genetically dealt. But she would not let herself dwell there. She had not been and would not be their victim.

She had learned to hold her own in a world of double standards, even enjoyed her repeated jousts with the vestiges of chauvinism. She was convinced that gender archetypes would someday disappear, though probably not in her lifetime. Nonetheless, she wanted to advance that vision. As role model, as mentor, help obliterate the inequities and hypocrisies of cultural biases. Help propagate a single standard whereby goodness prevailed on the merits of goodness alone. Where badness couldn't be extolled if goodness was to flourish. Poetry.

Since her earliest childhood she had noticed them … and saw them still today. The many silent expressions. So many people needing to believe, wanting to find that goodness. It was this basic human capacity that must be celebrated and nourished. Not the cynicism, not the manipulation. More poets, fewer pragmatists.

To be effective in the long run, she'd been willing to blur her convictions from time to time. She occasionally had doubled back on the double standards, exploited the exploiters. Minor ethical casualties when waging a war for enduring principles.

She had known what she must do with Gunner. That murderous act had been intended to seal off a lot more doors than the memory of a retaliatory rape. And it had. But it also had stirred something deeper inside, something unanticipated. An overwhelming feeling of satisfaction in having wielded a finalistic power over pains of the past. And not just her pains. She had wielded that power on behalf of hordes of nameless, faceless women who silently suffered the indignities of the Gunners and Uncle Paulies of the world. The Jack Lumpkins and, yes, the Kyle Burtons. She had savored that feeling, indulged in it. Once Gunner was passed out on his bed, simply putting a hammer to his skull hadn't been enough – the decision to castrate him with that kitchen knife had been spontaneous. A response to the silent voices, voices needing to make a statement with how his body would be found.

The feelings had continued to roil inside her. But she was a rational, talented, successful woman with virtuous hopes, not a murderer. She had contained and suppressed those voices for more than five years. Then she had stood before that hungry crowd in Memphis. She had seen it in their faces, their expressions. Not just the women, all of them. Thousands of well-meaning eager souls looking to her for help in finding a deeper goodness within themselves. Tired of falling short. Tired of seeing the wrong people win. Wanting to do something with that goodness. Unable to recognize that Clements and the others were belittling and using them.

She had watched Clements and his friends behave like disgusting animals, bragging about their conquests. So smug in their self-importance. Then they dared to stand before thousands who looked to them for inspiration. *They must be stopped, men like them must always be stopped.* On that electric stage in those electric moments, as the thoughts and emotions converged, she had known she must wield the power. She had touched the crowd. Their silent voices were screaming out and she could wield it on their behalf. She must experience the ecstatic joys of wielding the finalistic power on their behalf.

She had continued to reach out to them from other stages in other arenas. They had reached back to her with their heartfelt appreciation, but also their silent screaming voices. She wielded the power three times on their behalf.

Because the FBI had managed to connect those three occasions, she could never wield that power again. She wouldn't need to. The inner conflict could cease, the doors could remain sealed forever. She at last would have a broader platform to see if her grandest hopes could be achieved … if she could help inspire a more lasting goodness with the millions who sought it. If she could help the silent voices finally speak for themselves.

She recognized the darkest of ironies. She would have such a chance only because of the bottom-feeding ways of the cable news networks that had indulged in the very murders she committed. Networks that had made her an integral part of their indulgence. Now she was poised to alter their bottom-feeding ways … and this was the brightest of ironies.

Part III

"Life may change, but it may fly not; Hope may vanish, but can die not; Truth be veiled, but still it burneth; Love repulsed, -- but it returneth."

Percy Bysshe Shelley, British Poet, 1792-1822

Chapter Thirty-Five:

Tuesday; January 13, 2009

"So, did you think about me today?"

"No 'hello.' No 'Hey, Andie, this is Zach.' Lucky for you I've got caller ID or I probably would have hung up on you. And, of course, your first question is, 'did you think about me?' Me, me, me … it's always about Zach, isn't it, pal?"

"Hardly, princess. Let the record show that I was asking if 'you' had been thinking about me. So, let's get back to the subject at hand. Did you think about me all day, or just every free minute?"

"Actually, I believe it was just the one time. In fact, I'm sure of it. Yes, it was right after I finished reading up on that guy whose arms and legs were lopped off by an ax in Hayward, Wisconsin back in 1987. Which means it would have been right before I dove into the one from '99, in Amarillo, when that male scalp was found in a convenience store freezer. Something about those cases triggered thoughts of you."

"Gee, Andie, I'm touched. And I'm also sorry I'm not in Kansas City to take you to dinner. Could've been a cheap date … sounds like you won't have much of an appetite."

"Yeah, but I'm sure I could run up a pretty sizable bar tab. Zach, there's no end to the sickos out there!"

"And don't think we're not grateful for their business."

"Very funny … and where might you be calling from tonight?"

As soon as one of them kicked things off, Andie and Zach might banter back and forth for many minutes before normal, more serious conversations occurred. These types of exchanges had become a valued part of their natural chemistry. Each appreciated the other's quick mind and irreverent sense of humor. But the easy flow of retorts also reflected the uninhibited comfort they had for one another, for their relationship together. For them, an appropriate affirmation of their growing intimacy.

Working the P.E.T. murders together, the outward appearance of their relationship remained completely professional. Inwardly, Andie Morrison and Zach Peterson were falling headfirst. Tonight she was wishing she could see his smile in person, especially those dimples when he laughed. She'd finally decided that of all his physical attributes, it was the dimples she liked best.

One of Andie's primary assignments was digging into past crimes that held any potential of a remote tie to the P.E.T. homicides. She peeled through layers of details from cases that reflected even a hint of similarity, constantly searching for some obscure, heretofore unnoticed new layer to peel further. Hours upon hours, days upon days, weeks upon weeks, search upon search, Andie was convinced there was an answer out there to be found. The more she explored old crimes and the twisted minds behind them, the more fascinated she became with the mindset and motivations of the P.E.T. murderess.

Had these three been her first killings … were there others in her past? Only men … why? What role did the sex play … what part in her past? How did it make her feel … why did she want or need to feel it again? Why these three men? Why the connection to the tour cities and dates, the tour itself? What statement might she be making about personal empowerment?

Andie's role in the investigation required her to assume the murderess had killed before, then somehow figure out whom, when and where. Geographically, there were no boundaries. Mobility already had been demonstrated; the murderess was capable of killing anywhere.

Obvious matches weren't going to pop up at this stage of her data searches; those would have shown themselves well before now. The longer the effort required, the more cryptic the eventual connections. Andie trudged through gory, grizzly details of one horrid murder after another, intensely examining the bizarre circumstances and locations – reading verbatim accounts from witnesses and interviews. She pored through the pasts of every victim, of every suspect. Not simply reviewing the original case files, but launching her own probes into media reports and whatever additional source links she could think to reference.

In her years with the Kansas City Police Department, Andie thought she'd delved into enough murders, rapes and violent crimes so that no one incident could surprise her anymore, but this daily regimen of heinous acts was something else. Her stomach turned on a regular basis. Often times the irreverent exchanges with Zach provided exactly the desensitized distance she needed; but sometimes not. Somehow he seemed to know when to do nothing more than offer a commiserative shoulder.

"Zach, I spent most of the afternoon trying to piece together the background on a bizarre murder victim from 2001. Some guy named Nicholas Parravano was found with his severed genitals forced up his rectum, all of which was done after he'd expired from having his head bludgeoned."

"Did they get the murderer?"

"No, not even close. When you look at the file, it's obvious the locals barely conducted an investigation. This Parravano had done a few years in prison, and there were all kinds of notations about his history with prostitutes and known homosexuals. It was like his life wasn't worth worrying about."

"Unfortunately, Andie, there are resource constraints. No one wants to admit it, but every crime isn't going to get solved."

"But a violent murder? Even the guy's parents didn't apply any pressure. His dad was Joey Parravano, the college basketball coach.

"Probably didn't want any additional attention drawn to the kind of life his son had led."

"Sure seems that way. How could one life have become so meaningless? And what kind of demented mind decides to kill like that?"

"Andie, it's like you said earlier … a lot of sickos out there. I wish I was there to buy you that drink."

Chapter Thirty-Six:

Monday; January 19, 2009

"Thank you for watching tonight, let's talk tomorrow."

Stephanie Burton closed the inaugural telecast of *High Road* as though it had been a phone conversation with a friend. Hardly the grandiose statement most TV personalities would have chosen for signing-off a news program that had received so much press attention. But that's exactly why WNL's senior executives knew they'd just watched something very special.

Stephanie could feel the electricity through the camera's lens. She knew the first hour indeed had been special. Millions of people would find their voice.

～∙∽

Much to Gordie Jacklin's chagrin, the weekly Nielsen's for *Beneath The Surface* had reached all-time highs in December. Normally, this would have been cause for Jacklin to break out the caviar – but in this case, the show's ratings pinnacle happened to be reached while he was on vacation. Regular viewership had jumped the first night Stephanie Burton filled in as host and continued to climb sharply on each of the next two. The only explanation for the ratings bump was that audience interest had been building over the prior half-year through Burton's various television appearances. A growing number of people must have been eager to see what this refreshing new personality might do with a full hour. Those viewers definitely liked what they saw the first night, because they apparently told others. WNL certainly hadn't promoted the fact that one of its preeminent personalities was on vacation. The sizable overnight ratings surge could only have been driven by word-of-mouth. Unprecedented.

As stand-in moderator, Stephanie Burton had inherited incendiary topics and outspoken panels that Jacklin's staff arranged in advance. She hardly was thrilled with the assortment of low-minded garbage, but figured she'd been handed an opportunity to prove that any subject could be treated with greater dignity. She navigated the minefields of reprehension and sensationalism with such graceful respect that even Jacklin's regular guests dialed back the hyperbole, quickly recognizing that their normal on-air theatrics wouldn't play well. Each person, each story was featured with uncharacteristic civility. Programming executives only could imagine what this woman might do without the constraints of someone else's format. The very next week they'd begun to ask those questions in earnest … little more than a month later they were watching it live.

Stephanie and Kelly Amaker had holed up in Stephanie's hotel suite for several days to fully develop the concept of *High Road*. Their initial proposals to WNL Programming had sailed through unscathed.

More objective, more uplifting news programs had been tried numerous times by various networks. Market research perennially revealed there were increasing numbers of people who would flock to a televised concept that finally got it right. But with most past attempts, audiences soon had grown bored with what they perceived to be bland, unworthy experiments. Or veteran broadcasters, who'd only known one way to report on current events, found it difficult to stay a new course and had slid back into old, opinionated habits. Either way, those different formats hadn't worked; that different voice had yet to be found. After closely tracking her appearances and appeal, WNL execs were willing to take the chance that Stephanie Burton might be that voice.

As executive producer of *High Road*, Kelly had pledged she would allow that voice to ring pure and true. Not trick up the news of the day with artificial weaponry from the sidelines, but plainly "discuss a story the way you would if the people in the center of it were sitting around your kitchen table." Without hesitation, WNL had committed its full support and resources.

Gordie Jacklin's reactions were mixed. He had seen through the network's decision to schedule Burton's *High Road* immediately preceding his *Beneath The Surface*. He wasn't thrilled with the prospect of becoming a poster boy for negativity in a nightly counterpoint of styles that the programming brass clearly intended. Not to mention the way they'd yanked his assistant producer from him the instant *the vaunted Miss Burton* had asked for her. On the other hand, Jacklin had a strong suspicion that his ratings were about to enjoy a measurable upswing with Burton as his lead-in. Plus, lest anyone forget, he was still the one who'd put her on the air to begin with. And if anyone did forget, he'd be damned sure to keep reminding them.

Chapter Thirty-Seven:

Late February, 2009

For months reporters had been rummaging through the life and times of General William Addison Clements, going all the way back to his ROTC days as a Yates Scholar. There were mounting speculations about a Congressional inquiry, so the media was turning up that rheostat. More and more questions were being asked about Clements' role in awarding military contracts during the Vietnam Era and the decade that followed.

Compared to the vivisection he was enduring from one inflammatory telecast after another, Clements should have appreciated the respectful manner in which *High Road* had treated his building controversies thus far. Nonetheless, the general harbored a festering animosity toward Stephanie Burton. From his perspective, she was the one responsible for the whole mess in which he found himself. She'd been disloyal to P.E.T., an organization that had seen fit to invite her into their ranks and pay her handsomely for the privilege. In the military, that behavior alone would have branded her an ingrate. She'd so deftly manipulated the public to kill his tour, with her phony concerns about safety and humanity. And if that hadn't been enough, she'd found ways to smugly interject those innocent little references to past financial ties between P.E.T.'s silent partners. He'd seen through it all. She comes out looking like some Polly Purebred while a group of true Americans gets trashed by a bunch of media liberals. She ends up a media darling with her own damned show; he ends up with his world tumbling in around him.

Anson Jacoby had founded one of the world's most prestigious corporate espionage firms. He also happened to be a retired Army colonel who'd served loyally under William Clements. Though Jacoby Protection Agency (JPA) generated annual revenues of $200 million through its 800 associates in eleven countries, the private company didn't approach the size of the behemoths atop this healthy multi-billion dollar industry. But its reputation for results was unparalleled, in great part due to the ability of Anson Jacoby to recruit superior talent from the most elite military forces around the world. General Clements had been highly influential in establishing those connections and Jacoby was grateful for any opportunity to serve his former superior again.

Stephanie Burton was human, which meant there had to be dirt somewhere in her past. Clements was determined to know what it was, then publicly exact his revenge. Let the sharks rip apart that pristine image of hers as mercilessly as they were dismantling his lifetime of accomplishments.

JPA, like any top espionage firm, had access to most of the same databases as law enforcement. But unlike police departments or government agencies, these companies weren't constrained by the salaries they could throw at technical expertise and headcounts. These private sector firms attacked hundreds of billions of dollars that were sacrificed each year to trade theft, financial improprieties and employee fraud. With thirty-five percent of American companies reporting they'd been targets of such activities, there was a huge base of clients who paid handsomely for the hard evidence that could stem these losses of revenue. Investing in world-class personnel and state-of-the-art resources wasn't difficult for JPA, which simply could turn around and bill its clients whatever was necessary to guarantee results. Clements was convinced that pulling a few skeletons out of the closet of one lone female wouldn't represent much of a challenge for Anson's people.

Chapter Thirty-Eight:

November, 2006

From her teen years until the point she wrapped up her ad career, Stephanie Burton had avoided a conversation that would answer the tormenting question. With every facet in her life she'd possessed the courage and conviction to confront whatever challenge, whatever obstacle she ran up against. From pushing the corporate ceilings on gender to balancing the ledger with the man who had raped her, she'd neither dodged nor deflected what needed to be done. But the potential answer to this particular question so sickened her that she'd vacillated tumultuously on whether ever to ask it. *Had her mother known?*

Growing up, Stephanie had experienced the repeated humiliation – the whispers in the background … on occasion, the insults flung maliciously in her face. Year after year, the associations ever front of mind. *Your mother, the town slut. Leslie Burton, the faculty whore.* More hurtful than hearing the aspersions had been the knowledge that they were true. Seeing her with those men, seeing how they treated her. Knowing what they expected and how rarely she disappointed them.

The full scholarship to Columbia had provided her the coveted chance to escape the stench that permeated her youth. A new beginning … the opportunity to interact openly with peers, to reach out to others, not wondering or worrying about the preconceptions they might hold. She could pull down the protective barriers she'd erected in order to face each dreaded day of high school. It was toward this chance for a clean slate that she'd applied herself so diligently to every high school test and assignment. In a household that relied upon the part-time salary of a bookkeeper and whatever generosity could be stirred from the men who visited, there never would be money enough for college tuition. Without a scholarship, her only choice would've been to remain in Athens and work part-time to cover the reduced tuition that was available to dependents of university employees. To Stephanie, staying in the small town was no choice at all.

Her determination had been resolute. Excelling in high school could provide her the geographic distance she desperately sought. Excelling in college could then provide opportunities to dissociate completely from her past.

Over the years since high school, she'd maintained modest contact with her mother. Occasional calls, overnight visits during holiday seasons. Anything more would have been too disturbing; her mother hadn't changed. The familiar undertones were still present when Stephanie ran into people in Athens. Her mother's lamentations and contrivances hadn't changed – ever the misfortunate victim, no notion of accountability. And each year Leslie Burton displayed more and more resentment toward her daughter. Not for moving away. Not because Stephanie didn't call or visit enough. No, Leslie resented Stephanie's audacity. The audacity of a daughter to have made something of herself. The resentment was evident in her mother's tone and body language, and with every cocktail became more pronounced.

The salacious lifestyle steadily had taken its physical toll on a middle-aged woman. The lines in her mother's face, around her eyes, were more noticeable … deeper each year. Leslie Burton's hair was still tied tightly in a waist-length ponytail – hardly appropriate for her age and now more gray than black. Her pendulous breasts swayed noticeably beneath her clothes when she moved – forever braless and awkwardly low as a result.

Their conversations were superficial. Leslie Burton seemed uninterested, or perhaps incapable of discussing substantive or sensitive subjects. Being cautious not to offend, Stephanie ended most calls or visits by asking if it was okay to deposit money into her mother's checking account. No umbrage was ever taken and many thousands had been accepted.

In November, 2006, after her month on a Greek island with Kent Gillespie, Stephanie had decided it was time for the oft postponed discussion with her mother. She traveled to Athens, Ohio. It had been a time for fresh starts as she prepared to open her consultancy and pursue grander hopes. She had answered hard questions about her feelings toward Kent. No longer should she allow the doubt to linger about her mother. If she simply applied common sense, let alone common decency, her mother couldn't have known.

But she had. At first Leslie Burton wouldn't talk about it, not seeing any reason to discuss what might or might not have happened more than a quarter-century in the past. Stephanie had seen immediately that her fears were being realized, but continued to press. Her mother even had suggested that Stephanie leave the house, "No good purpose is going to be served by this visit … by your questions."

Stephanie had persisted and her mother finally dropped her defenses. It was the first time she'd ever seen her mother cry – including her father's funeral.

"Yes, I knew what your father was doing when he was alone with you. Not everything, but enough. But who was I to judge? Who was I to condemn him for what he did with you when he knew the outrageous things I was out doing at the same time? To suddenly start passing judgment on him, after all the crazy and illegal things we'd done before you were born?"

"For God's sake, Mom, I was just a little girl. Didn't you ever worry about what it might do to me? Whether you felt yourself worthy of judging him or not, you should have thought about me and called the authorities."

"You can't understand. I had no way of supporting myself if he was taken away."

"You're telling me that you knowingly allowed your daughter to be molested so that you could continue partying and screwing your way through life. Can that really be true?"

That's when it happened, her mother broke down. "I was so weak … such a mess. I still am. You'll never understand because you'll never know what it's like to be weak." Even among the tears, the contempt was there.

The depth of the personal hell in which Leslie Burton resided had finally been exposed, her vulnerability fully revealed. At the same time, Stephanie had been contending with her own anguish over what she'd just heard.

She permitted a few moments to pass, watching her mother tear up, trying to select her next words carefully. But her mother spoke first, in a faint broken voice.

"Please leave now. You have your victory."

Chapter Thirty-Nine:

Monday; March 2, 2009

"Whoa there, time out. Before I attempt to respond to your unfounded accusation, a few facts need to be clarified. Technically, Lizzie Borden was not a serial murderer. Serial homicides require at least three separate killing incidents and adequate time between them to be considered a cooling off period … a widely accepted definition, by the way, that dates back to the early 1970's, when Special Agent Robert Ressler coined the phrase 'serial killer.' So let's review the facts."

Now Zach was on a roll. "Ms. Borden's celebrated crime falls short on two measures. She allegedly killed but two people and there was not enough intervening time to label the multiple murders anything but a crime of passion. Further, she was acquitted. No one was convicted in the murders of her parents. And to be precise, though Andrew Jackson Borden was her birth father, Abby Durfee Borden was actually a stepmother. Counter to the myth propagated by a children's rhyme, Madam Borden was not stabbed forty times, nor did Master Borden then receive forty-one. Testimony from the 1893 trial in New Bedford would place the number of combined hatchet whacks at a mere twenty-nine."

He held up his right hand and wagged his finger at her from across the table. "So, Andie, for someone whose profession is tracking down facts, I'd suggest you get yours straight before you go around making careless statements like, 'Zachary, I bet when you were a teenager you had posters of serial killers like Lizzie Borden hanging in your bedroom instead of Madonna and Metallica'. And by the way, how many people did this Madonna or Metallica kill?"

He had made her laugh and he loved that. Her eyes danced when she laughed.

"I rest my case, Agent Peterson, you're a certified crime groupie. You should know that I'm not really attracted to you, but I feel it my civic duty to help you get a life … so maybe it's time we ask for the check."

They'd intended a quick stop at Beck Street Grill, nothing more than a few brews and some onion rings. His previous stopover in Kansas City had been the first time he'd spent the night at Andie's apartment. Though neither would acknowledge it outwardly, both were anticipating another long night of sleep that would be interrupted multiple times. But the conversation had fascinated Andie … partly out of relevance to the investigation, mostly from gaining insights into what made Zach tick. They'd get to her apartment later than planned and make do on a little less sleep.

A lengthy discussion had been prompted by Andie's curiosity regarding what was known about the criminal minds of serial killers. Because of a directive from Washington, she'd been reviewing archived files on serial cases that went back more than a half-century.

Zach didn't know exactly when he'd become the Bureau's go-to guy for serials, it just seemed to have happened over time. He first had been called in to help wrap up a case of repeated euthanasia at an Arizona nursing home in late '97, because he'd been in the Southwest investigating a murder-for-hire. Some good words from the senior on the nursing home case and the following year he'd been assigned to another apparent serial – this time, what was purported to be a string of Black-on-White shootings in the South. Local reactionaries had stoked a great deal of media attention, so Zach was among the agents pulled off other cases and airlifted into Alabama and Mississippi. Within a week, the field team led by Zach had arrested a suspect for two killings in Mobile and conclusively proven that he wasn't connected to two homicides in Biloxi. Since the Mobile shootings turned out to be White-on-White, the intense racial tensions dissipated. Solving this one scored serious Bureau points for Zach and his reputation for serial investigations had built from there. As did his interest.

Serial criminals were like no others. Even in prison, notorious felons of all kinds yielded a wide berth to the "serials" and the unimaginable demons lurking inside their heads. Zach had studied and restudied the facts and theories pertaining to all known serial homicides – more than five hundred documented cases in the country's history.

Justine Abernathy, Associate Director with the Database Section, had assigned specific decades in an e-mail directive to the data team members working the P.E.T. murders. "REVIEW RECORDS OF ALL SERIALS

FOR INDICATED DECADES. PLEASE EXPLORE DETAILS THAT
COULD PROVE BASIS FOR COPYCAT BEHAVIOR. POST DAILY
UPDATES TO ALL TEAM MEMBERS."

Andie had pulled the Thirties and Forties. She'd thought she might be
able to impress Zach, but the by-play quickly had turned into a pop quiz
on his serial crime expertise. He passed with flying colors.

"One of the esteemed gentlemen I learned about today was Joseph
Bell, The Alligator Man."

"One of my favorites, Andie. It's too bad they didn't have DNA testing
back then. Though it was believed he killed close to twenty women, they
couldn't verify any body parts for most of them in that alligator pit he dug
as a tourist attraction. So it was impossible to get an exact count."

"Very funny, hotshot. How about Anna Marie Hahn?"

"First woman to end up in Ohio's electric chair for first bilking and
then killing five elderly men as a live-in nurse."

"Raymond Fernandez and Martha Beck?"

"You mean 'The Lonely Hearts Killers.' They lured more than twenty
women into their web before robbing and murdering them. Have you gotten
to Bruno Ludke, Eddie Leonski or Cleveland's 'Butcher of Kingsbury Run'
yet? The Forties weren't much, with the war and all ... but The Thirties
had some pretty colorful serial killers."

"Okay, uncle. I surrender. You obviously need a new hobby ... but
please permit me to at least derive some benefit from your obsession before
I disavow ever knowing you."

Having lived non-stop with the P.E.T. killings for nine months, Andie
had become fixated with trying to understand the mind of their murderess.
In answering the avalanche of questions that followed, Zach had described
what had been learned about serial killers over time.

Serial killers often were loners – but almost as often, quite socially
interactive, even charismatic. They tended to be highly manipulative,
usually testing at above average I.Q. levels – in several known instances,
geniuses. A disproportionate number of serial killers had come from broken
homes, had been sexually abused by parents or relatives, or had experienced
other emotional trauma in their youth. At last count, more than fifteen
percent of these murderers had been adopted once or multiple times as
children.

The differences between male and female serial killers were stark.
Females had accounted for less than ten percent of serials, but it took
more than double the time to capture them – with an average of eight

years from the time of their first murders. Male serial killers exhibited more brutality with their victims and were more likely to desecrate the bodies. Men typically shot, stabbed, bludgeoned or suffocated; women most often used poison. Nearly three-quarters of female serial homicides had been committed for financial gain. Males killed mostly out of sexual deviance or control issues. With females, victims almost always included individuals with whom prior relationships existed – most often, husbands or relatives. Whereas with male serials, it was a mixed bag that included numerous instances of random or anonymous killing.

By the time they finally headed to her apartment, Andie had gained a greater appreciation for what Zach had been mulling since the beginning of the investigation. Not only was it highly unusual that they were pursuing a female for the serial sex murders. But on virtually every known criterion, the P.E.T. murderess had killed more like a man.

Chapter Forty:

March, 2009

Stephanie Burton's presence was being felt on the media landscape. More importantly, her affirmative messages were starting to find their way into the national psyche. Audience ratings for *High Road* were doubling anything else on cable TV. Her pictures and quotes were hitting the pages of national magazines; numerous blogs and a few unofficial websites were now dedicated to her. It didn't hurt that male viewers had taken notice of her natural beauty or that young men described her as "hot." But men and women alike, adults of any age, were drawn to what she had to say, the new civility she was bringing to the discourse on current events.

In six weeks, Burton had become WNL's hottest property. Entire network departments had gone into overdrive to dream up ways of capitalizing on her rising stardom. At a minimum, they wanted to carve out more daily airtime for her beyond the one-hour *High Road* telecasts. Each of her shows already was rebroadcast during late night hours, so perhaps it made sense to run them a third or fourth time in other day parts. She could post a daily thought piece on WNL's website. She could do regular guest appearances on other WNL panels and programs. She certainly should become the centerpiece of WNL's advertising and on-air promotion. The network's public relations staff would launch a full-court press to get her featured in magazines and radio interviews.

Stephanie Burton was bound contractually to none of these ideas being thrown at her. On the heels of her success as guest host for Gordie Jacklin, WNL had been eager to ink her to a long-term deal before another network got the chance to back up a Brinks truck to her door. Stephanie had been satisfied with the multi-million dollar contract she ultimately signed, even though she'd known she could have held out for much more.

She had represented herself in the negotiations rather than involve an agent or attorney. The network's sense of urgency had been obvious, but she chose to apply her disproportionate leverage on what WNL could or couldn't require her to do once she was under contract. She'd observed how the networks zealously overplayed their past successes … squeezing out eggs as fast as humanly possible from whatever golden geese that had come their way. She had watched distinguished personas be transformed into cartoonish caricatures of themselves. Left to its own devices, WNL willfully would overexpose another welcomed new voice and dilute the longer term potential.

A meteoric career in advertising already had made Stephanie Burton wealthy by anyone's measure, but money never had been a primary motivator. Materialistic trappings held little allure to her. What remained most important was the achievement of bolder goals and not relinquishing control over matters that might obstruct them. Through daily interactions, Kelly Amaker had been gaining the same appreciations, so together they rebuffed the network's endless suggestions on how to leverage *High Road's* early success.

When the network attorneys had consented to Burton's request to retain various approval rights in her agreement, none of them had conceived that she might turn down opportunities for increased exposure and income. No personality signed by WNL, or any network, ever had done that. The senior-most attorney had been eager to strut into the rarified air of the sixty-second floor and plop a signed contract onto the boardroom table – taking personal credit for closing the deal before Stephanie Burton might "come to her senses and hire an agent." To the benefit of the network's bottom line, she'd left hundreds of thousands of dollars a year on the table. But now in retrospect, the network's top execs would have paid that extra salary and more if their star attorney hadn't so willingly ceded her the power to ignore them.

Shortly after the contract was executed, a few wardrobe questions had been raised from a corner office on the sixty-second floor. "Why aren't we taking advantage of Burton's figure? Let's start putting her in clothes that show a little cleavage … and a lot more leg. It'll boost our male demos. Hell, Fox News does it all the time. For God's sake, this woman's got the goods, why aren't we flaunting them. And let's get some pictures of her with a sexy smile and put 'em up on our website."

The request had been relayed through Kelly. Stephanie hardly could get angry by the overt suggestions, having once found it necessary to "flaunt her goods" to gain an audience with Jack Lumpkin at the ad agency. Instead, she simply pulled a copy of her contract and drew a red circle around a paragraph that indicated the CEO's wardrobe requests had put the network in breach. She paid a casual visit to his secretary, politely asking her to place a sealed envelope on his desk. Nothing was said, but the next day Stephanie was notified that WNL was donating $50,000 in her name to a scholarship fund for inner city girls. Henceforth, all decisions on wardrobe would be hers alone – just as her contract specified.

Stephanie Burton had a knack for bringing out the best in people.

In San Diego, Zach met with a semi-retired forensic psychologist whose contributions to prominent cases had been the inspiration for the fictional hero in a series of popular crime novels. Dr. Cory Caputo was well-respected by professional colleagues as a foremost expert and lecturer, but mostly as the driving force behind the Caputo Institute in Rancho Santa Fe. Anyone outside the field of psychology was more likely to know him as the shrink back in the Eighties who'd helped Ft. Lauderdale police recognize that their Spring Break Rapist was really a group of high school boys who had taken truth-or-dare way too far.

Over the course of a distinguished career, Caputo often had been called into cases by the FBI and police forces around the country. He neither pretended that psychological profiling was an exact science, nor that he possessed any unique insight into the criminal mind. Quite simply, he was extremely good at what he did and made himself available to assist and collaborate with no ego attached. With each new case, he advanced his understanding of deviant thought patterns; but mostly he wanted to see murderers, rapists, molesters and torturers captured before they could harm again.

Forensic psychology, or investigative psychology, dated back to the second half of the 19th Century. But as a meaningful part of criminal investigations in the United States, it didn't start gaining broader legitimacy until 1957 – the year Freudian psychologist, Dr. James Brussel, helped lead police to George Metesky, the "Mad Bomber" responsible for thirty New York City bombings in the preceding sixteen years. From the earliest hours of the P.E.T. Murders investigation, forensic profilers from the FBI's Behavioral Science Unit had begun working with Zach and his team. In the months since, noted outside experts also had provided input into the hypothetical profiles that were being refined continuously.

After studying the case files forwarded by Zach a few weeks earlier, Caputo had warned that a trip out to see him may not be warranted. He wouldn't have much to add. But Zach persisted – tenaciously adhering to a principle he'd picked up from a veteran agent early in his career. "Little things break a case, but only if you're physically present with your mind open to seeing them." So far, Zach had logged close to two hundred thousand air miles open-mindedly chasing the missing pieces in the P.E.T. Murders.

He was taken aback by how refreshingly humble and down-to-earth Caputo was. For a seventy-seven-year-old who had accumulated monumental wealth and reputation, his energy and cooperative spirit would suggest he was much younger with much still to accomplish. Dr. Caputo affirmed the core attributes that the FBI had been using to profile what types of people would be likely suspects for the P.E.T. killings. The problem remained that the investigation was not turning up any individuals to put against the profile.

"Zachary, I certainly agree with the opinions of the others. Your killer is apt to be a female harboring extreme animosity towards men … maybe toward males in general, but at minimum, men who could be perceived as exploiters of women. More precisely, men who view or treat women as inferior … men who are most likely inclined to demean or debase women for ego aggrandizement and/or sexual gratification … males whose chauvinistic tendencies cause them to assert whatever advantages, gender-specific or otherwise, they can gain over females.

"Based upon the common personality traits of the victims, and the means by which they were scouted and selected, the murderess probably sought males who displayed specific behaviors or negative personality types from her past. Considering the methods used to compromise and kill them, she seemingly associates this personality type with a man or men who, at a minimum, harmed her emotionally … and in great likelihood, physically. She may have been subjected to physical beatings or other traumatic behaviors that were nonsexual, but the probability is higher that she was a victim of sexual abuse. Incest or molestation. Rape or gang rape. Sadomasochism, genital mutilation. Some perverse activity or combination of sexual mistreatments that caused her great pain and emotional suffering.

"She exacts satisfaction by creating an intimate situation that she controls, then avenges previous abuses perpetrated upon her – symbolically settling past scores through the killing of surrogates for those who actually harmed her. The nature of the criminal acts would suggest this murderess principally seeks fulfillment of needs that are deeply personal and inward. However, the fact that she elected to affiliate her murders with an 'empowerment' tour could suggest a broader expression related to a woman's ability to gain adequate power and prevail amidst male-dictated standards ... that is, to beat men at their own game on what normally would be construed as their own turf.

"No doubt, the murderess was able to entice her targeted victims. This alone reflects nothing more than the fact she probably exhibits attractiveness or sexuality. However, the FBI theories on how events from the three evenings transpired would suggest levels of confidence and control that are sufficient to charm and arouse while also manipulating a complicated sequence of events."

Caputo was certain that the P.E.T. murderer would prove to be a woman of exceedingly superior intellect.

"I don't mean to sound dramatic, but she is perhaps as calculating, diligent and disciplined as any serial killer on recent record. The level of intricate planning required to select, lure and execute three anonymous men in three different cities, specifically correlating to the dates of the tour's speaking engagements, is unprecedented in anything I've studied. Spacing the first two murders by eight months, then seven until the next, reflects a patience and persistence for planning, but also a will strong enough to suppress her inner needs for extended periods. The fact that ten months have passed without an incident since the third known homicide and the national attention it drew, further punctuates her intelligence and discipline. Perhaps she will kill again, when she is comfortable she can do so safely on her terms. But perhaps she has the strength of will to stop – not necessarily because her emotional desires have been quenched, but because she is smart enough to avoid being captured now that her crimes have been exposed.

"The two characteristics that have undermined many of history's most ingenious criminals were either an unrelenting need to keep killing or the gratification derived from continued public attention. Based on her actions to date, it is quite possible she possesses the discipline and will to be an exception. She was smart enough to kill with absolute anonymity, then smarter still to stop. Agent Peterson, I fear we could be chasing the one who finally gets away."

Dr. Caputo's parting comment to Zach rang disturbingly true.

Chapter Forty-One:

Tuesday; April 1, 2009

Due to the severity and notoriety of the P.E.T. murders, Zach was required to present a monthly update to his superiors in Washington DC. His report for March reflected lots of work, hence lots of Bureau expense, but little in the way of progress since February. He could reel off hundreds of directions that so far had produced dead ends, but that would serve no purpose. Instead he took his medicine.

Despite endless minutiae analyzed from every conceivable angle, they still had few hard facts upon which to base anything. The female perpetrator had entered and departed three bars alone in a non-distinctive fashion. She twice had utilized fentanyl and some form of razor-like blade, and once a handgun belonging to the victim. She had lured and sexually stirred her victims, manually bringing two to ejaculation. Prior to finding her victims, she had stopped at local drug stores to purchase specific brands of body lotion, lip gloss and mascara. And for some inexplicable reason, the dates and cities of her crimes coincided with a national speaking tour. Basically everything else about the killer and her activities remained a mystery.

Though members of the panel reviewing the investigation recognized the murderer had done her job well, and could offer no substantive suggestions on where next to take the investigation, they were obligated to express the Bureau's disappointment. In the past, such admonition would have torn at Zach. He'd worked hard to avoid tarnish of any kind on an FBI career that was an all-consuming priority. This case gnawed at him relentlessly, but not because of what it might do to his reputation. There was some person out there with a superior talent for killing and he was determined to find her. For now, the rest didn't matter.

As he left headquarters that afternoon, he reflected on his current state of mind. Maybe with age, he finally was seeking more balance in his life. He smiled. Maybe with Andie, he was finding it.

Since the morning he'd been told the unfathomable news about his parents, Zach Peterson felt like he'd been dangling in a groundless search for more permanence in his life, something more substantial. Such a perceived void was unfounded, he knew that. He'd always had the unconditional love and admiration of his sisters, their husbands and kids. His devotion to them was unquestionable. Even after his parents' death, his youth had been filled with friendships, experiences and successes that came naturally. In adulthood, his talents and interests were many. But still, very little seemed to stick with him emotionally. The hole left by the loss his parents at such an early age had seemed permanent.

He'd excelled in his Finance courses at Emory, then Law School at Georgetown. Zach had considered "all that book junk" relatively easy. The hard part had been contemplating what to do with it, where to take it. The FBI had hosted regular recruitment seminars at Georgetown and for the first time he felt the inkling of a career tug. Zach signed on and committed his total best efforts – his career, a place-holding receptacle for pent up passions. The progression had been rapid during the first few years, but soon thereafter he began feeling less and less enthused about the prospects for longer term fulfillment – at least until he'd been thrown into the middle of his first hardcore cops-and-robber case. From then on, his passion for tackling "street crimes" had kicked in. It was the one part of his life to which he felt rooted, but it hadn't been enough. At age thirty-six, something, someone, some aspect in his life still hadn't clicked to make it all seem more worthwhile.

Zach had dated plenty of likable young ladies, a few on a steady basis, but none had come close to shaking anything loose inside him. Then he'd made eye contact in a KCPD briefing room.

In his latest monthly update meeting, he was instructed to start splitting Andie Morrison's time with KCPD, who wanted her back. Three days with the Bureau one week, alternated with two the next. With progress on the investigation virtually stalled, it only made sense. On a personal level, Zach wasn't concerned. Their relationship had progressed well beyond any need to stay connected through a serial homicide case. He was more worried about losing her skills and instincts for the investigation because this directive was an obvious precursor to her full reassignment to KCPD. It also signaled that his bosses might be worried about the prospects of ever finding the P.E.T. murderess.

Chapter Forty-Two:

Wednesday; April 9, 2009

By spring of 2009, Stephanie Burton was settling into her new routine as a nightly television host. She'd moved into a Midtown apartment not far from WNL's studios on 6th Avenue. Though *High Road* didn't go live until 7PM on the East Coast, her days started early. To accommodate her daily workouts, Stephanie was out of bed by 5AM. Then she spent an hour alone in the office reading up on overnight news events before her production staff started showing up around 7:30. Daily staff meetings began promptly at 8AM, with the first order of business being an objective assessment of the prior evening's telecast.

Many WNL personalities preferred to debrief with their teams immediately following a broadcast, but Stephanie had recognized a natural tendency. The instant the on-air lights dimmed, studios full of hovering people would feel obliged to pat every back within reach, glad-handing one another for how incredible they'd just been. Instead, Stephanie would exit the building right after sign-off to avoid the meaningless praise of network sycophants. Then behind closed doors the next morning, invite a more robust critique with just her trusted team – with all having had the benefit of time to gather their thoughts.

Stephanie had relied upon Kelly to hire most members of the nine-person production staff, but she had recruited two from her former FutureScape team. Besides Stephanie and Kelly, there was the show's director and six all-purpose players. Everyone had job titles, but none of them really remembered or cared what they were. Together they would research the hell out of what was going on in the world, conceive segment ideas for each program, then draft scripts or discussion guides, line up guests, dispatch camera crews and reporters, and find ways to do anything else that needed to be done. The *High Road* team was noticeably smaller than most, especially considering the ratings status that Stephanie quickly had achieved with the network. But they preferred it that way. They'd become family – a highly motivated, totally interdependent, never off-duty family that loved what they were doing. They loved being around Stephanie Burton, being part of her team, being part of something different and better, something that lived up to its name. And Stephanie loved being around them, just as she had her FutureScape team. These were families she could trust and respect, be proud of.

Though anyone else would recognize Stephanie Burton as the central figure in this *High Road* family, Stephanie herself viewed Kelly Amaker as the bedrock necessary to assure its legacy. The name on her birth certificate was Keetje Hayami Amaker, but an Irish housekeeper had started calling her Kelly before she'd entered pre-school. Born in Hong Kong, Kelly was a living, breathing, thriving product of the world's global economy. Her Dutch father was an engineer with Shell Oil, her Japanese mother, a foreign currencies specialist with Fuji Bank. The ancestral lines had converged to produce a young woman of exotic beauty. She attended prestigious private schools in Hong Kong, Brussels, Montreal and finally San Francisco. She possessed intelligence, people skills and boundless energy – which, combined with the diverse cultural experiences of her childhood, made her exactly the kind of person Stephanie Burton wanted in charge of *High Road*.

Still a few months shy of twenty-nine when Stephanie Burton named her executive producer, Kelly had been paying her proverbial dues in broadcast journalism. Though she worked tirelessly behind the camera, she possessed the talents and composure to be successful in front. She even had done a few stints of on-the-scene reporting while working her way up at local TV stations.

Stephanie had felt a kindred spark from the first phone call, when Kelly asked her if she'd be interested in appearing on *Beneath The Surface*. In the months since, they'd become close colleagues. Through constant interaction, they were collaborators, co-creators, co-confidants, at times co-inspirers with the production staff. Mostly they were friends. Friends, ten years apart in age, sharing a sense of optimism about the world around them. In Kelly Amaker, Stephanie Burton could see herself. The self she wished she could be. A basic human goodness from deep inside … with nothing in its way.

Within weeks of *High Road's* premiere, a trend took shape that drew concerns from other broadcasters. Encouraged by their publicists, highly desirable but usually evasive public figures started agreeing to appear with Stephanie Burton. Dignitaries, celebrities and executives who normally eschewed interviews were willingly accepting invitations to go on her show, and their newsworthy appearances generated even larger viewership for WNL's hot new property. Burton didn't give these guests a pass on difficult issues, but she could be counted on to treat them and their subject matter respectfully. Fair and equal time was assured, with none of the circus tricks.

She long had hoped that if highly accomplished people could feel more comfortable in dropping their media guards, the public at-large might benefit from seeing their depth of character ... the admirable attributes that had made them successful but were hard to discern in typical ten-second sound bites. These were the values that could serve testimony to the deeper human potential. Such faith had been rewarded.

An archbishop became teary while discussing the repercussions from child molestation cases within the Catholic Church. A secretive and curmudgeonly billionaire investor was revealed to be a wonderful story-teller as he warmly recounted the people and fortunate breaks that had saved him from his own bad instincts on numerous occasions. The Lieutenant Governor to a former Southern Governor jailed in a bribery scandal, had described the crisis of conscience when she first suspected the administration was corrupt.

In the midst of an investigation slowly going nowhere, the last instruction Zach Peterson had expected from headquarters was to fly to New York City for a television interview. Media relations for the FBI usually meant a standard press announcement with limited Q&A to follow. But this time the Bureau's public affairs officer had decided it prudent to accept an invitation from *High Road*. The serial murder case had been out of the limelight for months; it was only a matter of time before some reporter or public interest group started making noise about the lack of results. Better to pre-empt that eventuality by disclosing whatever they could regarding the case in an interview by a person who would conduct it fairly.

Like most senior agents, Zach periodically had attended FBI media training sessions, but he still was met in New York by a team that spent a full afternoon firing practice questions at him. As lead agent on the investigation, he was expected to reassure the public that the FBI hadn't lost its intensity for the P.E.T. Murders case, and go on to express the Bureau's confidence about breaking the case in the coming weeks or months. The first part would be easy because intensity was still evident among his teams. As to his confidence about breaking the case any time soon, expressing that would be one of those line-of-duty things for Zach.

When the idea of an update on the P.E.T. murders was first suggested in a staff meeting, Stephanie Burton had hoped it would be shot down by someone else on the team. The public's interest in the case had waned and it was hardly a subject she wanted to stir up again. But momentum for the idea had picked up as staffers reminded themselves of the role that the story had played in introducing Stephanie to the public. "Without those murders, there would be no *High Road*." If anything, they had a responsibility to stay on top of the investigation. Ultimately, Stephanie had no choice but to approve the idea of contacting the FBI.

"Miss Burton, for reasons already cited I only can reemphasize that this murderess is unlike any serial killer ever encountered by the FBI … or for that matter, in the annals of law enforcement."

"Not to be argumentative, Agent Peterson, but it really wasn't the FBI that encountered this serial killer was it? It was three innocent victims who just happened to be in their favorite hangouts … and the concern is whether the FBI will be able to prevent any more innocent victims from meeting the same fate."

"That always has been the issue, Ma'am. The FBI didn't create this killer and we won't rest until she's captured. Fortunately, we were able to connect her homicides to the Personal Empowerment Tour and, with the help of people like you, draw attention to that unusual pattern. Of course, we can't be sure, but it appears she hasn't killed since we went public … however, we cannot assume she won't attempt to again. It is our intent to identify and arrest this woman before she has that opportunity."

Stephanie Burton came at Zach much harder than he or his prep team had anticipated. She put him through his paces for nearly the entire interview and he handled her interrogative style impressively. Before wrapping up the segment, she owed him and her audience the high ground.

"Agent Peterson, earlier you referenced the connections made to the Personal Empowerment Tour. On behalf of millions of grateful citizens, the FBI should be commended for discovering that link. As details around the three murders became known last June, I found it remarkable that you were able to do that with the limited facts you had. Who in the Bureau was really responsible for such incredible police work? Was it you personally?"

"Miss Burton, it most definitely was not me. In fact, the actual connection to the tour wasn't made by a FBI person at all. It was an accomplished professional with the Kansas City Police Department, whom we've since made an integral part of our investigative team. She probably should have been acknowledged months ago, but as I'm sure you know, the FBI prefers not to go public regarding specific team members or their particular contributions."

"Well, you've at least disclosed it's a she. You won't tell us her name?"

"I really can't. But I assure you she is a very special talent. In fact, a very special person."

Stephanie saw more gleam in his eyes than the mere praise of a colleague. "Indeed, she must be, Agent Zachary Peterson of the Federal Bureau of Investigation. Thank you for being with us tonight, and let's hope that on some future appearance you'll be discussing the capture of a serial killer. Who knows, maybe you might even identify that special person in Kansas City? She deserves a very special thanks."

⚜

"So what was she really like?"

"You mean to tell me that's the first question on your mind? I get raked over the coals for nearly thirty minutes on national television about a complicated investigation that we've been working together for ten months. I sneak as close as humanly possible to an official reprimand for singling you out to untold millions. And the pressing question of Andrea Morrison's day is what Stephanie Burton is like in person?"

"Quit stalling, Peterson. What was she like?"

"She had nice cans."

"Very funny. Do you want me to hang up?"

Their conversation was a brief one. Zach was catching a late night flight from LaGuardia to Philadelphia to interview P.E.T.'s former sound tech, who'd been busted on a narcotics charge. Zach wanted to know what kind of company the guy kept and whether he might have had easy access to fentanyl.

Andie actually had been very appreciative, even touched, by his efforts to recognize her contributions. "I want to keep thinking about it, Zach, but off the top of my head I can't recall another person ever bothering to talk about me on national television. So until I'm sure, please allow me to extend my provisional gratitude."

She also offered much genuine praise for how Zach had conducted himself during the interview, especially his ability to remain unflustered under fire. "You almost made the FBI likable ... if that were possible."

But she really did want to know what Stephanie Burton was like. Her fascination had taken root back in Kemper Arena and continued to grow with Burton's television appearances during the early months of the P.E.T. murder investigation. Now Andie was a full-fledged fan of *High Road*. She'd almost felt a personal bond develop when Stephanie Burton had extended that 'very special thanks' to her during tonight's broadcast.

"I'm giving you one last chance, buster. Tell me about Stephanie Burton."

"She was the real deal ... in every aspect, the real deal." Zach hesitated to find the right word then continued, "She was just so decent."

"Decent?"

"Yeah, nothing complicated. No pretensions. Exactly the way her fans would want her to be. Humble, easy to talk to. When she asks people questions, she really wants to hear and understand their answers. And talk about a people person ... you should have seen her with everyone in the studio. They all adore the ground she walks on ... and you could tell, she deeply cares about them, too."

"So, other than her cans, I guess you didn't much care for the lady."

"Andie, you'll like this. Remember when I made those references about the special talent back in Kansas City? After the show was over, she told me she'd noticed something."

"That you had your fingers crossed?"

"No, that she detected I must have special feelings for this person with the special talent."

"Did she caution you about keeping work and play separated?"

"No, just the opposite. She told me how important it is to let people close to you know that they're special ... to treat them as special."

"Well, Stephanie Burton would be delighted to know that Agent Peterson does a stupendous job of making me feel special."

"Andie, there was one other thing she said."

"I'm not going to be jealous am I? I don't want to compete with someone who has their own nightly television show."

"After hitting me with all those tough questions during the interview, before I left she wanted to make sure I knew that she thinks I'm a genuinely good man."

"Zach, you are."

"Whether I am or not, she didn't need to go out of her way to compliment me. She explained that there are never enough good men in the world … how uplifting it still is for her to meet the good ones. Do you know how rare it is for some average guy to hear those things from someone like Stephanie Burton?"

"First off, you're anything but average. But maybe that's what makes her someone like Stephanie Burton."

Forty-Three:

November, 2006

Stephanie had hoped that finally getting a grasp on certain realities might open inner doors that could free her to experience life's poetry. It had been painful to hear her mother confess how she'd closed her eyes to the sexual molestations by her father. Even more troublesome had been seeing the depth of bitter resentment that her mother harbored toward her. Combined with the hollowness that Stephanie carried home from her month with Kent on Mykonos, the journey for answers and introspection so far had been a difficult one. But she needed to persist.

The next leg was Tallahassee and the campus of Florida State University, for a chat with Paul Scanlon. Following Kyle Burton's death, Scanlon had remained one of Leslie Burton's frequent visitors for several years, until he accepted a faculty position at Iowa State. After another interim stint at Auburn, he was recruited to chair the political science department at FSU. Until she called him in advance to set up the appointment, Stephanie hadn't seen or talked to "Uncle Paulie" in twenty years.

At first he gruffly waved her into his office from behind the desk, as though she was but another of the pesky students that insisted on distracting him from the stratospheric musings of his academic genius. Then he'd caught himself and shuffled over to the door to greet her personally. Had she passed this man on the street, she wouldn't have recognized him. The cocky way he used to strut his compact size, the playful grin, the curly red hair and freckled complexion … all that had vanished. Here was the man who'd so retained a perpetual boyishness that no one could stop calling him Paulie, but now he stood before her looking like someone had crossed a mad scientist with a troll. The only feature of his appearance that remained the same was the beige buckskin shoes – and based on their condition, they might have been the very same pair she remembered.

The top of his head couldn't have been more hairless, yet a border of thick, gray sprigs spiraled in every direction around his ears and temples. His face was ruddy, his nose swollen and veined – sure signs he'd been losing the lifelong contest he waged with a vodka bottle. His wire-rimmed glasses teetered atop a bulbous nose, the lenses so thick it had been difficult to see his eyes or gauge the depth of the surrounding creases. Vertically challenged already, he appeared to have lost another inch or two in height. On the plus side, the swollen jowls of his neck and chin seemed to have expanded in proper proportion to his sizable midsection.

Throughout her life, Stephanie had strove to rise above pettiness and superficiality. For Scanlon she could make an exception; she had taken great satisfaction out of seeing him look so horrible. Yet nothing about his unattractiveness seemed to bother him in the least. He'd turned into one of those far-off professorial types, his mind forever mulling something elsewhere – and wherever that might be, it was obvious that grooming and fitness didn't matter there. Paul Scanlon the pretty boy, Paul Scanlon the party boy, had aged into Paul Scanlon the academic distortion.

Once she'd fully absorbed his looks and erudite demeanor, Stephanie had grown more comfortable in his presence. One particular misgiving about coming to meet with him already had been laid to rest. It seemed a safe assumption that this new incarnation of Paul Scanlon wouldn't waste his or her time with flirtations and innuendo. She couldn't imagine that a lecherous thought had entered his mind in years.

Paul Scanlon had spent much time in the Burton home and, as a result, Stephanie often was left alone with him. He'd never quite crossed the legal lines of impropriety but he frequently made her uncomfortable – extremely uncomfortable as she'd progressed into her teen years. He had teased her about the "delicious bumps" forming under her sweater. He repeatedly would swat her on the rump, letting his hand linger way too long. He routinely had offered to give her "neck rubs, back rubs, any rubs at all" … and upon every rejection, retorted, "I know, Steffaroo, I just love seeing those pretty cheeks of yours blushing so brightly." But the redness in her face was a reflection of anger, not embarrassment.

There had been the incessant, inappropriate questions.

"Steffaroo, are you having those thoughts about boys yet? Ask your mom … you're better off waiting for full-grown men."

"Steffaroo, do you have any questions for your Uncle Paulie about the facts of life?"

He claimed he was doing his best to stand in for his best friend, Kyle – "the way your daddy would have wanted me to." A statement with implications that sickened her on every level.

She'd stopped calling him Uncle Paulie shortly after her father died. It hadn't been exactly clear what uncles were supposed to do inside a family, but it probably wasn't what she'd spied him doing with her mother in the driveway. Then, within a week of the funeral, he was the first of Leslie Burton's male companions to show up for dinner and leave before breakfast. For several years thereafter, he remained the most regular late night guest – at least once or twice a week. Stephanie had wanted to start calling him "Mr. Scanlon" … in fact she would have preferred "Creep" or nothing at all. Instead, her mother had said it was okay to address him plainly as "Paul" … familiar enough for someone in her mother's bedroom rotation, but in no way suggesting little "Steffaroo" wanted any special bonds with this unwanted interloper.

Two decades later, he sat like a potentate in his high backed leather chair as Stephanie took her seat in the single, diminutive guest chair that was centered in front of an oversized mahogany desk. The layout, the scale obviously calculated to preserve a commanding angle and presence for Scanlon in his conversations with whoever might enter his hallowed domain. She couldn't help but think of the steady stream of students and faculty members who might be granted an audience with this over-inflated authority figure … the same lowlife who frequently had left morning lines of cocaine on her mother's dresser to express his appreciation.

"Miss Burton, it has been a long time."

"Please call me Stephanie. Let's just not go all the way back to Steffaroo, Professor."

He tried for a friendly smile but came up short. "Of course, Stephanie. I take it your mother is doing well. I've lost track of how many years have passed since I last spoke with her." This comment had seemed to come off like a disclaimer – as if to clarify he was in no way accountable for whatever self-destructiveness she might be practicing currently.

"I was with her a few days ago and she is very much the same as always."

He paused, the momentary look of sadness indicating he was sorry to hear that. But he quickly regained his aloofness, "Please offer Leslie my best."

"I appreciate your agreeing to see me, Paul. I hope you'll indulge a number of awkward questions concerning my parents. For a variety of reasons, I would like to better understand some of the things that went on between them."

"I won't make any promises, Stephanie; your parents had an abnormally complicated relationship. Besides, from what I've been able to read, their lifestyle choices haven't precluded you from succeeding quite well. You've made quite a name for yourself in advertising."

"Thank you, but I've decided to move on from advertising, and I also would like to move on with other aspects of my life. Some answers might prove helpful."

A game of verbal hide-and-seek was played for a solid ten minutes before Stephanie tactfully worked her way behind the fortress he kept around his past. Over the remainder of their ninety minutes together, information flowed forth in almost cathartic fashion. Because of the close friendship he'd enjoyed with her father and the intimate relations with her mother, both of her parents had confided many of their most private thoughts and secrets with Scanlon over the years.

For the first time she heard the genesis of her parents' relationship – a subject which always had caused Leslie Burton to go icily silent. For reasons Stephanie was determined to understand, it had remained a forbidden topic in her conversations with either parent. Scanlon repeatedly stressed the importance of context to Stephanie, as though he was talking to one of his classrooms. "One must be careful in drawing conclusions from events that occurred during the late Sixties and early Seventies. Contemporary standards aren't applicable to this era of unparalleled social upheaval and experimentation." The reminders seemed to be as much for his benefit as hers.

He explained how an old Victorian near Ohio University's campus had housed a "free love" commune and, surprisingly, that her mother had been the driving force behind its formation. Stephanie found it hard to imagine how a woman who'd never displayed an ounce of conviction could have been the driving force behind anything – but as details were revealed, it made sense.

"After weeks of round-the-clock dating, your father, Kyle, had suggested that he and Leslie find a place to live together. Several evenings later, during one of their nightly marathons of lovemaking and pot smoking, she tossed out the alternative notion of a commune. Such unstructured living arrangements were popping up across America's campuses and your mother was intrigued with the possibilities. Your father was so infatuated with her body and beauty that he habitually humored her frequent whims in order to remain close to her.

"By the next afternoon they had located the perfect house, leaving the simple matter of which kindred spirits to unite in cohabitation. Kyle advocated numerous acquaintances that might evoke stimulating dialogue on social issues. Candidly, your mother's criteria were much more primal. She simply considered the possible individuals with whom she'd prefer to get high and have sex ... and I'm afraid, your father deferred to her selections.

The truth came flowing forth from Scanlon in unfiltered detail, as though he was sending Stephanie a message. *So you think you can march in here and demand to hear how screwed up your parents were ... well, let's see if you really mean it.* No matter how unsavory the facts, his pompous attitude suggested he felt neither remorse nor responsibility for their actions. Nor was he the least bit reluctant to be outwardly judgmental.

"Your father made two tragic mistakes that caused him constant misery during the balance of his abbreviated life. First, he allowed his physical obsession with Leslie Sutherland to become emotional. The poor man was so desperate to feel loved. Second, because of her most exquisite exterior, he never properly comprehended the permanent damage on the inside. She will forever be wrestling with the turmoil from her childhood, searching for ways to rebuke a father who abused her. I'm sorry, dear, but your mother is incapable of true love or intimacy. But I'm sure you've recognized that."

As Scanlon shared his observations, Stephanie tried to contain the palpitations she was feeling. He couldn't possibly know the multitude of nerves he had struck. *Incapable of true love ... intimacy. My God, he could be talking about me.*

She had too many new questions all at once. Her head, her pulse, her stomach – everything was pounding. She excused herself to the restroom to regain her composure before Scanlon might notice she'd lost it.

Stephanie had known her mother was raised in a strict Catholic family. The only time she'd met any of the Sutherlands was at her father's funeral, where she was introduced to her grandmother and an uncle, Leslie's lone sibling. Her grandfather had chosen not to attend. Growing up, it seemed curiously sad not to know one's relatives, but what Stephanie learned from Scanlon convinced her that she'd been fortunate.

"Acid trips were like a truth serum with Leslie. Only then would she open up about her father, but she obviously needed to get it out. I suppose those particular drugs made everything more third person ... the pain wasn't really hers when she talked about it."

It quickly became evident that Leslie had left little to the imagination in her drug-induced revelations to Scanlon. Leslie's father had managed a car dealership in Sydney, Ohio – having worked his way up from used car salesman. He was a two-fisted drinker and an iron-fisted head of his family. He had counted on eight or ten kids, like any hard-working Catholic, but was forced to settle for two due to his wife's "female problems." As children, when Leslie or her brother stepped out of line, they were marched into the living room and whipped with his belt. After closing the car lot each night, he and some of his salesmen would stop off for a few rounds.

"Unfortunately for your mother, there was an inverse correlation between the number of rounds he drank and the distance out of line that Leslie could step before she was ordered to lift her nightgown for his belt. It was the early Sixties, and in those days how a man raised his kids in the privacy of a household was his business. And your grandmother chose to do nothing but stand silently by.

"As Leslie matured into an unusually attractive young lady, her father apparently liked what he saw when she lifted her nightgown for punishment. Your mother related three occasions when she was sixteen years old that he came home intoxicated and entered her bedroom. After the third, Leslie finally confronted him at the dinner table ... ironically enough, following Sunday Mass. She threatened to go to the authorities but ultimately succumbed to the pleas of her mother and brother ... that her father be given another chance for the sake of the family's reputation.

"Her father never again touched her, and her mother and brother continued to pretend that nothing really had ever happened. So Leslie spent the remainder of her high school years lifting her nightgown for lots of young men in Sydney, flaunting her ruined reputation to her father and family. Included in the price for her silence was the cost of a college education, which she chose to squander spitefully."

Scanlon became so carried away with describing the lengths to which Leslie would go in hurting her family, that he was well into the details of a planned abortion before he considered the implications for Stephanie. He had no option but to complete the story.

"Leslie so wanted to pull the Catholic foundation from under her father's house with that abortion. She had found a local doctor who would do the procedure and phoned her parents to insist that they forward the necessary funds. But for one of the few times in their relationship, Kyle prevailed and convinced her to have the baby ... which obviously was a good thing for you. In fact, it was for that reason alone that Leslie's mother and brother came to your father's funeral – to pay respect to a son and brother-in-law they'd never met, but who had saved their family from disgrace and the eternal damnation of their beloved Church." Scanlon practically snickered.

"Your mother may have enjoyed her bodily pleasures with sex and drugs, but the real pleasure she has always been seeking is payback. Living in the Victorian house, Leslie pushed every limit. Sex with any man, woman or group that was willing to experiment. LSD, cocaine, heroin, and her daily staple, marijuana."

Scanlon paused and stared into Stephanie's eyes, as if to make sure it was all registering. *So there ... had enough yet?*

"The whole scene got to be too much for Kyle. He naively had hoped that starting a family would lead to something better ... but all that was rubbish to our Leslie. She was in such obvious need of professional help, yet Kyle still thought he could find his Ozzie and Harriett. We all watched in amazement."

"Excuse me, Professor Scanlon." Stephanie Burton had managed thousands of people and many hundreds of millions of dollars over the preceding decade without once losing her temper. But on this day she couldn't contain herself any longer, having masked her contempt since entering his presence. She stood and leaned over his desk.

"You have the audacity to question my father's judgment in wanting to marry my mother because you knew what a mess she was. You knew what damage her father had done to her, what she was out to accomplish through all the sex and drugs. You just admitted how obvious it was that she needed professional help. But did any of that ever once stop you? Stop you from taking advantage of the easy access to her body ... the good times she brought your way? From screwing the brains out of a woman whose looks were so far out of your league that you couldn't have touched her if she hadn't been some sort of head case? From getting her high and living out your little fantasies as often as possible? Not just in college, but for all those years that followed? Even after the death of her husband, your alleged best friend? In fact, did any of those keen insights into my mother's problems stop you from hitting her up for a blowjob in the driveway of our house while her husband, your good friend, was dying inside? Or from banging her in his bedroom a week after his death, while his daughter was forced to listen in the next room? Or those hundreds of other times?

"How dare you pass judgment? How dare you sit there like you've made something of yourself, when you know how often you took advantage of my mother's sickness to gratify your sexual needs and pitiful male ego? How dare you, when we both know that you even tried to take advantage of me when I was a minor? Hey, why not … like mother like daughter, right? Scanlon, you're pathetic."

Anyone outside his office would have heard her raised voice … in fact, she hoped they had. She hovered above him for several more minutes, glaring. Not saying another word, wondering if he had enough character to respond in some fashion. Her eyes locked upon him as he fumbled with his chubby little fingers, fidgeted with his glasses and squirmed in his high backed leather chair. After permitting his uncomfortable silence to make its cowardly statement, she gathered herself and calmly exited the office.

Rage was an emotion that Stephanie Burton had disciplined herself to contain and channel appropriately. With Scanlon, the appropriate channel had been to let it out. She originally had intended to probe deeper into her father's background as well as her mother's … to see what "best friend" Paulie might be able to share about Kyle Burton. But the more she had watched him behind the scholarly veneer, listened to his detached assessments and thought of how often he had taken advantage of her mother's weakness, she couldn't hold back … hadn't wanted to hold back. She thought of the many men like him who so often took advantage of human weakness to satisfy their fragile maleness.

So much about her mother had become clear. How could she have been so blind to her mother's emotional damage? One of her college majors had been Psychology; she'd studied the symptoms, yet never considered that her mother might have been abused by her own father. After the conversation with Scanlon, it now was so obvious that Leslie Burton had devoted her life to the repudiation of a father who had whipped and raped her. She had wasted all talents, ambition and self-respect repudiating an entire family that had swept the filth under a carpet of outward appearances. Leslie Burton had surrendered in weakness, wearing her emotional scars like badges … a victim for all to behold. *She should have been stronger.*

Stephanie now recognized why Leslie Burton might have convinced herself to ignore the unthinkable when she'd left her own daughter alone with her husband. Her mother had wanted to abort that daughter to punish her parents … perhaps to avoid bringing a child into a world filled with so many unthinkable actions. *But she still should have been stronger.* Perhaps Leslie Burton thought it fitting that her daughter be subjected to the very same deprivation she had suffered. Let her daughter's tainted life serve as proper tribute to her own disgusting father ... and to Kyle, the needy husband who'd talked her into motherhood and tried trapping her into convention. Let another damaged child serve as living testament to her own weakness and failure to cope. *Why, Mother? Why couldn't you have been stronger?*

So too, Stephanie could better understand her mother's resentment toward her – having watched the unwanted daughter accomplish what she could not. Stephanie had been able to move forward with her life, to overcome the pains and dysfunctions of her youth, to push toward making something of herself. The unwanted daughter had been able to shed the demons of her past. At least on the surface. If her mother only could know how those demons had lurked beneath her thoughts at every waking moment ... how they had caused her to commit cold-blooded murder with Gunner. But, of course, her mother never would know. No one would.

⁓⁌⁍⁓

Scanlon had piqued her interest with his references to Kyle Burton's need to feel loved. After Tallahassee, Stephanie next traveled to Upper Arlington, a prosperous white-collar suburb of Columbus, Ohio. Her father had been raised in Upper Arlington and the elder Burtons still lived in the same house. Stephanie had been introduced to them when her father died. She'd even spent an evening with them at their motel because Leslie Burton had wanted to keep Stephanie away from her own family, the Sutherlands. At the time, none of that made much sense, but after recent discoveries it finally did.

Having been introduced to various relatives during those days surrounding her father's death, Stephanie had hoped the wider family interactions might continue. Instead, following the funeral her mother promptly cut off communication. Stephanie had received an occasional birthday or graduation card from the Burtons while she was growing up, but otherwise there'd been no contact.

By the time she departed Upper Arlington, Stephanie was quite certain that she would never see her grandparents again. They were insufferable. They'd been "thoroughly charmed" by the unexpected phone call and "so looking forward to getting together for tea."

Somewhere between the phone call and her arrival, they must have forgotten the part about tea. Granted, they were in their eighties and their memories were poor, but it also could've been that they were permanently pickled. During her afternoon with them, Stephanie counted four bourbons for Grandfather Burton and three for Grandmother. No tea in sight.

The requisite tour of the house would have been all Stephanie needed. The wall-to-wall photographs from country clubs and gala tables, the pretentious memorabilia jammed into every available space, it all had spoken volumes. The Burton homestead was nothing more than a fourteen-room curio cabinet heralding one couple's lifelong quest to bring Gatsby to Central Ohio. So noticeable through absence was any priority placed on family. There had been another son and two daughters besides Kyle. Yet nowhere in evidence was there a current family picture … not a single clay sculpture or finger-painting from a grandkid. Occasional family portraits from years long past hung in a few obscure places, but the multitudes of more recent photos featured only the exaggerated smiles and tanned leather skins of an aging social circle.

Stephanie had asked which bedroom was her father's. After debating back and forth, they narrowed their "best recollection" down to one of the two rooms up on the third floor. They "so rarely found much cause to go up there." Stephanie segued into questions about what kind of boy Kyle had been.

Mother Burton needed to reflect for several moments to make sure she properly captured the essence of her son's memory. But the best she could manage was, "Kylie was normal enough, I suppose."

At which point the old man weighed in, "He was a pretty good looking boy, but not much of an athlete. Certainly a disappointment when he went off to college. All that long hair and such."

To say the least, the Burtons weren't the types to go overboard with praise for their children. As it turned out, in one way or another, all the Burton kids had managed to disappoint their parents – which probably was why they didn't merit much treasured wall space.

A pair like the elder Burtons hadn't somehow changed in their golden years. The levels of materialism, superficiality and self-absorption they'd attained would have taken all eighty-plus years. It became evident why Kyle Burton might have been so desperate to feel loved. It became evident how hurtful it must have been to be routinely ignored by his parents, only to see his later dreams of a nurturing family life be trivialized by the emotionally impaired woman with whom he'd become obsessed.

Her father must have been spiritually broken, with deep and unfulfilled emotional needs. Nonetheless, she couldn't accept what he had done with her. *He should have been stronger.* She truly had loved her father as a little girl, but he had trivialized that love through his own weakness. *Better that you died when you did, before I understood. Better I never faced the decision of how to deal with you if you'd been alive.*

By exploring secrets and uncertainties that had gnawed at her for as long as she could remember, Stephanie uncovered answers. But instead of resolution or inner peace, she was left with greater torment ... now further convinced she was unlikely to ever feel the poetry. But she still could help others. To this purpose she became more resolute.

Fresh were these thoughts when she'd opened her consultancy in December of 2006. Fresh were these thoughts when she received that invitation early in 2007 ... the opportunity to share her messages of hope and encouragement with tens of thousands at a time. Fresh were these thoughts and emotions when she took the stage in Memphis.

Forty-Four:

Friday; April 11, 2009

"General Clements, I was sorry to read about the military inquest into your past financial dealings. I'm sure you'll come out with all stars still shining, sir."

"Thank you, Anson. I'm confident we can get through this; however, I didn't anticipate attacks on two fronts. With a Senate subcommittee already digging into my every orifice, you'd think Army brass could be more sensitive to one of their own."

"Sir, it's all about managing public perceptions these days and the Army has to look like it's not trying to hide anything." Anson Jacoby glanced around the restaurant to be certain no one was watching or listening to them.

"Before I forget, General, please know there's no reason to worry about your business arrangements with the Jacoby Protection Agency. The paper trail is clean and thorough. You provided legitimate services when we were building this company and appropriate taxes were withheld on any commissions we paid you."

"Thank you again, Anson. I have utmost confidence regarding any scrutiny JPA might come under. There's a reason you're the best in your line of work."

"With much help from you, sir, and I never forget that."

"Let's talk about Miss Burton. What have you found?"

William Clements had grabbed a morning train from Philadelphia to Washington to meet Anson Jacoby for lunch. He was looking for the assurances he'd just received about his past ties to JPA, but had needed to hear them in person. He was having a lot more face-to-face meetings these days because he no longer knew what phone conversations were being monitored, or at a minimum how a sudden flurry of calls to past acquaintances would look on phone records that might be subpoenaed. For the same reason, he was traveling a great deal more by train or automobile than usual, rather than leaving a trail of flight records with the airlines.

Jacoby normally would have chosen one of his private business clubs where the General loved being seen, or taken him out to Congressional in Bethesda where he loved being treated to several rounds of golf a year. But Clements specifically had requested that they meet somewhere less conspicuous and Jacoby had understood. Still, Anson Jacoby wouldn't have contemplated that he ever could be sitting in a Denny's with the esteemed General William Addison Clements, former Chairman of America's Joint Chiefs. Just from the questions he'd asked the waitress, it was obvious the General never had stepped foot in a Denny's. It was unfortunate that the meeting must remain confidential, because there were legions of retired officers who would relish a play-by-play description of General Clements trying to order an honest-to-goodness patty melt from a waitress with purple hair and a pierced nose.

"Sir, this Burton keeps coming up clean. We're all the way back into her childhood. Last week one of my guys drove down to some small town in Southeastern Ohio where she grew up … Athens, I think."

"No dirt there either?"

"No, anything but. Her dad dies when she's nine years old. Her mom's some sort of small town tramp, yet the Burton girl pulls herself out of a background like that and earns a full-ride to Columbia. I'm afraid she just keeps looking better and better, General."

"Please, stay with it, Anson. Stay with it."

~~

"So nothing suspicious about your sound tech guy in Philly?"

"Nah, not really. Other than having an engineering degree from M.I.T. that he puts to good use by traveling around the country with rock bands and gray-haired speechmakers. Then, of course, there's his need to get high every night. If you were his parents, a lot about young Chase Noland probably would seem suspicious, but so far we haven't found a thing related to our investigation. But we'll keep him on the radar."

"Zach, I still can't believe you decided just to pop into Kansas City."

"Hey, I found a cheap ticket online and thought we might have a real weekend together. And no murder-speak tonight … this check's on me, not Uncle Sam."

"Then how about I flip you for it?"

"Dinner's my treat. But if you still want to flip me, I wouldn't be opposed … later, at your place."

The conversation, the laughter came so freely with Andie Morrison. When Zach had ended the phone conversation from LaGuardia on Wednesday evening, he'd finally said it to her. But it wasn't until he was descending into Philadelphia that it dawned on him what he'd done. He had told her he loved her. As easily and instinctively as please, thank you, or pass the ketchup. He never had uttered those words to anyone, not even his sisters. He'd often wondered if he would be capable when the time arrived. Yet now he had done it. Miraculously, unthinkingly he had done it. What's more, she hadn't fainted or hung up on him. She didn't go cool on the phone or warn him about slowing down their relationship. *What was it she had said? Oh yeah,* "I love you, too." He suddenly had felt this incredible urge to get to Kansas City, as fast as possible. A need to somehow commemorate what they'd been able to express to one another. To see if they could say it again, in person.

Zach had called ahead to hold their favorite booth, and upon arrival warned the waitress, "You'll probably need to add rent to the check tonight … I think we may be here awhile." Then they settled into conversation.

"I imagine the old gang at KCPD is glad to see you behind the keyboard again."

"You make it sound like we're a rock band. And yes, the Pit Bulls have welcomed me back graciously."

"The what?"

"The Pit Bulls … that's the name we ladies of the Data Pit gave ourselves a few years ago in retaliation to being labeled Honey Bees by Benny."

"You mean B-Cup?"

"You've got it, Zach. We avoid normal names at all cost."

"I'm afraid it won't be long until they get you back full-time."

"As a matter of fact, HR talked to me about that yesterday."

Zach was a bit miffed to be out of the loop, wondering why no one in Washington had felt obliged to share that tidbit with him. "So when do we lose you?"

"The discussion really wasn't about the timing per se, except that KCPD feels like they've been team players long enough. The reason for the meeting was to offer me the senior slot when I return full-time. I guess I became more valuable in my absence."

"Fantastic, congratulations." He stood up, bent over the table and planted a light kiss on both her cheeks, like some French dignitary. Then shrugged, said "what the heck," and laid a more serious kiss on her lips. He paused for a second. "Oh, I like that." He kissed her again before finally retaking his seat.

"I'm not surprised, Andie. I'm sure the Database Research unit had some awkward days without you around, and I'd bet that KCPD Human Resources had more than a few complaints about Benny Atkins. It's about time they stepped up and got him out of there."

"Not exactly. They still need to keep him around until he earns his pension, but they want to bump me up a couple levels and make me his boss."

"Wow. Sounds like another round of congratulatory kisses are in order."

"Not so fast, Pierre. I don't think I'm gonna take it."

"Oh, come on, Andie. You're not going to get hung up about leapfrogging over some empty uniform that they never should have put in charge to begin with. You've got to look out for yourself ... this is exactly the kind of thing you've been saying you need to work on. It's time to put Andie first."

"I've been giving this a lot of thought and I'm in total agreement with everything you just said. I'm ready to step up and absolutely do what I believe is in my best long-term interests. So at the end of this week, I'm giving my two-week's notice to the Kansas City Police Department."

Confused by where she was going, he only could stare blank-faced. She picked up on his befuddlement; then added to it. "Before I go on, Zach, let me just clarify something about what was said on the phone Wednesday night." She let that linger for a moment – which he now recognized as one of her endearing little tricks. "I meant every word I said ... all three of them. I love you."

Zach's eyes brightened, then he started chuckling, "Andie Morrison, I think you're losing your mind but I'll hold the call to the guys with the funny nets until after we get naked one more time. I love you, too, by the way ... and remember, I said it first. Now, is there any chance you might tell me why you're quitting?"

"For months, your noted Dr. Justine Abernathy has been waving an offer at me. Federal Agent Peterson, I've decided to become a permanent part of your very own FBI. I want to test my game in the Big Leagues, Coach … the Bureau's Database Section."

"Andie, that means a move to headquarters. What about all your ties here? Do you even know anyone who lives in Washington DC?"

"I do happen to know someone who travels there a great deal and I've been feeling pretty darned close to him lately. But this move isn't about whom I know where. It's about the clean break, the big leap I've always been afraid to make. I'm finally taking ownership for the fact that it isn't my bosses, parents, friends or anyone else that have caused me to play it safe with my life. It has been me, my own comfort with fitting in too easily … my own discomfort, my own lack of confidence to rock the boat a bit. Something has changed for me. I don't know if it's because of Stephanie Burton … how her comments started sinking in when I saw her last year in person … and now the inspiration I feel every time I see her on TV. Or if maybe it's because of how wonderfully good you, Zach Peterson, make me feel about myself. What I do know are two things right now. First, I'm one hundred percent positive about the decision to start a new chapter. Second, I most definitely love the guy sitting across the table shaking his head with those adorable dimples and that goofy smile on his face."

Zach never had imagined Andie would be able to speak that long or that insightfully about herself without a hint of self-deprecating humor. He never had imagined that with so many positive qualities and such obvious joy for life, she could have kept that kind of conviction bottled up for so long. He never had imagined how much he could love a woman like the one sitting across the table with those tears in her eyes … those magical, magical eyes.

Forty-Five:

Monday; April 27, 2009

The senior editors had been unanimous in their choice of covers for the April 27 edition of *Newsweek*. The issue featured a story on Stephanie Burton and one of the magazine's photographers had been permitted inside WNL's studios during a live broadcast of *High Road*. In the shot selected, there was a confluence of movement, expression and emotion that captured the essence of what was drawing so many ardent viewers. Burton was standing before the TV camera in mid-sentence, her hands in mid-gesture, chin angled slightly upwards with a hint of moisture in her eyes. Conveyed in that one frozen moment were her individuality and determination, her passion and concern, her heartfelt hopes. Instead of *High Road's* familiar set behind her, oversized red and white stripes from a fluttering American flag had been superimposed. The dark blue headline was bold across the bottom, "America's Moral Compass."

The WNL publicity folks constantly were scratching their heads, trying to anticipate what their hottest new star would or wouldn't do. One week she respectfully declines an interview with *People* and a cover story for *TV Week*, hardly pausing to consider either. The next week they wonder if it even makes sense to bother her with the offer from *Newsweek*. Again she doesn't hesitate to decide, but this time shoots them a smile and a very matter-of-fact, "Let's do it." These were all big-time exposure ops that would have prompted the network's other personalities to do handsprings up and down Broadway, yet she chooses which to pluck and which to toss as though they were nothing more than petals on some schoolyard daisy.

For many weeks it had been like this, an entire organization struggling to get into rhythm with Stephanie Burton's reactions and wishes, trying to mold around the personality that had become the network's overnight centerpiece. Stephanie and her tight little team, who had dubbed themselves "The Road Crew," meanwhile seemed to operate on their own private wavelength as ratings soared.

The *Newsweek* reporter had exhausted her most proven interview techniques in trying to get Stephanie Burton to open up about herself, her past and her ambitions. To no avail, as Burton gracefully found ways with each new question to pivot into broader themes … "how important it is for all individuals to find the will to pursue their loftiest ambitions" … "the latent power of society's collective strengths if that were to happen" … "the moral responsibility we each should feel to at least affirm one another's efforts."

"Public officials must take the lead by more consistently aligning their actions to their rhetoric. The news media needs to better balance the slice-and-dice cynicism it automatically inflicts on any issue, from global to the most local. And whether we're teachers, technicians or TV personalities, we each need to cherish and more willfully amplify our own basic desires for human decency in order to foster the same from others through our regular interactions."

The normally hardened journalist couldn't help but feel, respect and ultimately write about Stephanie Burton's genuineness. She also was undeterred in her efforts to learn more about Burton's past. *Google* led her to professors at Columbia and Northwestern, as well as former classmates. But those particular phone calls had produced little beyond the trite, glowing statements one would expect when people are asked by a national magazine to describe someone they now knew to be a highly acclaimed media personality. Stephanie Burton had been a hard-working student who earned repeated scholastic awards, but no one had foreseen the charisma and convictions that would make her a national phenomenon.

The writer concluded that Stephanie Burton had begun to hit her stride when she was building FutureScape for the ad agency, GA&J, and made appropriate note of the irony. "Burton not only helped some of America's most recognized brands shape more relevant strategies for their future success, but the ethos and pathos that would shape her future rapport with the American public blossomed during that early stage of her career."

The lengthy article included quotes and descriptions from former GA&J clients and associates. "No doubt, she was a superior business strategist and a uniquely gifted speaker in front of business audiences of any size or composition, but what I remember most was her ability to evoke the best in people. Through collaboration and encouragement, she made us believe in our own untapped potential then held us accountable to deliver on it." The retired Jack Lumpkin had lauded her from his Monterey home – one of his three.

In an interview that took surprising turns, Kent Gillespie offered effusive descriptions of what Stephanie Burton had accomplished for the agency and the ad industry, plus how much she'd personally taught him about both business and life. He hadn't been the least bit resentful in acknowledging that he was her early boss before she passed right over him, or that they'd lived together for nearly ten years before she broke off the relationship.

But the sincerest tributes and most meaningful insights had been carried in the accounts of people she recruited in the earliest days of FutureScape. Not because of their quotes per se, but because these individuals' later accomplishments were living testimonies to what Stephanie Burton espoused.

The public was able to read how an ex-bartender that Burton had convinced to take a stab at advertising, recently had become president of GA&J's European network. Or how a college dropout, driving a cab, had gone back to night school after joining FutureScape, and now was a tenured professor at Fordham. How a failed options trader, listlessly attending seminary classes, was lured back into the business mainstream by Burton and had gone on to make tens of millions. With her spiritual faith rejuvenated, the woman now funded annual scholarships at three different seminaries.

The *Newsweek* piece most definitely reflected the impact Burton had on people, but not just the ones referenced in the story. Like so many others, the reporter, the photographer, the various editors and anyone else associated had gained a sincere admiration for their featured subject. "America's Moral Compass" was more than a clever title to sell magazines; it was an expression of hope about a role that had been vacant too long.

Forty-Six:

May, 2009

"I'm telling you, Will, don't wait too long. Get your attorneys asking around … see if the Feds will cut you a deal."

Carl Henderson had agreed to meet the general for coffee at the house of Sam Cummings in Bryn Mawr, a tony Philadelphia suburb. The conversation no doubt would be uncomfortable, so better to get it over with. The time had come for Henderson to look out for himself, but he didn't want to hang a long-time associate out to dry without first trying to warn him – not that the hard-headed general would ever listen.

Henderson's ties to Clements always had been more business than friendship. The two were introduced many years earlier by Harry Yates, who had envisioned mutual advantages to their acquaintanceship. The relationship proved to be quite lucrative, but Carl Henderson still hadn't seen the need to cavort with Clements the way that Yates and Larry Mendel did. Never had he met anyone who worked so hard to namedrop the expensive wines he drank, the expensive cigars he smoked, even the expensive women he bedded when he was away from his wife. Clements was a self-important braggart who forgot that they all had known him way back when – when Harry had handpicked a bug-eyed high school senior and offered him a shortcut into wealthy, powerful circles. If it weren't for his personal exposure in their business dealings, Henderson would enjoy watching this nouveau riche bag of wind go down and go down hard.

Henderson had been contacted by a federal attorney – he assumed because relative to the others, he had less of a personal friendship with Will Clements. Or perhaps it was because the contracts that Clements had brokered to Henderson Industries weren't nearly as large as those with Yates and Mendel. He wasn't sure of the reason, but he knew that the immunity granted by a Senate subcommittee wasn't something he could turn down. He was eighty-one years old and, God willing, might have another ten or fifteen left. Damned if he'd spend them in some minimum-security prison with a bunch of inside traders and corporate con artists. He had to take the deal; his attorneys were adamant.

As expected, Clements didn't agree. "Carl, if we remain calm together, they'll find it very difficult to prove anything. Think about what you'll be doing to the rest of us."

"Will, you're not listening; they're probably sitting on the proof they need already. The hearings and interrogations are just for show so that a bunch of Senators can make bigger names for themselves on C-Span. I saw enough of what they have on us to know that I'm cooked. All those large contracts we were awarded to make hand tools ... well, someone is finally asking why our bids weren't ever the lowest ... and why every one of the exception letters on file with Procurement has your initials somewhere in the approval chain. Under the scrutiny we'd be facing, there's no way we can document or demonstrate the superior performance those letters assert ... not when the Army had other reputable manufacturers to choose from.

"And even if we could ... it's the actual invoices that give prosecutors their smoking gun. Right there in black and white, the amounts we invoiced were consistently a percent or two higher than the specified contract rates ... and your officers always signed them right through. We never overbilled enough to draw attention, but over time ... Jesus, it was sweet for everyone, Will. All those years, not even a sniff ... but now that it's all laid out ... hell, a first-year law student could put us away."

"What have you told Harry?"

"The same thing I'm telling you. I'm not the big fish they want. They've already called Larry ... they're working their way up to you and Harry. You're the two they want. For God's sake, Will, you were the Chairman of the Joint Chiefs. They want to slow roast you and Harry in front of the American public. It's time to cut your losses."

"Carl, if anyone believes that General William A. Clements will allow himself to be turned into some sort of political whipping boy, you can trust that I've been gravely underestimated."

Henderson and Clements stood, shook hands and left the den. Sam Cummings had no idea why two important men who could reserve any room in Philadelphia had needed to meet at his house on a Saturday morning. Whatever the reasons, when he saw their faces it was obvious that the meeting hadn't gone well.

As his driver pulled away from the house, Henderson shook his head and muttered to himself in the backseat, "Dumb bastard, you deserve whatever they throw at you."

He'd realized that Clements wasn't going to heed his advice from the moment the stubborn prick had started referring to himself in third-person again. *If anyone believes General William A. Clements will allow himself ... gravely underestimated ... my ass.* Will Clements was a certifiable megalomaniac. But deep down, he was still nothing more than a street punk. *Screw him.*

<hr />

Much about the *Newsweek* story pleased Stephanie Burton. It properly captured her beliefs and the messages she was determined to deliver by whatever means she could find. That was the reason she'd consented to be featured in a credible news magazine, hopeful the article would explore beyond the superficial, gossipy aspects of her rising celebrity. She wasn't being modest when she had sidestepped the writer's repeated probes into her personal life and past. More than anyone possibly could imagine, she knew she was unworthy of being placed upon a public pedestal. She was a cold-blooded murderer, praying for the strength to keep her demons in check. She could never experience what life was meant to feel like. The best she could hope for was to encourage others not to settle, not to dismiss or sacrifice their grandest dreams. However, she was caught off-guard by how those themes had been developed in the magazine.

Many of the quotes from people in her past had made Stephanie uncomfortable; the praise for her was too excessive. But she was thrilled to read the various turnaround stories that profiled former FutureScape associates. She delighted in their individual successes because each was worthy of the acclaim. These truly were the types of role models from which others should derive great hope.

Reading the positive comments attributed to Kent Gillespie, her eyes filled with tears. *Kent Gillespie ... he should've been "the one."* But now there never would be that "one" for Stephanie Burton. At last, she'd come to grips with the permanence of her inner void – the capacity, whatever it was, that allowed someone to love another person unequivocally.

She knew all the textbook reasons why scars from her past might have woven a curtain around her subconscious feelings, yet Stephanie had remained so sure for so long, convinced she could overcome the psychological damage. She'd always believed she could elevate above or beyond whatever obstacles that stood in the way of her hopes and ambitions.

The escapade with Gunner, the other teenage boys with whom she'd dabbled sexually – at the time she believed she simply was testing her mettle against the repulsive male behaviors that permeated her childhood. But had she really been evading deeper fears about an inability to experience a healthier relationship? Years later, while in college, she'd made persistent attempts at normal dating and more affectionate sexual encounters. Even after the events of her sophomore year, she had resolved not to allow a rape by a cretin like Gunner to deter her. She would deal with that remnant act separately. She continued to search for a feel-good storybook romance. Not because she'd been eager to find the one right man in her life, but simply to prove that at some point she could be receptive to the possibility. She needed to know if she was capable of opening up with a man, trusting a man, wholly caring about a man, of loving a man.

During college, grad school and her first year at GA&J, she had dated a number of men. Some revealed their chauvinistic tendencies and she'd ended those relationships before any unpleasantness might occur. There were other men who not only behaved admirably toward her and women in general, but with whom she also was able to enjoy fun experiences, engaging dialogue and mutual respect. However, no sparks ever had been ignited. Nothing in her being yet had suggested that one day she could enjoy the inexplicable energy of a soul mate. Nothing in the bedroom had suggested that sex could be anything more than mechanical or manipulative.

Yet, she had remained resolute ... always resolute. Throughout her youth in Athens, she'd found refuge from a mother's debauchery by immersing herself in the works of poets and philosophers. There, among timeless words and thoughts, goodness could reign, spirits could soar and love truly could triumph. *Uncompromised love with another person ... life's greatest treasure. Enough to lift one's hopes, enough to erase one's pain.* She would not be denied that fulfillment because of what others had done.

As soon as she'd started working for Kent Gillespie, there'd been unexpected chemistry. For one thing, he made her laugh – which was something she rarely had done. Since escaping her hometown, she'd worked hard to stress the positives in her life and thus found much to smile about. But she could count on one hand the few outright fits of laughter, let alone the uncontrollable guffawing that made eyes water and sides ache. That wasn't her personality, or so she'd thought. Then she'd met Kent. His mind was bent; he saw the world through bizarre-colored glasses and was uninhibited about letting loose with off-the-wall observations. *God, it had felt good to laugh like that.* But it was never pure silliness. Kent's irreverent wit and barbs were spurred by the insights of a fertile mind. He was both funny and smart. *If only he had been taller.* She would tease him, because she was almost as tall as he was. And he would tease her back – actual teasing, something else she'd never done previously.

In truth, Kent was average in height. In fact, he was average in overall appearance, but that hadn't mattered at all. Stephanie had liked the way his mind worked – the quick humor, the intellect, but most importantly the common sense and common decency. He was a legitimately good man, the product of a normal family with normal upbringing that had produced abnormally good values.

If anything, Kent Gillespie might have benefited from a modicum of selfishness. From the beginning, he felt awkward about taking charge of FutureScape when it had been her idea. But he also recognized how things had worked at GA&J in those days. If he'd turned down the senior position, Stephanie and her brainchild would've ended up under someone else, someone less receptive to a female talent and exciting new ways of conducting business. He'd been blown away by the proposition of FutureScape, and within a few weeks of working together, he'd been blown away by her. And he wasn't shy about telling her. "Stephanie, I've never met anyone with your ability to inspire people. Just being around you, I want to think bigger … behave more boldly."

Undoubtedly his boldest action had been telling her, "You need to feel free to build FutureScape according to your own instincts and passion." He then stayed out of her way, other than offering encouragement and running interference with the old guard whenever necessary. She'd recognized that his selfless actions weren't normal in business, nor anywhere else. She'd been completely caught off guard when less than a year later Kent proposed to Jack Lumpkin that she be named the president of their up-and-coming business unit. By then they were dating seriously, yet he hadn't even hinted that he was going to make such a recommendation. The surprise announcement reversed their reporting relationship, but he in no way tried to exploit her obvious gratitude. No, this had been classic Kent Gillespie, a good man doing what he thought was right.

She'd felt more attachment to him than any man in her life, immeasurably more. She still did. But it hadn't been enough. She had liked and cared about him, enjoyed being with him … greatly admired him. Surely with that foundation, the rest should have come. But year after year, at least for Stephanie, the love she desired never took hold. Their live-in relationship was comfortable, but the emotional connection remained plutonic. The sexual gratification was one-sided, in no way due to lack of effort on his part. That clawing emptiness, the void, had been strictly hers. Year after year, the longer she held out, waiting and hoping, the more it had gnawed at her.

She'd placed so much hope into that month in the Mediterranean. Perhaps, too much, as she reflected on the past. Whatever the possibilities might have been, maybe she had squeezed the breath from them. Regardless, nothing had stirred. She had become convinced the psychological damage was real. And permanent. Her yearnings turned to anger, and the anger to contempt. Not toward Kent, but to men from her past and the others like them – men who had rendered her powerless to change, to feel. Powerless to experience the true love she coveted above all.

Seeing his name in the *Newsweek* piece had surprised her, but the positive things he said had not. She always could count on him to take the highest road. But she was saddened to read the references to their past relationship printed in black and white. Sad for him, because she knew he still loved her. Sad for herself, because she knew she was incapable of adequately loving him back.

After breaking off the relationship in early 2007, she'd allowed several months to lapse before touching base with him. Kent Gillespie was too good a person; she couldn't stop caring what happened in his life. Since then, they'd spoken every few months. He even had teased her about the sexual frolic of their last night together, but on that subject she hadn't teased back.

In casual phone conversations, they continued to share an interest in music, feeding each other names of obscure artists across assorted genres. In their years together, they repeatedly had hooked into new sounds before they'd become popular – Michael Buble, The Corrs, Alison Kraus, Ben Folds. He'd introduced her to rugby, Peruvian food and Native American art. She introduced him to the joys and nuance of poetry. On rainy Saturdays, they together would search out interesting old volumes at antiquarian book shops. On Sunday mornings, they would attend various church services around Chicago, discussing the sermons and hymns well into Sunday afternoons. How much she missed the comfort of his regular presence.

If only she could have ripped down that curtain. No doubt, Kent Gillespie would have been the one. He should have been the one. But with the unspeakable things she'd done since, there never could be that one special relationship in her life. Now to be hailed as America's Moral Compass. *Oh, dear God, if only …*

Forty-Seven:

Monday; June 1, 2009

"It was Evelyn Salmich." Zach said nothing else. He just stared at Andie, waiting for a reaction.

"What a relief to finally know it was her." She froze his teasing stare with one of her own.

They sat in silence, eyes locked, smiles on both their faces. Zach finally tossed out another taunt, "You don't know, do you?"

Andie stared a while longer, then grabbed her napkin and buried her face in it. "Okay, you broke me, G-man. What is the 'it' we're talking about?"

"Come on, Morrison, you've gotta stay with me if you have any hope of making a name for yourself here in Washington."

"That's great, Zach. I invested close to an hour packing up my worldly possessions, just so I could move to our nation's capitol and play Twenty Questions."

"Okay, no gold stars tonight. Evelyn Salmich was the last of our unknown tour attendees … and Agent Katrina McGlocklin talked to her in Zionsville, Indiana at approximately ten o'clock this morning. So as of June 1, 2009, we can officially shut down our longest blind alley to date and declare but one more total failure."

"I know how frustrated you are … and I imagine your monthly review with the big shots wasn't a lot of fun this morning."

"I was reminded no less than a dozen times that last month marked a year. But if I had to guess, they weren't referring to when you and I first met."

They were seated at the bar waiting for a table at Bucks. It was much swankier than Beck Street Grill back in Kansas City, but they'd decided it was worth a shot because "Buck" sounded so much like "Beck" – plus it was near the Residence Inn where the Bureau had put up Andie. Policy gave her two months to find a place of her own, which promised to be a challenge based on the monthly rent of the apartments she'd seen thus far. Once she figured that out, they'd get more serious about scouting a regular hangout. But they agreed it wasn't going to be Bucks as soon as they'd gotten to the bar and noticed all the kiwi martinis being sipped. Bucks – the restaurant's name pretty well identified what patrons had better have plenty of. The likelihood of decent fish and chips on the menu seemed pretty low.

An evening with Andie helped soothe the frustrations of an investigation mired in its own tedium. Somewhere in the bowels of Washington's bureaucracy, there were people who could print out the total hours expended thus far by Bureau personnel investigating the P.E.T. murders. Zach just hoped those individuals wouldn't accidentally hit a computer key to set that report in motion. The required paper would wipe out a forest and he didn't need that guilt adding to his burden.

One of the first tasks initiated by agents assigned to the P.E.T. offices in Philadelphia had been indentifying not only who purchased the 53,000 tickets for the events in Seattle, Indianapolis and Kansas City, but also who actually sat in those 53,000 seats. By the time this process was complete, field agents in all three cities and others nearby had participated, not to mention scores of Bureau office personnel. They'd hoped to identify repeat attendees or ticket purchasers across the three cities, plus any number of "persons of interest" when the thousands of names were screened for police records and known associations.

The original ticket purchasers had been relatively easy to determine from order forms and credit card receipts, but the process of confirming who actually had used the tickets was a great deal more cumbersome. Letters or e-mails were sent to all purchasers, with follow-up phone calls to those not responding. These contacts produced the names of all but several hundred of the eventual attendees. For those exceptions, tickets were traced to their end users through old-fashioned legwork. Some tickets had been passed along several times as gifts, winding up in the hands of people unknown to the original purchaser. Others had been sold when original purchasers ran into schedule conflicts or changed their mind about attending. So the ticket trails had included classified ads, bulletin board postings and Internet auction sites ... plus a dozen tickets that were bought and sold by Zig Schneider, a professional scalper in Indianapolis. And it was that dirty dozen that had required several extra months to chase down. But Agent McGlocklin finally had pinned down the last of them – Evelyn Salmich, an Amway rep from Zionsville, Indiana.

After all the chasing, and all the names, there were no worthwhile leads to show for the effort. Not a single incidence of anyone purchasing tickets for all three events, or likewise anyone who attended all three. However, one middle-aged gentleman did purchase tickets for both Seattle and Kansas City. Personally inspired by hearing the tour's speakers in Seattle, he'd sent two tickets to his daughter in Kansas City – hoping her live-in boyfriend might be motivated to find a job.

As to other "persons of interest," Zach's teams quickly had discovered that motivational speaking events didn't attract many questionable characters or known felons. Perhaps a disproportionate number that had filed bankruptcy, or were delinquent on their child support, but few with ties to murders or sexual misconducts. But even these few had been tracked down … their whereabouts on the nights of the murders corroborated.

"So, Bright Eyes, as the one who started this whole mess with that trusty computer of yours, do you think I can convince the Director that we were wrong all along … that we've now concluded Wegman, Huggins and Calloway each committed suicide?"

"Zach, I've been getting an odd feeling. You know how we keep digging through the background of the tour's speakers … looking for enemies or outspoken detractors? Well, I've seen a pattern."

"They have enemies in common?"

"No, nothing like that. But as I scan through past speeches they've given or articles that they've written … and as I look at organizations they supported or didn't support … I'm sorry, they're all a bunch of chauvinists."

"Stephanie Burton, a chauvinist?"

"No, not her. She joined the tour later. The rest of them go back to the beginning, when Clements personally invited them to become part of his tour. When you read what they say and believe … it's pretty much an old-line, man's world view. As best I can find, not one of them has ever given a dime or volunteered a minute to affirmative action, women's issues or anything resembling more balanced, progressive perspectives. Pretty surprising in this day and age for a bunch of admired leaders."

"So what got you going on this?"

"When I try to put myself into the mindset of the killer, I keep coming back to the connection with the tour. What about this tour of famous people might tie to the mental state of a woman whose crimes most definitely make a sexual statement?"

"Any other thoughts?"

"Only that our murderess may have taken the time to get beneath the public images of these respected gentlemen and not liked what she found … just like our theories that she didn't like what she saw in the sexist behaviors of her three victims."

"Pretty provocative, Andie … I want to bounce it off Caputo and the other profilers. I may have been wrong about no gold stars for you tonight."

※

For lingering skeptics inside the broadcast industry, the latest "Sweeps" report eliminated any doubts about Stephanie Burton's popularity. She most definitely was more than a passing fancy with the American public.

Sweeps periods were the four months spaced across a calendar year when the Nielsen rating service measured minute-by-minute audiences of every program on every channel in the country's 210 media markets. In May of 2009, ratings for *High Road* more than tripled the highest levels ever recorded for a cable network and cut a sizable chunk out of viewership for the four major broadcast networks.

Since the price of advertising time was based upon a broadcaster's proven ratings, an additional tenth of a point during any Sweeps month represented millions in potential revenue. Hence other cable news networks were unveiling a flurry of compassionate faces and more dignified formats to blunt the momentum of *High Road*. Stephanie was elated to watch the competition adjust, having hoped television executives would respond in their familiar follow-the-leader fashion. Impact also could be seen beyond cable news, with the major networks and newspapers making their own adjustments. The chord struck by Stephanie Burton was becoming an orchestrated movement with the American public.

Her vantage atop the ad industry had afforded Stephanie Burton a close-up view of television execs hiding behind their chicken-and-egg defense as they'd presided over the downward spiral of on-air content. She'd heard them argue that their news departments merely covered events in ways that paralleled the public's changing interests … that broadcasters couldn't foist unwanted programming upon audiences. With such self-justifications, the networks had turned to more and more cartoonish personalities and sensationalized angles to draw interest ... blurring the lines between news and entertainment, between truth and opinion. Reported events and individuals were upended with increasing speed so that their undersides could be publicly picked apart with less and less concern about balance. Regardless of the industry's circular arguments, she finally was in a position to prove that both chicken and egg could move rightfully back up the food chain.

Among the cable networks, WNL executives were committed to extend the leadership advantage Burton had provided. Throughout the spring months, they'd retooled one program after another. In a closed-door meeting at the beginning of April, the president of the network left no room for misinterpretation, "Within sixty days, we need to be all-decent, all-the-time."

One by one, WNL's stable of on-air personalities had been pulled into special meetings where new ground rules were spelled out. In deference to Gordie Jacklin, Gwenn Townsend and the other fixtures on the network's lineup, voluntary releases from existing contracts had been offered at the outset of the mandated sea change. Not a soul opted to leave. With WNL owning the hot hand, there was no better place to be; with the tide also shifting at other networks, there was no place to run. Each of the seasoned egos was assigned a private coach to help reshape his or her on-camera demeanor. New boundaries were drawn. "News will not be sugarcoated, controversies will not be avoided. However, all reporting and analyses are to be handled with new appreciation for the greater public's desire for decency and fairness."

Proprietary survey panels, commissioned by the major networks, continued to confirm the public's connection with Stephanie Burton. But they also reflected a desire for higher broadcast standards that could extend beyond news programming. There were rumors of emergency meetings in New York and Los Angeles. Key audience segments were registering a growing weariness for the concocted realities of Reality TV and the frivolous manner in which other primetime fare too often devalued common decency.

Forty-Eight:

June, 2009

With each passing week, Kelly Amaker was receiving thicker stacks of unsolicited résumés attached to impassioned requests for job interviews. Recent college graduates were looking to start their real world climbs as part of something that could inspire them. Women and men in their thirties, forties and older, folks with established careers in unrelated fields, were willing to start over for the opportunity to work with something and someone they deeply believed in. Many offered to work without pay for however long required to demonstrate their commitment to the lofty principles of *High Road*. Experienced broadcast professionals offered to take pay cuts for the chance to feel good about the product they put forth to the public – reporters, writers, researchers, editors and others from TV stations across the country, as well as every other network.

The mailbags full of letters from prospective employees, the tens of thousands of e-mails each week from appreciative viewers, the letters to editors featured in hundreds of newspapers, the totality made a startling statement to everyone associated with WNL. Pride filled the control rooms, hallways and elevators. *High Road* represented more than a welcomed, fresh sound amidst the jaded din of America's airwaves. To growing numbers, it represented a cause, a higher cause worth caring about. A cause for decency, respect and optimism.

Though The Road Crew put in ridiculous hours, they didn't really need extra bodies to get their work done. There was no place they'd rather be, nothing they'd rather be doing than pouring all of their energy into *High Road*. But after fully vetting the issue at a staff meeting, they were unanimous in their decision to make room for additional team members. Stephanie kept silent and was delighted by the outcome. They would add a few recent grads, one or two seasoned production pros, but importantly, a handful of folks looking to jump from other fields. Real estate developers, chemists, martial arts instructors, the same eclectic approach that had worked in Stephanie's past. Granted, The Road Crew would benefit from new talents and points of view, but mostly they'd be adding new believers, new proof points. In fact, they chose to more than double their tight family to twenty members. With the ratings and ad dollars the show was pulling in, Kelly could have requested four times the staff and no one on the sixty-second floor would have blinked.

The anniversary came and went with the news media making only minor references to the murder of Prize Calloway. A year had passed since that death was connected to two others, plus a popular tour, to become one of the most unexplainable serial homicides in the nation's history. Months earlier, the Touring Temptress had been the feature of two primetime docudramas, which still continued to syndicate their way through late night time slots on local TV schedules. In the short span of a year, from a public perspective, the investigation into the Touring Temptress Murders appeared to have gone dormant. It soon would be categorized as one of those deliciously mysterious "cold cases" – another pop culture staple.

To Zach Peterson and the many agents he'd been assigned, or to Andie Morrison and the FBI Database Section, the year since Calloway's murder had been anything but short and the P.E.T. Murders investigation was anything but dormant. It might be slowed and devoid of meaningful leads, but it wasn't "cold" and Zach remained convinced they could make something break. Nonetheless, he and everyone else from the Bureau had been relieved that the media hounds didn't use the occasion of the anniversary to stir the whole case up again.

Stephanie Burton also had been pleased to watch the one-year milestone pass relatively unnoticed. Having left no trails, she wasn't worried about public attention fanning any flames that might burn a path to her door. She simply preferred not to be reminded. She was in no way proud of her perfect crimes, or the fact that she'd used them as the perfect vehicle for her ascension onto an expansive public platform. For her the ends had justified the means, but best those means stay buried in the past.

In a planning meeting with the *High Road* staff, the suggestion was made that one of their upcoming segments focus on the Touring Temptress

Murders. Considering the one-year anniversary and the fact that Burton had interviewed the FBI's lead agent earlier in the spring, it seemed a natural. Nonetheless, Stephanie had closed off the discussion.

"Continuing to dig up picked-over skeletons from an investigation with nothing new to reveal will serve no constructive purpose." Her statement conveyed her heartfelt opinion on levels The Road Crew couldn't fathom, but her team conceded on the surface logic alone.

However, a different suggestion was made during the first week of June that she accepted enthusiastically. She'd been waiting and wondering when someone might raise it. The Senate subcommittee hearing into the business interests of General William A. Clements was scheduled for the week following Fourth of July Weekend. Stephanie had enjoyed seeing this firm date finally cross the newswires. *How timely for such a patriot.*

Out of respect for the position Clements once had held, federal attorneys and public officials were making no advanced statements about the exact charges to be leveled. All indications were that the government was building a strong case and not only was the man's reputation in jeopardy, but he very likely would be facing prison time. For the growing audience that more closely followed the story as a public feeding frenzy neared, the witness list alone seemed to confirm suspicions about the general. Among those scheduled to appear on behalf of the government were three CEO's whose large companies had benefited from extensive military contracts over many years. It now also was widely known that these same gentlemen had enjoyed lifelong friendships with Clements. Stephanie had patiently watched as, one by one, connections were made and behaviors fell in line. *How poignant … the old boys so willing to blackball the general from their tight little club in order to preserve their manhood.*

Over the months in which more and more questions were surfacing about Clements' past, Stephanie had needed to reference the story several times on *High Road*. It was an important national news event and couldn't be ignored. But she'd confined her comments to simple updates, with repeated and respectful reminders that judgment should be withheld until all facts were known. Unlike other programs on WNL or competitive networks, she dispensed with any deeper dives into the details and personalities behind the mounting claims against Clements. As more explicit dirt piled around the former Chair of the Joint Chiefs, Stephanie had bided her time, knowing there would be eventual advantage from not further fueling the fray.

The notion that the general might agree to be interviewed on *High Road* should have seemed preposterous. He'd made no media appearances since the demise of the Personal Empowerment Tour. No doubt, attorneys had instructed him to avoid public comments prior to his committee hearing. Stephanie Burton certainly knew that Clements detested her. First, for being a woman who dared to hold her own with powerful men like him, but even more for the role she'd played in dismantling his prized tour. The media attention on the tour and its partners had started the chain of events which now could prove to be the general's total undoing. Nonetheless, she also had seen his ego in action and knew that he wouldn't be able to refuse the offer. So when the "wild hare idea" had been thrown out by someone on The Road Crew, she'd jumped on it.

"Hey, it's worth a try. I'll call and invite him myself."

No one in the room really had thought there was a chance Clements would break his silence with the hearing fast approaching. No one except Stephanie Burton. If he took the call, she knew she could sway him.

~∿~

"General Clements, thank you for taking my call. I know what stress you must be under."

He didn't wait to lose his temper. The anger was evident from word one and continued to rise with each word thereafter.

"You have a lot of nerve calling me, lady. When I was told you were on the phone, I needed to hear it for myself. I always knew you were nothing but another phony who loves to strut her pretty little fanny. This proves it. In spite of all that high road crap you shovel, you're no better than all those other parasites. You've resented me since we first met, so now you can't wait to gloat. Well don't gloat too soon, sweetheart. General William A. Clements isn't done yet."

"I'm hardly gloating, General, and I think you're anything but done."

She went on to convince him to appear on *High Road* during the last week of June. She would devote an entire hour to just him, his life, his values, his service to the country. The current accusations against him would remain off-limits – not only for legal reasons, but also because they had nothing to do with what she really wanted America to see. She didn't bother to point out that *High Road* was the lone news program that hadn't seen fit to attack him. She knew he would have been closely scrutinizing the media's coverage and keeping score.

Putting down the phone, he realized exactly what he'd done. He knew his attorneys would be furious. *Screw them … let 'em wet their pinstriped pants.* The public needed to see the true essence of General William A. Clements before watching him get grilled by a bunch of scumbag politicians. He didn't like Burton, but her show was popular and she played fair. The way his friends were turning on him, he couldn't rely on anyone else anymore. It was his ass; he had to go with his own instincts.

⌒⁄⌒

"Do you think we should go back and take a deeper look into the history of the partners behind P.E.T.? Maybe our murderer is some woman that one of those gentlemen managed to tick off … a female veteran … some military wife or daughter … a mistress?"

"Andie, our Philly teams have chased that one pretty hard. You know how many data runs you guys have already done on Clements and his buddies. Plus, there's another group in the Data Section compiling background on those birds for the Attorney General's Office … and the federal prosecutors have agreed to share anything they turn up for the Senate subcommittee. I'm not sure how much more we can do."

"So I suppose you think I should take that as a no."

"Or maybe we could start calling every person drafted or enlisted into America's armed services since Yates and Clements hooked up in 1961 … ask them if anyone might happen to have a little story they'd like to share."

"Which years do you want, Peterson, odd or even?"

Andie Morrison sat amidst the boxes she hadn't gotten around to unpacking in her studio apartment. Zach Peterson had flown out to meet with Dr. Caputo again and was nursing his third cranberry juice in a lounge at Lindbergh Field, waiting to hear the next estimated departure time for a delayed flight out of San Diego. Since he'd had plenty of time to spare, he waited until that evening's telecast of *High Road* was over before calling. No need to interrupt Andie during her favorite show. He watched it himself whenever his travel schedule permitted … like tonight, when he'd watched alongside the other travelers seated at the bar.

At the end of the broadcast, Stephanie Burton acknowledged that General William Clements graciously had accepted her invitation to do a live interview the following week. That reference, amidst rampant press speculations on what the subcommittee hearing would reveal about Clements' insidious ties to his old friends, had caused Andie to wonder if they might have missed a possible link between the tour murders and the tour partners. Perhaps something in the pasts of Messrs. Clements, Yates, Mendel and Henderson had triggered a rage inside their Temptress. As soon as she'd seen Zach's name on caller ID, she answered the phone by hitting him with her concerns. Eventually she deferred to his assurances that the various paths to the tour partners had been thoroughly explored.

"Zach, isn't it amazing that Clements would do a live interview now, when he's been keeping up a cone of silence for months?"

"He must feel like he needs to start a little damage control."

"It hardly will be a little damage control. I can't imagine how many millions of people are going to be watching."

"Since I'll be in DC next Tuesday, we can catch it together. Pretty hot date, huh?"

"Yeah, but I'd better not catch you staring at Stephanie Burton's cans."

Like millions across the country, Andie and Zach had become more than devoted viewers; they'd become true admirers of Stephanie Burton. But they also enjoyed a feeling of special kinship. At times it seemed this charismatic woman had been interwoven into their relationship like some celebrity guardian angel. Just days before they'd met, Andie had decided at the last minute to attend the Personal Empowerment Tour event in Kansas City and been blown away by Burton's presence on stage. Her message and persona had pierced Andie's natural resistance to self-reflection and stirred her long-denied ambitions.

Within days of that event, a multiple homicide investigation had brought Andie and Zach together. They had watched Burton play a pivotal role in closing down P.E.T. while ardently defending the FBI investigation that Zach headed. Months later, Zach had been a featured guest on *High Road* ... coming away mesmerized by the utter decency of the woman. Throughout these months, Burton's on-air messages and example had been uplifting, helping each to better confront their personal shortcomings.

Amidst so many popularized voices of cynicism, Stephanie Burton dared shamelessly to evoke a faith in the power of human potential. Andie increasingly drew courage to step from behind her cavalier exterior and show a serious side, her convictions, her aspirations. As Zach continued to bring more balance into his life, he was finding it easier to express what was in his heart. He was making the effort to check in with his sisters more often, actually telling them one-by-one that he loved them. And it felt good … Stephanie Burton had been right. It was important to let people close to you know that they're special.

Forty-Nine:

General William A. Clements sat on a Queen Anne loveseat with his wife, Deanna, demurely at his side. Behind him a bookcase filled with leather-bound volumes, a flag stand to either side. One posted the Stars and Stripes, the other the official flag of the United States Army. Silver hair freshly trimmed, tanned skin affirming his love for the outdoors, dark blue suit with starched white shirt and patterned red tie, he looked exactly the way he always imagined himself in the history books – except the part about having his wife next to him.

Usually Stephanie Burton left studio set decisions to Kelly and the production team, but this time she'd been prescriptive with every detail. She wanted Clements to feel that his stature was being properly dignified by the preparations for his *High Road* appearance. Based on reactions thus far, their efforts had managed to live up to the high opinion he held of himself.

As host, Stephanie would sit in a matching Queen Anne chair across from the General, between them a coffee table with his military medals and other awards on display. She briefly greeted and fawned over Clements and his wife when they arrived at their appointed time, two hours before the cameras went live – but since then, Burton had avoided contact. Kelly Amaker had taken full charge, reviewing how the interview would flow, introducing them around, escorting them to make-up and their final bathroom stops.

Two hours was double the time necessary, but excessively early arrivals were standard practice with live broadcasts, in order to allow time for unexpected occurrences. With a subcommittee appearance imminent and the recognition that millions of viewers soon would be rendering their own judgments, such prolonged idle time was somewhat discomforting for Clements. It gave him more time to think about the impact this interview might have on his future ... to feel more and more pressure about keeping his cool under the heat of the studio spotlights.

The guest couple had been positioned on the love seat for more than twenty minutes as the production crew adjusted final lighting and camera angles. Neither Clements nor his wife had said a word to the other. Stephanie guessed the seat was getting pretty warm for the arrogant bastard. She hoped so. She would take her place just before the program started, not wanting to engage in unnecessary small talk ... not wanting to offer the slightest hint of her intentions.

Over the coming hour, Stephanie Burton knew she would travel a fine line along the high road. Here was a man in the center of a national controversy, an important story that deserved fair and decent treatment. Her audience expected no less. But here also was a man she'd watched as he paraded his assorted chauvinisms no differently than the uniform he stood accused of disgracing.

The retired General Clements had been audacious enough to bring a mistress to the P.E.T. event in Memphis, then again in Phoenix, Salt Lake City and elsewhere. Not the same mistress, but different women, all much younger than him. The man believed himself so bulletproof after retiring from public life that he flaunted his amorality. His masculinity so shallow that he'd needed to show off in front of the cronies he had recruited to speak with his tour. Chest puffed in manliness, a blushing companion on his arm, he had boasted of the exploits he could still perform in a hotel room.

He crassly had pulled Stephanie Burton aside in Memphis and asked her to "honor my tour's unwritten code of secrecy" – the accompanying wink and nod like some fraternity handshake. The imagery and associations with this loathsome rooster's behavior had become another shrieking voice inside her head. As she settled into the chair facing Clements and the pleasant-looking wife he'd betrayed many times over, Stephanie's smile and outward temperament in no way reflected the contempt she was feeling. The hour ahead would be an interesting ride for General William Addison Clements.

⌒⁄↶⁀

After *High Road's* opening module and her welcoming comments, Stephanie Burton immediately veered from the discussion outline that

Kelly had reviewed in advance with the two guests. It had been General Clements's choice to invite his wife and park her at his side like another one of his medals. Deanna Clements wasn't in the eye of the looming political storm, so he had specified that few, if any, questions be directed to her. It had been obvious what role Clements intended her to play – the loving, supportive wife who smiled and nodded her head in agreement to whatever brilliance he imparted, on occasion verbally affirming his greatness as husband, father or American. A role she probably had been required to play many times in their years together.

By directing the very first question at Deanna Clements, Stephanie instantly wanted to clarify that regardless of whatever rules of engagement the general thought he'd decreed, total control was now hers. Not only would the power shift be unsettling to him, the departure from normal protocol would be an affront to his masculine pride. This was the lone media interview granted by a man of significant reputation and authority; to him, it would be unthinkable to start with comments from the wife he had expected to occupy her proper place in his shadow.

"Mrs. Clements, this evening we need to steer clear of the substance of next week's Senate subcommittee hearing, but it's still appropriate to ask how events of recent months might have affected you and your family. What has it been like for you?"

Deanna Clements not only wasn't anticipating this question, she wasn't accustomed to being asked anything at all – let alone a question assigning significance to her feelings. Hers was a life permanently superseded by the dominant figure in it. She struggled with what to say and where to start, so she wisely bought a little extra time to collect her thoughts.

"Miss Burton, I watch your program so regularly that I feel I already know you. I hope you don't mind if I call you Stephanie?"

"Of course not, I'm flattered."

"It's a pleasure to meet you in person. I very much admire how you treat every subject and guest with such respect."

At first, Stephanie couldn't determine whether the comment was a veiled appeal for gentler treatment in the coming interview, or if it had been intended as a subtle message aimed at her self-absorbed husband who showed little respect for anyone but himself. Either way, there seemed to be more to the compliment than the woman's obvious need to buy time. And either way, General Clements clearly wasn't happy to see his wife patronizing a female interviewer who already was throwing curve balls now that she had him trapped in front of millions of people.

"Deanna, I wish such praise were unnecessary, because respect shouldn't seem unusual. It shouldn't be something that any of us has to earn. Respect is rightfully ours to begin with, unless we might do something to un-earn it."

Not yet had he been addressed or even uttered a word, but Clements was seething inside. How precious that Burton and his vapid wife were now on a first-name basis. He wondered what kind of swipe the manipulative bitch might have intended with her clever little comment about un-earning respect.

Mrs. Clements finally was prepared to tackle Burton's original question, "To be honest, Stephanie, these months haven't seemed all that unusual for me or the children and grandchildren. The General has always been a proud and private man who chose not to share much about his military life with his family. As with other matters related to his career, there has been minimal discussion in our home about the pending subcommittee hearing. The only difference would be that in this instance we could have learned more details on our own through the media. But I think The General would have been disappointed if we lent further credence to any portion of this whole unfortunate situation by paying much attention to what was being said."

Stephanie hadn't expected such a smartly crafted response. The general's attorneys would have counseled Deanna Clements on the importance of establishing that she knew nothing, and therefore could divulge nothing about her husband's military dealings. She successfully had done that. Yet in describing how little she knew, she had communicated so much more – and, it would seem, not by accident. Though her husband was smiling smugly, satisfied the question had been handled to his liking, wives across the nation would be simultaneously cringing. Stephanie recognized an inherent goodness in this woman, an unassuming spouse who probably had been underestimated and taken for granted for most of her adult life. The glimmers of a strong, virtuous character were evident, but also there was a sadness. Here was another well-meaning soul who had compromised her potential because she lacked the conviction or the encouragement to reach higher. Another woman who had sacrificed her ideals and ambitions for the sake of a man.

It was time to attend to that unworthy man. "Good evening, General Clements. In view of recent events, there are many people watching who are eager to learn more about you."

"Good evening to you, Miss Burton, thank you for inviting me." He gave the camera his most appreciative smile. At last, the attention on him, the opportunity to start working his messages.

"General, after hearing from Deanna, I'm most curious to hear your observations on a thirty-eight year marriage. With all the accomplishments in a distinguished career like yours, this longevity stands out as one of the most notable. What attracted you to your lovely wife ... what keeps you together? Please reveal to us the secrets of your marriage."

The man inwardly fumed – already drawing upon his limited emotional reserves to keep it together in front of the cameras. What kind of garbage was this? There'd been an agreement to focus on his military service, his effective term with the Joint Chiefs. Yet right out of the box she goes after his marriage ... with that knowing gleam in her eye. All that extra emphasis she'd put into asking him to "please reveal the secrets of your marriage." A public shit storm coming his way and she chooses now to taunt him about a few women he'd kept on the side. It didn't really seem to bother her at those tour events, so why now? The conniving bitch was trying to get under his skin. He must remain calm ... beat at her own game.

"Wonderful question, Miss Burton ... you don't mind if I continue to call you Miss Burton?" Two could play her game. "I've always kept Deanna, my children and grandchildren as top priorities. Please understand that I've had a sworn duty to serve my country first, but simultaneously I worked hard to uphold the duties of a devoted family man. No matter where I was stationed or needed to travel, I was thinking of them ... eager to hear their voices on late night phone calls from opposite sides of the globe ... finding little gifts or mementos that recognized their individual interests and personalities. It hasn't been easy, considering the enormity of what was on my plate, but what in life could be more worthwhile?"

"Well done, General Clements, we applaud your ability to balance those different lives. But please, sir, don't be timid ... even you hard-edged generals have soft spots. Can we hear in your own words what your wife has meant to you?"

"Very well." He reached for the bottle of water on the floor beside him and took a slow drink – fully recognizing the bumpy road he faced. Seething. Completely vulnerable to a woman he despised, a woman who had tricked him.

"As the proverbial wife behind her husband, Deanna has been a genuine unsung hero. Commanding our nation's forces took me all over the world for extended periods, but her vigilance on the family's home front never wavered. I can't imagine any woman doing a better job than Deanna in fulfilling the responsibilities and duties of devoted mother and loyal wife. We have respectful, hard-working adult children who do honor to our family, their respective communities and this great country. Some of the medals on this table should be hers. She has more than earned a commendation from a most grateful four-star general." For emphasis, he turned to his wife and placed his palm over the folded hands in her lap, "Thank you, dear."

Stephanie responded playfully, "Deanna, I believe salutes are in order. You're one terrific soldier. I can't imagine any higher praise from your husband, The General." She emphasized 'The General.'

Clements was oblivious to how shallow his praises for his wife had sounded, but he certainly recognized that Burton somehow had tossed a jab his way. And so it went for the duration of the interview, a grueling hour for William A. Clements, The General. Question after question, volley after volley, he was kept constantly off balance. Underneath her pleasant façade, she tormented him at every turn. He battled the upper hand she wielded so deceptively, simultaneously battling his ever-rising anger.

Stephanie gracefully transitioned through a sequence of seemingly natural questions – none of which providing Clements an opportunity to frontally address what he'd planned. He awkwardly inserted what he believed to be his laudatory qualities and achievements wherever possible, but in so doing, repeatedly came across as egotistical and desperate. All the while, Stephanie's external demeanor remained one of interest and compassion. Along the way, she found additional reasons to direct questions and comments to Mrs. Clements – each time more irksome than the last for The General.

Whether aware or not, Deanna Clements only referred to her husband as "The General" during the course of the interview. Never William or Bill … not once a "dear" or a "honey" or any such pet name. Only, "The General." No descriptions or anecdotal stories could better have revealed the kind of relationship this man had with his wife and family. This was a man who commanded the respect of every person close to him – literally.

As he'd done throughout his career, Clements worked hard during the interview to give the impression that he was a military warhorse. His frequent references to "commands" and "tours of duty" seemed to suggest that he often had been placed in harm's way. Stephanie recognized that he wanted to leave the impression that his wits and leadership in dangerous, hostile environments were the basis for his ascension to the top of the military pyramid. But by having done her homework and carefully framing questions, Stephanie Burton helped The General dissect his own myth and paint a more accurate picture. General William Addison Clements had built his legendary career through repeated administrative assignments – a world-class paper pusher, combating more red tape than Red Armies.

She kept him on a roller coaster. At times, the hotness of his temper burned through. Other times, he simply looked lost and disheveled. As the interview wound down, The General knew she had won. He was spent and beleaguered, yet she hadn't revealed her true intentions to anyone but him. Viewers had seen the same Stephanie Burton they always did. It galled him, but he privately conceded her mastery over the battlefield she'd lured him onto.

His final act of desperation was to reach out to Stephanie Burton through laudatory comments, in the hope she would accept them as an olive branch. At least he could attempt to end this disastrous hour on a more positive note. If she recognized his surrender, perhaps she would grant him a few closing minutes on his terms. He figured it couldn't get worse.

He was wrong.

"Miss Burton … Stephanie, this hour together is nearly over, so I hope you'll forgive an interruption. There is something I must say before we run out of time."

His bold move left her no choice. "Please, General, proceed."

"I was privileged to first meet you at the beginning of 2007, when you joined the Personal Empowerment Tour. I was proud to have started that tour, but obviously saddened by the horrific murders that compelled us to take appropriate action and disband it. From the very first time you spoke to those thousands of people in an arena, I could see you held a special connection with your audience. It is no surprise to me that you now enjoy your remarkable success with *High Road*. Not only are you a woman of immense talents, but the principles you espouse and represent need to be reinforced. You do this country a great service."

Stephanie wasn't buying any of it and had no idea where he was going. She tried to cut him off, "Thank you for that, General …"

"Please, let me finish. The point I want to make is how much you are to be admired for overcoming the adversities of your youth in a small Ohio town. I have great empathy. I, too, had parents with limited financial means and needed to lift myself above a multitude of negative influences inside my home. I don't think your audience has any idea that your father died when you were young, or that you and your mother were left …"

"That's enough, General Clements, you've said enough."

"I was just trying to …"

"Enough. I think it is rather obvious what you were trying to do. Neither I, nor a most intelligent audience, can be fooled by your faint praise and self-serving analogies. Furthermore, I resent your references to my private life when I have resisted disclosing the things I know about yours. Let me conclude by wishing you luck with the Senate subcommittee next week, as I suspect you'll need it."

She held her stare on Clements as he went red-faced. His volatile temper won out and he finally erupted, "I've put up with your condescending games all night, and now you dare to judge me. The daughter of some small town tramp back in Athens, Ohio doesn't pass judgment on General William A. Clements …"

"You're right, sir, we'll leave that to the federal authorities and the American people." She signaled the director to go to commercial, then immediately instructed Kelly Amaker to escort Clements and his wife from the studio. She was irate and needed to compose herself during the break so that she could properly close the program.

William Clements had trespassed into her personal history and Stephanie Burton felt deeply violated when he pulled his insolent ploy. She'd been careful since the day she first left Athens to avoid discussing details about her youth or family. No one since had seen much reason to dig into that part of her life. She regularly screened whatever information could be found about her on the Internet or in published articles. Nothing was out there that touched on her family's composition or financial situation, and certainly no details about her mother's reckless lifestyle.

It was obvious that for some reason, Clements had put significant effort into digging around in her past. His ulterior motives alone were disturbing. But the intensity of her rage arose mostly from seeing those distant doors being opened. Now she must wonder who else might follow Clements through them. She was ashamed of what people might find about her mother – ashamed for herself, ashamed for her mother. More importantly, she didn't want anyone's empathy. Much less, their pity. She didn't want acknowledgement for whatever challenges she might have overcome. She didn't want anyone suggesting that she ever was or ever could have been a victim to anything in her past. She hadn't been, she wouldn't be. The unexpected violation had been jolting to her sense of control. With those doors open, there were too many dangers if others started digging into people and events from her past.

Stephanie Burton never had cut off an interview or seen fit to censure a guest, but from an audience perspective her anger still had been contained. She would draw no further attention to what had transpired with Clements. She closed the telecast with one of the short human interest stories that her staff kept on standby, then thanked her viewers in usual fashion.

Clements was waiting for her as soon as she stepped into the hallway adjacent to the studio. He was livid. She had sabotaged and minimized him. She had outwitted and toyed with him. Pushed every unseen button. Provoked him into blurting out what he had learned about her mother. He'd been disgraced publicly, his legacy tarnished. In a matter of days, more still would befall him in front of the subcommittee. The whole chain of events had been her fault from the beginning and now she'd plotted to play another pivotal part in his final downfall. Why? Why was she hungry to bring him down?

He pounced, "You lying bitch. You set me up with all those promises about letting the public get to know the man behind the controversy. About letting me tell my story in my own way. You purposely were out to destroy me all along. Your moral superiority and your high road bullshit … it's all a pack of lies."

Stephanie smiled at him. "Not all lies. The public did get to see the real General William A. Clements. As to the rest of our dealings, I now simply ask that you honor my program's unwritten code of secrecy." A wink and a nod followed.

She turned her back on him and walked toward the lobby in search of Deanna Clements. The general wanted to continue his rant and started after her, but Security was already there to intercede. Stephanie realized that Deanna Clements might share her husband's anger, but still she felt obliged to speak to her face-to-face. Mrs. Clements stood calmly at a window, taking in the New York skyline as though nothing had happened.

"Deanna, I apologize for any embarrassment or discomfort that tonight's incident might have caused you. I truly am grateful to have met you and was most impressed with how you handled yourself during the interview. It may seem horribly inappropriate for me to say this, but I hope we might meet again."

"Miss Burton … Stephanie, I would welcome that. You know, I've been reflecting on something you said earlier. Respect is rightfully ours to begin with, unless we do something to un-earn it. That's very good … I think I'll use that."

Fifty:

She'd popped for the pizza; Zach had brought the bottle of Chianti. They'd dined among Andie's still unpacked boxes, wanting to catch the entirety of the Clements interview.

"Stick a fork in that guy, he's done. If he can't keep his cool with Stephanie Burton, what's he going to do when a bunch of blood-thirsty senators start firing fast balls at him?"

"Yeah, nothing like self-destructing in front of a few million people who already think you've been pocketing their tax dollars. Andie, that final exchange escalated from out of nowhere."

"Zach, we've never seen Stephanie Burton get like that? She cut him off at the knees, or maybe it was a body part a little higher up."

"The old fool deserved it … bringing up her childhood like he did … then that comment about her mother. If that poor woman's still alive, I smell a libel suit."

Though they'd had no previous reason to ponder Stephanie Burton's family or upbringing, they like anyone else would have presumed her to be the product of wall-to-wall normalcy. The woman personified the Ten Commandments and the Golden Rule all rolled into one. In their continued discussion about the telecast, Andie and Zach agreed they were even more impressed with Burton than before – if that were possible.

"Andie, if she really did overcome the kind of background that Clements suggested, it's incredible that she never makes reference to it. Her humility is truly astounding."

As they polished off the wine, they wrapped up their post mortem on the Clements appearance. What had he hoped to accomplish … what was that back-and-forth innuendo about each other's secrets? Eventually they moved on to the rest of their evening, but Andie couldn't entirely let go of the final awkward exchange from the interview. An inkling. She didn't want to voice it quite yet, but one particular reference was tugging at her memory. "Athens, Ohio." Somewhere amongst the thousands upon thousands of files she'd reviewed, there'd been something about Athens, Ohio. She was almost certain.

Fifty-One:

Wednesday Morning; July 1, 2009

Overnight ratings for the interview had shattered the audience records previously established by *High Road*. For the time period, the show annihilated everything else on cable and pulled more viewers than all but two of the major broadcast networks. The audience interest wasn't surprising, considering it had been the sole media appearance by a former Chair of the Joint Chiefs slated for a Congressional hearing that could put him in prison. The only surprise was the way in which he conducted himself. In morning-after conversations across the country, people were scratching their heads about how and why "the guy had just plain lost it."

There'd been nothing unusual in the discussion that should've caused him to start patronizing Stephanie Burton so desperately, or then to come unglued when she pulled him up short. From the public's perspective, no matter what charges might await him with a subcommittee, Clements already had pleaded guilty through his behavior. The stress of knowing his indictment was unavoidable was the only plausible explanation for why a man of his accomplishments would have acted so irrationally. To have launched into that pathetic rant about her mother, the man must be verging on a nervous breakdown.

⌐⁓

The phone lines at WNL were overloaded. Most of the network's internet servers hit their e-mail capacity sometime during the first few hours following the interview. Viewers of *High Road* wanted to formally register their disgust for General William Clements, but at the same time offer words of encouragement and compassion to Stephanie Burton.

It hadn't been deplorable enough that "the traitorous prick" had "lined his sleazy pockets with blood money on the backs of real soldiers who'd protected his cowardly white ass." Now he had dared to take unwarranted cheap shots at a woman who'd become an intimate part of countless American families.

"Way to go, Stephanie. If it'd been me, I'd have slapped the jerk. But you keep showing us a higher road!"

"I don't know why you allowed that general (William Asshole Clements) to appear on the most important show on television, but he blew it. I hope he rots in a cell for the way he repaid you."

"Miss Burton, you are my favorite person on television EVER. I wish that Clements clown hadn't tried to embarrass you about your childhood roots. You have every right to keep your life private. You're a true beacon of inspiration."

"Stephanie, if your mother is still living, please tell her we're sorry for what General Clements said. Even if she did make mistakes in the past, she surely can be proud of the honor you now bring to her."

Calls poured into the network's press relations staff. Reporters from all over the country were hungry for details about Stephanie Burton's childhood. Late into the night, journalists scoured the Internet, looking especially for more background on Burton's mother. But other than her graduation from Athens High School in 1989, there were no available facts about Stephanie prior to her enrollment at Columbia University. As for Leslie Burton, the only item that could be found was that she was listed as an employee of Ohio University. She didn't have a police record, so whatever Clements was intimating about salacious activities, they hadn't been bad enough to get her arrested.

Anticipating the wave of curiosity, Stephanie had placed a prepared statement on the desks of everyone at the network who handled press calls – long before any of them arrived for work the morning after the interview.

During a live telecast of *High Road* last evening, June 30, I regret that General William A. Clements made reference to the nature of my childhood. Further, in the heat of a rage I do not understand, he made an inappropriate comment about my mother. This also, I do not understand. Like all families, mine has experienced the breadth of joys and sadness that life entails. I hope that you would respect the boundaries of my private life, just as I would yours. General Clements never has had occasion to meet my mother. So in particular, I hope the ill-chosen derogatory toward her will not be dignified with additional intrusion into her peaceful existence.

I will neither comment further nor answer questions regarding this matter. Thank you for understanding.

Stephanie Burton

This statement was read verbatim to the hundreds of reporters and journalists who called. The public's curiosity had been piqued by General Clements's vitriol, but everyone eventually got the idea. Stephanie Burton had nothing more to say to anyone about the matter. Period. Even her staff restrained from inquiring. The firm yet respectful insistence mirrored the "high road" approach she unfailingly demonstrated with newsmakers and guests. Stephanie Burton consistently had stayed away from personal issues that weren't pertinent to the stories at hand, no matter how juicy or controversial. Because of whom she was and the standard she continued to set, her wishes were honored. Within a matter of days, the flow of calls to the network trickled to a stop. Likewise, the calls to her mother's home in Ohio – where the phone had been yanked from the wall.

✒

Inside a conference room of a preeminent D.C. law firm, the discussions underway were bound to stretch late into the evening. The hearing was a week away and every aspect of their strategy needed to be rethought. In the TV interview that Clements had accepted against advice of counsel, he and his wife successfully managed to avoid any specifics pertinent to the government investigation. Nonetheless, the destruction done by the *High Road* appearance was massive. The general's crazed conduct would cost him any chance of public sympathy – even among the most hardcore critics of Congressional politics. Any senators or federal attorneys on the panel now could discard their kid gloves and dig their sharpened teeth into Clements when he took his chair to testify.

The normal checks-and-balances tied to potential voter repercussions no longer would be operative. Months of extensive legwork on the Hill by his attorneys had been neutralized. Senators predisposed to attack the general could do so without constraint. Those previously inclined to defend or protect him would now sit silently by and watch a public stoning.

Fifty-Two:

Wednesday Afternoon; July 1, 2009

The printout read the same as her computer screen, but somehow holding the actual hard copy in her hands made it more real. Her hands trembled. For thirteen months they'd been grinding, twisting and hoping for a breakthrough lead. Perhaps finally she was staring at it, but she prayed to God she wasn't.

Whenever she completed the review of any historical case file as part of an active investigation, Andie Morrison appended a preface summary of the key facts so that accessing it in the future would be more efficient. She reread the top section of this particular summary for what had to be a twentieth time.

NICHOLAS J. PARRAVANO: VICTIM/SEX MURDER (11/01)

- Goddard Cabins, outside Toledo(OH)
- Nude corpse/mutilated.
- Throat slashed/severed genitals in rectum
- Case open/no suspects
- Police theory: revenge, gay sex partner; victim has reputation for physical violence/forced sodomy (multiple arrests & dropped charges)

Then she scanned down through the rest of the page that bullet-pointed what she'd learned from digging into his background. The employment at a driving range, his time in prison, the college basketball career, the identity of his parents, everything she'd chosen to highlight until she came to a bullet near the bottom of the page.

- 1986-1988: Athens High School (all-state/basketball, mediocre student); Nicknamed, "Gunner"

After watching the General Clements debacle on *High Road*, she'd awakened wide-eyed a couple of hours before sunrise. She hadn't bothered kissing Zach good-bye, wanting to avoid his questions about her early departure. Better to avoid than resort to evasiveness. Clements had referenced Stephanie Burton's hometown and Andie was almost certain she'd come across Athens somewhere in her research. Before mentioning a word to Zach she wanted to see if there was anything worth mentioning at all.

Armed with two chocolate doughnuts and a bucket-sized coffee, she'd jumped into the thousands of case files retained on her computer. It was late in the day before she got to PARRAVANO: SEX-MURDER/OHIO, 2001. Moments later, any doubt about the need to tell Zach was eliminated.

When she'd first reviewed the official police reports on the brutal homicide, there were no details about Parravano's background prior to Bowling Green. College basketball marked his arrival in northwest Ohio, so detectives apparently had felt no need to dig further back. By searching various sources on her own, Andie had filled in whatever blanks she could – just as she and her Data Section teammates had done with many other archived incidents that became part of the P.E.T. Murders investigation. They tenaciously had sought people, places or dates that might connect to some random detail surrounding the tour murders. Two such random details now had connected.

It was difficult for Andie to process the implication. Perhaps they barely had known each other. Athens High School, Class of 1988 … probably nothing more than coincidence that Stephanie Burton had been Class of 1989. Yet words from a training session nine years earlier still resonated with Andie. "In this job, you can park coincidence right over there with Santa Claus and the Tooth Fairy."

She tried to make sense of the possibilities. What kind of lunatic with ties to Athens would have had reason to bash Parravano's skull and then six years later start following Stephanie Burton around the country and slashing throats? Had Parravano and Stephanie dated … did she steal him from another girl who developed some bizarre obsession as a result?

There could be any number of explanations. Sure Stephanie Burton was in all those cities, but we know she departed before the murders occurred. No way, that it could have been her. Not with everything she stands for, everything she has accomplished in her life. *Why would she ... how would she?*

But Andie could feel that gnawing instinct telling her otherwise. And at that moment, Andie Morrison regretted ever having had hunches about anything in her life. It was incomprehensible. She'd been drawn so completely to Stephanie Burton. Thinking of her as a potential suspect belied common sense. Worse, it belied common decency. Yet, so many stillborn pieces of the protracted puzzle had started tumbling into place.

The first murder had occurred the month after Burton joined the tour. She'd spoken at all three events.

What man wouldn't be lured by her beauty ... couldn't be lured into believing anything she might say?

Who more than Stephanie Burton could fit the near-epic profiles that forensic psychologists kept constructing? Charismatic. Superior intelligence. Patient, disciplined, measured.

Then last night ... the way she'd reacted when Clements mentioned her childhood ... the immediate need to protect her privacy. The insinuations about her family's hardships ... about a mother with a sexual closet of her own.

Suddenly everything was pointing in one direction ... the way tough cases so often came together. *But please, not this case.* At first Andie had wanted to vomit. Now she wanted to cry. Zach and his teams surely could uncover facts and explanations that would prove her wrong. Of course they could. She picked up the phone to find him.

Not counting college students, the population of Athens, Ohio had stalled at twenty-one thousand more than a decade earlier. Sure, there'd been the typical Main Street upheaval when Wal-Mart restructured the commercial landscape of another small town, but otherwise the changes had been minor. For forty years, Leslie Burton had shopped the same local stores, dined the same local restaurants and attended the same local functions as pretty much everyone else in Athens. Disapproving glances and whispered conversations had followed her no matter where she went, but somehow she'd never really noticed them.

She hadn't been one to pay much attention to the news or current events. She couldn't honestly remember having heard of General William A. Clements – in fact, she wasn't sure she'd even known there was such a thing as a Chairman of the Joint Chiefs of Staff for America's Armed Services. But last night she happened to have her TV on. Sometimes she watched her daughter's show, other times she couldn't force herself. It all depended on her sense of self-worth for that day. She barely was awake when she heard Clements refer to the negative influences that her daughter overcame in Athens, Ohio. Then from out of nowhere, this retired big shot labels her a tramp on national television. Minutes later her phone had started ringing non-stop with rude people asking all sorts of rude questions.

All day she'd been seeing and hearing things. For the first time in her lifetime, she noticed the fingers being pointed, the voices being lowered when she neared. Her cocoon had been pierced and Leslie Burton sought the quickest path back to blissful anonymity. She found it where she always did, at the local liquor store.

As soon as he was handed the note in the middle of a late afternoon meeting, Zach knew Andie had discovered something important. She wanted him to call her immediately. She wouldn't dare draw attention to their personal relationship with this type of interruption, so it only could relate to the investigation. If not significant, she simply would have waited a couple more hours until they were together at dinner. But beyond his deductive reasoning, Zach also had noticed the difference after the *High Road* interview with Clements. Though she'd pretended to devote her full attention to the balance of their evening together, that mind of hers was churning elsewhere. Even when they'd made love, her body was with him but not the rest. Then she'd slipped out of the apartment at 4AM, not realizing he was watching her from the darkness. He wanted to sit up and kiss her goodbye, but had thought better. He'd become familiar with how her mind worked and knew she needed room to chase something down. Apparently she'd found it.

"Zach, I think you'd better come see something." The tone of her voice said more than the words.

She was waiting at the elevator doors to whisk him into the nearest empty conference room. There, she placed a single sheet of paper on the table. He'd never heard of Nicholas J. Parravano, but as he scanned down the bullet points beneath that name he recalled Andie's previous descriptions and disgust for the grizzly crime. Toward the bottom he came to the reference to Athens High School. His eyes locked, the relevance registering instantly.

She broke the silence, "Stephanie Burton graduated in 1989."

Silence again, he staring at the page, she staring at him. She allowed a few minutes for the other connections to play out in his mind. She knew first-hand how horrendously difficult it was to process those implications.

"Zach, I should have seen it sooner."

He finally lifted his head, shaking it slowly from side to side. His eyes may have been pointed in her direction, but he really couldn't see past the previous assumptions and decisions that now were haunting him. His muttered response may have sounded like it was for her, but he was talking to himself.

"We had no reason … we were able to eliminate all the tour speakers as actual suspects early on. We checked and double-checked. We even searched for enemies they might have made … but we focused on their careers … their public lives … as adults. Why would we have gone traipsing through their childhoods? My gosh, Andie, think of who those speakers were. For God's sake, think of who she is!"

She waited, knowing he wasn't finished.

"Andie, the facts were airtight … she'd already flown to other cities. She made it to all of her next appointments. How could it be possible?"

"Zach, we might be jumping to the wrong conclusion."

The best he could manage was a hopeful squeeze of her hand. They finally had the elusive lead that was likely to break the case. His mind automatically started sequencing the steps ahead – steps that must be taken with great care. But the feeling in his heart, the air in the room, the look on Andie's face, it all seemed funereal.

Zach needed to inform his superiors. With a high profile case now compounded by an even higher profile suspect, they would demand utmost speed, absolute certainty and maximum confidentiality. For a boatload of reasons, the Bureau would be hypersensitive about the faintest whiff of speculation leaking out.

He asked Andie to get the Data Section started with the airlines, seeking inconsistencies or explanations related to Stephanie Burton's flight records. After her documented departures from each of the cities, could Burton possibly have returned and departed again within the timelines required to make her next appointments in other cities? If so, would she have used a different name? What other explanations might there be?

Zach would take a team and head to Athens, Ohio to look for a few answers. How well might Burton and Parravano have known each other? What about the childhood adversities alleged by Clements ... or her mother's lifestyle? He dreaded their every step ... the answers to their every question.

Fifty-Three:

Fourth of July Weekend, 2009

As soon as they pulled onto Stimson Avenue on Friday morning, it was evident the town had started kicking back to celebrate the nation's birthday. No one seemed to be in a particular hurry and many already had reached into the rear of their closets for the red, white and blue outfits they dusted off once a year. Sacrificing a holiday weekend wasn't all that unusual for Zach and the two agents who accompanied him to Athens.

Prior to arriving, they'd identified residents who had graduated from Athens High around the same time as Nicholas Parravano and Stephanie Burton – likewise the faculty members who still taught or had retired in the area. In setting up interviews, their stated purpose had been simply to explore aspects of Nicholas Parravano's background because of potential ties to an unresolved FBI case.

A number of townspeople didn't even know whom the agents were talking about until his nickname was mentioned. As it turned out, most everyone had recollections and opinions about Gunner Parravano. When the local basketball star headed off to Bowling Green, the entire town had followed the ups and downs of his college career. Once his playing days were over, the Athens newspaper had continued to report on the notoriety he achieved – his arrests, his prison sentence, his release, and lastly his murder.

Twenty years after his graduation from Athens High, the only consistent positive the townspeople could cite was the quality of Gunner's jump shot. Otherwise, Parravano now was remembered for his misdeeds, for having wasted his talent and ultimately his life. No one seemed surprised that the FBI still might be looking into his nefarious activities nearly six years after a brutal death he somehow had brought upon himself. As one retired teacher said, "That boy just had a mean streak."

The subject of Stephanie Burton typically was brought up early in their conversations, but not by Zach or his agents. The locals could hardly wait to talk about her. The pride for this town's favorite daughter more than offset any embarrassment that citizens felt about how Gunner had turned out. With Stephanie Burton having turned into such an inspirational public figure, the people of Athens marveled over the irony that she and Gunner had been contemporaries. Some even recalled that they had dated.

As this coincidence was raised, it had been easy to segue into speculations about the nature of Parravano's relationship with Burton – how long it had lasted, when and how it had ended. Once Burton's name was referenced, even businesslike FBI agents could exhibit a little natural curiosity regarding a popular celebrity. "Oh, I didn't realize she came from here … what was she like back then?" "Did she date lots of local guys?" "How about that crack General Clements made about her mother on TV … any truth to that?"

Zach and his team compared notes. Parravano and Burton had dated rather seriously for most of a school year. Gunner had boasted extensively about their promiscuous activities. Stephanie had ended the relationship quite abruptly. At the time, there'd been divergent opinions on why. But given the context of events since, everyone now was certain that Stephanie Burton had chosen to take the high road away from whatever low road behaviors that Gunner Parravano must have inflicted upon her. When asked, none of the people who knew them could imagine that the pair would have had reason or occasion to reconnect subsequently. Parravano never even returned to Athens after high school because his father accepted a coaching position elsewhere and his family had moved. And, of course, everyone now knew that Stephanie had gone on to Columbia, a brilliant business career and a place in the hearts of most Americans.

When asked to comment on the recent allegations about Leslie Burton, most locals chose not to sink to that level. The town seemed to be experiencing a surge in neighborly love and civility. Yes, there might have been "occasional rumors" about Mrs. Burton's relationships with various men – some married, some not.

"But bear in mind, the woman had lost her husband at a young age and was forced to raise a child alone."

"Considering how that daughter blossomed, she surely must possess many fine qualities."

However, one fifty-something housewife wasn't subscribing to any of it. "Leslie Burton is a whore and the whole town has known it for years. When I got my divorce, the attorneys discovered that my husband had been paying her electric bills for more than six years. We've been apart for two years, yet he still loves to flaunt the fact he spends every Tuesday night with her. And I have a pretty good idea of who gets her on Wednesdays."

Zach decided they should hold on further probes into Leslie Burton. No need to stir suspicions in the community, at least for now. As to exploring how Parravano and Stephanie Burton might have stayed connected, the safest next step would be some careful digging away from Athens. The guy had spent four years in prison. Prisoners often felt irrepressible urges to brag about the sordid details from their pasts, and cellmates had an inescapable reason to listen.

~*~

On March 26, 2007, following the Seattle P.E.T. event, Stephanie Burton's flight for San Francisco had departed at 6:09PM. On October 16, that same year, Burton's flight from Indianapolis to Chicago had taken off at 6:47PM. Her Chicago flight from Kansas City on May 21, 2008, had left at 5:53PM. These times and her expended boarding passes had been verified the previous June, when the FBI first documented P.E.T.'s travel records for the speakers and staff who attended the three events.

Over a holiday weekend thirteen months later, Andie and her associates from Data Section reconfirmed that if Stephanie Burton had departed on those flights, she couldn't have made it back to any one of the cities and committed the complicated crimes. No configuration of travel arrangements would've worked within even the most liberal interpretations of the forensic timelines for the three homicides. Commercial flights, charters, train schedules, automobile travel at any speed … nothing was logistically plausible.

Stephanie Burton's gate check-in and seat occupancy for each of the flights had been reconfirmed. Agents already had confirmed that she made all of her morning appointments on the following days in San Francisco, Chicago and then Chicago again. As amazing as this woman might be, she couldn't have been in two cities at once. So somehow the amazing Stephanie Burton had subverted standard airline protocols on three different occasions without anyone noticing.

Fifty-Four:

Whatever bad days William Clements may have had in his sixty-seven earthly years, it would be hard to imagine any being worse than this July Wednesday. The floor seats and galleries behind him were at capacity. Television cameras fed live signals to C-Span, as well as the news networks that would carry portions throughout the day. In front of him on a raised tier, an enormous U-shaped table that accommodated eleven U.S. senators, five federal attorneys and contingents of aides behind them. The general's table was miniature by comparison, the three dark microphones standing in stark contrast to the white table cloth. He was flanked by two defense attorneys.

The Chair hurried through the formalities of her opening statement, slowing only to emphasize the potential charges facing Retired General William Addison Clements. Then for ninety minutes, two of the federal attorneys took turns summarizing the findings from a lengthy investigation into thousands of military contracts brokered or approved by Clements. Included were affidavits from Messrs. Henderson, Mendel and Yates that enumerated illicit agreements from which they'd benefited. Next came the tomes of photocopies that documented bank deposits into numbered accounts that had been traced back to the general. The evidence was excruciating.

Finally, the senators were unleashed. It was an unmitigated massacre of accusatory questions and long-winded admonitions. More firing squad than hearing. Clements became tongue-tied so frequently during the ordeal that he asked one of his attorneys to read the personal statement he'd been practicing for weeks. A Senate subcommittee wouldn't issue its final conclusions and recommendations without at least a pretense of further due process. However in her wrap-up, the Chair pronounced that the Attorney General's Office should begin preparation of formal charges immediately.

The next morning a spokesperson for the Pentagon announced that a date for court martial proceedings would be forthcoming as well. Retirement didn't preclude "The General" from the jurisdiction of the Uniform Code of Military Justice.

Clements still would have a few more months of freedom, but he hardly could enjoy them. The eventual trial outcomes were certain, substantial prison sentences were inevitable. He was ruined. His name and legacy, the wealth and its amenities, even the arrogant pride. All taken from him.

As for his cherished associations with Philadelphia's blood-lined elite, in the end they had failed him. To avoid serving time, Carl Henderson and Lawrence Mendel quickly had opened their books on Clements. In return they agreed to millions in reparations and the suspension of government contracts for a period of no less than five years.

Striking a deal to avoid jail had been harder for the eighty-five year old Harry Yates. Virtually all of Yates' sales and profits were generated through the production of military equipment. The company was to be banned permanently from bidding on any type of government contract; existing military business would cease immediately; and eighty-eight million dollars of ill-gained profits must be repaid. After 168 years, Yates Brothers Steel announced its doors would shut. The immense wealth and proud heritage that had been accumulated for future generations were wiped away by the lineal heir who'd seen no value in the sappy patriotism of his forefathers. Apparently Harry Yates had been destined to prove himself correct.

Fifty-Five:

July 9, 10 & 11, 2009

Over a period of forty-eight months in Youngstown, Gunner Parravano had averaged a new cellmate every eight. Prison officials had provided their identities and the FBI hurriedly tracked them down. Two were serving time – one still in Youngstown, the second having made a career move to the Commonwealth of Kentucky. Two others were traveling down successful roads of rehabilitation. Another had died of a drug overdose in 2007. The sixth had vanished into the world of the homeless in 2004.

The four who could be interviewed were, but only Dwayne Binder provided any worthwhile assistance – and that was by simply pointing agents to another source of information. Apparently when it came to sex and prison, Parravano was more doer than talker. Minimal details about his sexual proclivities prior to prison had been shared with his cellmates … but each had done their delicate best to explain to agents that Gunner had accessed the full range of available sexual outlets with great frequency during his incarceration. What Gunner had preferred to talk about was his basketball exploits.

Dwayne Binder worked on a dairy farm in Western Pennsylvania. He'd served sixteen months in Youngstown for selling cocaine to an undercover cop in Hamilton, Ohio. Now he was committed to his solid marriage, a baby girl and keeping out of trouble. In sharing a cell with Gunner Parravano for seven months, he'd needed to be resourceful to avoid sharing anything more intimate. Binder possessed a borderline photographic memory when it came to sports, so he kept Gunner sexually at bay by recounting many of Parravano's college basketball highlights. Apparently Gunner hadn't wanted to slip off Binder's athletic pedestal by trying to slip into other places where he wasn't welcome.

In a late night conversation with Binder, Gunner once had confided how his teammate, Jobie Williams, had rescued him with the Bowling Green coaching staff over a claim of sexual misconduct. Binder could remember the conversation almost verbatim. "Dwayno, I can't believe you remember Jobie, man. The guy barely played any minutes, but he sure saved my ass when some drunk groupie slut accused me of raping her."

Jobie Williams sold business stationery in Atlanta, and he definitely remembered having covered for Gunner Parravano with the coaches. He'd been at the same campus party and seen this girl come on to a number of teammates before begging Gunner to make her an honorary cheerleader. Amidst her morning-after remorse, she must have forgotten that she'd also invited Jobie to stay in the bedroom and observe her official induction. As a result, she eventually had been convinced to drop the rape charges.

Williams had been saddened but not totally surprised by what happened to Gunner after college. "After I saved Gunner's bacon during sophomore year, we became good buds. On road trips we shared rooms … and occasionally women."

Once Williams got going on Gunner stories, the FBI agent who was interviewing him just sat back and took notes. He related one story about a trip to Madison Square Garden, when Gunner faked a migraine to skip out of afternoon practice.

"He had this 'hot' high school honey who lived in New York City and she'd invited him to her apartment. Later that night, he was in one of his boastful moods and I remember him telling me, 'Bro, I never knew if I was her first screw in high school or not, but today I got her other cherry for sure. Jobie, you should have seen her when I put it to her ass.' For months he kept talking about how he taught that babe in New York the lesson she deserved. He'd even get this evil look when he talked about it. He never mentioned her name, but I always figured that Gunner must have forced himself on whoever that poor girl was."

It didn't take long for the FBI to figure out who she was. While Gunner was on the team, Bowling Green had made only one trip to New York City. On those particular dates in early November of 1991, Stephanie Burton had been a sophomore at Columbia University, living alone in a studio apartment.

Part IV

"Yes, there is a Nirvanah; it is leading your sheep to a green pasture, and in putting your child to sleep, and in writing the last line of your poem."

Kahil Gibran, Lebanese Poet, 1883-1931

Fifty-Six:

Sunday Night; July 12, 2009

In the midst of Nielsen's Summer Sweeps, Stephanie Burton appeared live on a special edition of *60 Minutes*. CBS Corporation owned a twenty-percent stake in WNL, so network officials were more than amenable to the idea. To the relief of WNL intermediaries, Stephanie had consented as soon as the concept was presented to her. The segment would be televised from *High Road's* studio so that Stephanie could be seen in her natural surroundings, which included Kelly Amaker and The Road Crew. The *60 Minutes* producers wanted to provide a behind-the-scenes glimpse of what went into the country's fastest growing television program, as well as the people behind the country's most fascinating new personality.

Stephanie had been thrilled by the notion that her team would be featured prominently. It was critically important to her that America understand the tenets of *High Road* were much stronger than Stephanie Burton alone. The number of viewers would dwarf the readership of the *Newsweek* piece. She'd recognized a chance to reach the largest audience of her lifetime – an offer she couldn't refuse.

Close to thirty million viewers tuned in, eager to meet the real Stephanie Burton up-close-and-personal. Then they watched with fascination as she found ways to recede gracefully from the limelight.

Instead, Kelly and the others effectively communicated the most important principles, as Stephanie had known they would. One by one, they related heartfelt messages about dreams and accomplishments, hopes and encouragement. But it was far more than the words. The Road Crew members embodied the values and inner peace of a religious faithful, but were tied to no single religion. They demonstrated the abiding support and devotion of a strong family unit, yet most of them had known each other for only months.

They didn't behave like some newborn sect who had discovered "the way" and might accost people at airports. They appeared exactly as they were ... plain everyday folks of different ages, from different backgrounds, who had found reasons to start believing more in themselves. And by believing more in themselves, had learned they could believe more in each other.

Near the conclusion, one question was directed at Stephanie that she could neither duck nor defer ... a question that caught her off-guard.

"Miss Burton, are you aware the latest Gallop Public Opinion Poll being released tomorrow morning, will reflect that you now are viewed as the most trusted voice in America? How do you react? And more importantly, how do you think all our national leaders who rank below you should react?"

Before responding she looked around the studio, making eye contact with each person on The Road Crew, her gratitude evident.

"No, Ed, I was not aware of the poll. But as I consider what it means, I'm not surprised. The survey reflects absolutely nothing about me personally, I assure you. I shouldn't even be mentioned in the same breath with those individuals who devote their entire lives to genuine public service.

"I have to believe the responses to that particular question are a powerful reflection of desires we all have to find our own higher potential. That's what we work so hard to impart on *High Road* ... that's what you heard, saw and felt from my close friends and colleagues here this evening. The opinion poll you're citing offers great encouragement that we're all on the right track together. I would hope that any leader or citizen would consider that to be promising."

As terrific as network executives might have felt about the segment, the overwhelming majority of the millions who watched it felt even better. The hard-nosed television critic for *The New York Times* took the liberty of speaking for them in his review.

"There have been those rare occasions when we've all been watching television in the privacy of our homes, but suddenly can feel the emotion and excitement swelling simultaneously in countless homes across the country. My personal list would include the first step on the moon, the U.S. Hockey Team in Lake Placid and a few others. To that list I now add the simplest of events. A mere interview, in fact. If you happened to miss Stephanie Burton and her very special team on *60 Minutes* last night, then TiVo it, YouTube it, do whatever you need to do to catch it. America was reminded last night that amidst all the magic of modern media, the greatest magic remains the human condition."

Fifty-Seven:

Wednesday; July 15, 2009

Letters swarmed the WNL mailroom following the *60 Minutes* segment. Network staff members would read them all, but only a representative sample was placed in Stephanie Burton's inbox each morning. As she read them, she experienced mixed emotions. Sincere expressions of gratitude that were intended as praise had the opposite effect. Knowing the horrid impulses she worked to contain, the horrid acts she had committed, Stephanie felt horridly unworthy of the public's esteem. When she was informed on live television that she'd become the most trusted voice in America, she had wanted to scream into the camera. *Please, just listen to what I say, don't be fooled by what I am.*

Stephanie had lived with intense inner conflict since childhood, but nothing compared to recent months. She was achieving a life's ambition of helping others step into their own potential, but in so doing she had attracted a following and adoration for which she felt completely unworthy. She now carried an emotional burden more troubling than any scarred memories. She was an imposter, a hypocrite to the very people for whom she cared most. But if the writers of these letters, the millions who watched *High Road*, were finding their own sense of self-worth, how could she stop?

Buried in one bundle, Stephanie found a letter she hadn't expected.

Dear Stephanie,

Much has happened in the short time since we met. As you must have followed, my husband faces difficult days ahead. I cannot comment on his tenuous legal situation, but suffice to say, the name of William Addison Clements will assume its rightful place in military history.

255

It is disheartening that the General continues to blame you for everything happening to him. Whether he ever accepts responsibility for his past decisions and actions remains to be seen. I suppose he will have much time to reflect.

Personally, however, the recent weeks have represented a period of soul-searching liberation. For too many years I hid from my own complacency and cowardice. To others, but mostly to myself, I pretended to be content with utter discontentment. By closing my eyes and settling, I steadily "un-earned" my self-respect.

Important seeds were sown as I watched and listened to you on television — seeds of doubt at first, but eventually seeds of hope. Then I was fortunate enough to meet you and closely observe your treatment of my husband. I recognized that the interview was not conducted as we'd been led to believe. I also am most aware that my husband has held little regard for his moral obligations to me, whether inside or outside our marriage. On national television, you discretely did what has been mine to do for way too long. You made him accountable for the consequences of his actions. Yet even as you recognized the hypocrisy of our marriage and the façade of our joint appearance on your program, you chose to treat me with a level of respect to which I've allowed myself to become unaccustomed.

I've informed the General that regardless of his other legal outcomes, I am filing for divorce. This, too, he blames on you, no matter how much I assert otherwise. Henceforth, I am resolved to pursue my own passions and higher potential. I am resolved to help others do the same. Encouragement is so little to give but so much to receive. You've shown me that.

We both have our reasons for keeping this letter confidential, but I hope you're not offended by the presumptuousness of my writing it to express heartfelt gratitude and best wishes.

Most sincerely,
Deanna Clements

Stephanie Burton neatly folded the letter and tucked it into a pocket inside the leather calendar on her desk. She couldn't remember the last time she'd experienced tears like this. Part of her wanted to linger and savor a moment of emotional fulfillment, but instead she burrowed deeper into a morning stack of mail.

Fifty-Eight:

Friday; July 17, 2009

With established links to the murder victim, Nicholas "Gunner" Parravano, Stephanie Burton had become the first and only legitimate suspect for the P.E.T. serial homicides. But according to travel records, she would have needed an accomplice to orchestrate them. Someone who did the actual killing after she had departed Seattle, Indianapolis and Kansas City. Or someone who had pretended to be Burton on those flights. In that case, a someone who looked like her, or who carried a counterfeit ID in her name. If she had employed a surrogate to clear security and fly in her place, then Burton could have committed the crimes herself. Timing may have been tight, but she could have pulled off the murders and still made it to her appointments on the following days by traveling as someone else.

Through the Transportation Security Administration, FBI agents accessed airport security videos for the dates in question. In screening the tapes, they carefully watched for reasonable look-alikes to Burton, or any females who displayed unusual behavior. Instead, what they'd seen was Burton herself clearing the security lines.

The probability of an accomplice always had seemed low. The killings had been too intimate, too seamless. Data Section had been charged with exploring other methods by which Stephanie Burton could have managed the three confirmed departures without stepping foot on the airplanes. Following a morning work session to confirm the details, Andie picked up the phone.

"Zach, I think we might have the answer. It was pretty complicated to find."

"I would hope so, Andie. I'd like to think that if it was easy, the combined resources of the FBI might have stumbled into it by now."

"Sorry … here goes. We've been checking passenger manifests for the flights that Stephanie Burton took out of Seattle, Indianapolis and Kansas City. In each case there were various seats that people paid for, for which boarding passes were issued, but then didn't get used. So far, nothing unusual … lots of people get advanced boarding passes and then change flights or miss them entirely."

She'd been talking pretty fast; she caught herself and slowed down so that Zach could absorb the significance of what she was about to reveal. "The unusual part is that among these unused boarding passes, there's one for each flight for which no subsequent flight change or refund was ever issued. In each case, there was no record of the designated passenger booking another flight to their original destination city. So three separate people on these three separate flights decided they no longer needed to travel to their destination at all, and each of them chose to forfeit the value of their tickets. For that to happen once is odd enough … but to happen on all three of the flights in question?"

"Can the airlines tell us who these people are that didn't use the seats they booked?"

"I just e-mailed the names to you, Zach. And guess what, all three were females traveling alone."

"So somehow Stephanie Burton found a way to exchange tickets without the airlines knowing?"

This ball was back in Zach's court. Field agents would contact the three women and inquire about their respective scheduled flights from Seattle, Indianapolis and Kansas City.

On one shoulder, he felt the weight of every brick in the J. Edgar Hoover Building. On the other, the looming potential of public reaction. In between, his head was filled with contradicting emotions. Zach Peterson was finding it difficult to get a good night's sleep. All those months with no leads, now this.

There still was much work to be done, but the FBI was well on its way to demonstrating that Stephanie Burton had the opportunity to commit the crimes … that she had remained in the three cities during the times of the murders. Teams were pursuing the logistics required for Burton to make her following day appointments in cities that were hundreds of miles away.

As to motive, they had pieces. A childhood with apparent hardships, a mother with apparent sexual appetites. A likely sexual assault involving anal sodomy by a former boyfriend who ended up dead with his severed genitals in his rectum. Zach instructed another team to determine the whereabouts of Stephanie Burton when Parravano had been killed in 2001, but do so without raising suspicions that she was under investigation. He also made a call to Rancho Santa Fe to lay out what they had so far; then followed up by overnighting a box of videotapes. Dr. Cory Caputo wanted to dig further into Burton's background and study her behavior in front of the television cameras.

Opportunity. Motive. All they needed was physical evidence. Zach recognized the difficulty of that hurdle. Right now they had nothing to link Stephanie Burton to the crime scenes and he wasn't optimistic. Maybe she had kept the clothes, weapons or assorted paraphernalia ... and maybe she mistakenly would disclose something that allowed them to be located. *Or maybe the victims themselves would come back to life and pick her out of a line-up.* These crimes were too well executed. She was too smart. Too much time had passed. Yet there remained one certainty. Unless Stephanie Burton somehow confessed, prosecuting such an admired personality with no physical evidence wouldn't be worth attempting in front of a jury.

Hell, without physical evidence Zach wasn't even sure he could believe she'd truly committed the murders.

Fifty-Nine:

Late July, 2009

The three female travelers related similar accounts. All had been approached by a businesswoman who needed to sit in coach. She'd been "so pleasant" … "so professional."

"How could you not accept her offer to move up to first class?"

"Did I do anything illegal?"

"I hope I'm not getting that nice woman in trouble."

The woman definitely had been attractive. They each remembered different aspects of her beauty – and all of which were consistent with the suspect the FBI now had.

"Quite striking."

"On the tall side."

"Black hair, worn long and flowing."

"Her hair was definitely pulled back."

"Beautiful skin."

"Dressed extremely well … classy."

"Shapely and fit."

"The kind of woman that draws attention from men."

According to one, "She had the looks of a celebrity … a Catherine Zeta-Jones or Stephanie Burton type."

⁓

Gerber, Alton & Jennings had installed a proprietary operating system in 1998, which included an electronic calendar system for scheduling meetings. "ADvance" software had been upgraded many times since, but historical data remained buried in the system for anyone who knew how to find it. Once Agent Melissa Woodruff from Cyber Division could get inside GA&J's system, it wouldn't take long to check Stephanie Burton's calendar for November 8, 2001, the date Nicholas Parravano had been murdered.

Zach liked playing things fairly straight with his investigations. Fairly straight, but not completely. He asked Woodruff to contact GA&J's IT officer directly, so they could talk tech to one another.

"So you're telling me ADvance's firewalls haven't been infiltrated by a Trojan Horse, a salami attack or an e-mail bomb ... and you've had negligible infection levels from Zap Seven and Agent Naranja. Very impressive considering the hit rate on other ad agencies."

That's all it had taken. The IT officer hardly could wait to show off his pride-and-joy to an expert from the FBI. Following the demonstration, Agent Woodruff had no difficulty finding what she needed.

According to her archived schedules, Stephanie Burton had picked up a rental car in Chicago late in the day on Wednesday, November 7. She'd made a presentation that Thursday morning in Detroit and was back in Chicago for meetings on Friday. Detroit was no more than an hour's drive from where Nicholas Parravano was murdered. Estimated time of death had been early evening on Thursday. Drive time back to Chicago, approximately four hours. Five, at most.

⌐ℳ⌐

Credit cards used to book the three rental cars had been issued to a commercial account, the former Stephanie M. Burton Consultancy. Final payments were made in cash, but the original bookings were still in the systems. Avis, Budget, Thrifty. She'd spread her trail across three different companies.

The cars from Indianapolis and Kansas City had been returned in Chicago. Downtown Portland, for the one from Seattle. Her means of transportation from there to San Francisco was still being investigated. Facts were falling methodically into place. Once the FBI had gained a better sense of what to look for, the assigned agents knew precisely how and where to look.

⌐ℳ⌐

Convening a federal grand jury seemed like overkill. The Senate subcommittee had issued its official recommendation. Retired General

William A. Clements should be tried on multiple counts of fraud and malfeasance.

The final counts totaled ninety-seven in the papers filed by federal prosecutors. A federal judge easily could have ruled the documented evidence sufficient for moving straight to trial, but the Justice Department had wanted to make sure the high profile proceedings were impervious to any claims about due process.

The grand jury was set for August 18. U.S. Army court martial proceedings would be scheduled at the conclusion of the criminal trial, to ensure that General Clements and his defense team could fairly and properly focus their preparations.

Clements was working every angle and connection he'd ever had, hoping to strike a deal. Any deal. The Hill, the Pentagon, any place he could get a meeting or even get a call returned. But he was radioactive from the standpoint of public opinion; no one wanted to touch him. There was no reason to; he offered nothing in return. He no longer held any political capital.

To the general, the inequity was outrageous – that all the others could strike their deals and leave him holding the bag alone. He had been the one who put everything on the line for them … the one who dedicated his life to serving his country.

Sure, he'd pocketed some cash … but hell, what about all those governors and members of Congress who end up wealthy? Just because of an uppity broad with some agenda up her ass, he becomes the convenient whipping boy. The whole thing was outrageous.

Clements reached out to the senior senator from Pennsylvania, a long time friend with whom he'd taken a few memorable jaunts.

"Herb, isn't anyone thinking about how this will look to the rest of the world? One more political scandal for our enemies to point at … the whole blasted world watching as a former Chair of the Joint Chiefs gets carted off to jail!"

"Will, I'm sorry. With what has come out, think how it would look if you weren't."

Sixty:

Tuesday; August 4, 2009

"Zach, she'll never admit to those murders and she's too smart to start making mistakes now. She knows we've figured it out. She even knows that we know she knows. But I could just tell, it doesn't matter. It's like she has this supreme confidence about some trump card she's still holding. And do you know what the weirdest part was?"

"That even knowing she committed the murders, you admired the hell out of her."

"Exactly. How'd you know I was going to say that?"

"Because, Andie, I felt the same way."

～⁊ル～

Headquarters had approved his idea. The once white pages of Zach's spiral notebook had darkened rapidly. Dotted lines converged into a solid one that pointed directly at Stephanie Burton. He was briefing his immediate superior on a daily basis. The prospects of physical evidence tying Burton to the crimes were understood to be low. Nonetheless, at some point, she would need to be arrested and interrogated, whether an airtight case could be constructed or not. It would be at that juncture when the public fur would begin to fly.

The FBI couldn't tiptoe in and arrest a Stephanie Burton until it was prepared to weather an onslaught. Even the public reaction from merely questioning her as part of an official investigation might quickly snowball out of control. That's why Zach had suggested testing the waters with a meeting that was unofficial. "See how she responds … maybe cause her to start making mistakes."

To propose his idea, he'd needed to disclose his personal relationship with Andie. A few eyebrows had been raised, but nothing serious. During the conversation he'd had with Burton in the studio, right after his appearance on *High Road*, she seemed genuine in her desire to meet the woman who had linked the serial killings to the Personal Empowerment Tour. Burton had sensed special feelings from Zach toward this woman and provided him encouragement. It would be natural enough to call Stephanie Burton and let her know that he and Andie were going to be in New York City together ... that they'd be thrilled to take her up on her offer. Breakfast, lunch, coffee, cocktails, whatever could be worked into her busy schedule.

It was Stephanie who suggested late dinner at a casual Cuban restaurant just off Times Square. She arrived punctually at 9:30, her appearance much different than that evening's broadcast. She'd changed into jeans and sandals, removed her make-up and pulled her hair under a Yankees cap, but that hadn't stopped restaurant patrons from recognizing her. It took more than twenty minutes before she could make her way to the back table where Andie and Zach had been waiting and watching. She thoughtfully had inked signatures on menus, shirtsleeves and whatever improvised items people thrust in her path. She'd posed for group pictures. She embraced an elderly man dining with his grandkids who stood and reached out to her – his eyes watering as she'd kissed his cheek. Most noticeably, she took the time to have legitimate conversations with anyone who called to her; each person from the diverse crowd was made to feel that their comments and salutations meant something to her. By the time Stephanie Burton reached Andie and Zach, every table somehow had participated in a spontaneous processional that left the entire restaurant feeling uplifted.

Andie had yet to meet this woman, nonetheless she was moved to stand and give Burton a brief hug. Zach extended his hand, which she took and clasped in both of hers, "Agent Peterson, I can't tell you how much I've been looking forward to this evening. After your appearance on our show, I've been hoping for an opportunity to get to know you both. And Miss Morrison, before we say another word, congratulations on the terrific police work last summer."

They were the last customers to leave, sometime close to 1AM. In part it was due to the number of interruptions from other patrons, not to mention the Cuban couple that owned the restaurant or the waiters and kitchen staff who wanted to express their admiration and gratitude. But mostly the evening extended into early morning because the conversation had been easy and enjoyable. Andie and Stephanie hit it off from the beginning. Any concern Andie or Zach might have felt about the awkwardness of the evening and the reason they were there seemed to vanish instantly. Stephanie Burton's outreaching, compassionate nature had made everyone comfortable.

Stephanie wanted to know about Andie's family and childhood ... likewise Zach's. She prodded Andie to go on and on about her relationship with Pops back in Missouri. She was empathetic without being maudlin when Zach described his parents' untimely death in Africa, affirming him for the positive way in which he'd moved on with his life. Andie opened up about her patterned behaviors of complacency and her willingness to take the easiest paths available. A year earlier, she would have glossed over those shortcomings and avoided a serious conversation about higher purposes. Now she unburdened her innermost doubts and dared to articulate formulated ambitions.

Andie acknowledged her attendance at the Personal Empowerment Tour event in Kansas City and admitted that Stephanie had been the only speaker to make an impression. A powerful one. "After you spoke, I first had to overcome my absolute jealousy ... but in the hours and days that followed, the things you said kept coming back to me."

She went on to describe how the seeds planted at Kemper Arena had been nurtured since by a great deal of soul-searching, the affirmation and support of Zach, as well as the reinforcement of Stephanie's continued presence on television. "So if you two have this urge to clink glasses over your collaboration on the Kansas City production of Pygmalion, don't let me stop you."

Stephanie low-keyed any praise that came her way, but repeatedly offered effusive encouragement to Andie and Zach. As individuals, as a couple. "Too often relationships are convenient stalemates rather than two people truly being unafraid to bring out the best in each other. I hope you can remember to let others you touch, see how special that can be."

Stephanie also managed to skirt most every question about her own family and childhood – skilled in the techniques of taking a pointed probe and quickly exploding it into a more general theme. But Zach and Andie kept at it.

"We watched the Clements interview and were surprised that a man of his stature would stoop to the personal comments he made near the end. It seemed totally unfair to you and your mother ... how'd she handle what he said?"

"Thanks for your concern, Zach. I've moved on. My mother and I really haven't spoken much about it. General Clements is learning first-hand that, at some level, we all must accept the consequences for our past mistakes."

Her response could be interpreted to have so many meanings that Andie and Zach just stared at her while they pondered which had been intended. Stephanie calmly returned their gaze, as though she knew she'd served up a riddle and wanted to allow them the time to work their way through it.

Andie broke the silence. "That reminds me, Stephanie. I think General Clements made reference to Athens, Ohio. Is that where you're from?"

"I am. Have you been there?"

"No, but in my research on the P.E.T. murders, I came across another pretty disturbing murder that involved someone from Athens."

"I'm sorry to hear that, but I don't remember anyone being killed there while I was growing up." Burton's inflection suggested no more curiosity than would be natural.

"The murder wasn't actually in Athens. The victim was from there. In fact, you might have known him ... he was about your age."

She remained unnerved. "The only one around my age who I know to have been killed was Gunner Parravano. Was that the murder?"

Andie, too, maintained a calm demeanor. "That's the one ... it must have been gruesome. Did you know him?"

"Yes, quite well. We dated in high school. I guess his life took some ugly turns in later years."

Zach finally chimed in, "Based on everything I've learned about the guy, he seems like another example of someone accepting the consequences of past mistakes."

There were a few more polite inquiries about Stephanie's connections to Gunner Parravano and Athens. On the surface, not enough to push too hard. Burton's pleasant tone and overall expression never wavered, but Andie had seen it deep in her eyes. When Gunner's name was first mentioned, their eyes met and locked. In that instant, Stephanie Burton's eyes revealed the acceptance. No anger, no fear. Nothing malicious. Just a knowing look so deep that her eyes truly did become a window into her soul. So much revealed in that instant. The acceptance of what had needed to be done to Gunner. Acceptance of what she'd needed to do with others. Acceptance of the consequences. On her time ... in this world or a next one.

This entire exchange had consumed only minutes, midway through dinner. The affable atmosphere before or after was unaffected. They emptied a second pitcher of house sangria, genuinely enjoying each other's company. Exiting the restaurant they'd hugged farewells on the sidewalk, trading hearty best wishes and meaning every word.

Sixty-One:

Friday; August 7, 2009

Leslie Burton's aimless solitude had been disrupted enough by an asshole general with some kind of vendetta against Stephanie, the morality princess. Now the FBI wanted to come poking around. Couldn't she just be left alone? Obscurity, invisibility; that's all she wanted. She wasn't hurting anyone. Certainly not her parents anymore. Certainly not the exalted Stephanie who'd managed to rise above those horseshit "adversities" – at least, according to some know-it-all general.

So why had she agreed to meet this agent? *I didn't even know my daughter dated that ex-con basketball star who got his pecker cut off.* But down deep, she knew why she'd agreed. It might feel good to see a little dirt land on Stephanie's shoes. Through the lens of a gin bottle, hell, the whole world could use a little more dirt.

Zach flew to Athens alone. When he pulled up to the Cape Cod, the overgrown weeds and peeling paint were in line with his expectations. Leslie Burton was barely lucid when he had reached her the first time. He called back twice to confirm the appointment and she was only slightly more coherent on those occasions. He offered to meet in her office, but she indicated the University had placed her on medical leave.

Inside the house, there were no liquor bottles in sight. But most everything else about the home and homeowner signaled the excessive consumption. The blended odor of cigarettes and booze that hung in the air. The feeble attempt to straighten up the main seating area in the living room, when all the surroundings reflected permanent disarray. The cigarette burns on furniture cushions, the watermarks from too many wet glasses on the coffee table. The stained spots on her poorly fitting dress. The low-cut nature of the dress for early afternoon. The hit-and-miss application of lipstick and eye make-up. The sad, surrendered look in her eyes.

"Mrs. Burton, you never met Gunner Parravano and you didn't know that he and your daughter dated during most of her junior year in high school?"

"Mr. Peterson, I thought I told you that on the phone. I apologize if I wasn't clear … my medicines occasionally make me tired. My daughter was raised to be quite independent. I wasn't aware of everything she did in high school, nor did she keep tabs on me."

"Ma'am, the FBI is currently exploring whether Parravano's murder somehow relates to the serial murders that coincided with the Personal Empowerment Tour. Since your daughter has ties to both, we're concerned for her safety … especially with her being such a public figure."

"I still don't see how I can help you. I don't know anything about that tour … didn't even know she was part of it until she started showing up on TV after those murders came out."

"We're just wondering if there were people in her past that gave her any problems. And I hope you can appreciate the FBI's thoroughness … we like to go as far back as possible. Did any kids ever torment her? Did she have any strong enemies in her youth?"

"Like I said, we didn't share much. I have no idea who her friends and enemies were when she was growing up. She never came home crying or anything."

"What was her childhood like? It must have been difficult losing a father at such a young age. What kind of adversities did the two of you face?"

There was that damned word that idiot general had thrown out. Her mind started spinning. So now some smart-ass, uppity FBI agent is wondering if those "adversities" really existed … which also means he's wondering if that crack about being a small town tramp is true. She needed to excuse herself; she was thirsty.

She asked Zach if he'd like some water, but when she returned and took her seat back on the couch, the glass in her hand held anything but water. Zach was sure it wasn't the first such glass she'd held that day.

"Mrs. Burton, your daughter has yet to marry. Do you know if she's had any serious men in her life?"

"Why don't you just ask her, Officer … Detective … whatever you are?"

"We will, but we're doing our homework. We don't want to alarm her unnecessarily. Is there anything you can tell us about how she gets along with men?"

"I haven't a clue … she may be celibate for all I know. Maybe she likes women, I've never asked."

"Did anything happen to her, or did she see anything as a child that might affect her adult relationships with men?"

She pulled the glass away from her lips, closed her eyes and held the liquid in her mouth for a moment before swallowing. "Look, Mister, I know where you're going with all this. The fact that I liked sleeping around with a few men when the famous Stephanie Burton was under my roof, doesn't mean I did her any damage. If she's got some kind of hang-up that attracts sex perverts, you can thank her father for that. But it all seems pretty far-fetched to me."

"Did something happen between Stephanie and her father?"

Leslie Burton gulped what was left in the tumbler. Her hands were noticeably shaking. "You'll need to speak with her."

"Mrs. Burton, was there abuse?"

"Please don't ask me these questions."

"Did he beat her?"

"Please."

"Was she molested?"

"Please, just talk to her. I was never sure."

"But you suspected something. Did you confront your husband?"

She stared at the empty glass in her hand. The answer was obvious.

"Did you contact the authorities?"

No response.

"Mrs. Burton, did you contact the authorities?"

She pulled herself up by the arm of the sofa. Tears that were building a few moments earlier had disappeared. Her expression was coarse. "Mr. Peterson, answering your pointless questions has left me rather thirsty. Please show yourself out." She turned and walked out of the room.

On the flight back to Washington, Zach squeezed more notations into his notebook. He needed to call Dr. Caputo and fill in more of the blanks from Stephanie Burton's childhood. Speculations about the mother's sexually active lifestyle had been confirmed. Stephanie probably had seen and heard plenty while she was growing up. It was obvious that mother and daughter were never close. In fact, he'd not observed a single maternal instinct in Leslie Burton. The resentment toward her daughter's success was palpable. And then the probable molestation by a father who had died when she was nine. It appeared the mother had known, or at least suspected, but had taken no action to protect her own daughter.

Stephanie Burton clearly carried extensive parental sewage from her youth. Plus added memories of whatever Parravano had done to her in New York. Zach had studied a multitude of sexual predators and serial killers whose psychological scars were mild in comparison. Stephanie Burton's murderous actions could never be condoned, but he was beginning to understand. What he couldn't understand was how she'd kept it all separate … her incredible success … the remarkable goodness.

⌒𝓂⌒

Stephanie couldn't remember the last time her mother had phoned her – not even for extra money. The regular amounts she continued to send always seemed sufficient. Stephanie often wondered if her mother even bothered to keep her phone numbers around. So when her assistant interrupted a walk-thru in the studio to tell her that "a Leslie Burton" was on the phone, Stephanie practically ran to her office, thinking her mother must be ill.

But it was merely the first time her mother felt she had something worth calling about … the possibility of bringing her daughter down a peg or two.

"Stephanie, I thought you should know that there was an Agent Peterson from the FBI here this afternoon. He asked lots of questions about you and that boy they found with his privates jammed up his backside up in Toledo. He was nosy as hell. Wanted to know if you even liked men. Plus all kinds of questions about what went on between you and your dear ole daddy. Told him he'd have to ask you about that."

"Is that all, Mom? You sound like you've been drinking."

"My drinking's nothing new, sweetheart. What's new is that America's Moral Compass may have some trouble heading her way. Sounds like you may have made some pretty strange friends along that little primrose path of yours … or maybe you've got some weirdo who's coming after you. But that Agent Peterson fellow, he can tell you all about it when you meet him."

271

"I already know Zach Peterson and he's a very thoughtful man. I have every confidence that he's looking out for my best interests. Thank you for the call, Mother."

She hardly was surprised the FBI was moving this quickly into her background. Since the dinner a few nights earlier, she'd started anticipating the inevitable. What surprised her, or at least saddened her, was that her mother's bitterness now bordered on hatred. All the different ways she had tried to keep her mom out of the gutter when she was growing up. Or once it was obvious she couldn't, how she at least had tried to give her mom the dignity and respect that any mother deserved. But her mother had wanted nothing of dignity and respect. All along her mother simply had wanted a daughter who could crawl into that gutter alongside her … a daughter to share her misery.

Sixty-Two:

Monday; August 10, 2009

Three days after the call from her mother, Stephanie heard a second unexpected voice on the other end of her phone. William Clements wanted to meet with her in private to clear the air prior to his grand jury appearance. His tone was hardly conciliatory and the conversation was uncomfortably stiff, but she nevertheless agreed to an appointment later in the week.

~*~

The phone conversation later that morning with Kent Gillespie was polar opposite. They shared opinions about a hot new recording artist and an obscure foreign film. They laughed about some of the weird movies they'd gone to see during their years together. They laughed about a lot, which was exactly what she'd needed. One of the reasons she had called was to let him know how much she missed the light-heartedness he'd brought into her life ... how much she would always appreciate him for that. She wanted him to know he would remain special to her.

~*~

"I'm not sure you really require my services any longer, Zach. I don't think there's much doubt that you've identified your murderess."

"Yeah, but Doc, you know how much you'd miss my calls. Besides, I was just about to suggest we double your hourly rate."

"Zachary, I'm touched." Cory Caputo chuckled. From the onset, he'd insisted that his work on the case be gratis. "I suppose I can tolerate you a tad longer."

The byplay was indicative of the friendship that had developed and, truth be told, Caputo now was fascinated by the enigma of Stephanie Burton. He most definitely wanted to see this one to its conclusion.

Zach could remember feeling compassion for the criminals in some of his past investigations, but never outright admiration. He continually found himself playing amateur psychologist on behalf of Stephanie Burton. Caputo needed to dissuade him of one notion or theory after another.

Like during a call the week before, "Miss Burton does not have a dissociative identity disorder … what many lay people mistakenly would label a split personality. In fact, she is quite unlikely to have any dissociative disorder … or even a depersonalization disorder, Zach."

Or the call a few days later, "No, I'm afraid not, Zach. She displays none of the characteristics of a schizophrenic – undifferentiated, residual or otherwise."

Or then the day after that, "Interesting concept, but post-traumatic stress and related anxiety attacks could not be so well contained over such a prolonged period. Internet excursions into the world of mind science are dangerous, my young friend. Aren't there some international drug cartels you should be penetrating with so much spare time?"

In actuality, Dr. Caputo had listened patiently to each possibility that Zach served up, before patiently leading him to the same basic conclusion.

"No matter how sad or unsavory the traumatic events of Stephanie Burton's past, from a clinical standpoint her behaviors indicate she has remained psychologically healthy – at least within the currently accepted boundaries of normality. But, Zach, the potential altered capacities of the human mind are in many ways as unexplored as distant galaxies."

New mental disorders might emerge or be recognized if genetics, brain chemistry and environmental influences converged into unforeseen patterns of behavior. But according to present definitions, Zach was forced to accept that Stephanie Burton would have to be classified as psychologically normal. Undamaged.

Caputo had studied the growing FBI dossier on Burton … the educational accomplishments, the career successes, the dozens of articles written about her, the personal accounts from people who knew her. He had observed her behavior during many hours of videotape – from her first

TV appearances related to the P.E.T. murders, through her most recent *High Road* telecasts.

"From a clinical standpoint, Stephanie Burton consistently exhibits efficient perceptions of reality, as well as voluntary control over her own behavior. She is able to convey adequate self-esteem and acceptance in how she carries herself, even though she clearly shuns praise for personal accomplishment. I submit that this tendency is even further evidence of her mental cognizance, because she understands the wrongness of her secret actions. She is able to relate well to people in a breadth of situations and vary her interactions according to circumstances. Most importantly, she sustains a high level of productivity ... indeed, a superior level."

Stephanie Burton didn't just meet every important criterion for psychological normalcy, she excelled in them. Given the context of her crimes that were anything but normal, she was the most supremely unusual case that Dr. Cory Caputo ever had observed.

Sixty-Three:

Finally they'd found a D.C. hangout they could call their own, a pub called Nonpartisan Crowd … "check your party affiliation at the door." The formal briefing with Zach's superiors had been a breeze compared to the interrogation he received from Andie over dinner. With the suits at headquarters, the latest from Dr. Caputo represented another layer of necessary detail in a high profile case that was destined to become much higher. With Andie, it was far more personal.

"So Stephanie isn't a Sybil?"

"Caputo explained that there are two schools of thought on whether separate and multiple personality systems can coexist in the same individual. He's in the camp that believes dissociative identity disorders occur, but, as he would say … rarely compared to the disproportions suggested by popular fiction and resourceful defense attorneys. When split personalities form, each develops its own motivations, memory patterns, relationships and character traits. One personality within a single individual might be aware that another coexists … maybe even be sensitive to the different needs of this other personality. But the shifts from one personality to another can only be prompted by emotional stress or impulse. They can't be switched back and forth to accomplish some ulterior purpose … like killing men who don't respect women. Also, the different personalities can't be controlled over long periods of time."

"Like the eight years that Stephanie was able to control her secret activities since killing Parravano in Ohio?"

"Caputo also said the altered states of consciousness in dissociative personalities are often subconscious escape mechanisms to avoid anxieties that the dominant personality might have. Having reviewed Stephanie's academic records and professional accomplishments, and watched tapes of her in a wide range of spontaneous situations, he concludes she has superior abilities for dealing with psychological and emotional stress. She doesn't need to escape into an alternative personality."

"But she needs to kill people?"

"Interestingly, Caputo describes the violent demise of good old Gunner as a cognitive act … meaning it probably was premeditated. And maybe over a number of years."

Andie nodded. "That makes sense, since the rape occurred more than ten years before the murder. But why wait and murder him … if he really raped her, why not just have him arrested at the time?"

"For whatever reason, she needed to inflict her own punishment to satisfy her psychological needs. Here's where it starts to get pretty heavy. Doc believes the ideals she demonstrates and espouses every night on television have been so evident throughout her adult life, that they must be rooted in a belief system she developed at a younger age. Yet we know her home environment was the antithesis of high values and virtue. According to her test scores and school records, Stephanie was exceptionally bright and perceptive. It is probable the negative influences at home created dissonance with what she knew to be appropriate behaviors and she yearned to be part of this more desirable world. The more intense the negative influences, the more idealized her inner desires became. She erected higher and higher standards for this envisioned code of conduct. To create such standards, she would have sought cues from outside sources … perhaps observing how other families interacted … or watching movies and television … perhaps from reading. Classmates and teachers indicated they rarely saw her without a book."

"And, Zach, you're going to get around to how seducing and murdering men might fit into those idealized standards?"

"Hang with me … and remember, Andie, none of this is for sure. It's merely Caputo's most expert opinion. He's hoping for the chance to sit down with Stephanie Burton once we arrest her."

"Keep talking, G-man."

"With increased maturity and broader perspectives about the world outside her home, the dissonance between Stephanie's utopian aspirations and the sordid realities of her real life became more and more acute. Growing up, all of us ran into contradictions between what we were taught was good, and what we actually experienced. The result was a series of practical compromises. Simplistically, everyone ends up somewhere on the continuum of good guys versus bad guys according to what compromises we make on primal virtues.

"Caputo believes that Stephanie Burton sought a means by which she didn't have to compromise or sacrifice her idealism. That idealism became paramount to her. Unable to make her home environment more suitable, she could well have wrestled with two courses of action for an extended portion of her most formative years. Should she devote her energies to shaping a more positive environment on a different horizon outside her home life … and attempt to displace the vivid disappointments? Or should she lash out at the very people and behaviors that had denied her what she most wanted?"

"Or do both?"

"Exactly. The people we met in Athens said Stephanie was very much a loner when she was young. That solitude could have resulted from feeling abnormal and embarrassed about things at home, and so much private time would have allowed her to fixate on the types of deeper thoughts for which we know she was capable. She might frequently have contemplated the challenges and consequences of her two courses of action. These mental struggles could have been accentuated by behaviors observed routinely with her mother – and having met Leslie Burton up close, I can only imagine what Stephanie might have been subjected to. Not to mention other traumatic events like her father's death, apparent molestations, and who knows what else? If she couldn't decide on the proper course of action, Caputo said she may have found ways to keep both options alive in her conscious thoughts."

"So how does Dr. Caputo explain that this loner of a girl ends up with a mega-career because of her people skills … then becomes a mega-star because she's able to connect with millions of people at once?"

"Andie, I asked Doc the same thing. First, we shouldn't assume that because she was a loner, she didn't possess inherent people skills. We're obviously dealing with a uniquely talented and complex individual … she may have been holding back. Somewhere after high school, there seemingly was a point when Stephanie Burton committed wholeheartedly to becoming a positive influence, and therefore had reason to unleash different skills. In college and early in her career, she also may have explored different ways to maximize her impact. And somewhere along the line her confidence and comfort gelled into the strong persona we've watched with amazement on television."

"But somewhere along that line, something also must have triggered the second set of actions."

"Apparently. And in response, she activated a second persona. Not a dissociative personality, but a parallel personality by conscious choice. She decided that two long-considered options should both be put into action. We know this conscious choice was made at least as far back as 2001, when she killed Parravano. We're pretty sure he raped her while she was in college, so maybe that act had been the final straw in her decision to lash out. But maybe it had come sooner, and there were previous crimes we haven't uncovered. Regardless of when … what once had been a philosophical struggle for Stephanie, now became a more complex self-image struggle because of the actions she actually had taken. If there had been difficulty finding inner happiness before, now it would be almost impossible. In observing her behavior, Caputo cites dozens of examples where she evades any form of praise. He believes she considers herself unworthy of acclaim, and probably unworthy of experiencing true joy or contentment. Whatever satisfaction she does permit herself is derived vicariously through the accomplishments of others and any sense of fulfillment those close to her express outwardly."

"Everything you're saying makes such horribly perfect sense based on what we know … but it's all so sad. When I saw her the first time, I couldn't conceive that I'd end up feeling sorry for Stephanie Burton … Zach, I would have sworn she walked on water."

"And while you were in the audience being wowed by her, who knows what was going on inside her head? Hours later she would be slicing Prize Calloway's throat. Had she been trying to fight off that urge, or was she savoring the thought?"

"Does Caputo have any ideas about why she tied the three murders into the tour?"

"Well, obviously, the tour provided a natural opportunity to spread the killings around, but it also added risk because of the increased chances we might connect the crimes to her. Maybe it had something to do with the whole notion of empowerment … it's another piece the doc hopes to probe with Stephanie."

"And maybe it's something you should also probe with General Clements. Based on the little blow-up during his interview with her, there's some sort of history there … and Stephanie sure doesn't seem to fit in with the rest of the speakers he assembled."

"Well, if I've learned anything during this investigation, it's not to take any of your hunches lightly. I'll make sure we talk to him when the time is right."

"Anything else from Dr. Caputo?"

"Only that he believes with Stephanie, inevitably one side must win the battle that rages inside her head. Her personal sense of morality requires it. One persona needs to prevail, one needs to disappear permanently. Given time, she'll search for a way to properly resolve the conflict on her own terms."

Andie shook her head sadly. "But she won't have that time, will she? When are you planning to arrest her?"

"In a few days ... early next week at the outside. We're verifying a few more facts and getting all the proper sign-offs. Subpoenas are being issued to search her premises in Chicago and New York, on the off chance she kept fentanyl, a wig, receipts, or anything else. In the meantime, she's under pretty tight surveillance, just in case she'd have some urge to lash out and murder again."

Sixty-Four:

Wisdom

Thursday Evening; August 13, 2009

The wine was flowing freely, but the stories and emotions even more so. With only a day's notice, Stephanie had invited her *High Road* family to a special night out. It had been a while since The Road Crew was able to kick back together. She reserved the backroom of a popular bistro down in the Village. All twenty gathered around the gigantic table that they'd formed by pushing smaller ones together.

Stephanie made a single comment before toasting the team, but it was enough. "Each and every one of you is a true friend ... you're a remarkable family of which I'm blessed to be a part." Later in the evening she choreographed a group hug for Kelly, describing her as "The Road Crew's heart and soul."

She engaged in a number of private one-on-one conversations, catching up on people's families and personal lives. But mostly Stephanie found ways to sit back and watch. The smiles, the teasing, the high hopes, the laughter, the genuine happiness. The genuinely good people. Maybe there was a tinge of envy for the outward happiness they all could feel and express, but only a tinge. In total, she experienced an overwhelming contentment. This one time she would allow herself to savor the warmth of it. Her smile was much more pronounced than usual – feeling great about the future.

Friday Morning; August 14, 2009

Stephanie Burton had just wrapped up a morning staff meeting and this time it was the General Clements's wife on the phone.

"Deanna, what a pleasant surprise ... your letter meant a great deal to me."

The desperation in her voice signaled there was nothing pleasant about the call. "Stephanie, I'm sorry to call, but is your appointment with my husband still on for today?"

"Yes, it is … in about half-an-hour."

Her voice took on a sense of panic, "Oh, God, I'm not sure how to say this, but I think he may be coming there to kill you. Please don't meet with him … have your security people intercept him … even the police if necessary."

"Deanna, please calm down, dear. I'm sitting here quite safely alone. What makes you think the general would want to do something so extreme?"

"You can't imagine what it's been like. Each day he's more belligerent than the one before. He drinks, he rants practically non-stop … about me, about friends who deserted him, about worthless politicians and attorneys … but mostly about you. Last week I finally asked him to leave the house and he went to a hotel. Yesterday he came home to pick up some papers … and this morning when I went into his study, I saw that he'd left the safe open."

"Okay, I'm still listening."

"Stephanie, the file folders in the safe didn't look like they were touched at all. My jewelry was exactly where it belonged. The only thing missing was his gun … a prized military pistol that he kept locked in there."

"Deanna, that's quite a leap."

"If you'd been watching his moods turn meaner and meaner … endlessly talking about how America can't see Stephanie Burton for what she truly is … that he's sick of how the media creates false heroes while it crucifies the real ones. After one afternoon of drinking, he went on and on about how it was up to him to deal with you properly."

"Was he coming to New York alone?"

"Yes, he planned to catch one of the early trains this morning."

"I know how difficult this call must have been … and I'm sure this morning will go just fine. Whatever thoughts he might have been having yesterday, his head is probably a lot clearer today."

"Promise me, Stephanie, that you won't treat this lightly … that you'll take the necessary precautions."

"I assure you that I'll be prepared in every way possible. You're an amazing woman, Deanna … I'll let you know how things turn out."

Stephanie Burton hung up the phone and hurried from her office.

Sixty-Five:

Friday Evening; August 14, 2009

"Good evening for Friday, August 14, 2009. And welcome to this special edition of *High Road* ... I'm Kelly Amaker. We know this could be a difficult and tragic day for all of us ..."

~~~

The television networks had been airing special reports throughout the day, piecing together the facts as they'd become available. Shortly before 1PM, Eastern Standard Time, the New York City Coroner officially ruled Stephanie Burton's death a homicide. Building security officers had apprehended Retired General William Addison Clements at approximately 11:20AM, turning him over to New York City Police minutes later. He'd offered no resistance.

At 3PM, New York City's Police Commissioner read a brief statement and took a few questions from the throng of reporters and cameras that were standing vigil outside Police Headquarters, across from City Hall. Miss Burton was hit by two bullets at close range, one that looked to have passed through her brain, the other her heart. Either could prove to be fatal ... autopsy results were pending. The victim had welcomed General Clements into her office several minutes before the first shot was fired. The two were alone behind closed doors in a meeting scheduled when they had talked by phone on Monday, the 10th.

A security officer, Frank Milligan, who was stationed in the 61st floor lobby of WNL headquarters, rushed to the crime scene as soon as the first shot had been heard. Upon entering Miss Burton's office, he found General Clements standing above the victim's body, aiming a pistol at his own head. According to Mr. Milligan, he ordered Clements to release the weapon, which he did; and then the general had put his hands to his face and begun sobbing. Milligan and another security guard had detained Clements until the police arrived.

An emergency medical unit took Miss Burton to Mt. Sinai Medical Center, where she'd been pronounced dead on arrival. Due to the nature of the bullet entries, her death was believed to have been instantaneous.

The pistol taken from General Clements, and presumed the murder weapon, was a .45 caliber, semi-automatic M15. This particular pistol had been presented to then Brigadier General Clements in 1982, by the United States Army's Rock Island Arsenal on the tenth anniversary of the adoption of the M15 as the standard issue for general officers.

NYPD would not disclose where Clements was being held, but the Commissioner confirmed that he had been arrested on suspicion of murder. The exact time of his arraignment had yet to be determined. Under no circumstance would it be feasible for General William Clements to appear at his grand jury hearing scheduled for the following Tuesday in Washington DC. An undisclosed source from within the police department indicated that the suspect was being kept on suicide watch.

By early evening there were breaking reports that Deanna Clements, the general's wife, had suspected her husband might try to harm Miss Burton. When asked why she didn't alert police officials, she related details of a call she'd placed directly to Stephanie Burton, "her friend." Mrs. Clements was said to be quite distraught. Phone company records had validated that the call to Burton did occur.

WNL suspended its normal broadcast schedule. Amidst unfolding details surrounding the murder, reflections about Stephanie Burton were being shared from different vantages. Highlights from previous *High Road* telecasts were shown, along with her most memorable TV appearances before *High Road*. Gordie Jacklin had assumed the central anchor role, conducting in-studio interviews with other WNL personalities, news personalities from other networks and public figures who'd been guests on *High Road*. Live remote interviews were conducted with former ad industry associates ... classmates from Columbia, from Northwestern ... the hometown citizens of Athens, Ohio ... and on-the-street citizens across the country.

There had been televised shock, televised tributes and many televised tears. Jacklin attempted to read a poem he remembered Stephanie once quoting, but was unable to finish. With the recognition that he spoke for millions of people, WNL's Chairman made the first on-air appearance of his life to express the grief he was feeling. There was growing speculation about the bad blood between Burton and Clements … their past interactions with the Personal Empowerment Tour and on television. No one close to Burton could fathom a single reason for the man's deep-seated hatred.

Upon hearing the news of Stephanie's death, Kelly Amaker had pulled the *High Road* family together in the same conference room where they'd sat only hours earlier in a morning staff meeting. It was a half-hour before meaningful discussion could take place. Kelly had understood the importance of that initial mourning process … the tears, the hugging, the blank stares, the shaking heads. After enough assimilation occurred so that words might begin to penetrate the level of shock, she spoke to the group.

"Last night, we enjoyed a special night with Stephanie. Coming to work this morning, none of us possibly could have anticipated how this day might end. We easily might allow this day to stand as one of the saddest in our lives. But I'm going to encourage us not to. We have a responsibility to make this day something more significant … for ourselves … for many others … but mostly, for Stephanie.

"I now believe I was the last person to see Stephanie alive, other than General Clements. About twenty minutes before her appointment with him, she came hurrying into my office. Even though we'd all just been together in a staff meeting, she gave me an especially long hug. Then she asked a favor.

"She said she'd received a phone call a few minutes earlier that got her thinking about tonight's program. When we gathered the team this afternoon, she wanted us to stay away from the news issues of the day, whatever they might turn out to be. And she'd stressed, 'whatever they might turn out to be.' She said she had an instinct that this evening's show needed to be different … really, really uplifting. She didn't have anything specific in mind, but was hoping we would come up with something. Her words were, 'You guys have always amazed me, so please nail this one. No matter what, tonight's show has to be uplifting.' Then she told me she needed to pull some things together before her meeting with Clements and headed off toward her office."

Kelly allowed the silence to linger. This close-knit team of Stephanie Burton, her family, needed time to absorb these new implications. Kelly was still struggling to absorb them for herself. Eventually one of the more recent additions to the team spoke up with an idea that was embraced quickly. They grabbed their notebooks and scurried to the elevators, deciding that the backroom of a bistro down in the Village was a better place to brainstorm the kind of special show Stephanie deserved.

✺

"… but for the next hour we're not going to dwell on the details surrounding today's unexpected events. We hope you'll respect this decision. Instead we're going to feature ten stories that profile people who turned their lives around to make positive differences in communities, both big and small. All are stories previously featured on *High Road*. The broadcast family of Stephanie Burton spent this afternoon vigorously debating which were her favorites, and we are unanimous with the final selection. Each segment will be introduced briefly by a different member of Stephanie's staff, her Road Crew."

Sixty-Six:

Earlier Friday; August 14, 2009

"You'd better get over here. There's been a shooting and it sounds like Burton might be involved. We're on our way up."

The daytime surveillance team assigned to Stephanie Burton had been positioned inside the building's main entrance when the four squad cars raced up to the curb. One of the two FBI agents flashed his credentials to a police officer who was sprinting through the lobby. "What's going on?"

"Shooting … sixty-first floor … Stephanie Burton's office."

*

Zach had arrived in New York on Thursday to coordinate the final details of Stephanie Burton's arrest, which was slated for Saturday morning. The media would be caught more off-guard on a weekend, so Bureau officials might better contend with the anticipated tidal wave of public reaction. But the two calls received Friday morning negated all the previous planning. Zach was working out of Federal Plaza, at the NYC field office, when he received the first call. He took the second call from the passenger seat of a local agent's car, as they raced to WNL headquarters.

"She's dead, Zach. Shot twice by General William Clements, who also intended to kill himself but lost his nerve. It's pretty chaotic … people crying all over the place."

When he arrived minutes later, he was told about a sealed envelope found on Stephanie Burton's desk – "To be opened only by Agent Zachary Peterson, FBI." An hour later, a NYPD Forensics tech finally handed it to him.

Dear Zach & Andie,

My life, like any, will be defined by my decisions and their consequences. Whether we might regret past choices is immaterial unless we've strived to improve. Every day, every existence is filled with boundless opportunity to better oneself and some piece of the world. Similarly, each of us, no matter our situation, confronts dispiriting realities that can misguide or limit our potential.

The responsibility is ours to make the most of our potential. We should try to encourage others in their pursuit of ambitions, but the final responsibility remains ours. We are human, there will be setbacks. But we are provided more than one chance; each lifespan, an unending series of second chances. We must have faith there will be new opportunities and that we ultimately can prevail. Our journeys are hollow without such faith in a greater goodness.

People may attempt to justify certain of my actions by rationalizing circumstances from my past. Others may focus on the manner in which my life ends. Let there be no mistake, I never was a victim. I am and must remain totally accountable for all my decisions and their consequences. Perhaps the divergent paths I traveled stand as testament to the range of choices ever before us.

I feel a special kinship with the two of you – for the work you have done together, for choices you will make, for your individual strengths and mutual support, and for the love so evident between you. Please cherish and celebrate what you have … for yourselves and for others to see and emulate.

Godspeed,
Stephanie

Enclosed in the envelope with the letter, Zach found three driver's licenses that had been used to rent cars in Seattle, Indianapolis and Kansas City.

Sixty-Seven:

Accountability

As news rapidly spread throughout that Friday, the public sought ways to express both its grief and fondness for Stephanie Burton. Many millions practically cemented themselves in front of televisions, finding whatever comfort they could from the nonstop reports and commentary. That afternoon, moments of silence were honored at schools and businesses across the country, then throughout the evening at sporting events, theatrical performances and most anywhere crowds assembled.

By mid-afternoon on Friday, a sizable pile of flowers, stuffed animals, pictures and letters had started to accumulate on the sidewalk outside WNL's Midtown headquarters. By Friday evening, similar piles formed outside GA&J offices in Chicago and Leslie Burton's home in Athens. Round-the-clock bloggers went to work. By Saturday morning, thousands of people were placing bouquets into massive floral wreaths taking shape on plazas outside the thirty-one arenas that once had hosted Personal Empowerment Tour events.

Among those placing flowers on the pavement outside Kemper Arena in Kansas City was Benjamin Atkins. In recent months, Benny had dropped forty-six pounds toward his goal of eighty-five, determined to pass the physical that would make him eligible for active patrol duty. Stephanie Burton's nightly influence on *High Road* had prompted the first serious soul-searching of his life. Long ago, Ben Atkins joined the police force with every intention of becoming the kind of respected cop his dad had been, but too early and too often he'd lost his conviction, then eventually his pride. With the final phase of his career, he believed he still could bring dignity to himself, his family and the Kansas City Police Department.

Public duty required that the FBI report the P.E.T. serial murders had been solved, along with the open homicide case of Nicholas J. Parravano. The only question had been when. To the materials they'd previously prepared to disclose, they now could add three counterfeit driver's licenses that served as Stephanie Burton's postmortem admission. Public reaction was sure to be incredulous. The nation was already in shock over the tragic loss of a beloved figure and now would learn that this paragon of virtue had been identified as the Touring Temptress. Impossible, a practical joke of hideously poor taste. Too unthinkable to be absorbed, yet undeniably true.

Zach realized the Bureau really was left no choice. *There was that word ... choice. Stephanie had stressed it in her final note.* Zach knew exactly what she would have advocated and she would have been right. It wasn't the FBI's place to worry about preserving Stephanie Burton's image or the sanctity of a mourning process. No matter what else she may have accomplished, she also had been the calculating, cold-blooded murderer of three random citizens. She violently had executed four men for her own gratifications. Stephanie Burton would have been the first person to stress that those facts be kept front and center. Let issues about respecting her death or her memory play out as they might. Such were the consequences of the choices she'd made.

At 2PM on Saturday, the FBI's Assistant Director of the Criminal Investigative Division read a prepared statement before turning over the podium. Then for twenty minutes Zach Peterson detailed specifics from the investigation, a litany of incriminating facts, and Stephanie Burton's possible motivations as best understood by forensic psychologists. He concluded by pointing to the enlarged photos of three driver's licenses and reading the non-personal paragraphs from her final letter.

Members of the press had wondered, even complained about the FBI calling a weekend press conference in New York City to announce that the P.E.T. murders had been solved. It had seemed odd that so many senior officials would have traveled there from Washington. The reasons became clear a few sentences into the Assistant Director's remarks. The large room went eerily silent during the prepared statements. Even when the floor eventually was opened for questions, the emptiness hung for several moments. Not out of shock, because by now weathered reporters would have had enough time to set aside whatever personal reactions they might have been feeling. The slow reactions were a reflection of due care and respect. They weren't quite sure what the appropriate questions were to ask about such unexpected revelations ... or how best to ask them?

The television networks had been ambivalent about even carrying the FBI press conference amidst their special coverage of Stephanie Burton's murder – not contemplating that the two stories would converge into one. A few, including WNL, merely had sent remote crews to grab excerpts that could be incorporated into regular news updates. But shortly after the press conference started, every network switched to full, live coverage. At the conclusion, the assorted familiar faces back at their various network anchor desks looked sullen. Mouths that normally didn't rest were slow to find words ... each in their own way struggling to find the right ones. Network executives and news chiefs scratched their collective heads. First, yesterday's bombshell about Stephanie Burton being shot ... now this. How should the story be covered, how best should the public interest be served?

The emotions across the country were palpable. In homes and buildings, across state lines, across age and ethnicity ... millions and millions of people individually absorbed the harsh, unbelievable reality. But feeling a connectedness, a shared sense of loss. Those millions collectively pondered the true measure of that loss. The hopes ... the meanings of Stephanie Burton's messages, the value of her constant encouragements ... what did any of it matter now?

There could have been no lower point in his life than his arrest on Friday morning. So thought William Addison Clements. Facing a lengthy prison sentence, a court martial and an infamous place in military history, he had shot an unarmed woman whom he blamed for his total demise. Then he'd lost the courage to at least end his misery honorably. He couldn't fire that third bullet and instead had wept. He'd been escorted out in handcuffs and in tears – disdain in the faces of everyone he passed.

On Saturday afternoon, his attorneys informed him that Stephanie Burton was responsible for the P.E.T. murders. The consequences were even more unthinkable. If he hadn't killed her, he could have watched her go down ... she wouldn't have won after all. But by killing her, he'd saved her the public humiliation she was due ... while his would now multiply immeasurably. It wasn't possible. He had been right. Despite all her pompous preaching ... a psychotic murderer ... a man-hater. Every bit the fraud he'd said she was.

But she had won. She had destroyed his tour, then his life. She had defeated him in every way possible. He was deader than any of her murder victims and he'd never seen it coming. *That conniving bitch smiled every step of the way ... even when she'd seen the gun.*

⌒∦⌒

No one had thought to call her. She learned about her daughter's death like everyone else – through the media. In her car late Friday afternoon, on the radio ... then hurrying home to flip on a new TV that one of her regulars had given her. She'd cried a little, but wasn't quite sure how to feel. She'd decided to have a few more cocktails and continue thinking about it into Saturday morning. But for sure all those flowers gathering on her front yard had bothered her. People from all over Athens ... it seemed like people from all over Ohio, were parading by her house like it was some kind of official mourning site. *Don't they have anything better to do?*

Then came Saturday and news that her daughter had killed those men. She'd sliced their throats like a whoring whacko ... and cut off that Gunner's private stuff, too. *Hell, there must have been a lot of loose screws inside that head of hers.* Leslie Burton wasn't quite sure what any of it meant yet, but she'd have a few more cocktails and keep thinking. At least now she could rake those damned flowers off her yard and toss 'em in the trash. *Folks gotta be feeling pretty stupid about wanting to make her out as anything special.*

Looking out the window on Sunday morning, she was confused. She could have sworn she'd cleaned up all those flowers. Throughout the rest of the day, she watched as cars continued to slow and stop. People must be nuts. *Go ahead, waste your time putting flowers and silly crap on my lawn ... but she still turned out no good, didn't she?*

She'd keep searching for answers the only way she knew.

⌒∦⌒

Deanna Clements slowly circled the enormous wreath that was forming on the concrete near the main entrance of The Spectrum, placing single white roses in the blank spaces she spotted while she walked. She'd wept often since receiving the news that her husband had killed Stephanie Burton.

292

She was ashamed for her husband and felt she'd lost a true friend. She had replayed the Friday morning phone conversation over and over in her mind … wondering if she could have said anything differently … wondering why Stephanie hadn't taken the precautions she promised she would. Then on Saturday she had watched the FBI's press conference.

It was Sunday morning and she watched as individuals, couples, families and groups of friends laid their flowers and wrote their notes. She replayed the phone conversation again. White roses seemed perfect for Stephanie Burton. Her eyes went teary once more, but this time Deanna Clements was smiling.

Sixty-Eight:

September, 2009

On the first telecast following the weekend of revelations, Kelly Amaker once again filled in. By the end of that week, network execs had decided that *High Road* should continue without Stephanie Burton. Kelly Amaker was announced as the new host.

Certainly The Road Crew agreed. None of them had any intentions of going anywhere. Neither Gordie Jacklin, nor any other WNL personality, had made a play for the plum slot in the network's line-up. The appropriateness was too obvious.

The public agreed. The ratings of *High Road* didn't miss a beat. Kelly Amaker didn't miss a beat. The same respectful demeanor, the same sense of decency, a genuine goodness. A goodness that emanated from her positive belief in the human spirit. An unencumbered belief.

⸙

"'Ah, but a man's reach should exceed his grasp, or what's a heaven for?' Those are the words of Robert Browning. Stephanie loved them all ... Burns, Frost, Longfellow, Bryon ... T.S. Eliot ... Emily Dickinson ... but Browning was her favorite. She was fascinated by the undying love he'd shared with Elizabeth Barrett, often commenting that the union of two such great and romantic poets must be the most divine love of all ... that the intersection of such souls surely proves that a heaven of some sort does exist. Stephanie admired the way that Browning used poetry to challenge the people of his time to find the goodness in even the most unsavory and immoral characters. Clearly she continues to remind us that this challenge is timeless. And indeed, we will continue to reflect on a woman who pushed us all to extend our reach for heavenly behaviors.

"Stephanie Burton never would have agreed to this gathering because of all the good things that might be said about her. But I do think Stephanie would have appreciated how we kept it to immediate family."

The laughter evoked by his comment caused Kent Gillespie to pause and look out over a crowd of several hundred that assembled on a September Saturday. He saw dozens of familiar faces from the old days at GA&J and FutureScape ... so many talented individuals who had gone on to accomplish so much. He also saw faces not as familiar to him. The Road Crew and their significant others who had flown in. Friends from college and graduate school who had felt Stephanie's encouragement. A couple from the FBI who were dating. The wife of a disgraced general. Other isolated individuals who were meaningfully affected by her in one way or another. Along with Kelly Amaker, Kent had organized the memorial service and coordinated the guest list. No cameras. No blood relatives. Just immediate family.

It was an old Baptist church on Chicago's Westside. After sampling many congregations around the city, Kent and Stephanie had agreed that this was their favorite because of the way the rafters rocked with joy when the choir cut loose. Kent had hoped they might someday be married there. Today the choir wasn't singing, but joy still permeated every corner of a sanctuary that was filled to capacity.

More than a month had passed since Stephanie Burton was shot and the events of her private past had been revealed. The ninety-minute service was intended as an upbeat celebration of her life ... at least the dominant part of that life. More than thirty people took their turn at the lectern; the tributes delivered through stories about her encouragement to others, her impact on lives. Only minor references were made to how she died or the private burdens she must have carried ... a total absence of judgment or pity. If they hadn't already, each in attendance would need to reconcile Stephanie's other activities on their own. This day was about the goodness, the poetry.

Toward the conclusion, Andie Morrison walked to the microphone. She abhorred public speaking and had managed to avoid standing at the front of a room since high school. She definitely hadn't planned or prepared any comments in advance, but now was moved to express her sentiments.

"Hi, I'm Andie Morrison … with the FBI. I haven't given a speech since I was seventeen years old, but I've been sitting back there thinking I'll need to do more of this in the future. You see, Stephanie has had me pushing the old envelope pretty hard over the past year, so I hope you don't mind if I use you guys to practice. Oh, by the way, it's probably not the right time to mention this, but I was the first person to realize she was a serial killer. Talk about a bad day. Anyway, when I first heard her in Kemper Arena …"

For the next seven or eight minutes, Andie Morrison entertained, touched and charmed a church full of strangers with her Midwestern friendliness. She calmly meandered her way to insights that captivated the crowd as much as her incredible eyes did. Zach Peterson smiled in wonderment, relishing the years ahead of watching this remarkable woman discover her untapped potentials.

Chapter Sixty-Nine:

February, 2010

After a brisk winter jog through their neighborhood, they found themselves where they often did – a table by the window and a pitcher between them. Kelly Amaker was on the TV screen above the bar. It was the one-year anniversary of *High Road* and Stephanie Burton was being remembered, her accomplishments and her crimes.

Zach and Andie looked up at the screen before angling their glasses until they touched. "To Stephanie."

⁓

None of the networks had wanted to be the first to revert to their old ways. Not abruptly, anyway. Programming execs had been certain they could orchestrate a more gradual slide back down the slimy slope. The public would grow tired of this "new civility" nonsense. There might be room for a *High Road* and a few shows like it … at least for a year or two. But not all the time. Surely a pent-up desire for slash and attack journalism would win out.

Six months after Stephanie Burton's death, the public was standing firm. They continued to vote strong preferences with their eyeballs and remote controls. Sponsors were standing firm with the public.

William Addison Clements had been tried and sentenced in federal court … additionally found guilty on all charges in the subsequent court martial proceedings. His trial for murder was still pending. But the media had covered his demise with fangs in check. The facts alone had been sufficient … the story of a man who had abused both power and privilege, and now faced the consequences.

The revelations about Stephanie Burton had been handled with unprecedented forthrightness. Her death and career accomplishments had been covered with dignity, her murderous acts recognized for what they were. Despite much supposition regarding her reasons, the severity of those crimes had not been glossed over. She hadn't been excused as a victim of her past ... not exempted by her celebrity. Regardless of what might have happened in her youth, or the many positive impacts she may have had in later years, the public was holding her accountable for her actions ... all of them. Her legacy, rich in poetic justice.

Novels by Mitch Engel

Deadly Virtues

Noble Windmills